You Can't Cheat an Honest Man

How Ponzi Schemes and Pyramid Frauds Work... and Why They're More Common Than Ever

---

James Walsh

Silver Lake Publishing

You Can't Cheat an Honest Man
How Ponzi Schemes and Pyramid Frauds Work...and Why They're More Common than Ever

First edition, 1998

For a list of other publications or for more information, please call +11 (323) 663-3082.

Library of Congress Catalogue Number: Pending

Walsh, James
You Can't Cheat an Honest Man
How Ponzi Schemes and Pyramid Frauds Work...and Why They're More Common than Ever.
Includes index.
Pages: 354

ISBN: 1-56343-169-6
Printed in the United States of America.

Acknowledgments

Putting this book together took almost two years and critical support from a small band of people with a passion for studying shady schemes—some fallen, some still running—in order to understand how and why they work. Sander Alvarez, Christina Schlank and Megan Thorpe helped me find examples and talk to people on all sides. David T. Russell, who teaches risk and insurance at Illinois State University, asked me pertinent questions about particular schemes and broader analysis. Finally, a group of informal con scheme connoisseurs—including Jeff Barker, James Kenefick and Jason O'Malley—listened to various stories and theories and offered fresh perspectives.

Some readers may recognize the title of this book. It's taken from the title of a W.C. Fields movie from the 1930s. In that movie, the grouchy comedian played a crook whose greed was so intense that it got in the way of his own schemes. It seems like an appropriate metaphor.

One last note. Many of the experts that I interviewed for this book, both crooks and law enforcement types, joked that the people most interested in reading a book like this would be Ponzi perpetrators. In fact, so many people said this that it seems futile to contradict them. They may be right. But I hope they're not. There are many more potential targets of Ponzi schemes out in the investment marketplace than there are potential perps.

By arming potential targets with information, I hope we can make some progress toward pushing the perps out of the business.

James Walsh
Los Angeles, CA
July 1998

Table of Contents

INTRODUCTION

Some Background to the Current Situation

Ponzi schemes have a strong—almost addictive—grasp on the people who perpetrate them and the people who invest in them. Why? Consider the original scheme.

Carlo Ponzi was a loser. He knew this. Everyone who knew him knew this. But he was desperate to be something more.

Floating from job to job in the hard-scrabble Boston of the early 1920s, the formal little man (he was 5'2" and irregularly employed but elegantly dressed) was, in one sense, loosely moored to reality. He would stay up late nights dreaming up ways to get rich.

Ponzi had been born in Italy but arrived in New York in 1893 at the age of fifteen. He immediately set to the task of finding a fast way to make a lot of money. His impatience lead him into the most basic kind of swindles—and an itinerant lifestyle. He served short stretches of time in prison in both Canada (for mail fraud and passing bad checks) and Atlanta (for an illegal immigration scheme). He ended up moving to Boston in 1919.

Boston has always been a particularly tough place to be poor. Frustrated by the luxury he saw being casually enjoyed by the local swells, Ponzi kept dreaming of ways to take his piece. And he wrote letters home to various members of his extended family. Living in the aftermath of World War I, they were anxious for their traveling son to strike it rich in the New World.

His letters home provided Ponzi with the origin of what he would later—famously—call his "Great Idea." Although Ponzi himself probably couldn't describe it, the scheme was essentially a crude form of currency exchange speculation.

In the early 1900s, a person could enclose a coupon with a letter to save a correspondent the cost of return postage. An organization called the International Postal Union issued postal reply coupons that could be traded in for postage stamps in a number of countries around the world.

Ponzi figured that the coupons could be bought on the cheap in nations with weak economies and redeemed for a profit in the United States. He decided to stake some of his hard-earned money on a test of his Great Idea. But he quickly discovered that there was a lot to the scheme that he hadn't anticipated. Most importantly, the red tape among postal organizations absorbed his profits. Delays prevented him from moving enough money through the system to make his plan work.

But, as his Great Idea wilted, something unexpected bloomed. Whenever he discussed the scheme with people, they quickly caught on and seemed interested in what he had to say. Friends and family members would ask him—unprovoked—how his tests were going. People were interested in the investment because it made sense to them...even though it didn't work.

So, near the end of 1919, Ponzi made a decision which would make his name an icon of modern-day thievery. He stopped buying international postal coupons and dealing with endless bureaucracy—and focused instead on bringing in investors.

The Original Ponzi Scheme Is Born

In December 1919, with capital of $150, Ponzi—who'd started using the first name "Charles"—began the business of borrowing money on promissory notes. He started out by inviting friends and relatives to get in on the ground floor of what he dubbed the "Ponzi Plan."

Ponzi claimed that he was making 100 percent profit on his money in a few months. His problem was that he didn't have enough capital to exploit postal rate discrepancies fully. Because there was room, he was willing to include investors on his deals.

Like many of his disciples in years since, Ponzi targeted people with the same ethnic identity.

Ponzi made his presentation...his pitch...shine. He would explain that he had received a letter that contained a reply coupon that cost the equivalent of one cent in Spain but could be exchanged for a six-cent stamp in the U.S. "Why can't I buy hundreds, thousands, millions of these coupons? I'll make five cents on every one," he'd ask convincingly. His tone was described as something between a plea and a command.

Whatever it was, it worked. A few wary acquaintances decided to take a gamble, and Ponzi collected about $1,250. Early investors included extended family members, his parish priest, and players at the local bocce court. Ninety days later, he returned $750 in interest. Stunned investors told their friends and soon Ponzi's office was filling with greedy people eager to fork over their money. He promptly moved his operation to a tony address in the city's financial district.

With a written promise to repay $150 in 90 days for every $100 loaned, Ponzi convinced thousands of people to lend him millions of dollars. He placated investors' fears by offering to pay his 90-day notes in full at the end of 45 days. Within eight months, he'd taken in $9 million, for which he'd issued notes with a paper value of $14 million. He paid his agents a commission of 10 percent. Including the 50 percent promised to lenders, every loan paid in full would cost him 60 percent.

But Ponzi's financial method was not based on actual earnings. Instead, it used incoming investors to pay the returns promised to earlier investors. Although he was cash-rich, Ponzi never actually made any money. As one court would later point out: "He was always insolvent, and became daily more so, the more his business succeeded. He made no investments of any kind, so that all the money he had at any time was solely the result of loans by his dupes."

In time, Ponzi was taking in $200,000 a day...and paying out dividends of 50 percent in 90 days. He later upped the promised payout to 100 percent in three months. Investors literally lined up at his offices to give him their money.

Keeping Up Appearances

Ponzi was a genius about maintaining certain parts of his scheme. One example: When investors went into his offices to redeem their notes, they had to walk all the way to the back of the place, to one of two or three redemption windows. There was usually a long line at this window.

Once the investors had their money, they had to walk past dozens of investment windows, with shorter lines and eager people investing hundreds and thousands of new dollars. Most didn't make it all the way out the front door again. They'd reinvest.

At the height of his liquidity, Ponzi went on manic shopping sprees, buying scores of suits, dozens of gold-handled canes, diamonds for his wife, limousines and a 20-room mansion in the Boston suburb of Lexington. As would hold true for many of the con men who'd follow in his steps, Ponzi seemed most in his element spending money.

By early July 1920, Ponzi was taking in $1 million a week. On one particularly flush afternoon, he walked into the Hanover Trust Co. with $3 million stuffed in a suitcase and bought controlling interest in the esteemed bank. But his success would not last long.

While hundreds of people lined up at Ponzi's offices every day, an editor at the *Boston Post* asked the opinions of several financial experts and concluded that—while it might be possible to make a few thousand dollars trading the postal coupons—the Great Idea couldn't support the amount of business Ponzi was doing.

Soon, skeptical reporters called for interviews. Nervous about the image he would make, Ponzi hired a public relations executive named William McMasters to handle publicity. It was a major misstep. McMasters spent a couple of days in Ponzi's office, realized the operation was a scam and went straight to state authorities. "This man is a financial idiot," McMasters said. "He can hardly add.... He sits with his feet on the desk smoking expensive cigars in a diamond holder and talking complete gibberish about postal coupons."

Ponzi was summoned to the State House in Boston. He was cheered by Italian admirers on the way in, but when auditors got hold of his ledgers they found only an addled mix of names and numbers. His employees, when questioned, had no idea how Ponzi's huge returns were earned.

A month later, fearing his scheme was about to collapse, Ponzi drove to Saratoga Springs with $2 million in a suitcase. He hoped to win back in the casinos money he'd spent living like a tycoon. He lost everything.

In August 1920, the *Boston Globe* published an exposé on Ponzi. A near riot ensued, with thousands of scared investors storming Ponzi's office and demanding their money back. In short, it was a run on the bank. A court would later explain the details:

> *At the opening of business July 19th, the balance of Ponzi's deposit accounts at the Hanover Trust was $334,000. At the close of business July 24th it was $871,000. This sum was exhausted by withdrawals on July 26th of $572,000, on July 27th of $228,000, and on July 28th of $905,000, or a total of more than $1,765,000. In spite of this, the account continued to show a credit balance, because new deposits from other banks were made by Ponzi. The scheme was finally ended by an overdraft on August 9th of $331,000. Bankruptcy was then filed.*

At the height of his scheme, Ponzi owned only $30 worth of postal coupons—against which he'd borrowed $10 million from 20,000 investors in Boston and New York.

In less than 10 months, Ponzi had catapulted to greatness and then crashed back down to ignomy again. Most investors there at the end lost their life savings. Ponzi was arrested by federal agents and eventually sentenced to four years in Massachusetts' Plymouth Prison.

The Supreme Court Offers Its Opinion

A number of lawsuits followed the collapse of Ponzi's scheme. The most important of these was the civil suit *Cunningham v. Brown et al.* Cunningham was the heir of one of Ponzi's investors. Brown was another investor, who'd received preferential treatment—that is, had been paid—by Ponzi. Cunningham wanted the money Brown had received to be returned to Ponzi's bankruptcy estate for even division among all creditors.

In April 1924, the case went all the way to the Supreme Court. The resulting decision, written by Chief Justice and former President William H. Taft, set a precedent for dealing with wreckage left in the wake of a Ponzi scheme. Among its conclusions:

> *Both [lower] courts held that the defendants had rescinded their contracts of loan for fraud and that they were entitled to a return of their money.... We do not agree. [W]hen the fund with which the wrongdoer is dealing is wholly made up of the fruits of the frauds perpetrated against a myriad victims, the case is different.... [This] is a case the circumstances of which call strongly for the principle that equality is equity, and this is the spirit of the bankrupt law. Those who were successful in the race of diligence violated not only its spirit, but its letter, and secured an unlawful preference.*

So, the money repaid to Brown was what lawyers call "voidable"—which means it could be ordered returned to the bankrupt estate. The concept of voidability is critical to the legal battles that usually follow the collapse of a Ponzi scheme.

Ponzi served some time in jail. But, like many of the people who would follow in his steps, he got right back to work after his release. He set to selling Florida swampland. Eventually, he was deported to Italy, divorced and destitute. "I bear no grudges," he said in his final interview with an American newspaper. "I hope the world forgives me."

Forgets is closer to what the world actually did. In the 1930s, under the mistaken impression that Ponzi was a banking wizard, Benito Mussolini gave him a senior job in the Italian government. Treasury officials soon figured out that the wizard couldn't handle basic math. Realizing he was about to be discovered...again, Ponzi stuffed cash into several suitcases and boarded a boat for South America.

But no one made bags big enough for the little con man. When Ponzi died in Brazil several years later, he was in a hospital charity ward.

Elegance and Financial Alchemy

Ponzi schemes have a larcenous elegance. They're a kind of financial alchemy, promising to turn basic human impulses like greed, trust and fear into piles of cash. For a brief time, they can make losers look like winners and satisfy people's reptilian impulse for easy wealth.

In legal terms, a Ponzi scheme is one in which money entrusted to the perpetrator is never invested in any legitimate for-profit venture. Instead, it's handed back to the investors under the pretense that the returns are profits. They aren't. They're just small pieces of the capital invested.

The Ponzi perp will usually divert some portion of the money received for his own use. This creates a need to expand the number of investors in order to cover repayments of principal and promised returns to the existing investors. The more money the perp siphons off, the more rapidly he needs to find new investors.

Typically, greedy investors are promised large returns on their money with little chance of losing it. "Low risk" and "no risk" are defining promises made in the early stages of most Ponzi schemes. Initial investors are actually paid the big money as promised, which attracts additional investors. But, eventually, the schemes get so big that they run out of new investors willing to support the structure.

Pyramid schemes and chain letters—close relatives of Ponzi schemes—induce people to participate in a plan for making money by means of recruiting others, with the right to encourage or solicit new memberships in the pyramid passed on to each new recruit. These schemes get their name from the flow of cash, from new members to old. The person at the top of the pyramid collects cash from all the people at the bottom.

Members are enticed to join a Ponzi scheme by promises that they will earn a lot of money on a modest investment. They're often told that all they have to do is convince friends and family members to make similar investments. In reality, more people must lose money than make it. The only way for the perp to get his ill-gotten gains is to keep the money moving long enough to complete a couple of wire transfers to Zurich or the Cayman Islands. When the money finally stops moving, everyone at the base of the pyramid loses his entrance fee or investment.

As far as most cops and prosecutors are concerned, though, Ponzi schemes and pyramid schemes are victimless crimes. People who lose money in the things have usually participated willingly.

Ponzis Versus Pyramids

The terms *Ponzi scheme* and *pyramid scheme* are used interchangeably by most consumer advocates and many law enforcement people. And the schemes are quite similar. Technically, the main difference is that in a Ponzi scheme money is handed over to be invested; in a pyramid scheme, money is handed over in exchange for a right to do something (most often to open a franchise or to solicit new members). Ponzi schemes are always illegal; pyramid schemes are sometimes, depending upon how they are structured.

The result, in both cases, is usually the same. As a Utah court wrote in the 1987 bankruptcy decision *Merrill v. Abbott*:

> *A Ponzi scheme cannot work forever. The investor pool is a limited resource and will eventually run dry. The perpetrator must know that the scheme will eventually collapse as a result of the inability to attract new investors. The perpetrator nevertheless makes payments to present investors, which, by definition, are meant to attract new investors. He must know all along, from the very nature of his activities, that investors at the end of the line will lose their money.*

This book will treat Ponzi schemes and illegal pyramid schemes like identical twins. In the contexts and circumstances in which the two are not the same, the differences will be highlighted and explained. As is often the case, these subtle differences shed important light on the mechanics and uses of each version.

Ponzi schemes thrive in cycles. They were big in the 1920s, late 1940s, 1970s and—most recently—have started to flourish again in the mid-1990s. Starting in 1995, the Securities and Exchange Commission began a campaign warning investors about a rise in Ponzi schemes and investment pyramids—especially ones using religious organizations for exposure and ones targeting the elderly.

In 1995, the SEC investigated 24 Ponzi schemes involving losses of more than a million dollars—a record for a single year. "We're finding Ponzis these days with a depressing regularity," Tom Newkirk, the SEC's associate director of enforcement, told one newspaper in late 1996.

Andrew Kandel, who handles securities fraud cases for the New York State Attorney General, sees one major reason for this: In the age of personalized pension plans (401ks, Keoughs, IRAs, etc.) more people have direct control of substantial amounts of money. "They can easily recall 10 percent CDs. So, a smart Ponzi scam doesn't offer a 25 percent promissory note—which might excite suspicion—but a quite plausible 12 percent piece of worthless paper."

The SEC's Newkirk goes one step further to offer a theory about why this is so: "Ponzis often seem to be an appeal to the populist streak in Americans."

The subtext of many of the schemes is that achieving wealth is a matter of knowing the right techniques and the right people—secrets that the rich are in on and that the Ponzi perp is willing to share with the little guy.

The Schemes Often Spin Out of Control

A Ponzi scheme is structurally simple, hard to control beyond its first few levels and ultimately doomed to fail. For these reasons, the schemes often grow in directions—and take turns—that even the crooks creating them don't anticipate.

One of the common side-effects: Publicity. Because people tend to associate financial success with wisdom, courage and other virtues, Ponzi perps are often heralded as geniuses or heroes. A scheme will build the illusion of a highly successful business that's paying big money to people "smart" enough to have bought in. Of course, these impressions are all as bogus as the underlying promise.

The truth is usually that the Ponzi perps aren't either wise or brave. In fact, they often aren't very smart at all. Most Ponzi schemes collapse dramatically because they expand so suddenly that the perps can't keep up with the lies they've told. (The smartest perps try to limit the speed with which their schemes grow. Doing so, they can let time build trust and blur memories.)

Amtel Communications, a San Diego, California-based telephone equipment leasing company, had a Great Idea to pitch to investors. The premise was simple: Amtel would sell pay phones to investors for several thousand dollars and then lease them back, locate them and service them.

The investor never had to take possession of the pay phones. He'd just get leases, a description of where the phones were located and a check for $51 per phone each month. The monthly payments worked out to an 18.5 percent annual return.

The pitch worked well...and for a long time. From 1992 to 1996, Amtel took in more than $60 million. But, as early as 1993, salespeople hired to bring in investors were complaining to Amtel management that delays in getting the pay phones placed were causing problems. One salesman wrote Amtel's sales manager: "Listed below are phones that I sold [recently] for which no phones have been provided. Some of these participants have purchased additional phones since and are apprehensive that we are conducting a Ponzi scheme."

The salespeople—and the company's on-time monthly payments—were persuasive enough that Amtel stayed in business for more than three years. The company was placing some pay phones...just not enough to generate income to cover all the investment money it was taking in. This is a common tactic in larger Ponzi schemes: Do some legitimate business in order to ward off the most skeptical inquiries.

By mid-1996, though, the scheme was collapsing. Amtel filed for bankruptcy protection and regulatory scrutiny followed. In October 1996, the SEC and a California bankruptcy examiner determined that Amtel was, in fact, a Ponzi scheme.

Lawsuits were filed from various sides in late 1996. The bankruptcy court allowed investors to vote on a reorganization plan proposed by new management. Although the plan would mean waiting even longer to recoup money, most investors supported it. The alternative was to accept a two-cents-on-the-dollar settlement that would protect the company's previous management from liability.

Minor Schemes Can Do Major Damage

Ponzi schemes don't always have to be as big and official-sounding as Amtel. Interior designer Cynthia Brackett had a simpler story for people in Greensboro, North Carolina.

Brackett said that she made as much money selling antique furniture to yuppies as she did in actual design fees. The markups on old furniture were plenty rich. Her only problem was that, while she had plenty of clients, she didn't have much capital. So, she was having trouble getting as many Queen Anne chairs and Chippendale dressers as she needed.

Her pitch: Short-term financing would help her buy the right things at bargain prices from estate sales, dealer closeouts and other sources that required a buyer to move quickly and pay in cash. She'd pay well—as much as 10 percent for a 30-day note.

A lot of Brackett's story checked out. She did have a design firm that seemed to be doing well. She was charming, attractive and traveled in the right circles. There were a lot of yuppies moving into the area. And banks did shy away from lending to "creative" businesses like interior decorators. So, some wealthy locals invested. However, "no money was used to purchase antiques," an FBI agent would tell a federal court some time later. "It went to pay back investors and finance her own lifestyle."

That lifestyle included a Mercedes, a home in Greensboro's high-end Irving Park neighborhood, a vacation house in nearby Myrtle Beach and tuition for her children at the trendy Greensboro Day School.

Like most smart Ponzi perps, Brackett was careful to repay her loans on time and with full interest. She was so conscientious that lenders were happy to increase their loans with her when she came back to them later.

But the most impressive part of Brackett's scheme was that she was able to convince each of her investors that he was one of a small group of big shots with whom she did business—that is, borrowed money.

By 1991, when the scheme collapsed, Brackett owed almost $1.5 million to more than 60 investors. In the early part of that year, Brackett had hit the wall. She'd run out of swells willing to loan her more money. Her checks started bouncing and her company declared bankruptcy.

In May 1995, the 46-year-old Brackett pleaded guilty in a Greensboro federal court to one count each of mail fraud and tax evasion. She was sentenced to 30 months in jail—the maximum time allowed under federal sentencing guidelines.

Ponzi Perps Are a Distinct Type

How was Brackett able, single-handedly, to keep her fraud going for more than five years? As we'll see through the course of this book, it takes a definite type of personality to organize and execute a Ponzi scheme. Unfortunately, these people usually combine two key characteristics: They're persuasive and they have few scruples.

Joshua Fry owned a small investment advisory firm near Baltimore, Maryland, called Stock and Option Services Inc. He impressed clients with detailed explanations of the program he'd developed for investing in the volatile derivatives markets. He was also witty and charismatic.

Fry said he had a method for maintaining the profitable upside of derivatives investments while reducing the downside risk. In the years before derivatives investments destroyed the prestigious British bank Barings and wounded giant American consumer products maker Procter & Gamble, this talk was convincing. Nearly 200 investors gave Fry a total of more than $5 million. "There'd always be some risk, but he said he had it down to no more than what you've got buying [stock in] General Motors," said one investor.

In fact, there was no risk at all...because Fry wasn't buying any derivatives. Rather than investing the money in an ingenious investment program, he spent indulgently on himself. He used more than half a million dollars to start a stable of race horses. He spent almost that much in Atlantic City casinos. (Like many Ponzi perps, Fry loved to gamble and usually lost.)

Throughout the scheme, Fry kept a jokey attitude that disarmed doubters. The vehicle that he used for collecting investors' money was called the GTC Fund. Fry would happily tell investors that "GTC" stood for Good Till Canceled or Gamblers Trading Consortium.

As often happens in these situations, the insouciant smirkiness made Fry all the more convincing. Who else but someone who knew what he was doing would treat serious money so unseriously?

In the end, the joke was on Fry's investors. During 1993, dividend checks to investors started bouncing. Angry investors called state authorities who promptly got a court order freezing Fry's assets, both personal and corporate.

Fry fled, leaving a note which said—in shades of his old form—that he was going to a place where "the weather will be warm and the primary tongue one other than English." But, again like most Ponzi perps, he didn't run anywhere exotic. He was arrested in Cincinnati 14 months after he'd left Baltimore.

Fry pleaded guilty to four counts of theft, securities fraud, lying to the Maryland securities commissioner and willfully failing to file a tax return. In early 1995, he was sentenced to eight years in state prison and ordered to pay restitution of $3.8 million to his investors.

State law enforcement officials seized a little less than $1 million in various assets under Fry's control. They doubted there was much of the GTC money left.

But the state couldn't keep an ambitious felon down. Less than a year after Fry moved into a Maryland prison, he posted his resume on an Internet website that offered fee-based financial advice. For an annual fee of $500, he would teach investors the intricacies of the stock options markets.

The posting made vague reference to "an unfortunate event" in which a client had defaulted on several hundred thousand dollars worth of trades and that Fry had made the "tragic mistake" of diverting other investor funds to cover the loss. (He didn't mention that he was writing from jail.)

Fry tried to put a positive spin on his bitter experience. His posting beseeched, "who better to advise against the pitfalls of...options trading than one who has been sucked into the abyss by utilizing them?"

Investors also Define the Ponzi Equation

The perps are only part of the equation, though. In order to understand why these schemes are becoming so common, we need to consider the greedy investors who enable the crooks.

In August 1996, the Nevada attorney general's office arrested five women and filed suit against 27 other people in what it called a "classic" Ponzi scheme[1] taking place in a city that wouldn't seem to need one: Las Vegas.

Actually, the Las Vegas scheme was more like a pyramid plan than a Ponzi scheme. It was surprisingly simple. Participants would receive $16,000 from a $2,000 investment if they could recruit a large enough number of family members, friends and co-workers. Time didn't matter that much, only the number of people a person could convince to join. The scheme's organizers didn't hesitate to admit that people who joined early would be paid by the people who followed.

The organizers of the pyramid scheme tapped a rich source when they got involved with the Las Vegas Metropolitan Police Department. Police sergeants, patrol officers and corrections officers were among the people actively recruiting co-workers to join the scheme.

By early 1996, the scheme collapsed and more than 200 people in the Las Vegas area lost their $2,000 entry fees. The fact that many of the participants were cops upset many people. A local newspaper complained:

---

[1]Law enforcement officials almost always refer to Ponzi schemes as "classic." A California lawyer who has prosecuted the things says, "It's a way that the cops can say these people should have known better than to get involved in a get-rich-quick scheme." In other words, it's a way for them to show the contempt they feel for the greed of the people involved. In the Nevada case, those people included some of their own.

> *Not only have they embarrassed themselves, their badges and their department, but they also have spent their precious credibility by recruiting others into the basest sort of get-rich-quick scheme.*

Like more flagrant forms of corruption, Ponzi schemes thrive on the kind of special, intense level of trust that police officers have in one another. And, like the more flagrant forms of corruption, the schemes undermine that trust.

One Las Vegas cop added some insight that seems to support the populist/class envy theory of why the schemes work. "This is a place where all kinds of bad people are making all kinds of good money. It's very hard to toe the straight line as a law enforcement professional. A lot of [police officers] looked at the scheme like a kind of honest graft."

A Global Phenomenon

Ponzi schemes aren't limited to San Diego leasing companies, North Carolina decorators or Las Vegas cops. Though the schemes are distinctly American phenomena, their resurging popularity is global. During the early and mid-1990s, several eastern European countries, newly relieved of the financial burden of Marxism, plunged into Ponzi schemes that were national in scope.

In Albania, which had suffered for 40 years under a Marxist regime too extreme for even the Soviet Union to support, private money-making schemes that promised huge dividends soaked up the savings of between 50 percent and 90 percent of the population. Most of these cons promised big money from the development of technology companies and international banks to people who barely understood the concept of currency. Almost $3 billion flowed into the schemes from people who could barely feed themselves. As ever, the first few successes created huge demand.

By late 1996, when the schemes started to collapse, street riots and political chaos followed. The outrage was understandable. The Albanian government, long suspected of being corrupt, had licensed most of the schemes. Although the government acknowledged what it called a "moral responsibility" to pay back at least some of the losses, its treasury didn't have enough cash to make a significant dent.

International Monetary Fund officials had warned the Albanian government about the schemes in 1995. Two years later, the same economists worried that the government could only meet its moral responsibility by printing money...and courting hyperinflation. "There can be very serious implications," said one IMF official. "There are risks to the stability of the currency and to the long-term economic stability of the country."

Albania wasn't alone in these troubles. In Romania, more than 500 pyramid schemes were hatched in the five years following 1989's overthrow of Nicolae Ceausescu. The biggest fund, known as Caritas, promised 800 percent profit within 100 days. In early 1994, the scheme collapsed with more than $1 billion in debts to three million investors.

"People Are Greedier Than They Are Smart"

As the eastern European countries develop their economies, they may find—as the West has—that people have short memories when it comes to get-rich-quick programs. As one investor in a New Jersey real estate pyramid said, thinking about all the money he lost, "People aren't stupid. They're just greedier than they are smart."

And perps are forever coming up with variations on Ponzi's scheme. In the precedent-setting Ponzi scheme decision *Kugler v. Koscot Interplanetary, Inc.*, the New Jersey State Supreme Court wrote:

> *Fraud is infinite in variety. The fertility of man's invention in devising new schemes of fraud is so great, that the courts have always declined to define it.... All surprise, trick, cunning, dissembling and other unfair way that is used to cheat anyone is considered as fraud.*

Almost all modern Ponzi frauds contain some semi-plausible business "explanation" for the astounding growth of the initial investors' money. It might be quick gains made from equipment leases, bridge loans, mortgages or currency futures. These things are echoes of Carlo Ponzi's Great Idea.

Also, the schemes always have perpetrators and promoters desperate enough to sell hard. These people are echoes of Ponzi himself.

PART ONE

How the Schemes Work

CHAPTER 1

The Mechanics Are Simple Enough

A Ponzi scheme isn't a complicated thing, mechanically. The perpetrator collects money from investors, promising huge returns in a matter of months or weeks. Then, he has to do one of two things:

1) return a portion of the invested money as "profit" while convincing investors to keep their "principle" (which is dwindling fast) invested; or

2) recruit new investors, whose money is used to produce the promised windfall to the earlier ones.

Even if the perp does the first thing, he'll eventually have to do the second.

Finding the second level of investors is usually the hardest part of the scheme. Once they are recruited, the scheme often drives its own growth. This is why a certain level of word-of-mouth publicity is essential to a scheme's success. When word of early profits and ritzy investors spreads, new investors pour in. With more dollars, the Ponzi perp is able to pay off more people.

Basically, a lot of cash is moving around but none...or very little...actually goes to anything that could legitimately turn a profit. The Ponzi perp can maintain the charade and skim off money for himself only as long as new suckers are feeding him with dollars. When this cash flow dwindles—even slightly—the whole scheme collapses.

The schemes can yield large returns for those who start them or join early on. As long as there are enough people to support the next level of the scheme, people above are safe. In financial circles, this is known as the "greater fool" theory. As long as you find someone willing to take your place in the scheme—a greater fool—the fact that you were a fool to invest doesn't matter.

The greater fool theory applies to more than just crooked schemes. Paying $40 million for a French Impressionist painting, $500,000 for a baseball card or a year's salary for a tulip bulb might make sense if there is someone willing to pay even more. But it's absolute folly if there's not. This fiscal relativism blurs many people's judgment about all investments.

The Numbers Never Add Up

"There's not a lot to be done about pyramids" or Ponzi schemes says Larry Hodapp, a senior attorney for the Federal Trade Commission in Washington D.C.. "People just have to be educated that the return rates these operations suggest are ridiculous."

A Ponzi scheme or pyramid plan, like a chain letter, is dependent on each new level of participants securing more persons to join. The new participant makes payment to the person on top of the list or pyramid, who then is removed, and replaced by those at the next level.

The fraud in the scheme is that when participants pay, they must assume that they and those that follow will be able to find new participants until all of the levels are filled.

In a four-level scheme, for all of the first group of new participants to be paid, 64 people need to join. After 20 levels of new participants, 8,388,608 additional investors would be needed. And there would be a total of 16,777,200 people in the scheme. These numbers are a practical impossibility.

Ponzi schemes are usually more secretive about these details than pyramid schemes. Ponzi perps keep their growing need for new money quiet—while pyramid perps usually announce their growing need as part of their pitch. In either case, the ultimate problem is the same: The schemes have to keep doubling, tripling or quadrupling in size just to avoid collapsing.

A Simple Four-level Pyramid

In 1987, a number of Wilmington, Delaware, residents were drawn into a pyramid investment scheme which was so simple in structure that it serves as a good primer for the basic mechanics.

The investors attended meetings where promoters pitched what they called an "airplane" scheme. If an investor bought a "seat" on an imaginary airplane for $5,000 and brought in two other people, he or she would receive $40,000. The scheme was a four-level pyramid:

1) When you paid your $5,000, you joined the group as a "junior sales executive."

2) After recruiting two other investors willing to pay $5,000, you moved up the ladder to a "senior sales executive" position.

3) After each new junior sales executive introduced two new investors (a total of four) to the group, you were promoted to "branch manager."

4) After each of those new people introduced two new investors (a total of eight) to the group, you became a "division manager."

The division manager would receive the money invested from each of the eight junior sales executives several levels below. At that point, he or she left the group or started the process anew.

The Delaware pitches were made by two men: John Ferro and Robert Jorge. They assured potential investors that the investment was risk-free and that the scheme was legal as long as investors declared the income.

Ferro and Jorge also waived off another possible problem: not having the $5,000 to invest. They could arrange financing in the form of personal lines of credit through several sources, including Chrysler First Financial Services Corp. Jorge passed out Chrysler First application forms at some of the meetings and introduced potential investors to Larry Doub, an employee of Chrysler First who attended several pitch meetings and participated as an investor in the scheme.

Chrysler First approved dozens of personal lines of credit connected to Ferro and Jorge's scheme. Many of these people borrowed the money (very expensively, with loan origination fees and high interest rates considered), invested in the scheme and got nothing out. The scheme collapsed after a few weeks when Delaware state police arrested Ferro and Jorge.

A group of investors sued Chrysler First, arguing that the loans were part of the fraudulent scheme and, therefore, not enforceable.

Delaware courts didn't show much sympathy to the fast-buck investors. In a March 1991 decision, *James M. Burns, et al., v. John J. Ferro, et al., and Chrysler First*, a trial court ruled that Chrysler First was not responsible for the fact that its borrowers spent their money in a Ponzi scheme. It agreed with Chrysler First that the borrowers knew they were getting into an illegal scheme and did so willingly:

> *It would be far easier to turn straw into gold than to turn $5,000 into $40,000 legally under this scheme. The fact that [investors] had knowledge of the pyramid scheme is not in dispute. The promotional materials made it plain that the investment idea was a pyramid scheme from the beginning. They participated in promoting the "airplane" by recruiting new members to perpetuate the scheme. [They], therefore, may not seek relief.*

"Commonality" and "Efforts of Others"

In the 1974 federal court decision *SEC v. Koscot Interplanetary, Inc.*, the Fifth Circuit Court of Appeals defined some basic issues and terms. Koscot was a subsidiary of Glenn W. Turner Enterprises (an umbrella organization that operated a number of Ponzi and pyramid operations). Through Koscot, investors could make money both by selling cosmetics and by recruiting "supervisors" and "distributors" to sell cosmetics and recruit others.

To obtain the right to make money through the recruitment of others required an investment of at least $1,000. That investment qualified a person as a "supervisor" who could then recruit other supervisors. For every supervisor recruited, the recruiting supervisor received $600 of the $1,000 paid by the new supervisor. For $5,000, an investor could become a "distributor" who could then recruit both supervisors and distributors in return for a share of their investments.

The details of the scheme were fairly standard. But the court decided that it was important to distinguish whether the Koscot distributorships counted as a security—like a stock, bond or promissory note—and, therefore, whether Ponzi scheme precedents could be applied.

In order to be a security, an investment needs to be made in a common enterprise in which investors give over control of assets to another entity. In discussing the *common enterprise* element of the scheme, the court recognized that "[t]he critical factor is not the similitude or coincidence of investor input, but rather the uniformity of impact of the promoter's efforts."

It quoted an earlier appeals court decision which held:

> *A common enterprise managed by...third parties with adequate personnel and equipment is therefore essential if the investors are to achieve their paramount aim of a return on their investments.*

This may sound like a pretty generic description of any investment vehicle—but, in the context of a Ponzi scheme, it's what distinguishes an elegant con from simply sticking a gun in someone's face and taking his money.

Using this analysis, the Fifth Circuit ruled that "the requisite commonality is evidenced by the fact that the fortunes of all investors are inextricably tied to the efficacy of the Koscot meetings and guidelines on recruiting prospects and consummating a sale." These meetings and guidelines were very much like those of most pyramid schemes—they were almost evangelical in their intensity and they focused more on getting paid than on the substance of the investment.

This left one other key pyramid scheme issue for the *Koscot* court to consider. Ponzi perps often argue that an investor's losses are the result of investors not working hard enough to keep the scheme going. In other words, the reason that Grandma lost the $20,000 she pumped into her cosmetics distributorship is that she didn't do enough to sell lipstick or recruit salespeople. She *deserved* to lose the money.

And, technically, the fact that she had to do some work to keep the scheme afloat means that the cosmetics distributorships didn't count as securities in the first place.

In this narrow sense, the perps might have a point. The Securities and Exchange Acts of 1933 and 1934 defined *securities* in part as investments whose success or failure came "solely from the efforts of others." But some courts had allowed broader interpretations of that phrase.

The *Koscot* court agreed that "solely from the efforts of others" wasn't meant to be a tool for protecting Ponzi perps. It ruled that a literal interpretation of the requirement would frustrate the original intent of the law. Instead, "the critical inquiry is whether the efforts made by those other than the investor are the undeniably significant ones, those essential managerial efforts which affect the failure or success of the enterprise."

Since, in most Ponzi schemes, the answer to that question is *Yes*, the court concluded that the perps don't have a right to Grandma's $20,000.

Case Study: Elliott Enterprises

From 1980 to 1987, Charles Elliott managed a collection of investment companies that included Elliott Real Estate, Inc., Elliott Securities, Elliott Mortgage Company, Inc., and Elliott Group, Inc.

Elliott Securities was a stock brokerage. The other companies marketed investment vehicles created and managed by Elliott. The brokerage operated primarily as what one former employee called "a fish pond." Clients with the money to buy and sell large amounts of stock were invited to meet Elliott. The sales pitch was simple: "We can get you 7 percent down here but if you want 18, you'll have to go upstairs to see [Elliott]."

Most of Elliott's 1,400 investors were retirees who believed they were gaining a high-yield tax haven for their life savings.

In fact, they were being sucked into a Ponzi scheme.

Like many smart Ponzi perps, Elliott made a big show of religious devotion. In his newsletters, he often quoted the scriptures. "Every letter we got from him made me think this is one of the most religious men I've ever dealt with," recalled one investor.

In his first newsletter of 1987, Elliott wrote floridly:

> *I am reminded of my strong commitment and relationship with God. I believe that spiritual strength is the only strength because it is capable of infinite renewal....I personally approach 1987 inspired to be honest, humble, courageous, clean-hearted, patient and noble.*

In the meantime, he was using gullible investors' money to collect conspicuous signs of God's favor—flashy things like rare jewelry, vintage cars and trendy art. He also threw lots of parties, including a big Christmas party every year for employees and investors.

Less piously, Elliott decorated his offices with photographs of himself with politicians and celebrities. He'd boast especially about his ties to Republican power-brokers. Some potential investors were told that Elliott was one of Ronald Reagan's "personal financial advisors."

The political boasts weren't Elliott's idea. He'd grown up in rural North Carolina and still saw most things—including confidence schemes—from a farm boy's earnest perspective. William Melhorn, chief executive officer for Elliott Enterprises, was the man who saw the obvious connection between power and money.

Melhorn had begun as a special assistant to Elliott and quickly worked his way up to chief executive officer. The two men had met in the mid-1970s. Melhorn was out of a job, following the collapse of an earlier enterprise, and Elliott needed people with ... particular ... experience.

In public, Elliott said his special expertise was municipal bonds and other tax-advantaged investments—and that investments with his firms were insured by the Securities Investor Protection Corp. In private, though, the most common investments he peddled were so-called "repurchase agreements." Essentially, these agreements were loans made by investors to Elliott (and, therefore, not insurable by SIPC). The loans may have been *collateralized* by municipal bonds—but investors never actually participated directly in the investments.

The SEC would later charge that most of the loans weren't really collateralized at all. (Elliott kept a small portfolio of muni bonds, which he pledged dozens...and possibly hundreds...of times as collateral.)

Free to use investment proceeds any way he chose, Elliott tended toward speculative start-ups and boneheaded real estate deals. But he was disciplined about keeping payments current with investors. "Elliott paid like a slot machine," said one associate. "He lulled everyone to sleep."

He had to borrow extensively to maintain the appearance of a thriving business, though. And his precarious circumstances always pressured him to chase new investors to pay off old ones. All the while, Elliott used investor funds to pay for his personal living expenses—including medical expenses and mortgage payments on his various houses. His sole employment during the lifespan of the scheme was as president of Elliott Enterprises—for which he never received a salary. Instead, he compensated himself by commingling investors' money with his own.

There was no legal mechanism to prevent him from doing this. Because Elliott Enterprises was an unincorporated business, Elliott could

draw upon company bank accounts as tho
funds. He kept a separate personal acco
Enterprises and moved money into this a
it. At several points during the scheme
more than $1 million.

The SEC was first alerted to Elliott in 19
that year, Elliott Realty employee James Gersonde co
to invest about $400,000 with Elliott. Gersonde's brothe
lived in Michigan, felt the deal was too good to be true. John a
questions but didn't like the answers he heard. His mother and brother claimed that they were earning a guaranteed 10 percent on money placed with Elliott—and that this income was tax-free. John rightly suspected a tax-free investment which paid as much as 10 percent—let alone a "guaranteed" 10 percent. So, he contacted the SEC office in Miami. (Though his mother was later happy she'd been able to get her money out of Elliott Enterprises, John Gersonde said at the time "she was furious with me for ruining her tax-free investment. Livid.")

The Feds called Elliott to their Miami office for questioning. He showed up at their offices but refused to explain his operations in any detail. Surprised by Elliott's brashness, the SEC agents let him go. But Elliott Enterprises was in their investigative sights.

In the early part of 1987, which was the peak of its larceny, Elliott Enterprises owed approximately 940 investors about $60 million in repurchase agreements and other loans. However, word was spreading fast through south Florida that the Feds were after Elliott. And interest checks started coming less reliably. Through this all, Elliott maintained a kind of crazy impetuousness. One worried investor who telephoned the company was told by an Elliott Enterprises employee that Elliott had been called to Washington by President Reagan for emergency financial advice.

There's no question that personal charisma was one of Elliott's keenest tools. "He would make decisions that weren't logical at all," one former associate said. "You'd wonder. Then you'd look around at the office, and all he had put together, and you'd say 'This guy must know oing. Maybe he sees a bigger picture than I do.'"

ny persuasive Ponzi perps, Elliott was able to convince some ors that the Feds were the villains. "I don't think the SEC is g very nice to Mr. Elliott," one investor told a local newspaper. /e honestly feel he hasn't done anything all that wrong."

Nice or not, the SEC filed a civil suit against Elliott and his firms in early 1987. The SEC suit was the final blow for Elliott Enterprises. The Ponzi scheme collapsed and all payments ceased.

In the immediate aftermath of a court-ordered receivership, Elliott's investors and creditors stood to recover a little more than 10 cents on the dollar. For any more, they would have to sue someone. Within a few months, Elliott and Melhorn were facing a major criminal indictment—which included 22 counts of fraud under the Investment Advisors Act, six counts of securities fraud under the Securities Act, 10 counts of mail fraud, and one count of conspiracy.

"I'm not sure that apart from market forces and unwise investments that he has an explanation for what happened," said David Pollack, Elliott's lawyer. "I think [it was] just a series of investments that didn't work out the way he thought they would."

But one former Elliott employee offered a more likely explanation: "His ego told him he could stay ahead of the game and it would all pay off. I don't think he had any criminal intent. He really thought he could give them what he promised."

The legal proceedings didn't go well for Elliott. In August 1988, a federal judge ordered him to "disgorge" $1 million for the receiver's benefit. Elliott was not able to comply because he didn't have any money. In January 1989, he was ordered in a civil suit to turn over his personal jewelry and household effects to the SEC. In March 1990, a federal trial jury returned a verdict of guilty on all but two of the criminal charges Elliott and Melhorne faced. Elliott was sentenced to three consecutive five-year prison terms. Melhorn received three consecutive four-year prison terms.

In April 1994, a federal appeals court considered Elliott's last gasp at arguing his innocence. Elliott claimed that the trial court should have listened to testimony from his *satisfied* customers when considering his intent to defraud. The appeals court didn't agree:

> *No amount of testimony from satisfied customers could "average out" Elliott and Melhorn's intent to defraud when they continued to solicit new investments and reassure old investors while concealing millions of dollars in losses per year with fictitious audits and phantom collateral....*

But Elliott remained free on bail while he filed other appeals. "Last time I heard, he was living up in Tallahassee," one burned investor said. "They just keep appealing and appealing. He's never served a day. I hope he winds up in jail, though. He should serve some time."

CHAPTER 2

Location, Location, Location...Then the Money's Gone

Real estate seems to beg Ponzi schemes.

Historically, Ponzi perpetrators have focused on commercial real estate development programs. They'd often use the so-called "four-from-three" formula—which is often used by legitimate developers.

In this kind of deal, the developer finds a good property, lines up potential tenants and may even arrange partial financing. To find the money he needs to complete the project, he looks for investors who will each put in a set amount of money in exchange for an equal ownership interest. In the case of three investors, each one gets a 25 percent interest and the developer gets an equal 25 percent interest for the time and effort that went into setting up the project.

Since legitimate developers use this formula, it provides credibility for Ponzi perps who either collect the investments and don't actually develop anything or sell dozens of 25 percent shares in a single project.

An example: In May 1997, Stephen J. Murphy was arrested on a 25-count indictment charging him with mail fraud and money laundering related to a Ponzi scheme that bilked more than 200 southern California investors out of more than $13 million between 1990 and 1993. The indictment resulted from a cooperative investigation made by the FBI and the IRS Criminal Investigation Division.

Murphy promised phenomenal returns to investors from across the United States if they invested their money in one of several commercial real estate projects being developed by his company, American Capital Investments Inc. (ACI). He invited people to invest in dozens of limited partnerships managed by ACI. The self-proclaimed real estate investment expert had advertised heavily on television and in magazines. He'd also co-written a book called *One Up on Trump.*

According to the U.S. Attorney's office in Los Angeles, Murphy commingled money from various limited partnerships and improperly diverted a large portion of that money to pay, ACI's operating expenses and his own personal expenses. Allegedly, Murphy also used funds from later investors to pay supposed profits to earlier investors. The indictment charged that Murphy lied to obtain his investors' money and continued to hide the truth to avoid having to repay principal and promised profits.(The Securities and Exchange Commission had begun a civil investigation of Murphy and ACI for fraudulent practices in early 1993. Murphy did not tell the investors about this investigation, as required by law.)

As many Ponzi perps do, Murphy persuaded investors to roll their supposed profits into new funds rather than cashing out. Those who demanded their money were paid with funds from later investors. Unfortunately, only a few investors demanded their money back. Of more than $18 million that Murphy collected from investors, he returned less than $5 million.

About the time that the SEC was opening its investigation into Murphy's limited partnership Ponzi, it was closing the lid on another.

In September 1993, the SEC filed a lawsuit against Atlanta real estate developer H. Ellis Ragland. The Feds asked U.S. District Court Judge J. Owen Forrester to make Ragland return $670,042 in "ill-gotten gains" derived from a Ponzi scheme.

Between July 1985 and December 1987, Ragland's company, Guaranty Financial Corp., raised more than $4 million from 165 investors in three limited partnerships and two blind pools. (Blind pools are investment vehicles in which investors don't know exactly how or where their money will be used.)

In each limited partnership, Ragland was the general partner or manager, in charge of scouting out real estate in metropolitan Atlanta. Investors who assumed they were putting their money in shopping centers, auto malls and undeveloped commercial land were instead supporting Ragland's social-climbing lifestyle, including a taste for fine wines, payments on his house, country club dues and a Mercedes-Benz, according to the SEC.

The SEC lawsuit had come too late to save Ragland's investors. A few weeks earlier, a group of investors who'd asked repeatedly to withdraw their money from Ragland's limited partnerships had forced him and Guaranty Financial into involuntary bankruptcy.

A court-appointed trustee investigating the assets of both Ragland and his wife didn't find much. He finally agreed to a settlement of only $10,000. This might seem like a surprisingly small settlement—considering the large sums of money Ragland collected from his investors—but very little is ever recovered in the wake of a Ponzi scheme.

The "Zero-Down" Ponzi

Beginning in the recession of the late 1980s, a number of real estate Ponzi specialists moved from the commercial market to the so-called "zero-down" residential market. They filled the deregulated television airwaves with infomercials promising big profits from investments in distressed properties.

Zero-down Ponzi schemes can be complicated. The perp will offer information and support that helps investors find residential real estate owned by people who are late in paying property taxes, mortgage payments or both. (Some schemes focus, instead, on real estate tied up in probate or other estate disputes. But the ultimate point is the same.)

Just before a bank repossession or tax sale, the zero-down investor steps in and offers to take over the payments on the property—sometimes on an accelerated schedule—in exchange for taking the title. Usually, some heated negotiating follows. If the existing owner and lender or tax assessor are desperate enough, they will agree to easy terms.

Anyone with decent credit and strong nerves can do this. Where does the Ponzi perp come in? He's been "coaching" the zero-down investor through the process. If it goes well for the investor, she can end up owning a piece of real estate with some—though usually not much—positive equity value. *That's* what the Ponzi perp wants. Saddled with the right kind of second mortgage, it becomes cash in his hand.

Part of the Ponzi perp's coaching will be to convince the successful zero-down investor to borrow against equity in the newly acquired property and join the perp in other real estate deals. "It's a neat trick," says a veteran real estate Ponzi perp from the New York area. "You use other people's good credit, stupidity and greed to squeeze the last few drops of cash out of property that was already in trouble. And they're actually coming to you asking what to do next! Give me the money is what to do next."

Second Mortgages and Trust Deeds

In many cases, the zero-down investing strategy is really a funding mechanism for getting money into a Ponzi scheme. Once there, it will often disappear in a flurry of real estate-related transactions. And these will have something to do with second mortgages.

Second mortgages are a shadowy sideline to traditional real estate lending. In many states, they are regulated less carefully than primary loans. And, since traditional lenders shy away from them, second mortgages are often made by non-bank financing companies and entrepreneurial mortgage brokers placing money for people who want higher returns or more secrecy than traditional investments offer.

One FBI special agent puts it bluntly: "There's a lot of dirty money in the second-mortgage business. Stolen money. Drug money. Mob money. Money from con schemes."

In 1985, Guy Scarpaci started a mortgage brokerage called U.S. Funding in suburban Boston. The company advertised aggressively that it could get mortgages for anybody, regardless of financial status or credit history.

As a result of the ads, U.S. Funding attracted large numbers of low and moderate income borrowers, people with poor credit or who were otherwise in dire financial straights. In order to sell these loans in the secondary market, U.S. Funding manipulated the records of the motley borrowers to make them appear more creditworthy than they really were.

The company also prepared phony appraisals and, in some cases, created phony title histories. As a result, loans were granted based upon the security of properties which the borrower did not own or which were already encumbered, with multiple loans.

U.S. Funding often told borrowers and investors that the proceeds of loans would be used to pay off prior indebtedness on the mortgaged property. But the company would divert the money to other uses. As a result of these diversions, U.S. Funding was often in a deficit situation. It had to use the proceeds from later loans to pay off indebtedness associated with earlier borrowers. In effect, U.S. Funding operated as a massive Ponzi scheme.

By the fall of 1989, the company wasn't able to write enough new second mortgages to keep its pyramid standing. U.S. Funding employees prepared for the inevitable collapse by destroying some of the documents that showed how the company had inflated borrowers' creditworthiness and properties' value. But there were so many incriminating documents, they couldn't destroy them all.

The company collapsed in late 1989. A federal investigation followed.

Beginning in 1991, the U.S. Attorney's office in Boston reached plea bargains with various former U.S. Funding employees and people related to the company. In the end, they'd diverted more than $10 million through the scheme.

There are several signs that should warn an investor that a second mortgage operation is actually a Ponzi scheme.

First, very high interest rates are always suspect. When standard first mortgages are charging 7 percent to 9 percent annual interest, legitimate second mortgages should be charging between 12 and 15 percent. Promised interest earnings of 18 percent or higher could mean the company is in trouble and desperate to attract money.

Second, in most states, mortgage brokers must have a realtor's license, a special broker's license or both. An investor should ask to see these licenses and make a call to the government agency that issues them to ask about any complaints made against the broker. If a broker can't produce the licenses, he or she may be a crook.

Third, legitimate second mortgage brokers will record their loans or trust deeds at the county recorder's office (or with an equivalent agency). A broker who claims he's experienced but can't show any paper trail with the county may be a Ponzi perp.

Fourth, mortgage brokers who lend money without title insurance are immediately suspect. Among other things, title insurance makes sure the owners are real and the property doesn't have six or ten other mortgages already.

A final note: Lenders in the second mortgage market often "warehouse" mortgages. In a typical warehouse arrangement, a party lends against a large number of mortgages for a short period of time. Warehousing provides interim funding to the originator of the mortgage until the mortgage can find a permanent investor, and it is used to cover various other delays between origination and ultimate resale on the secondary mortgage market. While warehousing is legal, it makes keeping track of money difficult.

Case Study: Financial Concepts

The biggest factor that makes real estate a rich ground for running Ponzi schemes is the illusion many people have that it's somehow different from other kinds of business. "People think they understand real estate. They think it's a safer bet because you can go and see it," says one California law enforcement official who has prosecuted several Ponzi schemes. "That's not true. The land and the building may be concrete. But ownership and loans can be hidden and manipulated in a hundred different ways."

In the mid-1970s, Earl Dean Gordon and Kenneth Boula founded a real estate investment syndicate called Financial Concepts, consisting of dozens of limited and general partnerships, which were in turn comprised of hundreds of individual investors. The operation was headquartered in Barrington, Illinois, a conservative Chicago suburb. The low-key environment was a cover for a far-reaching real estate Ponzi scheme.

Billing themselves as investment advisors, Gordon and Boula ran folksy ads on radio and TV offering free "estate planning seminars" with euphemistic names like "Operation Snowbird" and "Life After Work, A New Beginning." The workshops purportedly offered a "psychological adjustment program, a physical adjustment program, and a financial program for retirees." The adjustment that Financial Concepts had in mind for these attendees was brutal.

The real aim of the seminars had little to do with estate planning; the sharpies used them to sell investments in Financial Concepts. Some 3,000 investors—many of them elderly—bit.

Among other things, Gordon and Boula used investors' money to buy expensive toys: 22 automobiles, eight motorcycles, four airplanes, and an aircraft hangar. They ran up $10,000 monthly charges on their credit cards, paying the bills with investors' funds.

Gordon and Boula offered limited income partnerships yielding annual interest of up to 15 percent. They also promised investors that their money would be used to develop a particular property. They didn't usually do that. Instead, they'd use newly acquired money to finance other partnerships whose properties had not produced promised cash.

And this was a major problem. Few Financial Concepts partnerships generated any income. As one court later noted: "Whether by criminal malice or poor business acumen, properties Gordon and Boula relied on to solicit investors did not yield the promised returns, and the two began to pay earlier partnerships with money garnered from more recent ones."

The high-risk nature of the partnerships and some of the conflicts of interest were spelled out in the prospectuses for the partnerships, which warned that Gordon and Boula were permitted to enter into "potentially adversarial relationships" with investors regarding construction, financing, management and virtually every other aspect related to the projects.

The problem for many investors, according to one salesman who sold investment programs for Financial Concepts, was that they didn't have access to prospectuses. He recalled:

> *We were told to do everything we could to avoid letting them see a prospectus until after we had their money in hand. Sometimes we even would tell people that we had run out of copies and our word processor was down when there would be a pile of 40 or so on a nearby table. Generally, we'd mail them out a month or two after we had the money.*

And even if investors *did* see the paperwork, they wouldn't have been able to deduce much. Unlike most limited-partnership prospectuses, Financial Concepts' deal books didn't contain analyses of cash flows or any other financial data. In at least one case, the prospectus did not disclose the address of the apartment building in which investors were supposed to put their money. Nor did any of the documents mention the fees and expenses that absorbed large amounts of investment and funds.

These fees were often steep. Up to 25 percent of investors' money was taken off the top by Financial Concepts as a commission. Investors were also charged an "acquisition fee" of 10 percent on purchased property, various accounting and management fees and a 15 percent "termination" fee if they elected to sell early. In one two-year period, Financial Concepts took $121,000 in "fees and commissions" and another $37,000 in "legal and accounting fees."

In late 1987 and early 1988, Illinois securities regulators started investigating Financial Concepts to find out whether money from new investors was—in fact—being used to pay off previous investors.

During the early stages of the investigations, Gordon agreed to address a meeting of nearly 1,000 Financial Concepts investors. He called the state inquiry "a total rehash of two-year-old news." He said the charges stemmed from a technical violation of securities regulations the company had committed several years before by failing to file a form and pay a $30 filing fee. "The day we learned of that, we voluntarily suspended doing that," he said. "We haven't done what we've been accused of for two years." And then he made his pitch:

> *I'm not asking for your sympathy...but evaluate in your hearts the relationship we've had to this day, outside of having the hell scared out of you. I'm asking for your strength, for the same friendship we've always enjoyed and for your prayers, to help us endure what we have to endure.*

After the meeting, a number of investors went away happy with their investments. But the grind of regulatory scrutiny continued.

The investigations forced Financial Concepts to start recognizing the money problems caused by their numerous distressed projects. In March 1988, the Illinois Securities Department obtained a court order barring Financial Concepts from selling real estate limited partnerships on the ground that the ones it had sold were not properly registered. With that order, the scheme collapsed. Gordon and Boula declared bankruptcy for themselves and Financial Concepts.

A federal lawsuit followed a month later, in April 1988. The suit claimed that Gordon and Boula had sold property to partnerships at prices far above their true market value, mailed false financial statements and juggled funds among partnerships.

Prosecutors estimated that as many as 8,000 investors entrusted at least $60 million to Gordon and Boula. "Equity" partnerships bought real estate, including homes and resort property, and "income" partnerships lent money to the equity partnerships to buy property. They claimed that many of the income partnership investors were unaware the assets of the equity partnerships were "significantly less in value" than amounts lent to them.

All entities owned or controlled by Gordon and Boula were eventually placed under the receivership. Illinois-based real estate expert Jeffrey Cagan was appointed receiver and charged with managing the remaining assets of Financial Concepts. Cagan's appointment meant that investors could not withdraw any money pending a resolution of the case. Worse still: Under the court order, investors could be required to make additional payments to the partnerships in which they invested.

At the time of the receivership, a preliminary review placed the value of property owned by the partnerships at $10 to $20 million. Investors hoped to recover between 30 to 40 cents on the dollar of their investments. That hope turned out to be optimistic.

Prosecutors charged that, just before they entered bankruptcy, Gordon and Boula transferred $270,000 in investor funds to Swiss bank accounts in an unsuccessful effort to conceal their wrongdoing. The two were charged with three federal counts of mail fraud.

Gordon and Boula pleaded guilty and to their surprise were sentenced to 108 months in jail. Using terms like "incredible greed," and accusing them of destroying people's "capacity to express love," U.S. District Judge Brian Duff told Gordon and Boula, "There will be no tears for the sentence I impose. It will be well deserved."

Duff ordered a deputy U.S. marshal to lock both men up immediately to begin serving their sentences. But, after court personnel informed the judge that additional time was needed to designate a prison for the felons, he begrudgingly allowed them to remain free.

Gordon and Boula's attorneys said they would appeal Duff's sentence. They contended that he had exceeded federal sentencing guidelines, which would call for a prison term ranging from 30 to 46 months for each man.

A federal appeals court later held that sentences for crimes arising out of a Ponzi scheme were not subject to enhancement on the grounds the defendants specifically targeted elderly investors. So, it asked Duff to reconsider his sentence. He did—and found stronger legal grounds for keeping the same, harsh sentences.

CHAPTER 3

A Better Mousetrap Makes a Good Scam

New technologies have a rich history of fraudulent promotion. Over the last hundred years, crooks have promoted perpetual motion machines, water engines and magic elixirs. In the last 20 years, real technological advances have made outlandish promises seem all the more plausible.

As recently as the early 1980s, few people would have guessed that hundreds of millions of dollars would be made in stock offerings for companies that make Internet web browsers. A few years before that, no one would have known what to think of recombinant DNA drugs. And these issues say nothing of more modest tech advances, like cellular phones and satellite TV.

Like predators sensing a kill, Ponzi scheme perpetrators are drawn to this high tech confusion. "Whenever a new technology comes over the horizon, we see the same types of scams," says Paul Huey-Burns, assistant enforcement director at the SEC. Though this remark could apply to any high tech issue, Huey-Burns was talking specifically about a favorite Ponzi scheme premise of the early 1990s—wireless cable.

The wireless cable television business centered on a new technology that transmitted television programming signals through microwave relay systems, rather than through wire cables. This eliminated the capital-intense process of connecting homes to cable networks. It removed the *cable* from *cable TV*. It also made it possible—at least theoretically—for small, scrappy start-up companies to compete with giant cable companies. And the actual product is virtually unregulated.

Ponzi perps didn't miss the chance to exploit this opportunity. They promise outlandish returns—as much as several hundred percent—in a few months. The pitch will usually have something to do with acquiring licenses for transmission access cheaply and then selling them to an established cable player. It has nothing to do with the truth. The perp takes a big chunk of money out immediately, never puts anything into the cable system and runs the pyramid long enough to blur his tracks.

Other wireless cable deals will have some basis in truth. The perp will actually acquire a license and will use at least some of the investment proceeds to build a system. The rest of the money goes in the perp's pocket. Then, he'll operate the company for a while or sell it to a larger company for less than the amount he raised in investments—hoping no one loses enough to sue.

As farfetched as they may be, these schemes were a booming business in the mid-1990s. In 1997, the SEC was prosecuting more than 20 wireless cable fraud cases, involving more than 20,000 investors and $250 million. In a single 1996 civil lawsuit, the SEC sued four companies and 14 stock promoters who pitched nearly $19 million in investments in wireless cable systems from 1992 through 1994.

Wireless cable is another example of an idea that makes more sense to investors than it should. Many people think they know the cable industry because they watch a lot of ESPN and HBO. "It was the largest mix of people I've ever seen," says a southern California perp who sold bogus wireless cable securities in the early 1990s. "When you're selling gold or real estate, you get wealthier people who think they know what they're doing. In wireless cable, you get all kinds. Doctors and dentists, sure. But also truck drivers and people working retail. They're greedy. They might have heard Peter Lynch or somebody say 'invest in things you understand.' And they think they understand TV."

The State of the Crooked Art: Pre-paid Telephone Cards

As the 1990s wore on, consumer complaints and SEC investigations chased many Ponzi perps out of the wireless cable business. Some moved into a field in which the technology issues were much more basic—but popular demand was much greater: long distance telephone service.

The deregulation of AT&T was a shining moment of 1980s small-government ideology. It allowed companies like MCI and Sprint to become billion-dollar giants and drove down the cost of most long distance telephone service. It also created dozens of small long distance companies that focus on finding cheap, aggressive ways of marketing their services. In short, the long distance telephone business became a commodity market, in which price drove market share.

While investment-oriented Ponzi schemes do best in industries with big markups and profit margins, sales-oriented pyramid programs do well in fields with thinner margins. This is one of the most important distinctions between the two. And it's the reason that some of the most devoted Ponzi perps have experience running either kind of scheme. They size up a market, a company and a population—then start an investment- or sales-oriented scheme based on which will work best, accordingly.

When an industry transforms from a regulated monopoly (or near monopoly) to a price-driven commodity market, legitimate multilevel marketing mechanisms will flourish. They're cheap and relatively effective[1]. Where legitimate multilevel marketing schemes flourish, illegal pyramid schemes—their black sheep relatives—will follow.

In early 1995, the Better Business Bureau of San Diego County warned that southern California residents were being exploited by a multilevel marketing operation that was engaged in the long-distance phone business.

The company was Irvine-based National Telephone & Communications (NTC). Its corporate parent was Incomnet, a publicly-traded company also based in southern California. NTC sold long-distance telephone service and prepaid cards which allow people to make calls from public telephones. It also sold distributorships for selling the service and cards. Critics claimed that it cared more about selling distributorships than signing up actual long-distance customers.

---

[1] For more detail on multilevel marketing and its uneasy relationship with Ponzi schemes, see Chapter 14.

For $95, a person could become an NTC distributor. But distributors were strongly encouraged to pay $495 to attend Long Distance University, a "leadership course." (According to an NTC newsletter, the course was "a requirement for becoming an area marketing manager.") Finally, for another $700, a distributor could become a "certified trainer"—and sell distributorships to other people.

The BBB was concerned that Incomnet made its money from a pyramid scheme—not from selling long-distance service. About 24 percent of Incomnet's 1994 revenue came from fees paid by distributors and trainers. "Based on our investigation, we believe the average sales rep for NTC can expect to make less than $100 a year," said Lisa Curtis, president of the San Diego BBB. Curtis went on to say that ethnic groups—primarily Hispanics—were being recruited with particular intensity by NTC.

Beginning in the summer of 1994, NTC and Incomnet started having some problems. A number of sales representatives were leaving NTC—and many of these were complaining that it hadn't paid them earned commissions. The Better Business Bureau noted: "Our complaint history shows a failure to eliminate the basic cause of complaints alleging problems with billing for long-distance service."

But, as the BBB group was making its announcement, word was circulating that NTC and Incomnet were being investigated by the SEC for operating an illegal pyramid scheme. Incomnet insisted the approach was legitimate and that it wasn't the pyramid critics alleged.

A January 1995 Incomnet press release said that rumors that it was under SEC investigation were "categorically false." But the next day, a company spokesman sheepishly said Incomnet wasn't under a "major" investigation. Two weeks later, the company issued a "clarification" conceding that it had indeed been under an SEC investigation since August 1994.

The SEC wasn't the only group looking into the companies. The California Attorney General's office was probing whether Incomnet complied with the state's "business opportunities" law. (The law requires marketers to register with the state if, among other things, sales representatives must pay $500 or more to join.)

As much as anything, critics of NTC were concerned about some of the people running it. The long-distance operation was designed by two people who were involved with Kansas-based Culture Farms, Inc.[2]—an infamous pyramid scheme in which some principles went to jail.

Jerry Ballah, NTC's marketing director, had settled a civil lawsuit over his role as a consultant to Culture Farms. (Ballah was also involved with another multilevel marketer of long-distance phone service, Arizona-based NCN Communications.) Chris Mancuso, NTC's director of product development for a brief time, had served nine months in prison for his role in Culture Farms.

NTC and Incomnet weathered the regulatory storms of 1995. By early 1997, NTC was still in business. But it had turned its focus more sharply on ethnic groups and selling pre-paid phone cards, rather than traditional long-distance service.

"Pre-paid phone cards are the perfect product for a Ponzi scheme trying to pass as legitimate multilevel marketing," says one former Ponzi perp. "They have the gloss of high tech...but they're actually inexpensive and need to be replaced constantly."

Even the most grizzled Ponzi perp can't predict where the next high-tech schemes will emerge. But a number of people who know how the schemes work guess the premise will be genetically-engineered cosmetics and dietary supplements. "You started to see hints of this when the FDA was holding back on approving new AIDS drugs," says a federal law enforcement official who's helped prosecute dozens of Ponzi schemes. "The combination of biotech sizzle with the tried-and-true appeal of makeup and vitamins is a great pitch for Ponzi scammers."

Case Study: United Energy Corporation

California-based United Energy Corporation operated at the intersection of technology, tax havens and larceny.

[2] In the Culture Farms scam, some 28,000 investors lost about $50 million buying kits that would grow milky "cultures" in a glass, supposedly to be processed into cosmetics. Most of the cultures grown were simply recycled into new kits and resold to investors.

UEC President Ernest Lampert, who claimed to have made a fortune in construction and other business ventures in Alaska and Hawaii, had a fairly utopian plan. His company would generate electricity from high-tech solar modules suspended in pools of water—and sell the juice to local utilities. It would then use the hot water produced by solar electricity to raise warm-water fish and produce ethanol and high protein cattle feed as by-products.

UEC installed a network of 3,000 photovoltaic solar-cell collectors on man-made, acre-sized ponds in the rural California towns of Borrego Springs, Barstow and Davis. From the air, the "solar farms" looked like huge checkerboards. The 20-by-20 foot photovoltaic modules were shallow boxes with concave surfaces that focused sunlight on solar cells. They were mounted on islands about 208 feet in diameter, with aluminum frames packed with Styrofoam. These islands floated in a few feet of water.

Water was piped through the modules to cool them; this would then heat the ponds for fish breeding. The whole process was part of what Lampert called an "integrated life system."

Better still: Lampert claimed that UEC's solar energy cash flow would be heavily tax-advantaged. The average module, over its 30-year life span, would produce net cash flow of $243,775, all for an out-of-pocket down payment of only about $15,000.

The promised tax benefits proved to be grossly exaggerated. Still, UEC sold 5,323 aluminum and styrofoam solar energy devices to 4,500 investors for $30,000 to $40,000 each. That was a total take of more than $200 million—though only about $83 million was collected. "Ernie was a consummate salesman," says Patrick Jordan, a lawyer who bought a solar module from Lampert.

UEC recruited life insurance agents and financial planners to sell modules on a commission basis. The contracts for the modules usually provided for down payments ranging from 36 percent to 43 percent of the purchase price, with the remainder financed by long-term, generally nonrecourse, promissory notes which were payable in semiannual or annual installments and secured by the modules themselves.

In a typical United Energy sales agreement, a person bought a $40,000 module with a $14,500 down payment and signed a 30-year promissory note for $25,500 in monthly payments. There was *some* truth to the tax-advantage claims. Federal and state tax credits created in 1982 to spur investment in renewable-energy programs allowed a UEC investor in the 50 percent tax bracket who put down only $14,500 on a module to reap tax benefits of $23,235 in the first year.

So, for UEC's investors, many of them lawyers, accountants or engineers, the company's sales pitch offered a chance to invest in a socially beneficial program and a lucrative tax shelter at the same time.

Early investors were paid for power their modules never produced. In typical Ponzi scheme fashion, UEC made it appear that the business venture was a success. It fabricated kilowatt hours of production for each module and paid owners more than $4 million for this phony productivity.

The truth: UEC solar farms produced a negligible amount of power. The farms actually sold a total of less than $3,500 of electricity, in part because about 1,200 of the modules bought by investors were either not built or not installed.

Almost half of those that were installed didn't have a critical element, the solar cells that chemically convert sunlight to electricity. Lampert said that problems with solar-cell suppliers forced him to install many of the modules without cells in order to meet IRS requirements that the devices be "placed in service" to qualify for tax benefits. Because the modules were capable of producing thermal energy—that is, heating the water—they functioned technically.

This kind of slippery logic was typical of Lampert's business ethic. He was also a virtuoso of self-dealing. Among his transactions:

- Renewable Power Corp., owned by Lampert's wife Delphine, actually owned the hardware and real estate at the three solar farms. It rented the integrated life systems to UEC.

- United Financial Corp., owned by Lampert himself, and operated as a financing unit whose sole income was a 1 percent interest markup on investors' money as it flowed from UEC to Renewable Power.
- Lampert executed an agreement with himself, as "exclusive designer" of various renewable-energy equipment, to receive a 4 percent commission on UEC's gross sales. Besides his $75,000 annual salary, the arrangement brought him about $2.7 million.

By early 1984, word was circulating among UEC investors that the company was being investigated by the IRS and California state regulators. In April 1984, eleven southern California investors who put a total of almost $400,000 in UEC filed a lawsuit claiming fraud.

John Bisnar, an attorney for the group, said that his clients intended to use the investments as a means of lessening tax liabilities. Instead, they learned that the devices were "never purchased and never installed," Bisnar said. "In the beginning, everything seemed to be all right. Perhaps [UEC] got too successful and got more investors than they could handle."

Bisnar said the investors would be pleased if they could recover their investments and attorney's fees. "If Lampert called tomorrow and said 'I'll give them their money back,' I'd be willing to drop the whole thing," Bisnar said. The call never came. But more trouble did.

In October 1984, UEC and Renewable Power were named in a civil lawsuit filed by the California Corporations Commission, which alleged violations of state securities laws. The state tried to get an injunction to put the companies out of business—but the court refused, insisting the case go to trial.

By early 1985, well before any of the 30-year benefits were seen, UEC filed for protection from creditors under Chapter 11 of the federal Bankruptcy Code. By the bankruptcy trustee's accounting, more than $40 million of the $83 million received by UEC went to manufacturing and construction of solar modules, the ponds and manufacturing equipment. About $7.3 million was spent on research and development, $12 million for operating and marketing costs, $12 million for sales commissions and $4.7 million in payments to module owners for "purported but fictional power sales" to public utilities. The payments made UEC a Ponzi scheme.

The trustee alleged that $20 million in UEC assets, including three condominiums valued at more than $600,000, four airplanes, two cars and nearly $2.7 million in "royalties" were "fraudulently or otherwise improperly transferred" to Lampert and Lampert-controlled entities.

In March 1987, a federal court ruled that the Lamperts had operated an abusive tax shelter that "perpetrated a massive fraud upon the public and the government." The ruling, by Magistrate Claudia Wilken, enjoined the Lamperts from selling tax-shelter-related investments without prior Internal Revenue Service approval. Wilken concluded that Lampert had "diverted money from UEC for the purpose of hindering the Internal Revenue Service. He has engaged in extensive deceptive and fraudulent practices and made it clear that he intends to continue these practices."

Wilken also ruled that Lampert had diverted $4.5 million from UEC into his own bank account. Finally, she wrote:

> *No buyer with reasonable knowledge of the relevant facts would buy a UEC module at any price.... Such a buyer would have realized that UEC's modules had no chance of producing any significant income and that tax credits would never become available because the modules would never be placed in service and because the...operation was a sham.... The best evidence of the modules' value is the Trustee's sale of them for scrap, which will bring at most several hundred dollars.*

One of Lampert's attorneys said the findings "[weren]'t supported by the evidence" and he intended to appeal the ruling. He said that Lampert already had been assessed more than $9.5 million in abusive-tax-shelter fines by the IRS even though the judge who had presided over the state actions had "found absolutely no evidence of any type of Ponzi scheme."

Lampert blamed investigations by the IRS and the California Department of Corporations for the company's demise. "If I wanted to do an abusive tax shelter," Lampert said, "I could have done it out of a 2,000-square-foot office on Wilshire Boulevard. We did not have a garage operation." He also accused the government of purposely delaying trial in its case against him, aware that bankruptcy and tax assessments would leave him hard-pressed to mount a defense.

By the late 1980s, Lampert had gone back into business, selling rooftop solar-power modules through a southern California company called Lampert Energy Co. He even solicited former UEC investors, asking them to invest in his rooftop modules and promising $18,000 in "positive cash flow" during the first five years.

In October 1989, Lampert was named in a 15-count criminal fraud indictment. He faced a maximum of 75 years in prison and a fine of $1.2 million. The indictment ended a four-year investigation by the U.S. Attorney's Office, the California Attorney General's Office and the Postal Inspection Service. "They were rolling over money from new investors to old investors, creating a classic Ponzi scheme," said Michael Baum, a San Francisco postal inspector.

In March 1991, the case went to trial. Lampert's one remaining attorney, Deputy Federal Public Defender Robert Nelson, argued that his client had perpetrated no fraud but had worked for years for low pay to improve his cutting-edge technology. "This case is about a solar pioneer who tried to live his dream of making clean energy from resources of the sun," Nelson said.

He said Lampert was on the brink of success when the IRS, upset that the investments had become popular as legal tax shelters, "harassed and blacklisted the company," leading to its demise.

The argument didn't work. Lampert was convicted and sentenced to eight years in prison.

CHAPTER 4

Paying First Class, Traveling Steerage

The travel industry might not seem like an obvious place for Ponzi schemes to flourish—but it is. Travel has all the seductive trappings any seasoned Ponzi scam artist needs to operate:

- Passion. People are passionate about travel; especially, vacation travel. The Ponzi perp is banking on the fact that passion makes people act without thinking.
- Ease. The travel industry is largely unregulated; therefore, it is easy to get away with otherwise questionable activities.
- Privacy. When travel is a personal expense, many people like to keep its financial details to themselves.
- Enthusiasm. People who like to travel usually can be counted on to do it often; thus, it's a continual source of revenue.

Personal travel has become a ruthlessly price-driven commodity. The deregulation of the airlines, which began in the early 1980s, led the way on this count. Low-cost carriers like Southwest Airlines and ValueJet (and, in another area, Carnival Cruises) keep prices down.

On the other hand, business travel is a market with fat margins, big mark-ups and, as a result, all kinds of special deals. There are advantages to being an industry insider—just ask the travel coordinator for any large company. He or she is usually laden with promotional perks and freebies.

Ponzi perps try to take advantage of the fundamental differences that exist between personal travel and business travel. The smartest perps choose between investment-driven Ponzi schemes and sales-driven pyramid operations as circumstances dictate. Both work in the travel business. And sometimes the scheme combines both elements.

Travel Agent Card Mills

For years, airlines, hotel chains, car rental companies and other companies in the industry have offered professional travel agents promotional discounts and free upgrades in order to earn recommendations to business travel customers. These perks are one of the reasons that people who like to travel become travel agents.

The pyramid perps are drawn by a critical market imbalance created by the perks. Personal travelers accustomed to the low prices created by no-frills carriers see the perks available to travel agents as their best chance of getting even deeper discounts...or regaining some of the nicer treatment that commodity travel has eliminated.

The simplest way to get around the market imbalance is to become a travel agent. But becoming a professional travel agent has traditionally taken years of training, accreditation by groups like the American Society of Travel Agents (ASTA) or International Airlines Travel Agent Network (IATAN), compliance with licensing and registration requirements and obtaining bonding and comprehensive insurance.

That's a lot of work for a free upgrade on a Newark-to-Chicago flight.

Enter the pyramid perps. They set up what established travel pros—the people in ASTA and IATAN—call "card mills." For fees ranging from hundreds to thousands of dollars, the perps offer anyone the chance to become a travel agent. The companies produce agent cards, which the newly-appointed travel agents are told can be used to obtain a variety of travel-related discounts.

The card mills can do this because the travel agency industry isn't regulated by any law or government authority. Its standards have always been self-imposed and self-regulated.

In all, this environment is conducive to pyramid schemes.

Of course, they don't *admit* they're running pyramid schemes. The perps doll up their promotions with high-minded language. They promise to train people to become so-called "outside travel agents," part of a network of independent operatives who can make commissions and enjoy discounted travel benefits—in exchange for channeling their sales through "inside" agents working for the parent company.

Established travel agents rightly point out that the outside agent programs are simply multilevel marketing operations. There's nothing wrong with that. But the establishment groups go farther, arguing that the outside agent programs rip off unsuspecting travelers as well as hotels and airlines. They also claim that the outside agent programs pay members more for recruiting other outside agents than for booking airline tickets or hotel rooms.

If true, these charges would mean the outside agent programs are—or come dangerously close to being—illegal pyramid schemes.

One High-profile Company

One of the largest and best-known outside agent travel companies is California-based Nu-Concepts in Travel, Inc. It emerged as a leader in the growing trend in 1994, when it started aggressively recruiting outside agents by means of carefully targeted seminars.

In its early stages, Nu-Concepts made a number of tactical mistakes that would later support the charges made by groups like ASTA and IATAN. One brochure for a seminar read:

> *You never need to sell one reservation to enjoy these courtesies, although some may wish to provide that service to family, friends and business associates (and receive part of the travel agency commission...).*

The company disavowed this particular brochure as the work of one overly aggressive independent distributor. However, other company spokespeople repeated similar things. Even the company's own "Passport To Success" training manual said:

> *You can make a good deal more money by developing your contacts into Independent Distributors of the Nu-Concepts in Travel Independent Distributor Network.... You teach your contacts—a firm foundation of 5-7 people—to follow the simple steps you have followed.... Then, with your help, they each teach 5-7 contacts who teach their contacts...(and so on and so on).*

Whatever these statements suggested to long-time travel industry pros, there was no doubt Nu-Concepts was successfully attracting recruits. By 1995, the company had 35,000 outside agents responsible for generating almost $25 million in travel sales. According to Ron Cummings, Nu-Concepts' marketing director:

> *What we do is enroll and train independent outside agents and allow them access to our highly experienced travel agents. We provide our agents with the most up-to-date training materials, and they are backed up by a full-service travel agency, so customers get the same level of service they would get with any other travel agency.... We don't encourage our agents to run to a hotel and say, 'I'm a travel agent. Give me a discount.' But, on the other hand, they're just as entitled to any travel industry benefits as any agent.*

The industry critics were persistent, though, finding problems even in Nu-Concept's success. The company's own numbers indicated each outside agent was generating only between $800 and $1,200 in sales a year. This, after paying between $495 and $1,000 to enroll in the program.

With those low sales numbers and high entry costs, ASTA said it believed that most of the company's agents signed up strictly for the travel agent perks and distributor fees.

To these charges, Cummings had a blithe response:

> *The only reason [ASTA] is screaming about us is because we are so successful. We believe we'll be the Wal-Mart of the travel industry. We have our critics, but they'd love to have our bottom line.*

In January 1995, the Pennsylvania state attorney general announced his office was investigating Nu-Concepts. Joseph Goldberg, a deputy attorney general in the Bureau of Consumer Protection, said the program resembled a pyramid scheme—although he warned that his investigation was "very preliminary." Goldberg's office had received complaints from consumers who bought Nu-Concepts cards but couldn't get discounts.

On the other coast, regulators were still investigating. "[Outside agent programs] are sprouting like mushrooms in California and the rest of the country," said Jerry Smilowitz, a state deputy attorney general in Los Angeles. "We're still trying to get a handle on them."

Later in 1995, Nu-Concepts settled a legal dispute with IATAN by paying some money and agreeing not to use the IATAN logo on its agent ID cards. But the company's problems reached a new level in November 1995 after an unfavorable judgment in a New York municipal court case, *Elizabeth Brown v. James E. Hambric*.

Long Island resident Elizabeth Brown wanted to be a travel agent. She asked James Hambric for his advise on how to become one. Hambric, an "independent travel consultant" working for Nu-Concepts, convinced Brown that the Nu-Concepts "fast start plan" would provide her with the kind of training and education necessary to follow her dream.

Hambric gave Brown the Nu-Concepts "Passport To Success" manual, which promised that Nu-Concepts would provide support, education and training. Relying upon the manual and Hambric, Brown purchased the Nu-Concepts travel agent package for $537.75.

Then, everything started going wrong. Neither Nu-Concepts nor Hambric provided the promised training and supervision. Hambric, Brown's contact at Nu-Concepts, refused to attend scheduled training sessions and didn't stay current with Nu-Concepts information. As a result, Brown felt it necessary to purchase additional educational programs at a cost of $490.08. But even this didn't get her where she wanted to be.

Brown sued Nu-Concepts and Hambric. The New York court came

down hard on Nu-Concepts, finding for Brown on charges of breach of contract and state General Business Law sections prohibiting pyramid schemes and unfair business practices. The court went even further, writing:

> *There is nothing "new" about Nu-Concepts. It is an old scheme, simply repackaged for a new audience of gullible consumers mesmerized by the glamour of the travel industry and hungry for free or reduced cost travel services. Stripped of its clever disguise as a recruiter and educator of outside travel agents, Nu-Concepts is nothing more than a pyramid scheme.*

The court ordered Hambric to pay Brown the maximum damages allowed under state law, which totaled nearly $1,500.

The *Brown* decision was the first time a judge ruled that a card mill was an illegal pyramid scheme. However, ASTA legal counsel Paul Ruden predicted it wouldn't be the last.

In May 1996, ASTA sued Nu-Concepts in federal court, alleging unfair competition and trademark infringement. In December 1994, the company had agreed to stop using the ASTA logo on its agent ID cards. In May 1995, a Nu-Concepts attorney had told ASTA that all cards with its logo had been recalled and destroyed. But Ruden said that "recent evidence" had been found proving that Nu-Concepts was still distributing cards with the ASTA logo.

Nu-Concepts insisted it was abiding by the agreement and that any ID cards with the ASTA logo had been destroyed more than a year before. Still, the tide of opinion seemed to be turning against Nu-Concepts. In October 1996, Hertz Car Rentals announced it would not pay commissions to travel agencies that booked a disproportionate amount of business in agent rates.

"We will not only cut them off, we will refuse to pay commissions on any business," said William Maloney, Hertz's division vice president of travel industry sales. Maloney made a point to add that Hertz would not work with Nu-Concepts.

The Lure of Travel Remains Strong

When the court ruling on Elizabeth Brown's lawsuit mentioned the "glamour of the travel industry," it was talking about a very strong draw. Travel is something that people—especially people of modest means—dream about. Those dreams are a great tool for pushing a Ponzi scheme.

One scheme based in Alaska took advantage of people's passion for travel—and mania for airline frequent-flier miles. In 1996, the SEC filed a complaint against Raejean S. Bonham, who operated a program called World Plus out of her home near Anchorage.

World Plus was supposed to make its money by reselling blocks of frequent-flier miles. The pitch was that, if you invested money with Bonham, she would repay in either cash or frequent-flier certificates worth 10 times what you put in. (For the record, frequent flier miles are only transferable under certain conditions and never redeemable—legitimately—for cash.)

The SEC said that World Plus was simply a Ponzi scheme that took in more than $50 million from 1,192 investors over more than five years, making it one of the largest scams in Alaska's rough-and-tumble history.

Case Study: LPM Enterprises

The standard against which all travel-related Ponzi schemes must be compared is Louisianan Lynn Paul Martin's LPM Enterprises. Like some character from a Damon Runyon story, Martin was equal parts villain and clown. He recruited investors to provide his company with capital to purchase huge blocks of airline tickets for Las Vegas gambling junkets. He claimed to have made arrangements with various hotel/casinos in Las Vegas to reimburse LPM Enterprises for the cost of the tickets plus about 10 percent as a "finder's fee."

According to the pitch, LPM Enterprises could make this 10 percent as often as it could send planeloads of players to the desert. Martin told investors that the ticket purchase/reimbursement cycle took about six weeks. Therefore, money invested with LPM Enterprises could generate about 80 percent each year in profits.

The mechanics of the deal were complicated enough that they should have sounded warning bells for experienced investors. Martin asked investors to make funds available in cashier's checks. In return, each investor received two post-dated company checks: One for the principal and another for a share—normally 75 percent—of the finder's fees generated by the principal. If an investor wanted to reinvest at the end of a month or quarter, he would simply swap checks with Martin, delivering another cashier's check to cover any increase in the principal.

In many cases, Martin's investors rolled over their principal investment, which meant they only cashed the interest checks. "If somebody asked to see [contracts or financial documents], he'd refuse, saying, 'If you don't like the way I'm handling it, here's your money, you're out.' But nobody had the guts to do that," one lawyer would later explain.

Martin insinuated that everything about LPM Enterprises—including details about other investors—had to be kept secret because most of the customers were sensitive to any publicity. "Most of those people going to Vegas weren't going with their wives, if you know what I mean," said one investor. "So they traveled under other names. They didn't want people to know what they were doing."

The way Martin approached potential investors was well thought out. He usually only approached people he'd already met in some earlier business context. And he usually invited the potential investor to bring along a friend or associate. The friend or associate was invited along to make the potential investor feel more comfortable—in theory, to provide a voice of skepticism. As often as not, though, the friend ended up investing, too.

In a one-on-two meeting over drinks or a meal, Martin would explain the LPM Enterprises deal and drop a few names of local bigwigs who were either investors or customers. One investor—the CEO of a local shipping company—believed Martin's promises that only a handful of bigwigs were in the deal. "I wouldn't have put a nickel in the son of a bitch if I knew there were so many people involved."

Investors believed Martin's pitch for several reasons. First, he was known in the New Orleans area as a legitimate travel agent who specialized in organizing packaged tours. Second, Louisiana was full of rich gamblers who preferred to travel incognito—like former Governor Edwin Edwards, who was famous for staying in Las Vegas under the name "T. Wong." Third, Martin's numbers weren't outrageous for the travel industry. Fourth, in many cases, friends had invested money with Martin and could vouch for the details of his pitch, the secretive nature of his deals and—most importantly—the reliability of his interest checks.

The scam attracted doctors, lawyers, accountants, bankers, corporate executives and, in one case, a state judge. "No one seems to have made any real thorough investigation of the deal," said David Loeb, an attorney for several investors. "No one asked the hotel people if they had heard of Lynn Paul Martin, if they had set up this travel deal, if they were reimbursing him for flights between the two cities. It's just incredible."

In late 1984, Martin was investigated by the FBI because of suspicious activity between accounts he kept at St. James Bank & Trust Co. and the Bank of LaPlace. The investigation could have broken the LPM Enterprises Ponzi scheme at an early stage. But the FBI agents and the U.S. Attorney's Office agreed that the check-kiting case—while triable—wasn't very strong. They decided not to prosecute.

One prosecutor summed up the decision: "Juries are in the habit of finding people not guilty when there's not a victim."

Besides, Martin never acted like a criminal mastermind. He came from a family of law-abiding tobacco farmers in rural St. James Parish. After graduating from Southeastern Louisiana University in 1968, he worked for 10 years as a ticket agent at New Orleans International Airport.

In 1975, there was a sign of trouble. Martin's gambling debts—he played in Las Vegas casinos and bet on horses—caught up with him. He filed voluntary personal bankruptcy.

In 1981, Martin joined a local travel agency as a sales representative. A few years later, he left full-time employment to become one of the company's outside contractors. Throughout, Martin's colleagues in the business considered him little more than an ambitious country bumpkin. "We thought he was a simpleton," said one former travel agency customer. "It's hard to understand how he could have masterminded an operation like [a $50 million Ponzi scheme]."

In the first few years of the scheme, Martin had only a handful of investors. But, by the end of 1986, word had started to spread about LPM Enterprises. One of the most active salesmen for the scheme was Johnny St. Pierre. As time went on, some LPM Enterprises investors were not personally acquainted with Martin—but they usually knew St. Pierre. A 25-year veteran in the insurance industry, St. Pierre (who was also Martin's uncle) had a large network of contacts in the Louisiana business world.

In 1987, checks worth as much as $50,000 began passing through the company checking account every day. (By early 1988, that figure had increased to between $100,000 and $200,000.) In 1987—the scheme's biggest year—more than $97 million passed through LPM Enterprises' account at the Bank of LaPlace. Through all this growth, the scheme was always pushing the edge of solvency. "[Martin] had to bring in cashier's checks every day to cover the overdrafts," one bank officer remembered.

In fact, the bank had a special policy for LPM Enterprises. Every morning, tellers would begin processing the post-dated checks written to investors on the account. They'd usually find that the company didn't have enough money to cover the checks. But the bank would cover Martin for a few hours. A teller would call LPM Enterprises with an amount and Martin or one of his associates would drop by in the afternoon with a bundle of cashier's checks to cover the overdraft.

Because Martin was careful about covering the overdrafts, the bank rarely returned his checks. Of course, it was making good money from the LPM Enterprises account. For each check that overdrew the account in the morning, LPM Enterprises paid a service fee. By one estimate, the bank was collecting $3,000 to $3,500 a month in services charges during 1987.

Martin kept his scheme alive by obtaining funds from new investors to honor the interest checks given to earlier ones. Through early 1988, all went well and most of the bogus profits generated by LPM Enterprises were returned by investors to be reinvested. Then trouble hit.

April 1988 was the cruelest month for Martin. A number of big investors had begun scaling back their involvement in LPM Enterprises. Some were cashing out large portions of their investments to help pay income tax; others had become uncomfortable with their level of exposure.

Whatever the reasons, Martin was having trouble covering his daily overdrafts for the first time in five years. The bank returned quite a few checks. Just about every day, Martin was having to explain to some angry investor that there'd been a foul-up at the bank.

On Friday, April 22, Martin phoned Lee Leonard—an attorney he had used occasionally in the past. "I thought it might be a tax problem or a speeding ticket," Leonard said. "I had no idea what he was going to talk about." Martin was visibly shaken when he arrived at Leonard's office. Some LPM investors had made threats; others had sworn out arrest warrants. Leonard convinced Martin that he would have to turn himself in to the authorities. But Martin said he needed the weekend to think things through. Sometime that night, he flew to Las Vegas...where he spent the next two days gambling heavily.

On Monday morning, April 25, Martin walked into the federal building in downtown New Orleans and surrendered to federal authorities. By the time LPM Enterprises finally collapsed, about 500 people had been swindled out of an estimated $50 million.

Compared to what might have happened to him outside, Martin felt relatively safe in custody. An Assistant U.S. Attorney said, "Without going into specifics [about death threats allegedly made against Martin], let me just say that we recognize the possibility in a confidence game like this where you have so many victims, so many people were defrauded, the possibility exists that someone may try to take matters into their own hands."

In the late summer of 1988, Martin pleaded guilty to one racketeering count, two counts of interstate transportation of money stolen by fraud and two counts of filing false income tax returns for the years 1986 and 1987. U.S. Attorney John Volz asked the court to give Martin the maximum sentence of 25 years in prison. Volz called LPM Enterprises "one of the biggest scams ever perpetrated in this state." In September 1988, Martin was sentenced to 15 years in federal prison and fined $1 million.

The criminal charges were resolved so quickly that most of Martin's burned investors weren't sure how to proceed. Many were frightened of being identified as participants in the deal. "This damn thing could destroy me," said one prominent insurance executive. "What I sell is knowledge, ability, integrity and judgment. Who's going to trust me if this thing gets out?"

One group of angry investors sued Bank of LaPlace for negligence, arguing that it should have known that Martin's activities were improper. In the course of covering his daily overdrafts, Martin had gotten to know several bank officers. He explained LPM Enterprises' supposed business to them—but never deposited checks from or wrote checks to Las Vegas hotels or airlines. The investors argued that the bank effectively aided and abetted Martin's perpetration of the fraud.

On the negligence charges against Bank of LaPlace, the trial court said:

> *The Court is of the opinion that the banks violated no duty to plaintiffs. The banks owe no duty to the plaintiffs to protect them against the type of harm arising from the fraudulent scheme.*

Several investors tried arguing that Martin's post-dated checks should count as securities under federal or local laws. A federal court ruled that "post-dated checks, issued in return for investments in a bogus air travel business, did not qualify as *securities* or *investment contracts* under federal or Louisiana securities law."

In 1993, Martin was released from prison after serving a third of his 15-year sentence. Out of jail—but still on probation for years to come—Martin moved to Florida and found a job as a sales representative for a travel agency. He started making his restitution at the rate of $100 a month. At that pace, he was scheduled to pay off the fine in 833 years.

Most investors, who considered Martin little more than a nervously ingratiating salesman, didn't believe he could have done it alone. "Lynn was the bag man," said one burned investor. "Someone else was pulling his strings." One common scenario: Martin had a silent partner in Las Vegas who made the important decisions—and was holding some $5 million in missing money.

Even the pros were suspicious. "I don't think Martin did it alone," U.S. Attorney Volz said. But, after months of interviewing Martin's associates, pouring over records and grilling the star witness, the Feds had no hard evidence linking anyone in Las Vegas to the operation.

Lee Leonard, Martin's attorney, offered a different explanation: "Maybe you don't have to be that smart to cheat greedy people."

CHAPTER 5

1040-Ponzi

Tax hedges and dodges are a major selling point for Ponzi schemes. There seems to be something buried deep in the subconscious financial mind that links the phrases *tax shelter* and *con scheme*.

There are some good reasons for this. One reason that Ponzi schemes work so well as tax shelters is that the secrecy on which they rely appeals to many people who have a strong aversion to paying taxes.

But secrecy isn't the only aspect that makes a tax shelter a perfect place for a Ponzi scheme to flourish. There are other elements, too—primarily, greed and fear. An investor drawn by greed and fear (of the IRS) is a prime candidate for being burned in a Ponzi scheme.

Columbus Financial, a company that packaged and sold tax-advantaged limited partnerships in oil wells, was founded in 1987 in Beverly Hills, California. The company's pitch: Taking advantage of specially-written language in the U.S. tax code, investors could put money into Columbus partnerships, take a tax credit for developing oil wells and later recoup the investment plus interest on a tax-advantaged basis from income generated by the wells.

The brokers selling Columbus partnerships worked through any hesitation. They insisted on sitting down with potential investors to deliver prospectuses—which had been filed with the SEC—in person and go over the fine print. To financially inexperienced people, the paper trail seemed to support the company's legitimacy. "I didn't understand how little it means to file something with the SEC," says one burned investor.

Still, the promises sounded suspicious enough that the regulators who oversee partnership sales looked at Columbus' operations carefully and often. The National Association of Securities Dealers inspected Columbus every year. The SEC periodically checked the NASD's work. Both gave the operation a clean bill of health for eight years.

The agencies weren't looking in the right places. Columbus was running a Ponzi scheme the whole time—using cash from new investors to pay old ones returns of up to 14 percent. (The supposed tax-advantage of the deal increased the effective rate of return to 20 percent.) It covered up the misappropriation with phony financial reports and geological studies.

The Internal Revenue Service, which was initially confused by Columbus' claims of tax advantage, uncovered the fraud where the other Feds missed it. But, by the time the scheme was exposed by IRS and U.S. Postal Service inspectors, thousands of investors had lost $139 million.

Columbus had put $10 million—at most—into wells. The legal and financial pros brought in to sort through the mess predicted that investors would be lucky to get back seven cents on the dollar from the bankruptcy liquidation. Many of the brokers selling the bogus investments claimed they had been conned, too. They'd believed that the oil deals (which paid them 8 percent to 10 percent commissions) were legitimate. "How were we supposed to tell something was wrong if the SEC and NASD didn't know?" asked one former salesman.

Columbus president Neal Stein spent a lot of the money on himself. He lived in an ostentatious Beverly Hills mansion. He owned at least five luxury cars, including several Mercedes-Benzes and a Bentley convertible. He had three nannies to watch two children. But, even considering these extravagances, nearly $60 million of the money raised by Columbus was simply missing at the end.

A number of angry investors argued that Stein may have moved what was left to overseas bank accounts. He pleaded guilty to tax evasion and securities fraud in September 1995 and faced up to 10 years in prison plus a fine of $1 million at his sentencing, which was delayed indefinitely. The

Justice Department was investigating several of Stein's compatriots—and wanted his cooperation.

One of the surprising aspects of the Columbus scheme was the failure of the regulatory agencies to pick up any sign of fraud. Many of the investors did their homework before handing over their money—and still bought in because the partnerships looked legitimate. "What you need to remember is that this was basically a tax fraud," said one burned Columbus investor. "All the stuff that was wrong from the beginning was stuff the NASD doesn't even know to look for. Their people focus on securities issues. The IRS people would have been able to see that Columbus was a scam."

But the IRS didn't get involved until Columbus had already sold tens of millions in limited partnership shares. As one IRS fraud specialist said: "We don't look for problems preemptively. A crime has to take place before we can begin."

Lump Sum Pension Payments

The lump sum payments that many employees receive when they leave a company or retire are prime targets of Ponzi perpetrators who promise tax advantaged investments. Often, the perps will exploit the common misperception that "tax advantaged" means low risk.

For several years beginning in the late 1980s, Harold Sherbondy convinced a number of his San Diego County neighbors to invest almost $5 million in what was supposed to be a tax-advantaged commodities trading partnership (that is, essentially, an oxymoron). Most of the money came from retirement buyout funds that pilots, flight attendants and mechanics received when U.S. Airways bought San Diego-based Pacific Southwest Airlines.

Sherbondy's pitch: He had discovered a novel way to obtain IRS approval to invest buyout funds in commodities and have the income be tax free. His plan would allow investors to realize profits of between 25 percent and 50 percent a year.

This was an unlikely proposition. Commodities trading is not only one of the most volatile forms of investment around, it's also taxed just like any other investment. Other than the tax breaks given—by law—to certain kinds of government debt instruments (muni bonds, T-bills, etc.), the IRS doesn't offer tax advantages to particular methods of investment. It focuses its tax breaks according to how the money being invested is intended to be used.

However, Sherbondy never got to the point of hashing out tax policy. He never really invested his clients' money—only putting about 1 percent of the funds in a commodities account he used for show.

Most of the money went directly into Sherbondy's personal bank accounts. Like so many Ponzi perps, he needed to keep up the impression of wealth. The trappings—the Mercedes Benz, the private plane, the big house—were important elements of his credibility.

He also used church membership and apparent religious piety to convince people to invest with him. Sherbondy and his wife were regular members of a Christian church in northern San Diego county. Through this connection, Sherbondy met the first investors in his commodities scam—and these people went even further, convincing their friends to invest.

Despite the carefully laid foundation, there were parts of Sherbondy's story that should have raised warning signs for his investors.

Most pointedly, Sherbondy made no effort to appear low-key or conservative. He boasted about his wealth and international connections. He claimed to control a British bank and several mortgage companies in Texas. He talked vaguely about a millionaire father who ran a European investment trust. He said that the Teamsters pension fund had invested in his tax shelters. And, as his scheme was beginning to unravel, he insisted that the Gulf War had frozen assets he'd invested with the Emir of Kuwait.

But even the Emir couldn't help Sherbondy avoid the inevitable.

By 1991, Sherbondy was desperate to raise money to keep the scheme going. He tried the usual tactics—increasing his promised returns to even more unlikely heights and offering existing investors finder's fees for bringing in new money. But he needed more than he could raise, so dividend checks started bouncing.

In 1992, a group that included most of Sherbondy's investors sued him in civil court for embezzlement and fraud. Tom Laube, the attorney handling the case, was able to produce a $4.5 million verdict in the group's favor—but Laube was unable to enforce the award because Sherbondy didn't have enough money to pay it.

When Laube tried to collect the judgment, he discovered that Sherbondy's father was not quite a jet-set financier. The old man was a penniless former laborer living in a trailer on the outskirts of Las Vegas.

In late 1993, the U.S. Attorney in San Diego filed a 51-count indictment against Sherbondy for the various frauds he committed in the course of operating his scheme. The indictment also included charges of filing false tax returns—an ironic conclusion to a story that began with promises of besting the IRS.

The Outlaw Mentality

People who have a strong aversion to paying taxes often are attracted to investments shrouded in secrecy. These people have an outlaw mentality which plays into the Ponzi perp's plans. As one attorney says, "People who feel the government is stealing their money are easy prey for swindlers. They're predisposed to cloak-and-dagger antics."

Despite the outlaw mentality and cloak-and-dagger approach, the basic parameters that apply to tax shelters are—relatively—straightforward.

In order to take a depreciation deduction with respect to an asset, the asset must be used in a trade or business or held for the production of income. Furthermore, the asset must be *ordinary and necessary* to carrying on a trade or business or producing income.

While a profit is not required (and, in many cases, not desired), a business must enter activities with the *intent* of making a profit. This rule applies to most Ponzi schemes, because they are not created with the intent of making a profit. They are, by definition, frauds created to steal money.

Another IRS rule that limits the effectiveness of Ponzi or pyramid schemes as tax shelters states that activities which serve no "purpose, substance or utility apart from their anticipated tax consequences" are disregarded for tax purposes. The tax code states, in relevant part:

> *In the case of an activity engaged in by an individual..., if such activity is not engaged in for profit, no deduction attributable to such activity shall be allowed.*

So, even if a particular pyramid scheme is not illegal, it may have no purpose other than to be a tax dodge. If the Feds find this out—and they scrutinize pyramid schemes—they'll deny any benefit.

The last tax rule to consider is the most general. Federal law prohibits anyone from claiming a deduction for personal, living or family expenses which are *not* incurred in the conduct of a trade or business or in the production of income.

So, aside from all the other problems a pyramid scheme poses, it isn't as safe a place to hide expenses as a more traditional business. Since the things are suspect mechanisms to start, it's not a good idea to load up tax-shelter pyramid schemes with questionable write-offs.

Federal courts have relied on a number of factors—the legal term is *indicia*—to determine that tax fraud exists in an investment scheme. Although no single factor is necessarily sufficient to establish fraud, the existence of several can be persuasive. These factors include:

- understatement of income,
- maintenance of inadequate records,
- failure to file tax returns,
- implausible or inconsistent explanations of behavior,
- concealment of assets, and
- failure to cooperate with tax authorities.

As you can see, all of these factors can apply to a pyramid or Ponzi scheme at the same time. As a result, the IRS will often have identified a Ponzi scheme as suspicious before it collapses.

Unfortunately, the Feds have a hard time moving on a scheme before it crashes. This is partly because federal regulators have so much ground to cover that they move slowly on any one case; but it's also partly because Ponzi schemes tend to collapse quickly—often in less than two years.

To help the regulators—and, in turn, investors—some federal courts have added other warning flags to identify illegal schemes. The U.S. Ninth Circuit Court of Appeals (which includes Ponzi-heavy states like California and Nevada) has been active in this regard. Indicia that it has offered include:

- a history of illegal activity on the part of principals,
- a preference for cash transactions of less than $10,000,
- failure to make estimated tax payments, and
- offering any "guarantee" of tax-advantaged status.

Case Study: Home-Stake Mining

Despite the IRS' efforts to identify the characteristics of an illegal tax scheme, tax-advantage Ponzi schemes have continued to flourish.

In late December 1996, a federal judge in Tulsa, Oklahoma, approved a settlement in a case that had started in 1973. It involved one of the biggest and most protracted tax shelter Ponzi schemes in American history.

During the early 1950s, Robert Trippet organized Home-Stake Energy Co. to develop oil and gas properties. He raised money for so-called "wildcat" exploration by selling percentage interests or units of participation to investors through private placements.

Home-Stake organized separate annual programs, units which were registered with the SEC and sold to the public. Each of the programs was supposed to develop a particular oil and gas property or properties in the Midwest, California or Venezuela.

Home-Stake's salespeople pushed the things hard. They told prospective investors that they would reap big profits from proven oil reserves and that the tax deductions for intangible drilling costs and oil depletion allowances were advantageous. An investor could shelter as much as $700,000 of $1 million in income in one of Home-Stake's yearly programs.

The Home-Stake salespeople also tailored each pitch to each investor or prospect. Often, the salesperson would find out the details of an investor's tax situation and then offer participation in a Home-Stake program as a perfect solution.

This customized tax planning was of dubious legality but had an outstanding effect on sales.

Home-Stake investors included the rich and the famous, such as entertainers Bob Dylan, Liza Minnelli, Barbra Streisand, and Walter Matthau. Also involved were some captains of industry, such as the entire board of General Electric Co.

Home-Stake salespeople closed their deals with written sales materials, which included unregistered "black books." For all practical purposes, a black book served the same sales function as a prospectus. It provided a general description of the program, explained the nature of participating interests, and contained engineering reports for the properties, descriptions of the various tax advantages, and projections of substantial profits.

At first, Home-Stake's operation seemed successful. Its quarterly progress reports indicated that substantial oil was being produced and early investors received large payments which were supposedly proceeds from the oil drilling program. In truth, however, very little oil was being produced. The payments came from money paid for units by later investors. And, as a tax shelter, Home-Stake was useless.

Even with the Ponzi payments, there were some investors who complained that their returns did not match Home-Stake's promises. This was due in part to the fact that Home-Stake was going broke from the day it started. Since there was no real profit from oil operations, each succeeding year reaped less bogus profit for investors than the salespeople had promised.

The dwindling return on investment (to use that term loosely, since no real investments were ever made) led to a number of complaints to Home-Stake management. Various efforts were made to deal with those complaints. In some cases, Home-Stake repurchased program units from dissatisfied investors; in others, it offered investors the opportunity to "roll over" their units, typically exchanging units in a past program for units in a program that was currently being marketed.

Nevertheless, these efforts couldn't keep up with the growing number of complaints. In March 1973, two investors who were dissatisfied with their investment returns and one who'd been told that the IRS was going to disallow his intangible drilling deductions filed a lawsuit in California on behalf of all participants in the Home-Stake programs.

These investors alleged that Home-Stake management and its professional advisors engaged in "an unlawful combination, conspiracy and course of conduct that operated as a fraud and deceit." They also charged that Trippet and his salespeople made untrue statements and failed to disclose material facts.

By July 1973, the investors sought to inspect Home-Stake's documents. The federal court in California ordered that they be allowed to begin discovery. At this point, the collapse of Home-Stake accelerated. Within weeks, new management had taken over Home-Stake and discharged Trippet, investigators from the SEC had arrived at Home-Stake's offices in Tulsa, and Home-Stake had filed bankruptcy. After the collapse of Home-Stake in September 1973, numerous other lawsuits were filed in federal courts around the country.[1]

Home-Stake had done many of the things that a Ponzi scheme often does at various points in its life cycle. These included:

- paying illegal commissions to various persons in connection with the sale of participation units;

[1]For more details on these Home-Stake lawsuits see Chapter 19, page 267.

Home-Stake had done many of the things that a Ponzi scheme often does at various points in its life cycle. These included:

- paying illegal commissions to various persons in connection with the sale of participation units;
- entering a management contract with Trippet that granted him 50 percent of Home-Stake's interest in any oil and gas drilling programs sponsored by Home-Stake;
- financing equipment receivables which were listed as assets when there was no reasonable probability that this asset would be realized; and
- including various loans receivable when there was no reasonable probability that the loans would be collected.

However, because the Home-Stake scheme was so complicated...and involved so many investors...it would take more than 20 years to litigate all of the issues surrounding the mess.

In the mid-1990s, Trippet had an opportunity to invest again in several companies related to Home-Stake but he passed. The 77-year-old said, "I have a bad reputation in Tulsa, and it would not have been good for me to surface [in the deal]."

You could say that.

CHAPTER 6

Sure-thing Investments and Sweetheart Loans

Managing financial investments is a complicated mix of science and art. Regulatory standards take this complexity into account—the SEC, IRS and state investment rules allow a fair amount of leeway in which good faith and trust are supposed to rule. So, investments remain an appealing market to con men and Ponzi perpetrators. After all, it's the market that attracted Carlo Ponzi in the first place.

According to the North American Securities Administrators Association, which conducts surveys of fraud in the financial planning business, some 22,000 investors lost about $400 million in financial planning frauds between 1986 and 1988. That's a stunning 340 percent increase from investments lost to fraud between 1983 and 1985—and the numbers continue to grow.

Some people are surprised that so many wealthy investors are drawn into these old-fashioned schemes. But they shouldn't be surprised. For generations, bogus deals have been a staple of idiot sons from successful families who talk about doing business in vague terms because they feel guilty that they'd rather be skiing than reading 10-Q filings.

People who know investments—like people who know any business—talk about their interests in detail. They will welcome the chance to explain the mechanics of what they do, because they know there are no secret recipes for success.

But the 1980s and 1990s have generated armies of loosely-defined "investment advisors" and "financial planners." Many of these have come out of the insurance industry—former agents looking for new markets. They can pose a considerable risk of promoting—knowingly or not—pyramids and Ponzi schemes.

Who Is an Investment Advisor?

In relevant part, the federal Investment Advisors Act provides that an investment advisor is:

> *[A]ny person who, for compensation, engages in the business of advising others, either directly or through publications or writings, as to the value of securities or as to the advisability of investing in, purchasing, or selling securities.*

In defining the business standard for investment advisors, the SEC notes:

> *The giving of advice need not constitute the principal business activity or any particular portion of the business activities of a person in order for the person to be an investment advisor.... The giving of advice need only be done on such a basis that it constitutes a business activity occurring with some regularity.*

Another important point: Federal securities law holds that anyone involved in a fraudulent scheme must understand that the scheme is fraudulent. (Bad investments made in good faith aren't illegal.) Courts refer to this knowledge as *scienter.*

While all courts agree that a scienter requirement exists in securities fraud cases, "at least to the extent that something more than ordinary negligence is required," they don't all agree on a single standard. Some courts require "knowledge" while others require "general awareness that [a party's] role was part of an overall activity that is improper."

Perhaps the best summary of the standard for establishing scienter is that "[s]ome knowledge must be shown, but the exact level necessary for liability remains flexible and must be decided on a case-by-case basis."

In this context, the surrounding circumstances and expectations of the people involved are critical.

One of the purposes of the Investment Advisors Act was to protect the public's confidence in the financial markets. As one Senator warned: "Not only must the public be protected from the frauds and misrepresentations of unscrupulous tipsters and touts, but the bona fide investment advisor must be safeguarded against the stigma of...these individuals."

The Investment Advisors Act sought to regulate "investment contracts," which it described as any of a variety of investment devices and securities.

In its 1946 decision *SEC v. Howey*, the U.S. Supreme Court set up a test for courts to use in determining whether an investment contract was, in essence, a security and therefore within the reach of the SEC. The court ruled that an investment contract is a transaction:

> *[W]hereby a person [1] invests his money in a [2] common enterprise and [3] is led to expect profits [4] solely from the efforts of [others].*

In the more than 50 years that have passed since the *Howey* decision, federal courts have had little difficulty applying the first and third elements of the test. They've had more trouble applying the second ("common enterprise") and fourth ("solely from the efforts of others") elements.

The confusion has centered on whether so-called *horizontal commonality* between one investor with a pool of investors is required, or whether a *vertical commonality* between an investor and a promoter will satisfy the common enterprise element.

Horizontal commonality exists whenever "the fortunes of each investor in a pool of investors [are tied] to the success of the overall venture." Strict vertical commonality exists whenever "the fortunes of the investors [are tied] to the fortunes of the promoter." Broad vertical commonality exists whenever "the fortunes of the investor [are linked] only to the efforts of the promoter."

In the 1973 federal appeals court case *SEC v. Glenn W. Turner Enterprises, Inc.*, the court held that a pyramid scheme involving the sale of certain "Adventures" and "Plans" constituted the sale of investment contracts within the meaning of federal securities law.

In the case, a program called *Dare to Be Great* offered investors four different Adventures and a $1,000 Plan. For Adventures I and II, at a cost of $300 and $700 respectively, participants received tapes, records, and other self-motivation material, as well as the right to attend group sessions. For Adventures III and IV and the $1,000 Plan, purchasers received the same things received by the purchasers of Adventures I and II, plus the opportunity to sell the Adventures and the $1,000 Plan to others in return for a commission.

The court held that Adventures III and IV and the $1,000 Plan were investment contracts because they met the tests established in *Howey*. Obviously, the Adventures involved an investment of money. The court found that the money was invested in a "common enterprise," in which "the fortunes of the investor are interwoven with and dependent upon the efforts and success of those seeking the investment of third parties."

It was with the final element, requiring profits "to come solely from the efforts of others," that the court had the most difficulty. Because the income opportunities through Dare to Be Great required individuals to sell Adventures and Plans to others, the income was not based solely on the efforts of others.

Still, the court held that the word *solely* "should not be read as a strict or literal limitation on the definition of an investment contract, but must be construed realistically, so as to include ... those schemes which involve in substance, if not form, securities." The court concluded that the Dare to Be Great scheme was "no less an investment contract merely because [the investor] contributes some effort as well as money to get into it."

So, this is how the courts connect Ponzi schemes to investment and securities laws. But it's just a technical connection. The practical applications take various forms.

Beware of Projections

Many investors are swayed by ambitious projections—which paint seductive pictures of big riches to be had in six months...or six years. For this reason, projections are heavily regulated in most legitimate financial markets.

Ponzi perps know both of these things—that projections are compelling and that they are regulated. So, they find artful ways to use projections without running afoul of regulations.

According to the SEC, financial projections are fraudulent if:

> 1) the promoter "disseminated the forecasts knowing they were false or that the method of preparation was so egregious as to render their dissemination reckless," and
>
> 2) the investors reasonably relied upon these projections in making their investment decisions.

That *reasonably* can be a tricky matter. In general, reliance on projections as a forecast of the future is unreasonable as a matter of law if those projections are accompanied by language that clearly discloses their speculative nature. That's why so many ads for financial services or investment opportunities will include disclaimer language that reminds investors that past performance is not a guarantee of future performance, that certain investments are speculative and that some investors do lose money.

The Ponzi perp's challenge is to make the stuff that comes before these disclaimers so appealing that investors don't pay attention to the "legal mumbo-jumbo."

But there's more than this. Just because an investment goes bad, the investor doesn't automatically win a lawsuit—even if the people selling it fudge on the risk issues. In order to make a successful case under the SEC guidelines, a burned investor must "allege facts which give rise to a strong inference that the defendants possessed the requisite fraudulent intent." That can be tough to pull off.

Beware of Loan Programs

One common variation on the standard investment Ponzi scheme is the loan program. In these schemes, investors are encouraged to put money into a fund which, in turn, makes profitable loans. The only problem: Often these loans are made to other investors in the scheme. The whole situation quickly becomes just one more pretense for spinning money.

In the late 1980s and early 1990s, Melvin Ford ran an operation called the International Loan Network. ILN's pretenses were few and flimsy. It was a scheme to move money around quickly, so that a lucky few could siphon off enough to get rich quick.

Ford's scheme shouldn't have lasted more than a few weeks. Instead, it lasted several years. In revival-like assemblies targeting black and Asian-American investors, Ford promised huge returns on investment in foreclosed real estate properties around the country. Among other blustery things, he said, "ILN is a financial distribution network whose members believe that through the control of money and through the control of real estate you can accumulate wealth and become financially independent."

True enough. But most people have to work for years in order to control enough money and real estate to be considered wealthy. Ford's shortcut? The ILN mantra: "The movement of money creates wealth." This was daring. The slogan came close to admitting ILN was a Ponzi scheme.

To become a member of ILN and have a chance of obtaining "the organization's stated goal of financial independence," a person had to pay a $125 basic membership fee. The basic fee entitled the investor to a variety of "benefits and services"—consisting mostly of discount coupons for travel, car rental and high-ticket consumer goods. It also allowed the person to become an Independent Representative of ILN.

Of course, the basic fee was only the beginning. ILN encouraged investors to join one of its select clubs. For an additional fee of $100, $500 or $1,000, an investor could become one of the cream of ILN's sucker crop.

Club membership entitled a person to the benefits provided to basic investors plus newsletters and seminars on money management. As a member of the $500 or $1,000 Club, a person could participate in ILN's Property Rights Acquisition (PRA) program, which offered real estate investment training courses. And, finally, there were the bonus programs.

By recruiting friends and family to join, ILN investors could participate in the Capital Fund Bonus System and the Maximum Consideration program. These programs directed portions of new investors' fees to the people who'd recruited them.

For each new investor recruited, an Independent Representative received 50 percent of the new member's fee for whichever club he or she joined. The Independent Representative also received a descending percentage of the club membership fees paid by new investors recruited "downline" through recruits (and recruits of recruits) to the fifth level of recruitment.

ILN summed the recruitment process up in a slogan often repeated in its literature and at its meetings: "First you join. Then you bring your wife and kids." Investors would invite potential recruits to so-called "President's Nights." These were the meetings that looked and felt like revivals.

Ford was always the featured speaker. He'd enter a crowded hotel ballroom to the soundtrack from the movie *Flashdance*. Then, he'd deliver a lengthy presentation—part motivational speech and part financial evangelism—rousing the crowd with chants like "I will not accept defeat" and "I'm the captain of my ship."

In a complaint filed during the peak of Ford's activity, the SEC summed up his appeal with typical understatement: "He is both engaging and persuasive." The engaging and persuasive man called ILN's Capital Fund Bonus System "the most powerful financial system since banking." And a disturbingly large number of his listeners agreed.

If Ford had stuck close to the original structure of his scheme, ILN would probably have continued even longer than it did. Although

ILN was pretty plainly a Ponzi scheme, Ford was cautious enough—at first—to avoid flagrant violations of investment and securities law. But, as time went on, he expanded his operation into an investment operation that would prove his undoing.

Offering Investments Instead of Advice

Ford had experimented with mechanisms for convincing ILN's winners to keep pouring their money back into his schemes. Beginning in 1990, he expanded these efforts into the expanded Property Rights Assignment Program.

According to promotional materials, the PRA program offered investors "an opportunity to acquire property below market value." Still part of ILN, the PRA program would assign tax lien sale certificates or rights to property acquired through foreclosures or government-assisted programs.

According to the PRA material, purchasers of $1,000 PRAs would be assigned property rights assessed at $10,000; purchasers of $5,000 PRAs would be assigned property rights assessed at $50,000; and purchasers of $10,000 PRAs would be assigned property rights assessed at $100,000. The property transfers would be made within 180 days of the purchase of the PRA investment units. If this weren't tempting enough, ILN salespeople added a cash kicker. They promised potential investors the option of cash payment of five times the initial investment.

In other words, 180 days after making a $1,000 PRA investment, you could choose between $10,000 worth of real estate or $5,000 in cash.

Many of the ILN investors lucky enough to get money out of the recruitment scheme jumped at the chance to parlay their profits. Few cared much about property rights assignments—most wanted five times their money in cash. During the entire two-years-plus lifespan of ILN and the PRA programs, only one property selection list was ever distributed.

But Ford had stretched his persuasiveness too far. ILN declared bankruptcy in the summer of 1991, after the SEC filed a lawsuit charging that it was a giant Ponzi scheme. Of $110 million invested with Ford, only $1 million was recovered.

Much of the SEC's complaint focused on the PRA programs. The Feds claimed that promises made in the programs amounted to guarantees, which meant the investment units were securities. Investors, most black and elderly, packed a Washington D.C. federal courtroom in June 1991 to hear the SEC make its case against Ford and ILN. They were there in support of the man who had taken their money. In this way, the trial felt like a replay of Carlo Ponzi's trials in the 1920s.

After three days of live testimony and one day of argument, the court was still unclear about the mechanics of the ILN operation:

> *Programs as described in testimony and in written material are frequently incomprehensible.... As the Court understands Ford's explanation, a person who purchases a $1,000 PRA, a $5,000 PRA, and a $10,000 PRA, for a total of $16,000, is eligible for...up to $80,000 because..."the velocity of money increases to such a point, the ability to create wealth expands to such a degree, that we could come back and give somebody an award for up to $80,000."*

Despite this gibberish explanation, the court found that the PRA programs fit relatively neatly into the framework established by the Supreme Court's *Howey* decision. It concluded:

> *Clearly, each involved an investment of money. Similarly, each involved a common enterprise in the sense that the fortunes of investors were inextricably tied to the efforts of ILN management....*

Ford insisted the investments weren't securities. In his presentations, he had been careful not to make guarantees. He emphasized that ILN bonuses were awards and not commissions. However, he urged people to participate by saying "the system does work.... No, we can't guarantee you any money, but we sure have got a system that can produce some."

The court didn't find these evasions convincing. It concluded that the PRA programs constituted an investment contract. Sarcastically, it added:

> *The Court continues to be puzzled about why neither defense counsel nor any of defendants' witnesses has been able to explain how the velocity of money creates wealth. The Court regrets that Melvin Ford did not take the stand to more fully explain his novel theory.*

Most Ponzi perps are immune to judicial irony, though. In June 1996, Ford—who ended up serving no jail time for the ILN debacle—was offering get-rich-quick seminars at a resort hotel in Antigua. He invited investors to make a fortune using some vague offshore banking techniques.

Things You Can Do to Avoid Being Cheated

Many people think of investments and the investment community as a secret society with a language and rules of its own. Of course, it's not. Ponzi perps simply take advantage of investor hesitation—and sell their shady investments against better judgment.

There are a number of things any investor can do to avoid being taken by a Ponzi perp peddling worthless investments. Before you put any money in an investment, do the following:

1) Get a prospectus and read it. A prospectus should contain details on where the money is going, who will be responsible for it, and—most important—what the risks are.

2) Understand that all investments entail some degree of risk. Ponzi perps like to say investments are *guaranteed* or *government backed.* But, in most cases, these terms don't really mean much.

3) Don't invest because a promoter is a member of your church, country club or ethnic group. Affinity groups are a big mechanism for promoting Ponzi schemes and various other shady investments.

4) Investigate the salesperson or broker—and the firm. Get the

salesperson's disciplinary history from the state attorney general's office or the National Association of Securities Dealers (NASD).

5) Don't put all your eggs in one basket. Scammers try to get investors to cash in their savings or retirement money, saying it'd be easier to have it all in one place. That's usually a good idea.

6) If you've already invested and are having trouble cashing out, watch out. Beware of promoters who cajole you into "rolling over" your money into a larger position.

And, perhaps most importantly, law enforcement officials always remind investors not to let shame or fear stop them from reporting fraud or abuse.

Case Study: Hedged Investments

In terms of capitalizing on geek chic, James Donahue was 20 years ahead of his time. In terms of getting prosecuted for Ponzi scheme larceny, his timing was perfect.

In 1974, shortly after the Chicago Board of Trade opened its Options Exchange, Donahue set to applying statistical theory and computer techniques to tracking and measuring trends in options. He was on the cutting edge of mathematics and finance; he wrote *Options Strategies*, one of the first textbooks on the subject, as well as a related newsletter during the mid-1970s.

In 1977, Donahue formed Hedged Investments Associates, Inc. for the purpose of operating an investment fund known generally as Hedged Investments. Donahue attracted investors to the fund by claiming he had developed a sophisticated, computer-based strategy for trading in hedged securities options. He boasted reliable, annual returns of between 15 percent and 22 percent.

Donahue appealed to wealthy investors in the Denver area. He had an advanced degree in mathematics from Stanford. And he looked like an academic—tall, overweight and owlish. He wore business suits awkwardly but spoke in a calm, deliberate voice. His lifestyle spoke to reliability. He was an elder in his Presbyterian Church. He'd been married for 33 years. He lived in a nice, but unassuming, house in an upper-middle-class neighborhood.

In the late 1970s and early 1980s, Donahue's reputation spread quietly around the Rocky Mountain states.

However, there was a dark side to the professorial analyst. Some investors said they suspected Donahue because of his reluctance to share information about the stock option trades. He didn't offer audited statements. "He complained about how dumb the auditors were.... Not many CPAs understand hedging," said one former colleague.

Donahue dealt with hesitant investors in a disarming way. Rather than working hard to persuade, he simply told people to take their money elsewhere. "[H]e used to say, 'Look, I could just as well take your money and throw it in the ocean. If you are not comfortable with the way I do things, don't participate,'" recalled one Denver-area financial advisor.

What Donahue did do was guarantee investors a 25 percent annual return on their investments. He said his options investment program always produced returns of at least 19.7 percent. These numbers were compelling enough to make many investors forget their skepticism.

When a person invested in Hedged Investments, Donahue would sell him or her shares in one of three limited partnerships. Donahue's strategy was to combine buying or short-selling a stock with investing in call (sell) or put (buy) options in that stock. Whether the stock went up or down didn't matter; Donauhue's goal was to exploit inconsistencies in the small niches of the financial markets. (Theoretically, the price of a stock corresponds consistently to the price of its options; but markets sometimes make mistakes. When they did, Hedged Investments would make money.)

Buying stocks and selling call options is considered a conservative investment strategy. But Donahue sometimes varied his positions so that he was investing more heavily in options—a far more speculative move. But, by using complex statistical models, Donahue seemed to make it work profitably. "There was always the possibility a stock would jump outside the range and cause a loss," says Gregory McNichol, a money manager who helped Donahue establish his system. "But if he had 20 positions, it's hard to imagine any one being bad enough to wipe out profits on the other 19. He used to preach the discipline of this thing."

But he practiced something far looser. Donahue failed to maintain separate accounting records for the limited partnerships and commingled investors' funds into a single checking account. In other words, he treated the investors as if they were direct participants in a single investment pool instead of investors in discreet limited partnerships.

Donahue made money his first three years of operation, from 1978 to 1980, when he managed less than $2 million in assets for a small group of investors. But for the rest of the decade, he lost money routinely. After a few years, the program was insolvent— in that its cumulative losses exceeded its cumulative gains. The true source of money paid to the investors as earnings was the sale of limited partnership interests to new investors.

Beginning in 1981, Donahue lost $2.1 million, then $1.7 million the following year, $2.6 million in 1983, slightly under $1 million in 1984 and slightly over that in 1985. In 1987, the year the stock market crashed, Hedged Investments lost $6.5 million. Far from admitting his losses, Donahue told clients and potential investors that Hedged Investments not only survived the Crash, but had achieved a 26 percent annual gain.

His losses nearly quintupled in 1988, when he dumped $29 million into the market. There was some relief the next year when he made $5.7 million, but it was short-lived. And then, in 1990, he gambled on a heavy investment in United Airlines for his financial salvation. And lost.

In the course of a few weeks, Donahue lost $90 million trading United Airlines options. There had been talk of a takeover at United; he believed it would come. As Wall Street concluded there'd be no takeover, the value of United options dropped—and Donahue kept buying. "There's an old saying in investment circles: The trend is your friend. Don't fight the trend," says one West Coast money manager who knew Donahue. "He knew this. He just lost his mind."

Normally, Donahue pooled all of his investors' money in to a handful of accounts. But, late in his scheme, he made one exception. This hastened his demise. In September 1987, Weyerhaeuser Corp.'s employee pension fund had made an initial investment as a limited partner in Hedged Investments. By February 1988, it had committed $17 million. Like most big pension funds, Weyerhaeuser allocates a portion of its assets to "non-traditional investments," such as short-selling, commodities and options. Donahue had come recommended by several money managers in the Pacific Northwest.

At the end of each quarter, Weyerhaeuser received a short statement showing its investment and its gains. Like most Hedged Investments investors, Weyerhaeuser staff didn't question the temperamental genius down in Denver. In the spring of 1988, Weyerhaeuser gave Donahue another $5 million. But this time, it made a request. It split the money into two brokerage accounts handled by Kidder Peabody and Morgan Stanley—but was available to be traded by Donahue as he saw fit.

This was a smart move. By looking at the monthly brokerage accounts, Weyerhaeuser could check for itself how Donahue was doing. This was the first time anyone had managed to audit Donahue's performance.

As it turned out, the timing was good for Donahue. He managed to make money steadily for about a year. In November 1989, though, he had to do some explaining. The brokerage reports showed huge losses from a large number of call options on United Airlines stock—which had dropped sharply in November. Even more disturbing: the reports showed no offsetting investments to act as a hedge against the United Airlines options.

Donahue reassured Weyerhaeuser. He said the calls had been fully hedged by puts in the main Hedged Investments portfolios, where Weyerhaeuser still had most of its money. To prove his point, he transferred money into Weyerhaeuser's separate accounts. He allowed Weyerhaeuser to assume that this money was its share of profits on the UAL puts. This is a typical tactic used by Ponzi perps trying to buy time.

Weyerhaeuser money managers were calm for a few months. But the monthly reports continued to show a large number of UAL calls; and there were still no hedges in Weyerhaeuser's separate accounts.

In February 1990, Weyerhaeuser contacted Donahue again. The finance people were worried. In April, the company's money managers flew to Denver for a face-to-face meeting. Donahue was able to convince them that he was sticking to his model.

In June and July, as the price of UAL common stock—and related call options—fell, the Weyerhaeuser people called Donahue several times a week. Finally, they couldn't take his word any more. In August, they demanded an accounting of the company's funds in the pooled account.

This demand broke Donahue. He admitted to Weyerhaeuser money managers that he couldn't provide an accounting—and that there was no hedge in Hedged Investments.

On August 30, Hedged Investments filed for voluntary bankruptcy pursuant to Chapter 11 of the U.S. Bankruptcy Code. On September 7, the case was converted to a Chapter 7 liquidation and the bankruptcy court appointed a trustee. In a videotaped message, Donahue tearfully told investors that he had lost all of their money. Specifically, he said:

> *It is with deep remorse that I inform you that the Limited Partnerships in which you are a member have incurred a very significant financial loss.... At the request of many individual investors to keep the extent of their participation confidential, the total dollar amount of loss will be disclosed to you through correspondence and after a final accounting, and not at this semi-public meeting. The loss is extensive and involves almost all of the total assets of the fund.... My words at this point cannot possi-*

bly alleviate the emotion or financial impact on each person involved nor can they express the deep sorrow I have over this incident.

He blamed the collapse on a general stock market decline caused by Iraq's invasion of Kuwait, which presaged the Gulf War.

However, after the initial panic over the losses subsided, two former employees said Donahue had told them as early as September that he had been "miscalculating" the returns on his limited partnerships for five or six years. In all, Donahue had lost $129 million in the stock market.

In the end, only Donahue knows the path the money took. He kept no financial books, all of the accounts were commingled and only he saw the records of investment transactions.

Donahue pleaded guilty to securities fraud in August 1991, almost exactly a year after his investment scheme collapsed.

In January 1992, Donahue was sentenced to five years in prison. At his sentencing, federal prosecutors called Donahue's scam the single largest securities fraud in U.S. history.

During questioning, Judge Jim Carrigan asked Donahue whether he'd committed the fraud. Donahue answered that he'd "technically" broken the law. But Carrigan pressed him, saying, "I'm not interested in technicalities. If you're not guilty, this court will not accept your guilty plea." Donahue muttered his confession.

In June 1992, as part of a civil settlement with the SEC, Donahue consented to a permanent ban from the securities business. The SEC had sought to seize nearly $1.5 million from Donahue—but the fine was waived because Donahue didn't have the funds to pay it.

Many investors complained that Donahue wasn't cooperating sufficiently with the bankruptcy proceedings. His lawyer, Denver criminal defense specialist Robert Dill, sounded coy in response: "He's attempting to cooperate in the case. He hasn't given them specific information because they haven't requested it."

Frustrated, the burned investors realized they weren't going to get much money from Donahue or the remaining pieces of Hedged Investments. So, they looked for deeper pockets.

In November 1994, Kidder Peabody & Co. and Morgan Stanley & Co. agreed to pay more than $40 million to Hedged Investments investors. The agreement topped a $5 million settlement recently made with Prudential Securities.

"It was a very fair settlement under the circumstances," said Bob Hill, an attorney for the investors. Hill said that proving Kidder and Morgan committed wrongdoing would have been difficult because the two firms did not actively defraud investors. Instead, they permitted Donahue to trade recklessly.

"Our view was, if they had followed their internal policies, they would have realized what was happening," Hill said.

"The problem with Donahue was that on every measure of a money manager, he pushed the limits of credibility," said another fund management analyst. "We have a number of tests that a manager should pass. In the case of Donahue, he didn't pass any. He had none of his own money [invested]. He was still accepting an unbelievably low minimum of $100,000. And, he had no industry references. But the clincher was lack of an audit or any credible third-party verification that assets existed and the record was real."

Again, the problem was one of suspicious consistency. All investment markets—and especially the options and commodities markets—are volatile. Good investment managers try to diversify their holdings and hedge this volatility—but not even the best ones can smooth out every spike.

CHAPTER 7

Precious Metals, Currency and Commodities

While vaguely defined "investments" and elaborate loan programs will probably always be the favored pretenses for Ponzi schemes, commodities programs usually run a close second. These financial mechanisms—which, for the sake of our investigation, include currency investments, precious metals deals and true commodity goods—are complicated and volatile things from the start. They offer a Ponzi perp plenty of cover in which to hide.

Even when they are traded legitimately, precious metals, currency and commodities can sound like schemes. They trade in markets which rise and fall dramatically—often in short bursts of activity. Trading them successfully requires steel nerves and good timing. Many transactions are heavily margined, which means an account with a few thousand dollars can make—or lose—tens of thousands of dollars in a few hours.

This trading is usually regulated by a federal agency called the Commodity Futures Trading Commission (CFTC), which is smaller, poorer and generally less sophisticated than the SEC or IRS.

Many of the same legal theories that apply to investment contracts connect commodities investments to Ponzi schemes. In practice, though, the connection between commodities deals and Ponzi schemes is usually more simple...and more crude.

One of the most dramatic and detailed commodities Ponzi scheme in recent history was operated by Thomas Chilcott, a Colorado-based financial advisor who desperately wanted to be considered an investment genius. As is so often the case, the most surprising thing about Chilcott is how many people he convinced.

From 1975 to 1981, Chilcott attracted nearly $80 million in investments for a commodities pool from approximately 400 persons. He talked grandly about his market perspective as a "quant," financial industry jargon for a *quantitative investor*. He didn't care for stories that might impact commodities markets—he focused instead on market trends and abstract formulas to keep ahead of everyone else.

On paper, Chilcott was entirely legitimate. He was a registered commodities advisor and investment pool operator with the CFTC. In person, he seemed to fit the part—with a young, aggressive demeanor and an office full of computers (still a novelty during his peak) blinking quotes from around the world.

It was all a fraud. Chilcott didn't make very many commodities trades...and the ones he did usually didn't do very well. (At one point, he invested heavily in worthless Oklahoma oil wells being peddled by *another* Ponzi perp.)

What Chilcott did do well was follow Carlo Ponzi's model. He pooled investment money into a few accounts, moved it around and then gave small pieces back to investors as dividends and distributions.

The Chilcott funds collapsed in the fall of 1981. No longer able to keep the illusion going, Chilcott started issuing distribution checks that bounced. He tried the usual delaying ploys—blaming the banks and trying to convince investors to reinvest their distributions.

Within a few weeks, the FBI had taken over Chilcott's Fort Collins office. The Feds estimated that the commodities pool had only about $8 million in liquid assets, more than half of which were held by Chilcott in his own name. The rest of the $80 million had been diverted into personal ventures, lost in speculative trading and returned to investors as bogus profits.

Denver lawyer James P. Johnson was appointed receiver. The court ordered him to take custody of all money and records and prevent further dissipation of assets. About that time, Chilcott was indicted on criminal fraud charges. He struck a plea bargain and avoided trial. Meanwhile, several civil lawsuits, filed by Johnson as well as groups of Chilcott investors, inched through the federal courts.

Chilcott was released from prison in early 1987 and promptly began a new commodities investment pool. Between March 1987 and February 1988, he attracted about $1.3 million—some of it from investors who'd put money into his old scheme.

In January 1988, a federal jury awarded $39.4 million in damages to the original Chilcott investors, who'd charged that Shearson/American Express Inc. had substantively helped Chilcott defraud them of $31.6 million, by referring clients to him. The jury found Shearson liable for negligent management, breach of fiduciary duty and conversion of funds. The award included the defrauded funds and an additional $7.8 million in punitive damages. Shearson lawyers said they would appeal—if only to convince the court to reduce the size of the verdict.

In the meantime, Chilcott's new venture was collapsing. This time, he skipped town before his distribution checks started bouncing. In the spring of 1988, a federal arrest warrant was issued by an Evergreen, Colorado, court charging Chilcott with wire fraud.

For almost a year, Chilcott evaded FBI agents and other law enforcement officials by moving around the west coast. Finally, in February 1989, he was arrested by federal agents near Del Mar, California. He'd been doing business in southern California since late 1988 as the supposed CEO of an oil exploration company.

"This guy was like an addict. He couldn't control himself," said one of the federal agents who'd investigated Chilcott in Colorado. "And it couldn't have been fun. You should have seen him when he came back [after the Del Mar arrest]. He was still barely 40. But he looked ten years older."

Precious Metals Are a Popular Premise

Just as the complexity of commodities trading and currency exchange rates invites bogus theories and Ponzi scammers, trading in precious metals provides a rich setting for scams.

"There's something about the idea that an ounce of gold fluctuates in value against the dollar that strikes most people as magic," says an FBI agent based in the Midwest who's investigated several goldbug Ponzi schemes. "For a big part of this country's history, the dollar was backed by gold. When that link was broken, both dollars and ounces seemed a little less legitimate." And may, in fact, have become less legitimate.

The recession of the mid-1970s planted the seeds of uncertainty in many people's minds. Those days were the most recent shining moment for goldbugs. While stocks and bonds floundered along with the economy in general, gold exploded in value. People who wouldn't normally invest in gold were hoarding gold coins: American Eagles, Canadian Maple Leafs and South African Krugerrands. The coins have been out of financial fashion pretty much ever since.

Theories about the gold standard, usually the realm of economists and conspiracy-minded novelists, have given birth to Ponzi schemes based on exploiting the shifting connection between dollars and gold.

David and Martha Crowe started Gold Unlimited, a multilevel marketing company based in Madisonville, Kentucky, in November 1993. The company conducted seminars to recruit people willing to invest $400 in the company. In return, investors would receive a gold coin and be placed on a list giving them the right to recruit additional participants.

Once investors recruited two other people to join, they were promised a commission on the recruits brought in through them. From the beginning, the company struck some people as a pyramid scheme. But its participants insisted Gold Unlimited was legitimate. According to them:

- people paid nothing to become representatives nor were they paid for bringing in others as representatives;
- participants could earn profits on goods they sold, but they could only earn commissions when they brought others into their sales networks who either bought or sold products;
- participants had to qualify to establish sales networks by producing $200 in "personal business volume credit."

For 1994, the Crowes' company claimed sales of $25 million. It boasted more than 90,000 sales representatives worldwide and with divisions in Canada and Hong Kong. The company's headquarters had once been a private mansion. There were walk-in safes on each floor to store the gold and silver bullion and coins, precious stones, jewelry and rare books the company sold through its independent representatives.

But, in early 1995, the company started running into trouble with state courts and regulators throughout the South and Midwest.

Mississippi Attorney General Mike Moore said consumers in that state should exercise caution about putting money in the firm. "Our main problem is that several representatives of the company appear to be concentrating on the recruitment of people into the company, not the sale of gold coins," said a spokeswoman for Moore's office. "We've also heard people saying that since our office met with the attorneys from Gold Unlimited, we've approved the program. Nothing is farther from the truth."

Iowa authorities reported that a growing number of residents had been lured into investing about $200 in Gold Unlimited. Each investor then had to recruit two more investors who also paid $200 each. After the company received the $600, the initial investor would get a gold coin worth about $300.

Arkansas Attorney General Winston Bryant called Gold Unlimited's plan a pyramid scheme and warned Arkansans to avoid it.

On March 13, 1995, while some of the state actions were just being announced, FBI agents and U.S. Postal Service inspectors seized Gold Unlimited's assets and sent its employees home.

The U.S. Attorney in Louisville said Gold Unlimited and the Crowes had "knowingly devised a scheme or artifice to defraud or for obtaining money or property by means of false or fraudulent pretenses, representations or promises."

The only way a Gold Unlimited representative could recoup his payment to the company was to recruit others who were, in turn, successful recruiters. Payments to representatives came from the cash sent in by new recruits. As the number of levels increased, more representatives would earn commissions on a set amount of business, requiring ever-growing profit margins and price markups just to cover the commissions.

Kentucky law enforcement officials said that Gold Unlimited was set up like an earlier Crowe venture, American Gold Eagle. That company had gone out of business in 1991, resulting in $367,000 in investor losses. But this record didn't seem to bother many Gold Unlimited investors.

At a hearing on March 22, 1995, more than 200 investors, some from as far away as Arizona and Texas, packed a federal court in a show of support for the company. The court ordered the assets and bank accounts of Gold Unlimited frozen. The company would, effectively, stay closed. "We've got to keep a positive attitude," said Kellan Lamb, the company's executive vice president.

But the legal moves were just beginning. Worried state officials filed a civil lawsuit, charging the Crowes with operating a pyramid scheme. In June, U.S. District Court Judge Thomas B. Russell indefinitely suspended the civil suit, saying that there was "apparently grand jury activity" involved in the case (that is, a criminal prosecution was underway). Russell said that he would appoint a receiver in the case to preserve company assets and to try to pay some outstanding debts.

The Crowes were indicted on July 12, 1995, on 22 counts each of mail fraud, securities fraud and money laundering. The indictment alleged the company induced "individuals to invest money for the right to receive compensation for inducing others to join the scheme."

Government prosecutors said the Crowes "perpetuated the scheme by paying 'commissions' to earlier investors, not from profits from the sale of...products but from the fees paid by new investors." The criminal charges carried penalties of up to 145 years in prison and fines of $5.5 million. The Crowes were released on $50,000 unsecured bonds each. After consulting with their lawyers, they reached a plea bargain with the Feds.

A Silver Scheme and How Ponzi Perps Are Punished

Con men are always a challenge for criminal courts. Since their investors are often willing, are they somehow less guilty than other criminals? Since they'll often give some useful advice or counsel to their victims in the course of a greater theft, do they mitigate their crimes? A Ponzi scheme that made big promises about silver futures trading brought these questions into focus.

Over a period of more than six years, Richard Holuisa convinced investors to give him $11 million. His plan was to invest the money in silver futures and high-yield government securities. He told potential investors that he'd developed a computerized program for exploiting discrepancies in the silver futures and government bond markets. His company, Certified Investment Co., could put their money in either market.

In this way, Holuisa was like Carlo Ponzi. He was touting a Great Idea.

Funds were used to cover Certified's operating expenses and were never invested as promised. Holuisa and a close circle of trusted associates sent investors fraudulent weekly and monthly statements detailing both the principal investment and the interest that had purportedly accrued.

And Holuisa lived high on the hog. He and his partner James Simpson had grown up together in gritty East Chicago, Indiana. They emphasized their roots to win over skeptical investors. "Hey, we're local guys," one investor remembered them saying. "You can trust us."

This was another way Holuisa and his cronies were like the old master—they claimed to be people of the people, in conflict with the ritzy financial establishment. Still, Holuisa and Simpson worked hard to not seem *too* hometown. They both drove leased Mercedes to underscore their success. They rented offices in the ritzy Crown Point, Indiana, suburb of Chicago and filled it with high-tech equipment.

But the stock market crash of October 1987 sent many investors to the sidelines, effectively drying up sources of fresh money needed to perpetuate the scheme.

In the early spring of 1988, Certified's dividend checks began bouncing. In April 1988, the Indiana State Police stepped in. Responding to complaints from investors, detectives raided Certified's offices. They seized 25 boxes of records for investigation. The company ceased doing business the same day.

When the scheme finally collapsed, Holuisa had spent $3.5 million on himself and his friends and returned the rest of the money—slightly more than $8 million—to his investors in monthly payments.

In 1990, Holuisa, Simpson and one of their salesmen pleaded guilty to charges of mail fraud, conspiracy to commit mail fraud and failure to report a currency transaction.

Holuisa received a sentence of five years on the mail fraud count and 57 months—the maximum sentence—on the other two counts. In sentencing Holuisa, the court considered that "he never intended to invest the money taken from the victims," and "that the intent of this defendant was to defraud all the victims of their money."

Holuisa's lawyer pointed out that he had partially repaid the investments. The court's sentencing calculation had been based on a loss amount of $11,625,739. The lawyer argued that, because over $8 million was returned to investors, the actual loss was approximately $3.5 million.

In contrast, the prosecutors argued that the full amount should be considered, even though much of it was returned, because the money was not invested as investors had been promised. The district court agreed with that rationale:

> *In this case the gravity of the completed crime was more substantial than the ultimate loss suffered by the victims. The defendant never intended to invest the monies taken from the victims; the intent...was to defraud all of the victims of their money.*

Nevertheless, Holuisa appealed the sentence as inappropriately harsh. The appellate court hearing Holuisa's case had considered the various calculations of fraud-related losses in an earlier case that involved another precious metals loan scam. In that case, it had written:

> *Both the Sentencing Commission's notes defining "loss" and this court's cases call for the court to determine the net detriment to the victim rather than the gross amount of money that changes hands. So a fraud that consists in promising 20 ounces of gold but delivering only 10 produces as loss the value of 10 ounces of gold, not 20. Borrowing $20,000 by fraud and pledging $10,000 in stock as security produces a "loss" of $10,000: "the loss is the amount of the loan not repaid at the time the offense is discovered, reduced by the amount the lending institution has recovered, or can expect to recover, from any assets pledged to secure the loan."*

In the Certified case, the full amount invested was not the probable or intended loss because Holuisa did not intend to keep the entire sum. Indeed, return of the money—that is, payment of earlier investors with the funds of later investors—was an integral aspect of Holuisa's scheme, essential to its continuation. And, in line with his intentions, Holuisa returned over $8 million to investors before the scheme was detected.

The appeals court concluded that Holuisa should not have been sentenced based on amounts that he both intended to and indeed did return to investors. The court vacated his sentence and sent the case back to trial court for resentencing—involving less jail time.

The appellate court's decision rubbed a lot of people the wrong way. In fact, there was a dissent, arguing Holuisa had rightly been given the maximum sentence.

> *How he planned to use the money is irrelevant...because each time he took money from investors, he put their money "at risk" and left them without a "ready source of recompense"....Holuisa did redistribute $8.6 million to many of his victims before his scheme fell apart; but...the money was stolen the day he received it from his victims. Instead of corralling money from a few investors, then skipping town, Holuisa extended his scheme by giving back some money and taking in more. He literally robbed Peter to pay Paul (whom he had defrauded earlier)....This case is no different than a series of thefts or embezzlements. An embezzler causes loss for the full amount taken, irrespective of his intention to repay.*

While many legal experts agree with this dissent, it remains a minority opinion in most judicial circles. The majority opinion—which seems crook-friendly to many wronged investors—holds that Ponzi perps lessen the severity of their crimes by distributing part of the money they steal to other people.

Case Study: Robert Johnson's Peso Scam

In the span of just a few months in 1988 and 1989, hundreds of people—including Oklahoma teachers, Kansas churchgoers and a Texas motorcycle gang—invested in a Ponzi scheme that was supposed to create huge profits by swapping money from U.S. dollars to Mexican pesos and back into dollars again.

The scheme's main perp, Australian-born Oklahoma resident Robert Leslie Johnson, told investors that he had extensive political connections in Mexico. Using these connections, he said he could buy pesos below the daily commercial exchange rate. Then, he'd convert the money back into dollars at current market rates.

Johnson told people that his plan was profitable; just *how* profitable was anyone's guess. He needed more money than he could raise by himself to test the upper limits.

The whole story was bogus. But Johnson's worldly attitude—and lilting Aussie accent—convinced people he was telling the truth. Political and financial instability in Mexico helped, too.

Initially, Johnson told investors he could get pesos for 5 percent under official exchange rates and that a complete cycle of currency swaps would take about a week to complete. But an annual profit of more than 250 percent wasn't enough to attract the volume of money his scheme would need. So, Johnson gradually increased his promised returns—to 22 percent per week. At this rate—more than 1,000 percent a year—the money started to flow in.

It was a good thing for Johnson that he could turn on the charm; he'd had a long history of trouble with the law. He'd come to Oklahoma in 1988 from California, where he'd been paroled from prison. But his arrest record dated back to the 1960s. "He was basically a con man," says one burned investor. "And always had been. I guess most of us kind of knew this. But who could tell? Maybe this was going to be his big strike."

While most of his currency-swap scheme was a basic Ponzi, Johnson did buy some black market pesos. He'd purchase the currency secretly from Mexican businessmen who embezzled cash from Mexican corporations owned by U.S. companies. These connections—not quite the political movers Johnson's investors envisioned—sent the pesos to Johnson at a San Diego address. In southern California, Johnson would convert the currency at various exchange bureaus, careful not to draw attention to any single transaction.

He wasn't very successful. The scheme first caught the attention of the Internal Revenue Service in 1987—just after it started. The IRS initially thought Johnson's operation was laundering money for central American drug smugglers. But, after watching Johnson for several months, the Feds concluded he wasn't moving enough currency to be connected to drug runners.

Once the Feds checked out Johnson's background, they guessed—correctly, as it turned out—that he might be running some kind of

Ponzi scheme. But Ponzi perps don't mean as much to the Feds as drug money launderers do. Johnson fell to a lower level of priority.

By the summer of 1988, Johnson had created enough of a track record for his bogus peso operation that he was able to recruit a network of shady seminar leaders and investment brokers to raise millions of dollars from hundreds of investors in Dallas, Houston, Oklahoma City and other cities throughout the Southwest. At his peak, he was also operating in California, Nevada, Tennessee and Florida.

Johnson and his main partner, Dallas native William Wayne Gray, started living flashy lifestyles. In the course of the scheme, Johnson would take in something like $50 million. In January 1989, he bought a new Mercedes for $92,000. A few weeks later, he wrote a check for $112,000 to pay off his mortgage.

But the peso pyramid was about to collapse. According to the IRS, to circumvent tax laws the men had established several phony companies. Income from the Ponzi scheme went to those corporations rather than directly to Johnson, Gray or their brokers. "The network of companies wasn't especially creative. It was just complicated," said one investigator who tracked Johnson's operations. "They figured if they moved the money around enough we wouldn't be able to find it."

In February 1989, Johnson and Gray were charged with violating Texas state securities law. Federal agents cooperating with Texas Rangers in Dallas seized about $3.2 million from a bank account one of Johnson's brokers had set up for the peso operation. The broker's account, which belonged to a shell corporation called FHL Group Inc. (FHL stood for "Faith, Hope and Love"), funneled money to Gray's WWG Investments Inc., which in turn passed it to Johnson.

State and federal investigators also confiscated more than $820,000 in cash in a search of Gray's home. They found 11 promissory notes, ranging from $1 million to $20 million, from Gray to Johnson. Nearly $2.4 million was seized from bank accounts held by Gray's firm and FHL.

Gray, who'd been arrested, was eventually free on $15,000 bond.

Johnson was arrested a month later, during an extended gambling trip to Las Vegas. Federal agents seized more than $250,000 in cash and property from Johnson's accounts in Tulsa and confiscated more than $1.2 million in cash and gold coins when they arrested him.

Incredibly, Johnson was also allowed to post a bond at his arraignment. He was free on $100,000 bond pending trial on securities charges. Even with all of the money seized during the arrests, millions of dollars channeled through the pyramid scheme had not been located. And, within a few weeks, Johnson and Gray couldn't be located either. Both jumped bail.

Johnson's flight didn't last long. In September, he was arrested near Anaheim, California. (Once again showing that Ponzi perps don't usually flee to exotic locations.)

In October 1989, he was charged in a 63-count indictment with laundering more than $216,000 in investor funds. The indictment also charged that Johnson engaged in a series of illegal financial transactions with proceeds from the investment scheme.

In a related move, federal officials also filed a civil lawsuit seeking forfeiture of Johnson's home in Tulsa and a $43,000 certificate of deposit and a $25,000 annuity purchased in his name. They contended that all had been purchased with proceeds from the fraudulent investment scheme.

Eventually, the IRS decided to drop the civil suit against Johnson. But the criminal cases proceeded slowly.

Burned investors were frustrated by delays in the federal investigation. The delays kept seized money...seized. Hundreds of people nationwide contacted the FBI to lay claim to the money. The Feds said investors had little hope of recovering their losses. So, the smartest investors took matters into their own hands.

Fort Worth-based H&O Marketing and Landmark Financial Network filed suit against Gray, Johnson and WWG Investments in February 1989 to recoup about $17 million in lost investments and proceeds. Two Fort

Worth investors, Richard Sims and Mark Pace, joined in the suit in July 1989. Sims and Pace bought into the scheme shortly before state and federal regulators began to dismantle it.

A judgment in the civil case was handed down during the summer of 1990. It sided with the burned investors, awarding them $4.5 million of their initial investment and about $16 million in other damages.

"It's definitely nice to have a big judgment," said John Proctor, a Fort Worth attorney who represented Sims and Pace. "It would be even nicer to collect. [The investors] would like to get a return *of* their money first, and secondly, they would like to get a return *on* their money."

The judgment was the first major development in the case since federal agents in Dallas had seized millions of dollars in assets from the investment organizers. "We were able to get our initial investment back plus the profit that the money made," said John Gamboa, an attorney representing dozens of burned investors. "We know where [Johnson] is, and we know where his assets are," he said. But Gamboa said he expected the judgment would be appealed. "With that sizable a judgment, I'd be surprised if they didn't appeal," he said.

While the civil suits mounted, Johnson was awaiting trial on the federal criminal charges in a Tulsa jail.

Gray's whereabouts were unknown, although he was believed to have fled the state. His former attorney, Don Crowder, said he did not know how to contact Gray. "Even when I was representing him, I just had a phone number that I would call and leave a number and he would call me back," Crowder said.

Gray was eventually found by federal agents and returned to Texas for trial. He was convicted and sentenced to more than 10 years in federal prison. But he insisted the Feds had seized all of his money. Informed opinion differed on this issue. "Bill Gray's an idiot...a pathological liar and a thief," says one of his former defense attorneys. "He has still got $10 million buried somewhere. I believe that with all my heart."

CHAPTER 8

Affinity Scams

We've considered the most common premises for Ponzi schemes—tax shelters, travel deals, loan networks and commodities investments. But, in a growing number of cases, the premise of the scheme doesn't matter. These schemes are sold by something other than a Great Idea.

Instead, they rely on another of Carlo Ponzi's tools: Exploiting the trust of members of tight-knit communities. This often means people who share a racial group or ethnic origin—but it can also apply to people in the same profession, church or extended family.

Law enforcement officials call these "affinity scams." (And even the law enforcement community isn't immune. The 1990s saw an explosion of affinity scams directed at police officers.)

Recent immigrants—particularly recent illegal immigrants—are particularly vulnerable to affinity scams because they're often unfamiliar with the operations of American banks and mainstream investment services. In some cases, the countries from which they've come have an unstable official banking structure—so the difference between official and underground investments isn't very great.

In the United States, this orientation has created informal savings institutions like Korean *kye* and Caribbean *susu*. These can be dynamic lenders—examples of free-market capitalism at its best. But they can also attract crooks who thrive in the shady regions of loosely-regulated money.

Another reason that affinity scams focus on immigrants: Securities regulators don't track foreign-language newspapers, radio or television as closely as they do English-language outlets. As a result, advertisements recruiting investors can make outrageous promises with less accountability.

Beginning in the late 1980s, the North American Securities Administrators Association began issuing a series of warnings about affinity scams, especially those directed at immigrant communities. And with good cause.

Immigrants as an Affinity Target

In five years, between 1987 and 1992, New York-based Oxford Capital Securities Inc. scammed scores of investors out of more than $10 million in a Ponzi scheme that was as crude as it was effective. Once again, the reason it worked was not its sophistication—but the strength of its affinity appeal.

Oxford Capital was started by Samuel Forson, a native of Ghana who'd grown up in Brooklyn idolizing business tycoons like J.P. Morgan. He completed his MBA at St. John's University in the early 1980s and eventually worked his way up to sales manager at First Investors Corp., a mutual fund marketing company in New York. But selling IRAs wasn't aggressive enough for Forson.

Oxford Capital focused its sales effort on recent immigrants to the United States, usually from the West Indies, living in the New York area. The company had been founded and was run by immigrants and people of Caribbean heritage. They stressed the importance of community support when convincing potential investors to hand over money.

Forson used company money to support a lavish lifestyle. Like so many Ponzi perps, he seemed most comfortable spending money. Among his purchases: a $730,000 apartment on Riverside Drive in Manhattan, a $2,000-a-month home on Long Island's North Shore, a $1,000-a-month Jaguar sedan (this was a nontraditional move for a perp—away from the usual Mercedes Benz) and a rack of $1,500 suits from Barneys.

When Forson married Yvonne Thomas, who'd started out as a clerical employee at Oxford Capital, their reception was held at the Plaza Hotel near Central Park. The newlyweds arrived at the hotel in a horse-drawn carriage.

The scheme began to unravel after one experienced investor questioned the statements she'd received from two mutual funds supposedly purchased through Oxford Capital. When the statements didn't make sense to her, she contacted the funds directly and learned her accounts, which should have contained more than $100,000, had been cashed out two years earlier—in 1989.

Mutual fund employees then contacted securities regulators, triggering an investigation that began in September 1991.

The collapse of Oxford Capital was ugly. Many of the people who'd invested money were far from rich swells who could afford the loss. A New York subway conductor who lived in a working-class Queens neighborhood ended up losing almost $47,000. (Worse still, two friends that she convinced to invest with Oxford Capital lost another $35,000.) A secretary and recent immigrant from Jamaica lost $46,500 that she had been planning to use to complete her college degree.

Forson's lawyers argued that Oxford Capital intended to make good on its debts—and could have if the company had had more time to work out its bad investments. One of the lawyers pointedly blamed regulatory agencies and prosecutors for frightening investors into demanding their money back. "It was a run on the bank, in simplest terms," he said.

The Manhattan D.A. took a harder line. Forson and several of Oxford's top executives faced criminal charges of larceny and running a corrupt enterprise. Each faced up to 25 years in prison. "Basically, it's a Ponzi scheme," said one of the assistant district attorneys prosecuting the case. "It didn't start that way, but it rapidly became one."

In the prosecutors' scenario, Forson ran Oxford Capital as a legitimate but unsuccessful money management firm for about two years.

At that point—sometime in 1989—he concluded that he could attract more money if he padded his returns with capital that was supposed to be invested in safe vehicles like CD's and T-bills and in minority-owned or Caribbean-based companies.

What followed was a series of disastrous investments, which were obscured by the Ponzi payments.

Oxford Capital invested in a modeling agency, a fashion design firm and a sports talent agency. They all lost money. Perhaps the most egregiously bad deal was Forson's attempt to buy a Nigerian freighter carrying fertilizer which had been stranded in the waters off of South America because of a complicated international trade dispute.

Forson needed $800,000 of Oxford Capital money to spring the freighter full of manure. Part of the money would go to honest bribes back in Nigeria—the rest would go to taking title on the contents of the boat and greasing wheels in the States. Forson told his employees that this was the deal they'd been waiting for—the deal that was going to make them all rich. When his employees asked what they should tell investors, who believed they were investing in conservative things like certificates of deposit and mutual funds, Forson "said to tell them anything."

In a common tactic, Forson's defense lawyers argued that Oxford Capital investors were blinded by their own greed—choosing not to notice that the outfit was offering a no-risk 100 percent annual return on invested money. This, they argued, was a deal that anyone could see was too good to be true. One investor responded a little too readily, voicing the fears that drive so many working class people into the arms of Ponzi perps. She admitted that Oxford Capital investors were greedy, "if being greedy means that poor people can do the same thing that people on Wall Street do."

The defense attorneys also tried another standard argument. They claimed that the real villains of Oxford Capital were out-of-control salespeople who lied to investors in order to boost their commissions.

But the Oxford Capital sales force was given specific directions in its efforts. Salespeople were told to target their own ethnic groups, as well as relatives and friends. "That's another thing that roped me in," said one burned investor. "I trusted [Forson] because he was West Indian."

Misplaced Trust in Ethnic Loyalty

Immigrants are vulnerable to affinity scams because culture shock and language barriers can make their new lives overwhelming. For the same reasons immigrants buy native-language newspapers and rent homeland videos, they feel compelled to put money with former countrymen.

"It's a familiar tongue...it feels solid," says one investor who was burned in an affinity scam directed at Eastern European immigrants to the United States during the late 1980s. "But it's not. If anything, you need to be more careful about fellow [immigrants] who want to invest your money."

In the summer and fall of 1991, Taiwanese businessman David Tsao advertised in San Francisco's Chinese-language newspapers for "employees" in each of his three California companies: Pacific Percentage Inc., East Ocean International and Green Tree Investments.

Tsao, who'd come to the United States in 1989, offered salaries and trading commissions totaling $1,600 per month, but only after applicants made initial investments of about $16,000 with the companies.

The pitch was unlikely—but Tsao was charismatic. With a big Mercedes and three houses in the Bay Area, he impressed employees and potential investors as a man of means. He was in his early forties (which seems to be about the median age of Ponzi perps). His businesses supposedly included a travel agency, a real estate firm and several other ventures. And he made efforts to fit the classic—and some might say stereotypical—profile of a rich Asian entrepreneur.

While he boasted about his business ties to Taiwan, Hong Kong and even mainland China, Tsao was vague about specifics. He talked about his passion for high-stakes gambling, at one point telling potential employee/investors that he'd recently lost $3 million at the tables in Las Vegas.

He also claimed that he was an accomplished commodities trader. This was the reason he directed so much of his effort toward speculation in the commodities markets—particularly trades in Standard & Poor's 500 stock index futures contracts. (If nothing else, this image was consistent with a man who'd show millions of dollars of action in Las Vegas casinos.)

Tsao told employee/investors that his dream was to buy a vast tract of land in China, where he would build new homes for his friends. This was the sharp point of his affinity hook—an appeal to the ethnic Chinese impulse toward the homeland. It worked well. Almost 300 employee/investors, most of them recent immigrants, signed up in San Francisco. Another 120 or so were recruited in Tsao's southern California offices.

The homeland scenario also made Tsao's employee-investors feel better about calling friends and relatives for investments.

For several months, Tsao kept his promises to pay lucrative commissions. But the money he paid out was coming directly from money the friends and relatives were investing. By early 1992, Tsao was already having trouble paying commissions. His Ponzi scheme was beginning to collapse—after less than a year.

In early March, Tsao disappeared. His employee-investors were left with the harsh realization that Tsao's companies were nearly broke...and his personal assets were encumbered with loans and liens. They called the authorities.

As it turned out, the San Francisco District Attorney's Office, the Commodity Futures Trading Commission and the FBI had already been looking into Tsao and his companies. They'd been tipped off by a few employee-investors months before.

With Tsao missing and almost $25 million hanging in the balance, the Feds moved more quickly. The CFTC got a court order freezing

Tsao's assets and those of his three companies. One investigator who examined Tsao's trading accounts said, "I'll admit, [he] had one good day.... But his accounts show that at each month's end, he was clearly losing money."

The employee-investors, some 400 in all, decided to take their case public. They appointed new leaders, who held a press conference at which they pleaded with Tsao to come out of hiding and explain the disappearance of the money. They said they still had confidence in his ability to turn their losses into profits. "Everything will clear up if [Tsao] shows up in public," said one employee-investor, speaking through an interpreter. "It's not like this is a robbery. We gave our money to David to invest."

The spokesman said that Tsao—who didn't speak English—didn't know much about U.S. law. "He is afraid of rumors that people will kill him."

As was the case when Carlo Ponzi was arrested, many of Tsao's investors insisted that he would come out of hiding and make their investments whole. "He said that if he lost any money he will play the market and return the money to us," an employee-investor told a local newspaper. It was the same old reaction. If the Feds would just leave their guy alone, the investors believed they'd get their money back.

The Psychology Means More Than the Details

Often, the details of the scheme underlying an affinity rip-off are surprisingly crude. The perps get away with this because their pitches rely on psychology far more than finance.

The Better Life Club—which targeted middle-class black families in the Washington, D.C. area—serves a good illustration of an affinity scam's psychological draw. As is the case in many American cities, a large number of black families in the nation's capital choose to live and socialize in essentially all-black communities.

Robert Taylor set up a system to exploit the separateness. Taylor—

who is black—traveled the African-American social, business and religious circuits in and around Washington. Like Carlo Ponzi before him, Taylor claimed to have developed a method that would allow average working people to enjoy the profits usually hoarded by fatcat capitalists.

Following the cynical steps of Washington's scandal-plagued mayor, Marion Barry, Taylor filled his talks with insinuations about racism...in his case, in the financial world. He played on long-held fears in the black community that minority entrepreneurs are kept down by establishment banks and commercial lenders. And he twisted legitimate calls for commercial self-reliance into support for his scheme.

Taylor's Great Idea was pretty simple—and basically, pretty absurd. He claimed to be building an advertising and 900 number telephone marketing company. He'd set up over-the-telephone personal and financial advice lines that would generate big money. He claimed that he could double an investor's money in 90 days. He made the promise well enough that few people questioned its validity.

"He said it was all a numbers game," recalls one person who heard several Taylor pitches. "As much money as he could raise, he could put into phone lines and advertising. Of course, the market would eventually top out at some point. But he was just scratching the tip of the iceberg."

An iceberg is an apt image for the scam, which grew to Titanic proportions. In a little more than a year, Taylor attracted about 6,000 investors who handed him more than $50 million. At its peak, the Better Life Club was taking in something like $2 million a week. And Taylor was traveling to cities all across North America, conducting what he called "wealth-building seminars."

Of course, none of the money went into 900 numbers or advertising. A large part of the money went back to investors in the form of payouts, but Taylor kept enough for himself to buy a million-dollar home, several expensive cars and trust funds for his children. "In one way, the name of the scheme was true enough," says a federal investigator who looked into Taylor's operation. "It just should have made full disclosure. It should have been called the Better Life for Robert Taylor Club."

In September 1995, the SEC filed suit against the Better Life Club and Robert Taylor. It claimed that his investors had lost at least half of the $50 million they'd invested. Taylor didn't put up much of a fight. His lawyers helped him reach a plea bargain—and he received a relatively light three-to-five year sentence for wire fraud. A series of civil lawsuits followed, which effectively bankrupted Taylor; but not even this served to faze him.

Considering how many Ponzi perps return to their conniving ways after jail stints, Taylor's cool approach to his legal problems may not be so surprising after all. Quite a few of the people familiar with Taylor—both as investors and investigators—say he's charismatic enough to make money promoting a new con when he's completed his prison term.

Religion Works Well as an Affinity Hook

Next to ethnic or racial groups, the most effective—and most disturbing—affinity hook is religion.

Los Angeles con man Rodney Swanson used Emmanuel Evangelical Free Church, the suburban Burbank enclave to which he belonged, as his network for recruiting investors into a real estate Ponzi scheme.

Swanson looked the part of a successful California real estate mogul. In his late forties, he had the features and physical attitude of a blandly handsome television actor. He lived in posh San Marino and drove a big Mercedes sedan. But what really made Swanson believable was that he didn't seem very excited about his business.

The thrill of pulling a con comes in pressing the envelop of credibility...putting a twist on the pitch that closes the sale. This can make the perp all the more believable, though it risks collapsing the entire premise.

It's a fact of life in upper-middle-class Los Angeles—and in most places—that successful people sometimes seem ambivalent about their work. Swanson played to this trend. He was, at least initially, more excited talking about his children and his weekends with his family than about real estate. His fellow congregants saw the proof of Swanson's priorities: He was a regular at church baseball games and in the choir on Sundays.

This was just the soft sell leading up to the hard sell.

Gradually, Swanson talked to friends from church about investment opportunities. He had deals on commercial properties waiting to close. He had trust deeds on prime land looking for investors. He had spots open in limited partnerships.

Swanson actually had a motley collection of minority investor positions and heavily-mortgaged properties. He manipulated and finessed new investments and title transfers so that his investors believed they were getting something for their money. Word spread through church circles that Swanson was making good investments for people.

And he made his early interest payments and distributions on time—with the money he was bringing from new investors.

Swanson kept the scam going for at least two years. It was the perfect Ponzi scheme: It started out with a few investors and less than $100,000; as time went on, people started coming to Swanson—offering money to invest. At the peak, his scheme was circulating $10 million among various investors and accounts.

Like most Ponzi perps, Swanson started to run out of new investors more quickly than he'd figured. By late 1995, he was bouncing distribution checks. Most of his investors were worried; some called the police.

The scam was complex enough that it took investigators months to unravel. In the meantime, Swanson declared bankruptcy and withdrew from the Burbank church. When he was finally arrested on more than 60 counts of fraud, grand theft and money laundering, he was driving a soft drink delivery truck and living in a low-rent neighborhood. (But he maintained his ability to charm people out of their money. Some parishioners at his new church put up their own houses to help bail him out.)

Eventually, the deputy district attorney who tried the case against Swanson explained the scam in religious terms. He called Swanson a "financial Judas—except Judas only betrayed one person, and he did it for less money."

Swanson's criminal trial lasted more than eight weeks. The testimony of his conned investors—including a police detective, a fireman, a clinical psychologist and a banker—was full of insights learned painfully. Most concluded that they'd allowed their friendship with Swanson color their investment judgment. "You just wanted to believe that [Swanson] was what he seemed to be," said an investor—privately, after Swanson's trial. "It was a difficult moment when I realized that this man...who was so much a part of my church...was a thief."

Not all affinity frauds take the form of pyramid or Ponzi schemes. Many crooks use the pretense of ethnicity, national origin or religious affiliation to rip off others in a more basic way. But Ponzi schemes have a kind of resonance with affinity fraud. The familiarity and trust of the one plays off against the familiarity and trust of the other—with the final result being a bigger rip-off than either device could have created by itself.

An investor who lost money in an Asian affinity scheme described the geometric impact well:

> *It was almost worth the monetary loss because of how good it felt [to believe] that this thing was working.... I've never been involved in ethnic pride movements. But they must feel like this felt. I was happy that [immigrants from the same place] were looking out for each other. Making each other rich. I'm not a big financial person, either. I've always believed in being conservative with money. Investing conservatively. But this appealed to me emotionally.... When I found out it was a [Ponzi scheme], I didn't want to believe it. It was like someone in my family had betrayed me.*

It's a tragedy that investors can lose money and feel this level of betrayal. But this kind of self-supporting trust is irresistible to Ponzi perps.

Case Study: Wild Irish Castles

Affinity scams that target ethnic or racial groups don't always limit themselves to poor, recent immigrants. From 1985 to 1988, a group of New York con men ran one of the most successful affinity Ponzi schemes in recent history. And this monster's tentacles reached across the Atlantic Ocean to the Emerald Isle. All involved, perps and victims, were of Irish descent. Carlo Ponzi would likely have approved.

William Dowling, Walter J.P. Curley and Adams Nickerson controlled Dowmar Securities, a real estate syndication firm based in New York. Dowmar had showy offices in Rockefeller Center. Its syndication experts were often quoted in the financial pages, talking about the real estate market and specific deals.

The principals had pedigree. Curley was a former U.S. ambassador to Ireland and France. Dowling had been one of the developers behind the late Daniel K. Ludwig's Princess Hotels chain. Nickerson was a member of a socially prominent Long Island family.

The affluent background of the three players might suggest a blase attitude toward social climbing. But Dowmar made a concerted effort to have its people move in high net worth circles. "Frankly, they were pushy about it," complained one investor through a rigid Long Island lockjaw. The pushiness could be explained easily enough: Dowmar was on a constant lookout for rich people with even the slightest inclination to invest in its shady real estate deals.

Ashford Castle was an ancient fortress in County Mayo, on Ireland's west coast. In the late 19th century, it had been rebuilt by Lord Ardilaun, a member of the Guinness brewing family. In the 1940s, Ashford and 11 surrounding acres had been converted into a luxury hotel. By the late 1970s, it was owned by an Irish businessman who couldn't get it to generate enough revenue to pay the mortgage.

In 1980, Allied Irish Banks (AIB) foreclosed on Ashford. It didn't want the hotel—but it couldn't find a buyer. In 1985, it teamed with

Dowling, Curley and Nickerson to syndicate the hotel in the U.S.

Dowmar sold rooms, or "units," to investors. Because investors could spend two weeks each year in their units, the deal had an attractive time-sharing aspect. Technically, though, the deeds were securities because the investors had a right to share in the hotel's total income.

The syndication raised $7.5 million to buy Ashford from AIB, which financed most of the investments itself at a relatively high interest rate.

For the big bank, it was a great deal, transforming a white elephant into the personal loans to a bunch of wealthy Americans. It was also a great deal for Curley, Nickerson and Dowling, who collected syndication fees. Better yet, through an entity called Ashford Castle Inc. (ACI), they gave themselves a contract to manage the hotel.

Numerous American investors were solicited through personal contacts, a slick direct mail campaign and an appealing private placement memorandum. "It sounded like a great investment," says Peter McSorley, owner of a New York taxicab company. "We were told that big dividends would pay off the mortgage."

Among the Ashford group's members were such notables as Jay Higgins, a former vice chairman of Salomon Brothers; the Rooney family, which owns the Pittsburgh Steelers football team; Prescott Bush, the brother of the former U.S. President; and, Dublin-born Anthony J. O'Reilly, president of H.J. Heinz.

Throughout the solicitation process, AIB made efforts to conceal its ownership of Ashford. The bank did this, primarily, to get higher prices for the property than it would have if the buyers had known the hotel was in foreclosure.

Two years after the Ashford deal, Dowmar was broke. So, it found another old Irish castle to sell to the same American investors.

Dromoland Castle, near the town of Shannon, had been home to various lines of Irish royalty since the late 1600s. In 1963, it had been converted into a luxury resort hotel. In 1987, it was acquired by Curley, Nickerson and Dowling. Acting as Dromoland Castle Inc. (DCI), they raised almost $13 million. AIB had no equity in the castle this time; but it did serve as the project's sole financier and escrow agent.

The Dromoland private placement memorandum contained misrepresentations about the financing and the use of proceeds. Also, the syndication was consummated even though the requisite minimum subscription level stated in the Dromoland PPM was never reached.

The Ashford deal's financial structure created a hidden drain on shareholders' equity; the problem was much worse with Dromoland. For one thing, Dromoland needed extensive renovations. For another, the perps were using Dromoland money to keep Ashford investors current.

Andrew Schlafly, a lawyer for some of the investors, said: "If Dromoland Castle's promoters had to siphon off revenues and capital to pay down Dromoland's [AIB] financing, they also had to use Dromoland's funds to continue paying the older Ashford loans."

So, in the same period of time that the Ashford investors lost one-third of their equity, Dromoland's investors saw their equity sink to zero under a debt that eventually reached $9 million. "It was a classic Ponzi situation, where later investors lose more than earlier investors," Schlafly said.

The cash infusion from Dromoland smoothed things over for a little while. But, pretty soon, the Dromoland project needed money to make up for the proceeds it had transferred over to Ashford—which, for its part, was still soaking up development money.

By late 1991, the continued diversion of funds from one project to another had put the various Dowmar projects under great financial strain. In December, it was apparent to most of the people involved that the projects were irrevocably insolvent.

In 1992, about two dozen of the investors filed a lawsuit in New York federal court, accusing Dowmar of running a Ponzi scheme and AIB of aiding and abetting. The charges included: common-law fraud, breach of fiduciary duty, breach of contract and violation of the federal RICO statute. The fraud charges focused on the fact that the Ashford and Dromoland deals were closed even though the minimum subscription levels hadn't been reached. Instead, they were filled out with bogus stand-in investors backed by illusory loans from AIB.

The repayment of the bogus loans put the real estate syndications into debt from the beginning—and assured the need for future rigged offerings. Also, the stand-ins violated the investment contracts that Dowmar itself had drafted. The Ashford PPM expressly stated:

> *Investors will be required to represent that they are acquiring Castle Interests for their own account, for investment and not with a view toward resale or distribution thereof.*

The Dromoland PPM contained virtually identical language.

After the Ashford and Castle deals closed, Curley, Dowling, Nickerson and AIB directed the companies to "make substantial payments...to themselves and to Dowmar, purportedly for fees in connection with the closing." Lawyers for Dowmar and AIB said the fees were proper. One of their lawyers sneered:

> *The Ponzi scheme is baloney. It's a figment of someone's imagination.... The reason the Ashford investors are not making money has nothing to do with the defendants. Had there not been a global recession in 1989-92 resulting from the Gulf War, I doubt there would ever be litigation. These big hotels had huge operating costs and not enough guests. Once you fall behind, you never really get back on your feet.*

In a move that Ponzi perps often make when an affinity scheme collapses, the perps' lawyer tried to paint the scheme as ethnic intramural bickering. "I'm sorry that Mr. Dowling and they are all of Irish descent, and that there are hard feelings among them," he said, "but I don't think anyone was duped." By late 1996, the lawsuits were still grinding through court.

PART TWO

Why the Schemes Work

CHAPTER 9

Gullibility

Affinity scams aren't the only rip-offs that rely on trust. All pyramid and Ponzi schemes do. Of the key factors that allow Ponzi schemes to flourish, gullibility...or misplaced trust...is most important. It's the point on which burned investors—once they learn they've lost money—most often blame themselves. Invariably, the person will offer some version of "I can't believe I trusted that crook...."

Law enforcement officials, who don't usually feel much sympathy for Ponzi investors, often turn unexpectedly sociological when they are asked about the high level of misplaced trust. "It's the age we live in," says an East Coast assistant D.A. "Even smart people have no idea who to trust."

Essentially, the theory holds that information overload has made people confused and vulnerable. Telephones, television, computers and the Internet have shattered the traditional sense of social proportion. People don't trust their neighbors but believe they have a personal relationship with Oprah Winfrey or Hillary Clinton. This is an encouraging environment for Ponzi perps.

G.W. McDonald, the enforcement head of the California Department of Corporations, deals with the fallout of Ponzi schemes almost daily. He looks at Ponzi investors as the interesting phenomenon—and the perps as something more like a natural response.

McDonald says that most Ponzi perps dismiss their investors harshly—as nothing more than willing suckers, destined to lose their money.

This is a rationalization for crime as old as mankind. The fact that so many people are willing to believe these crooks is the news. McDonald describes the basic telephone scammer:

> *They're courteous, sound concerned about your well-being, listen to your complaints, flatter, try to be the surrogate son or friend you seldom see, tout their financial successes, offer some financial advice, tell you they can get a better return on your money. [Then] they take every penny.*

Another West Coast law enforcement specialist makes a more media-savvy observation:

> *The perfect Ponzi investor is a person who buys a lot of stuff from QVC. [QVC] isn't a con, but it requires an abstract level of trust that most people didn't have twenty years ago. That person is conditioned to invest money in [a] scheme with a person he doesn't know. He'll put bars on his windows and lock all the doors in his house, but he'll let [a Ponzi perp] waltz right in, over the phone.*

The same lack of perspective applies even more dramatically to distinguishing among people that we actually meet. Ponzi perps thrive on the inability of some investors to tell the difference between a friend and an acquaintance. This is particularly true in business circles, where the networking mentality of the late 1980s and early 1990s often confuses business cards in a Rolodex with time-tested relationships.

Strivers of all sorts—not just Ponzi perps—are attracted to real estate and insurance. In most states, you don't need much education to apply for a realtor's or insurance agent's license; and getting one puts you on an even professional footing with some of the smartest people in business. This is part of the reason that so many Ponzi perps use broker or agent licenses as fulcrums for their frauds. A license often suggests more legitimacy that it actually means.

How Misdirected Trust Works

In the classic nineteenth century crime novel *Lombard Street*, Walter Bagehot summed up the role that misplaced trust plays in many thieving schemes. The novelist described it this way:

> *...people are most credulous when they are most happy. And when much money has just been made...when some people are really making it, when most people think they are making it...there is a happy opportunity for ingenious mendacity.*

Michael Rosen knew something about ingenious mendacity. He got started in business in the late 1970s as a real estate agent in the San Francisco Bay area. He didn't have much formal education, but few people who met him would have guessed that. Rosen could talk with authority—and a certain level of self-educated accuracy—on a wide range of topics.

In a relatively short period of time, Rosen was able to schmooze his way into the Bay Area's local business and political scenes. He was particularly good at collecting contributions for Republican candidates and politicians. "The guy had radar," said one acquaintance who said he'd always been intrigued by Rosen—but never trusted him. "He'd sense who's the most important person in the room and he'd be over working the guy."

Rosen lived and worked in Rohnert Park, a relatively conservative enclave of San Francisco County. He eventually was named to the Rohnert Park Chamber of Commerce—which gave him access to politicians like Governor Pete Wilson and various state legislators.

Rosen's problem was simple. While he seemed to be doing well financially, he was usually spending more time chatting up rich people and politicos than actually selling real estate. So, sometime in the mid-1980s, he started building an elaborate Ponzi scheme.

His first step was selling bogus second mortgages. (As we've already seen, this is a disturbingly easy thing to do.) Rosen would approach one acquaintance and explain that a mutual friend—usually someone with a higher public profile—was having money problems and needed a quick, discrete loan. The loan would take the form of a second mortgage. Rosen would say that, in order to make things go smoothly and quietly, the borrower would be willing to pay a bonus and a high interest rate.

If the first acquaintance was willing to make the loan, Rosen would draw up paperwork. He would even, on occasion, show the potential lender things like personal financial statements. The whole deal would usually take less than a week to complete. And it would be completely fraudulent. The first acquaintance would never know that any loan had been made. The personal financial information was almost all made up. The lender was simply adding money to Rosen's Ponzi scheme.

Rosen did this dozens of times. He exploited the trust of friends, partners and political allies. If any of the lenders had contacted any of the supposed borrowers, the scheme would have collapsed. But people never made the connections. They trusted Rosen.

The bogus second mortgage business in Rohnert Park could only support a limited amount of fraudulent activity. As the 1980s turned into the 1990s, Rosen needed more room to keep his scheme growing. After listening and watching other real estate bigshots operate, he moved on to selling limited partnerships in real estate development projects—a relatively unregulated part of the market. Although the deals were different and the dollars larger, Rosen's modus operandi was the same: He'd sell many times the value of the deals.

His centerpiece was a project called Sky Hawk. It was supposed to be a large development like Blackhawk, a successful subdivision of $1 million homes about an hour north of San Francisco. "I went out with Michael and his brother Chuck," said one investor. "We physically looked at this property. We were walking around trails."

But Rosen didn't own the land. All he had—and even this would become a matter of dispute—was an option to buy the land. Most importantly, development agencies in the area never received plans for building Sky Hawk.

Rosen sold limited partnerships, anyway. And he even paid some distributions. He claimed these were from the early sale of Sky Hawk lots; in fact, they were from later investments. He planned his scheme carefully...and grew it slowly. But the most careful management only allowed Rosen to borrow more time. The inevitable outcome was the same.

There were some hints of trouble in early 1996. Several of Rosen's interest checks bounced. He blamed the problems on a jam-up with his bank and made good on the payments.

His scheme finally collapsed at the end of August 1996. Despite the walking tours of the area, Sky Hawk wasn't drawing enough new money to support the list of people who expected interest checks every month. Between 60 and 100 people had invested $6 million with Rosen. That meant monthly interest expenses of almost $100,000. And Rosen hadn't made investments which could generate that kind of cash flow.

He filed for bankruptcy protection in September 1996. His company listed almost 200 creditors—and a negative net worth of several million dollars. Because Rosen had used the banking system to perpetuate his scheme, the FBI was called in by local law enforcement authorities to investigate. Rosen cooperated with the Feds from the beginning, providing what paperwork he had and explaining the details of his con. As a result, a month after his scheme collapsed, he still hadn't been arrested.

"He should be in custody," said William Duplissea, a former state assemblyman who lost several thousand dollars with Rosen. "There are a lot of records and things like that he could do away with."

Duplissea had first met Rosen at a state Republican convention in the late 1980s. The two men turned out to have similar backgrounds, growing up in families that owned dry cleaning businesses in northern California. Soon they were attending baseball games at Candlestick Park, vacationing together in the Napa Valley, socializing with fellow Republicans. Rosen eventually invited Duplissea to join his real estate ventures. "I'd been in and out of them," he said. "They'd mature and I'd be paid, and we'd go into another one."

Another investor said, "[Rosen]'s smart. Since he declared bankruptcy voluntarily, he could argue he'd surrendered. Since he cooperated with the FBI all along, he could say he was making amends. He can't say his investments were legitimate, but I won't be surprised if he doesn't spend too much time in jail."

Building Confidence...and Then Exploiting It

A question—which may be impossible to answer—shows how trust shapes criminal schemes. Does the Ponzi perp create trust in order to exploit it...or does the perp pervert genuine trust to disingenuous ends?

This isn't just a philosophical abstraction. Courts consider the same issues. One federal appeals court dealing with the fallout of a collapsed Ponzi scheme noted:

> *Often there is a component of misplaced trust inherent in the concept of fraud. One must hold a position of trust before it can be abused, however. Fraudulently inducing trust in an investor is not the same as abusing a bona fide relationship of trust with that investor.*

The most effective Ponzi perps—the ones who can keep their schemes going for the longest time—are usually people who have built a track record of trust with the people from whom they're stealing. This level of trust also gives the Ponzi perp the option of skimming a little money at a time from the scheme, rather than stealing a big piece right away.

Saul Foos was a Chicago-based talent agent who specialized in working with radio disk jockeys and local TV newscasters. Like most agents, he had to deal with fragile egos, temper tantrums and complicated personal lives. He also dealt with his share of dirty laundry and hard-nosed negotiating. For almost 30 years, he maintained the appearance of calm resolve. Sitting by the swimming pool at his weekend home in Michigan, Foos would tell friends that his strength came from the fact that he had no debts. "I can sleep like a baby because I don't owe anything to anybody."

He was conspicuously generous. "You could never pick up a bill within a 100-yard radius of him," one longtime friend said.

Foos had come from a humble background in New York. He'd moved to Chicago in the early 1960s to go to law school at De Paul University. As a young lawyer, he'd done some high-profile personal injury work; but, by the early 1970s, he'd moved into the entertainment market. The move suited Foos well. "People sometimes forget that [he] spent years building a career as an agent," says one former client. "He was good at it. And his reputation was that he was fiercely loyal. He wouldn't screw you like many people in the business will." Or so it seemed.

Beginning in the mid 1980s, Foos began to take a more active role in investing his clients' money. Rather than simply placing it with professional money managers, he told his clients he was arranging commodities investments, purchases of radio stations, renovation projects and purchases of tax-delinquent real estate.

Some investors said Foos told them he owned a seat on the Chicago Mercantile Exchange. (He didn't.) These investors received periodic letters on Foos' stationery stating the amounts of capital invested and profits earned. Some claimed that he "guaranteed" them against any losses.

He told other investors that their partner in a series of radio station deals was former Texas Governor Mark White, whose political connections allowed them to buy stations that had received regulatory approval to move their broadcast towers closer to major cities and resell the stations for a quick profit. (White later said that he and Foos had "talked of doing deals" but never made investments together.)

All of the scenarios—the commodities and the radio stations—were bogus. Foos simply paid older clients with newer clients' money. "He was able to entice these investors because of who they were," namely clients, said one of the federal lawyers who'd later prosecute Foos. "Because they trusted him, they were a little slow to ask questions."

While there was some question of exactly when Foos began his Ponzi scheme, there was little doubt that it was in full form by 1987. He grew the operation slowly, skimming off just enough to supplement his legitimate income. Because he was cautious, Foos kept his scheme going for at least six years—by any standard, a long time for a Ponzi scheme.

The trouble started in the fall of 1993. By this point, Foos had already made over $13 million in bogus interest payments and had more than $7 million circulating through his scheme. It had grown big enough that he was having a hard time fending off questions. A handful of his clients had put enough money into Foos' deals that his letterhead reports weren't telling them everything they wanted to know. They asked for specific information about the investments. Foos offered only evasive answers.

Two or three of the clients asked for their money back. Foos continued to behave suspiciously—taking several weeks to cut the checks—which promptly bounced.

By early November, the collapse had begun. First a few—and, within days, dozens—of Foos' clients took their complaints to federal prosecutors. Foos turned his assets over to a bankruptcy specialist on the day before Thanksgiving. A week later, he was forced into bankruptcy court when four investors filed an involuntary bankruptcy petition.

When the scheme collapsed, more than 100 investors lost $7.2 million. In a telling twist, the ones who pressed Foos the hardest weren't his traditional entertainment people; they were a group wealthy professionals who'd been attracted late in the game by promises of 100 percent annual returns.

In December, Foos had started cooperating with federal prosecutors. But, at a January 1994 creditors meeting, his attorney read a letter from a therapist saying Foos suffered from "clinical depression" and couldn't attend. Among the disbelieving moans from the angry crowd was a clearly audible protest, "Save us the bullshit."

In April 1994, the Illinois Attorney Registration and Disciplinary Commission began disbarment proceedings against Foos. In May, after several delays, Foos finally faced his former clients—as required under federal bankruptcy law. Although he apologized for his actions, he often turned testy under questioning. He talked about living under the "daily strain of perpetrating this fraud." After 1988, "I didn't expect to get out of it.... I lived in fear of it being exposed for years."

In January 1995, the Securities and Exchange Commission sued Foos—to keep him out of the investment business for the rest of his life. The SEC asked that he be permanently barred from future transactions, repay his "ill-gotten gains" with interest and be assessed unspecified civil penalties.

In February, Foos accepted a plea agreement with the government in which he admitted that he "retained and used for his own purposes" between $6.8 million and $7.2 million. Four months later, he was sentenced to five-and-a-half years in prison. Foos opened his presentencing remarks by saying, "When a man loses his honor, he's a dead man. That's me, I'm a dead man. I chose the coward's way out."

Judge Ruben Castillo also ordered Foos to pay $500,000 in restitution and perform 300 hours of community service. The judge placed him on five years of supervised release after he completed his prison term. Castillo went on to say, "You betrayed the [legal] profession, you betrayed your clients and their trust, you did something incredible in betraying your family and ultimately you betrayed yourself."

Using a Legitimate Business to Build Trust

Some Ponzi perps will do something which only makes sense to an especially avaricious criminal: They'll set up legitimate businesses to camouflage their schemes. When the schemes collapse, investigators and burned investors are left wondering why someone who could build a real business resorts to theft.

The answer usually has something to do with bad impulses overwhelming good skills. It's a psychological variation of Gresham's Law. In this context, the urge to steal money devalues legitimate efforts—which the perp considers only a means to the thieving end.

Or, as one New York prosecutor says, "It's really amazing how much work some of these [Ponzi perps] will put into their schemes. They're smart and make a good impression. You can't help wondering what they could do if they put the effort into honest work."

Ponzi perps know they have to build at least a pretense of trust with their investors. Most tell stories or use tricks that, in retrospect, seem plainly dubious. In these cases, the best practice for avoiding a loss is to keep your eye on the traditional tells of a Ponzi scheme—exceptionally high returns combined with anything resembling a *guarantee* or *no risk offer*.

Few perps go to the length that Michael Rosen or Saul Foos did to exploit investors' trust. But, of course, the ones who do are the most dangerous criminals in this field.

A perp like Foos is probably the hardest to detect. He builds trust legitimately for a long time and then decides, long after a relationship has been established, to exploit it. The same red flags apply in this scenario that work in all Ponzi schemes. But they are harder to see. There's no doubt Foos' clients already trusted the man and were—as one lawyer pointed out—"slow to suspect."

To discourage people from following the tracks of these perps, investors have to rely on aggressive enforcement by prosecutors and judges. If fear of the lowest rung in Hell won't stop another Saul Foos, maybe fear of the darkest cell in San Quentin or Marion will.

Case Study: Joseph Taylor

People trusted Joseph Taylor. To everyone who knew him, the Knoxville, Tennessee, financial planner embodied integrity and perseverance. He was a dedicated husband, father and friend. In business, he quoted inspirational speakers like Zig Ziglar. If he gave you his word, he kept it. "He always espoused doing the right thing," said one investor. "In his dealings with his kids he was like that. He required them to be respectful and the old-culture thing of 'Yes, sir,' and 'No, sir.'"

Taylor was a Tennessee native. Born in 1949, he grew up on a farm in rural Jefferson County. In the late 1960s, he attended the University of Tennessee; he graduated in 1971 with a degree in agricultural science. But Taylor was too ambitious to spend his life plowing fields. He went into insurance, selling policies, investments and financial planning services.

During the 1970s, Taylor built a business based in the Knoxville area, but growing out over most of eastern Tennessee. He concentrated on small towns and suburban communities. Methodically working through the ranks of professionals and successful business people, he always based his deals on a foundation of trust.

"He would sit down with [investors] and talk about his family. They loved him," says one person familiar with Taylor's operation. "He was a likable guy. But—and I don't want to be unkind—he was not a handsome guy."

The homeliness only seemed to add to Taylor's credibility. Besides securities, he was authorized to sell insurance for 25 companies. He was a top performer in a down-home state. And he was clean. Tennessee's Department of Commerce and Insurance recorded no complaints against him.

By the time the roaring 1980s were under way, Taylor was selling mutual funds, life insurance policies and even real estate limited partnerships. His client list continued to swell in size and significance.

Taylor began attracting a wide circle of friends and acquaintances. He was making a six-figure income. He and his wife started to socialize with Knoxville's elite. "You couldn't have a better bunch [than this group] to vouch for you if you were selling something," said one investor.

Flush with success, Taylor began to describe his work in more "visionary" terms. He talked in New Age jargon about using financial planning as a means to achieve less specific life goals.

Then things took a darker turn. Taylor's clients had typically received official paperwork confirming their accounts through a wholesale brokerage. In the early 1990s, Taylor started pitching his own securities deals, like private debt offerings and limited partnerships. These deals didn't produce a detailed paper trail. This change should have tipped investors off that something was wrong. But the returns were so high—as much as 10 percent in a few weeks—that they went along with his slightly eccentric ways.

"I think he was a charming gentleman, obviously," said one local attorney who knew Taylor. "I think he had to be. He came across to people very honestly. Even if they thought that it was irregular that they could not get paperwork, that they all attributed it more to Joe's disorganization than to his dishonesty."

Besides, rumors swirled about Taylor's platinum connections. People in Knoxville talked about his contacts in the J. Peter Grace family, his friends at the state capitol who'd tip him off to hot muni bond deals and his ability to extract prime real estate at rock-bottom prices from probate and divorce court. "I used to say, 'Joe, you're one of the most well-connected people I've ever met,'" one investor marveled.

In fact, Taylor had started operating a Ponzi scheme with investors' money some time in the late 1980s or early 1990s. By most reckoning, Taylor had stolen a six-figure sum from investors' accounts in late 1992 or early 1993 and started the Ponzi scheme to cover his tracks.

Like many Ponzi perps, Taylor had a considerable ability to keep a complex web of detailed lies in his head. In another common move, he controlled what his clients knew about each other's investments. He'd often tell investors to keep the details of their deals private because he wasn't making them available to anyone else.

One of those investors was Jim Rogers. Rogers was the president of Ben Rogers Insurance Agency, Inc. in LaFollette, Tennessee. Rogers met Taylor in the late 1970s and made a series of investments through Taylor & Associates. The investments went conservatively and successfully until the spring of 1994, when Rogers told Taylor that he was interested in some more aggressive investments.

A pattern emerged. Taylor would contact Rogers and ask for a cashier's check in exchange for several post-dated checks from Taylor & Associates in the amount of the investment plus a hefty return. In a short time—often between seven and 30 days—Rogers could cash the checks.

However, Taylor would usually offer Rogers the chance to roll over his investment in another short-term deal. In these cases, Rogers would cash the interest check but hold on to the principal check. At the end of the next investment cycle, Rogers could make the same choice again.

Rogers thought that he was a limited partner of Taylor & Associates, L.P., because he received investment income tax reports from the limited partnership and was issued individual partnership checks at the time he delivered cashier's checks to Taylor. He assumed each of his investments, regardless of whether the check was made payable to *Taylor & Associates* or *Joe Taylor*, was being made with Taylor & Associates.

In a little more than a year, Rogers gave Taylor about ten cashier's checks and cashed about eighteen Taylor checks. All but two of the cashier's checks went into Taylor's accounts; the two that didn't were endorsed over to third parties—other investors anxious to get their money back.

This was the surest sign that Taylor was running a Ponzi scheme. But Rogers never noticed the third-party endorsements.

In September 1995, Rogers gave Taylor a cashier's check in the amount of $62,000. The money was supposed to be used to buy short-term municipal bonds that would be liquidated in 30 to 60 days. Taylor gave Rogers four checks for $16,759.78, $11,173.18, $22,346.37, and $18,994.41—for a total of $69,273.74.

If all went as planned, Rogers would make a 12 percent profit in less than seven weeks. But he was never able to cash any of the four checks.

Taylor became noticeably erratic in the fall of 1995. He seemed in a constant hurry and—for the first time in his working life—could be tough to reach. He confessed to at least one investor that he was getting psychological counseling for stress. "He probably had psychological problems," said one person close to Taylor's operation and who added, "Some people have said he was a manic depressive."

September and October proved a particularly frantic time for Taylor during which he called on dozens of investors, pitching an array of weird deals. He called one of his richest investors with a big one. Taylor said he had an exclusive option on a Memphis muni bond deal. If the high roller could raise $2 million immediately, he could make about $200,000 profit in about a week.

Taylor's deals had always worked before, so the high roller agreed. He wired the money the next day. A week later, Taylor said it was going to take a couple of extra days to liquidate the bonds.

Two weeks later, the high roller told Taylor he wanted to cash out his account. Taylor agreed, promising to hand over the money within five days. On the fifth day, Taylor showed up at the high roller's office and gave him a stack of 18 cashier's checks totaling $2.5 million. It was a 25 percent return in less than a month.

The high roller noticed that many of the checks bore the names of third-party remitters—other Taylor investors. This seemed suspicious. But the bank had no problems with the checks.

A few days later, Taylor stopped in at the Rose Mortuary in suburban Knoxville and made burial plans for himself and his wife. He picked his casket and named his pall bearers—all investors. As soon as he was finished, he drove his black 1995 Mercedes into the mortuary's rear lot, parked the car and shot himself in the head.

At his funeral, Taylor was carried by people whose money he'd stolen. A rumor circulated around Knoxville that, right before he killed himself, Taylor had called his wife and asked her to join him at the mortuary. But investigators who checked Taylor's phone records said this didn't actually happen.

In the last three months of his life, Taylor had made 174 deposits totaling more than $52.3 million into his limited partnership account; in the same period, he made 322 withdrawals totaling $53.2 million. Once again, frenzied banking marked the end of a Ponzi scheme. "It's on the same scale as some of the largest [Ponzi schemes] in the country," said Assistant U.S. Bankruptcy Trustee William Sonnenberg.

Taylor's investors moved quickly when word of his suicide got out. Within three days, several restraining orders had been issued freezing assets and records related to Taylor & Associates, Joseph C. Taylor L.P. and Taylor's estate.

Within two weeks, retired FBI Agent William Hendon had been appointed trustee for most of Taylor's operations.

Hendon didn't find much at first: $36,814.52 from the limited partnership's NationsBank account and $25,000 from the settlement of a lawsuit. He said that he expected to exercise his right under federal bankruptcy law to force those who'd received money within 90 days of the bankruptcy filing to give it back.

This proved easier than Hendon expected. In an unusual move, some clients who'd received money from Taylor before he died volunteered to pay it back. Knoxville was still a small town, in many ways, and trust was important. They didn't want to be linked to dirty money.

CHAPTER 10

Greed

Ponzi perps are moved by greed. In most cases, they'd rather steal money quickly than earn it gradually. (It's the exceptional perp who has the discipline to move slowly; typically, they are more crude) But they also count on the greed of their investors to make the schemes work.

No exploration of pyramid and Ponzi schemes would be complete without a consideration of what *greed* means in this context—and how it works.

The greed that leads an investor to make a foolish investment in a Ponzi scheme may not be an obvious thing. In an age when 25-year-old computer software designers can become millionaires overnight and even conservative investments like stock mutual funds have given investors returns of 30 percent or more in a year, many people lose perspective on how hard it is to make money.

"You hear about Bill Gates being worth $40 billion. You hear about Netscape or Yahoo! going public and making receptionists millionaires. You hear about the guy who started Dell Computer being a billionaire—and he's not 30," says a California prosecutor. "And you believe there's got to be some quick money for you out there somewhere. It may be subconscious, but you believe it. And this affects your decisions."

When lots of money is being made, scam artists will be there trying to take some. They rely on the greed of potential investors.

This reliance gets to one of the key issues that law enforcement agents face when dealing with the schemes. They tend to look at these things—like prostitution and certain forms of illegal gambling—as victimless crimes.

"There's a long tradition of ambivalence about 'protecting' people who get involved in con schemes," says another West Coast prosecutor. "You have to be a lot greedy and at least a little stupid to get sucked into a chain letter or Ponzi scheme. If you lose money, that's the price you pay. You're not going to be on the top of anyone's victims list."

On the other hand, it's hard to tell someone who's just lost her life savings that she was greedy and stupid. This is especially true if the scheme involved her family or church.

This is why other law enforcement types give the Ponzi investors a break, drawing an important distinction between *greed*—which perps and investors both may have—and *dishonesty*—which usually only the perp has.

Arthur Lloyd, director of investigations and financial risk management with Control Risks Group, says that there are important differences between a greedy person and a dishonest one. He says, "An honest person can still be greedy, and you could fool him. A bank that sees profit in fees may be greedy, but it does not come by the money dishonestly."

Applying the Greed-vs.-Dishonesty Distinction

In late 1995 and early 1996, an illegal pyramid scheme swept across southern California's Coachella Valley. All kinds of people got involved—from the country club set in resorts like Palm Springs to working-class families in dusty desert towns like Cathedral City and Indio.

Most believed the scheme, known as "Friends Helping Friends" and the "Gift Exchange," was no more dangerous than an office football pool. But a number of lower-middle-class people invested thousands of dollars that they couldn't afford to lose.

The scheme's participants rented banquet rooms in local hotels to hold their meetings—and recruiting campaigns. The meetings had the feel of a pep rally. As players forked over $2,000 in cash, a hundred-dollar bill at a time, giddy participants shouted aloud: "One hundred! Two hundred...."

Charts decorated with foil stars showed the structure of four-tiered pyramids: eight places on the bottom, then four, then two, then finally one at the top. When the bottom eight people each paid $2,000 to the person at the top, the recipient "retired," the pyramid split in two and everyone moved up a level. Eight new participants then had to be recruited to sustain each new pyramid.

"It was amazing how much these people were motivated by greed," said one undercover police officer who attended several of the meetings. "These were supposedly upper-crust people acting like junkies. Screaming and whooping for the money."

The people running the meetings seemed to understand that the scheme had a problematic relationship with the law. Promotional material handed out at the meetings touted the scheme's supposed legality. One brochure said vaguely and rather lamely that a player's neighbor who was "a judge" had looked at the plan and concluded, "Go for it!"

Players were warned to pay "all appropriate income taxes" on their profits from the pyramids. Brochures announced an ending date of December 31, 1996. By that date, new players would be "weaned off." This deadline, the promoters said, made the scheme legal.

Even if it were legal (a big *if*), the scheme wasn't any more financially sound than any other pyramid or Ponzi scheme. It collapsed during the summer of 1996.

People at the top of the pyramid had taken out as much as $100,000 while people at the bottom lost between $5,000 and $6,000. Of more than 1,000 people who allegedly exchanged an estimated $1 million during the scheme's lifespan, nine were eventually indicted by a Riverside County grand jury. They were charged with enticing people to pay money into an endless chain. "Many Riverside County residents lost thousands of dollars as a consequence of this criminal activity," District Attorney Grover Trask said.

Some residents were surprised by how many community leaders were in the scheme. Among the people indicted were: the president of the area's only higher education institution, the College of the Desert; the superintendent of the Desert Sands Unified School District; and the executive director of the McCallum Theatre—the region's performing arts venue.

An internal investigation by the College of the Desert had found that at least 20 employees put in money, though there was no evidence that anyone had been pressured to take part. Still, it accepted President David George's resignation.

It had been a College of the Desert employee—Joyce Moore, president of the local college employees union—who'd first brought the scheme to public attention. When she heard that George was involved, Moore had confronted him and then complained to the local newspaper and television station.

Deputy D.A. Edward Kotkin, who was prosecuting the criminal cases, said the area's tight-knit social and business circles provided the perfect environment in which the scheme could incubate. "My office is most concerned about people who may have used their influence or positions of public trust to bring others into the scheme," he said.

But the argument that the investors were as greedy as perps resonated with many people who lived in the Coachella Valley. One teacher at the College of the Desert noted that the area's country club set bred a lot of "country-club wannabees" who tried to act the part but didn't really have the financial resources to keep up.

Social climbing—which one loser called "the greed for recognition"—certainly was a major factor. With so many of the local swells involved, the social element of the scheme was important. One local society columnist explained:

A friend said...the pyramid party was the damnedest thing he ever saw. So I went two nights later. There were 150 people there—people who own art galleries, charity chairpersons, real estate people, members of the Daughters of the American Revolution—very respectable people. And people were turning over money and hugging one another, like a spiritual revival. And it was the damnedest thing I ever saw.

Moore—the original whistle-blower—offered her explanation to a national newspaper: "We think we're sophisticated, but we're an isolated community. Greed was what did it."

Case Study: Michael Scott Douglas

Like most compulsive behavior, the greedy rush for money makes little sense to outside observers. Michael Scott Douglas was a twice-convicted felon who used a little bit of computer knowledge to build a Ponzi scheme that bilked investors out of more than $20 million. His effectiveness is a testament to greed—his own and his investors'.

From August 1987 through November 1989, Douglas operated a bogus investment firm through which he induced investors to purchase limited partnership interests in four entities: D&S Trading Group, Ltd., Analytic Trading Systems, Inc., Analytic Trading Service, Inc. and Market Systems, Inc.

The companies were headquartered in a single, fancy, computer-equipped office suite on LaSalle Street—the heart of Chicago's banking and financial district. The pitch was simple. Douglas claimed he'd developed a proprietary system for exploiting price differences between stocks and related stock options or various kinds of commodities futures. He promised returns of 10 percent to 20 percent per month on investments.

As a federal court later explained:

Although some trading of commodities was done, most of the money raised from the sale of the limited-partner interests was used simply to pay the promised return. These payments gave the scheme credibility, enabling Douglas to sell additional limited-partner interests.

In a little more than two years, Douglas raised $30 million from the sale of limited-partnership interests and paid back less than $10 million in phony profits. During the same period, Douglas paid himself $3 million in salary. He bought 19 cars, two condominiums near Palm Springs, and homes, commercial property and vacant land all around metropolitan Chicago.

Despite the ostentatious spending, Douglas hadn't come from poverty. He was born and raised in the suburbs around Milwaukee. His father owned a successful company that made plastic containers for household use. The future Ponzi perp went to good private schools—but he wasn't a keen intellect. He fumbled his way through several colleges, finally dropping out and marrying his high school sweetheart.

The newlyweds moved to Chicago, where Douglas worked in several local banks while attending night school. He had his first brush with financial trouble in 1980 when, as a commercial loan officer at a community bank, he was fired by supervisors who accused him of stealing a $2,000 cash deposit a customer had left on his desk. The charge was never proved.

Later that year, a grand jury indicted Douglas on charges of theft by deception. In a crude confidence swindle, he'd written two bad checks totaling $99,000 to a former Chicago Bears football player. He pleaded guilty and served 18 months in prison.

On his release from jail in 1983, Douglas took a job as a sales manager for a retail outfit called Lake Shore Computers in yet another Chicago suburb. The job was a chance for Douglas to go straight. But his greed got the better of him. Within a few months, he was running another crude con scam—stealing customers' credit card numbers and using them to buy computer equipment which he would sell on the black market. Again, the scheme wasn't particularly smart. Douglas was back in prison for two years in 1985.

A few months after his release from prison in 1987, Douglas landed a job writing software programs for a trading firm that was a member of the Chicago Board Options Exchange. The programs that Douglas was hired to write tracked the firm's trades and generated client statements. This was considered basic back-office administrative work by the firm; but it was a revelation to the felon. It taught him the operational details of how stock option trading worked.

Though Douglas hadn't been much of a student in school, he learned enough in six months to embark on a new level of criminal activity. He left the trading company, teamed up with a veteran con man he'd met in prison and started D&S Trading.

Douglas refined his pitch with D&S Trading. He offered investors huge returns through an arbitrage strategy exploiting differences between prices in blue-chip stocks and options on those stocks. He'd learned enough about computer programs and options trading to sound expert. And as one family friend put it, "[Michael] is brilliant with numbers, so options would really be his niche, and that's partially why he was so convincing....He really dazzled people because of his command of numbers."

What sold D&S Trading even more than the technical jargon were the guarantees Douglas made. The firm would receive a management fee equal to 25 percent of monthly profits, which was high by industry standards. The trade-off: Douglas personally guaranteed to cover any losses.

This was a hollow promise, since his net worth was only a few thousand dollars. But it worked. By the middle of 1988, less than a year after he'd started D&S Trading, Douglas had taken in about $6 million from more than 100 investors. Instead of segregating customer funds, as required by law, Douglas kept all of the money in just two bank accounts—a D&S Trading account and one under his name. (This is a common sign that an investment firm is running a Ponzi scheme.)

Like many Ponzi perps, Douglas made great claims of religious piety. Though he was raised a Roman Catholic, he had become an evangelical Christian during one of his prison stays. He used the connections he made through church donations to lure ministers and members of their congregations to invest in D&S Trading. "He used the cloak of Christianity to lure these investors to their financial slaughter," one lawyer representing investors would later say.

Almost from the beginning, D&S Trading had problems making its dividend payments as promised. Douglas didn't have the mental discipline that some Ponzi perps use to keep things running smoothly. Instead, he talked about investment strategy and vision—explaining to investors that he was an idea person rather than a detail person. But his vision was no more reliable than his command of details. Within a year of starting D&S Trading, Douglas had abandoned his arbitrage strategy for a series of high-risk investments in stocks the firm had "carefully researched."

Although D&S Trading was a long way from collapsing, some investors made complaints to the SEC and state regulators in Illinois and Wisconsin. The SEC sent letters to D&S Trading, seeking information on its investment program and principals. In September 1988, under the auspices of Illinois securities regulators, Douglas agreed to be barred permanently from selling securities in the state and made a full refund to all his clients.

But Douglas would not be sidetracked. In an astounding act of brashness, he asked the D&S Trading investors to put their refund checks into Analytic Trading Systems (ATS), a new company he was starting. Many of them were still happy with the performance of their investments with Douglas, so they agreed.

ATS continued to operate the Ponzi scheme started by D&S Trading. Early winners spread the word that Douglas was an investment *wunderkind*. More money flowed in.

Douglas did make some investments. He boasted to anyone who would listen about a $4.2 million profit he made on 42,000 shares of RJ Reynolds Inc. stock he bought and sold during a three-week period in February 1989. "He probably did make that money because he was so impressed with himself about it," recalls one investor. "It should have been a sign. He was too excited. It's like [college football coach] Joe Paterno says: 'When you get in the end zone, you should act like you've been there before.'"

Douglas didn't. And, still, more money kept flowing in. By September 1989, ATS had raised almost $40 million from more than 300 investors spread across seven states.

The SEC and the local authorities weren't far behind. The SEC made a series of requests for information about ATS and the money it was managing. In late October, Douglas supplied the SEC with a document showing that ATS investors had $35 million deposited in segregated trading accounts. The document was a fake, though. It was based on a single trading account which actually contained less than $28,000.

In November 1989, the Feds arrested Douglas and charged him with stealing about $12 million from his investors. The SEC ordered all of Douglas's operations closed. A federal court appointed Chicago lawyer Steven Scholes as receiver of ATS to untangle its finances and recover as much money as possible for its investors.

Douglas had divorced his first wife and married a second time. The second marriage collapsed after his arrest. Douglas—who often spoke about himself with a strange detachment—said, "When my wife found out about all this, she simply could not fathom how I was able to commit such a huge fraud and keep it hidden from her."

More family shocks followed. Four months later, Douglas's father was accused in a civil racketeering lawsuit of illegally pocketing more than $800,000 in "finder's fees" from the scam.

Scholes argued that Douglas *pere* was paid the finder's fees for acting as a middleman who solicited investors by phone and at meetings. "David Douglas knowingly joined, combined and conspired with Michael S. Douglas and others in schemes to defraud investors in connection with the sale of interests in investment partnerships," the suit charged.

The father reached a quick, quiet settlement with Scholes. The settlement limited his ability to help his son.

In October 1990, Douglas *fils* pleaded guilty to three counts of mail fraud and one count of lying to the Securities and Exchange Commission. At his sentencing hearing a few months later, Michael Douglas offered a tearful explanation for his actions:

> *The investor money was coming in too fast—so fast, in fact, that I couldn't find a place to invest it.... I could see the handwriting on the wall, but I did not want the train to stop. The money's coming in at $2 million a month, and I'm stretched nine ways to Sunday, $15 million in the hole at one point.*
>
> *People want to know how I slept nights. It was easy, because I am a winner. I'm goal oriented, and in my mind I'm saying, "One more trade. I can make up the difference. I can be all things to all people." I tried to trade my way out of my losses.*

That statement could be part of a psychological profile (egocentrism, insecurity) as easily as a legal tactic. In any case, it didn't have the intended effect. Douglas was sentenced to 12 years in prison by U.S. District Judge William Hart, who called the fraud "a cruel crime."

By early 1995, Scholes had recovered $12 million, consisting mainly of real estate that Douglas had bought with stolen money. Scholes was also trying to recover about $2 million in charitable donations, another $1 million in undocumented personal loans that Douglas had made (including money he'd given his first wife) and some money early investors had taken out of the scheme.

Citing fraudulent conveyance laws that bar giving stolen money to someone else, a federal district court and an appeals court both said the charitable groups had to turn over the contributions. One lawyer involved in the case called the charities to whom Douglas bestowed donations "the real victims," because they ultimately were "the ones that had to pay the money back."

But the court ruling was a fitting close to the Douglas story. His greed overwhelmed and obliterated his charitable acts.

CHAPTER 11

Family Ties

One of the most surprising—but most telling—factors that control the size and shape of pyramids and Ponzi schemes is the involvement of family members. Many pyramid schemes actively encourage investors to recruit family members. This recruitment serves several purposes. It provides an easy source of new investors. But, in a more Machiavellian sense, it co-opts the most likely critics of someone pouring hard-earned money into a scatter-brained scheme.

On the flip side of the family structure, a consistent theme among Ponzi perps is to divorce long-time spouses as the stolen money begins to roll in. A spouse who's been around long enough often falls into the thankless role of the conscience to his or her significant other. A perp who's decided to throw morals to the wind will often decide to throw the potentially most incriminating witness out with the morals.

Finally, and most perversely, some families actually seem to cultivate scams as a common activity. These people usually share a cynical view of money and business—passed from a parent or spouse to other family members.

It's a cliché of the 1990s that many families are *dysfunctional*. Ponzi schemes offer some of these families the chance to project their eccentricity—and, sometimes, malevolence—on the wider population.

Father-and-Son Ponzi Perps

Sidney and Stuart Schwartz were father and son—but they were also partners in Schwartz & Topper Co., an accounting firm in Nassau

County, New York. They also ran STS Acquisition Corp., which set up bridge loans for small businesses and financiers in the midst of mergers, acquisitions or other transactions.

Bridge loans are short-term financing mechanisms that most traditional lenders find too risky to make. For this reason, lenders who are willing to make the loans—most often Wall Street investment banks—make a lot of money from them.

The father and son used their social setting to create a sense of legitimacy in potential STS Acquisition investors. The Schwartzes were regarded as pillars of the community in their section of Long Island; the focal point of their business and social circles was The Old Westbury Club. Sidney was the club officer in charge of membership and former president of his synagogue. (Old Westbury was a "Jewish club," opened in reaction to other country clubs that excluded Jews as members.) Stuart, with his good looks, wit and gregarious personality, flirted with the women and made friends easily with the men at the club.

Of course, the appearance of legitimacy was only part of the equation. As is often the case, some investors were motivated by simple greed. The Schwartzes offered high interest rates on money invested in STS Acquisition, as much as 18 percent plus bonuses on 90-day loans. These numbers meant annual interest rates ranging between 64 percent and 216 percent.

Bridge loans are profitable—but they're not *that* profitable. Despite the impression Sidney and Stuart cultivated with their neighbors and friends, they were crooks. STS Acquisition was a Ponzi scheme. And the father and son used Old Westbury as a proving ground for investors. "I gave them money because I felt, how could a family so involved with the temple and their country club...steal from me," said one.

For at least four years, from 1988 to 1992, the Schwartzes sloshed investors' money through a series of pyramid transactions. As their bogus empire was reaching its limits, the Schwartzes claimed a joint net worth of $5.7 million. In truth, their companies were running in the red.

Like many Ponzi perps, the Schwartzes had some problems which they managed to resolve but which pointed to the bigger collapse ahead. The crisis came in early 1992 when the Schwartzes defaulted on interest payments to their biggest client—who would eventually lose $2.4 million in the scheme. Stuart used his personal relationship with the big investor to plead for more time. His story was that STS Acquisition was growing so fast that all of its money was out working. Better to be cash-poor and collecting big interest than just sitting on the money.

The big investor would later say: "[Stuart] came to weddings and birthdays. He was like a son to me. When he asked for money, I said, 'What's the collateral?' He said, 'Collateral? I'm dealing with millions of dollars and bank presidents.' So I gave a series of loans, and he gave me promissory notes. But now there is not a day I get up that I don't wonder how could I be so stupid."

By late 1992, the Schwartzes couldn't charm investors fast enough to prevent the collapse. Dozens of STS Acquisition interest checks were bouncing. Sidney and Stuart were suddenly hard to reach. Panicky investors got together and demanded a meeting.

The first meeting took place in Florida, where many STS Acquisition investors had either winter or full-time residences. Because the Schwartzes had been receiving physical threats, they hired a security guard to keep order. At one point Stuart put his head against the wall of the conference room and cried, one investor who attended the Florida meeting recalled. Another investor said: "One man was so agitated, saying, 'This is not just my money, it's my son's money, and he can't afford to lose this.' He leapt across the table and tried to strangle Stuart."

After this meeting, the Schwartzes decided that the best tactic was to admit their theft. The candor was disarming. An investor who attended the second meeting, in Manhattan, recalled: "I looked straight at Stuart and said, 'Did you ever invest any money? Did you ever have any bridge loans?' And he said, 'No, we used it personally.'"

Most of the STS Acquisition investors were so shocked that they left the meetings without extracting any repayment—let alone liquidation—plan from the Schwartzes. But the shock wore off and, by early 1993, various investor groups turned the case over to prosecutors for criminal charges and moved in civil court to have the Schwartzes declared bankrupt.

When word of the fraud spread, the Schwartzes became pariahs in the Old Westbury social circle. In a strangely naive turn, Stuart was surprised by this. He continued going to the club and acted insulted when one member said "Hello, crook" in the locker room.

Ponzi perps don't usually play stupid about their deeds. And acting indignant about being called a crook after admitting to investors that he'd stolen their money seems downright weird. But, one Old Westbury member offered this insight into Stuart Schwartz: "He was the son of a well-known man. He probably didn't have the brains or the guts that [Sidney] had. It might be true that he didn't mean for things to turn out the way they did. But that would be because he didn't have complete command of what was going on."

What was going on was that the Schwartzes really were—by just about any standard—crooks. Government investigators discovered that they'd duped two pension funds and dozens of individuals into giving them nearly $8 million. (And they may have taken even more. Investigators for the U.S. Attorney only checked records back to 1989, though several STS Acquisition investors said the scam started earlier. One problem: Many investors failed to file complaints because they were embarrassed or because they invested to avoid taxes or to launder illicit money.)

Instead of using the money to make bridge loans, the Schwartzes paid off other investors and spent on themselves. Over the three years that investigators checked, Sidney and Stuart bought several Mercedes, homes on Long Island and in Florida, fancy dresses for their wives and various other trinkets of wealth.

In May 1996, Sidney and Stuart were both named in a 50-count federal indictment accusing them of conspiracy and mail and wire fraud. Their lawyers quickly arranged a plea bargain.

The Schwartzes claimed that all of the money raised in the scheme was gone. But many investors had doubts. Their homes were in upper-middle-class neighborhoods—but they weren't mansions. (And, because they were both mortgaged, the lenders quickly foreclosed.) Their tastes may have been *nouveau riche* and vulgar, but the Schwartzes didn't spend the big money that some Ponzi perps do—on things like yachts and private jets. Neither had a gambling or drug habit to eat up the cash. So, some of the old boys at Old Westbury grumbled that Sidney and Stuart had stashed the proceeds. "I'm sure there's money in a shoe box or a vault," said a member who'd invested in STS Acquisition.

In July 1996, Stuart started a 43-month sentence at the federal prison in Fort Dix, New Jersey. "I think he's contrite," said Stuart's court-appointed lawyer. "He's suffered from the day he was arrested. He has lost all his friends. He's lost his assets."

Sidney had wrangled several medical postponements but, in August, he was sentenced by U.S. District Court Judge Arthur D. Spatt who said, "There have been few cases involving a defendant of 80 years of age—in fact I could not find any. Maybe the reason is that people, when they get to [this] age, don't commit crimes like this."

Federal sentencing guidelines suggested 30 to 37 months. Sidney's lawyer pleaded for a reduction because of the old man's age and history of a stroke and heart irregularities. Spatt noted that the guidelines allowed for reduced terms for illness but not age: "This defendant is a youthful 80 years. He played golf up to the time these occurrences took place, and while in his 70s he knowingly cheated his friends and relatives of millions." In the end, however, the judge took pity on Sidney and sentenced him only to 18 months in jail.

At his sentencing, Sidney read a prepared statement in a halting but unemotional voice. "I must confess that I have sinned," he said. "I have been shamed and disgraced." He said his health problems were God's punishment for the money he stole from friends and family.

God's punishment for leading his childish and naive son into a major criminal enterprise would, no doubt, come later.

What Constitutes an Innocent Spouse?

If your husband or wife runs a Ponzi scheme but keeps you in the dark, will the courts hold you liable for the resulting damages? Usually not. However, the Feds may try to tax you for your significant other's ill-gotten gains.

The IRS has practice guidelines for dealing with married couples who have big legal problems. When one of the spouses turns out to be a crook, the other will usually try to avoid responsibility for the wrongdoing by claiming protection under the *innocent spouse doctrine*.

The twin 1992 U.S. Tax Court decisions *Phyllis M. Curtis Berenbeim v. Commissioner of Internal Revenue* and *Jerome P. Berenbeim v. Commissioner of Internal Revenue* deal with this issue.

Jerome and Phyllis Berenbeim had each been married before when they met in the mid-1970s. However, they got along well and decided to try once again—with each other.

Since graduating from UCLA in the mid-1950s, Jerome had been an insurance salesman and a financial advisor. From 1972 to 1974, he sold tax shelters to high-income neighbors in suburban Orange County. As part of this business, he held himself out as a financial consultant with expertise in insurance, real estate, pension and profit sharing plans, tax shelters and tax return preparation.

Phyllis was also well-educated, with a master's degree in education and a supervisory credential for teaching in California. She worked for the Orange County public school system in various capacities as a music teacher and administrator.

When they got married, Jerome—who had a history of money problems—didn't own a house. But he compensated for this by spoiling Phyllis with smaller indulgences. He gave her a grand piano and a diamond ring. He leased her a Datsun 280ZX, even though she already owned a late model Toyota Celica and an older Jaguar. And, most personally, he paid for some plastic surgery for Phyllis in the early years of their marriage.

The Berenbeims' day-to-day financial arrangement was fairly standard. Phyllis paid household expenses out of her checking account and Jerome would contribute any amounts in excess of Phyllis's salary needed to run the household.

He was in charge of the long-term financial planning. Which was too bad, because he was running a Ponzi scheme the whole time they were married. Selling tax shelters was just Jerome's premise to getting to know potential investors. His real job was convincing neighbors, friends and acquaintances that he was a successful financial dealmaker who earned huge profits on money that wealthy clients invested with him.

Although Jerome's pitch varied somewhat according to each potential investor, the basic premise remained consistent. He said that he worked with a regular group of entrepreneurs whose small, fast-growing business needed growth capital quickly—and somewhat unpredictably. These businesses were accustomed to paying high interest rates and bonuses for loans. This was the nontraditional world of venture capital and factoring, high-risk financing that potentially paid big money.

Jerome said his operation was different because, by diversifying his loans, he eliminated the risk that other financiers faced. He called his operation "The Fund" and told potential investors he'd pay between 20 percent and 30 percent on invested money.

An investor would send money to Jerome, who would then execute a note in the amount of the investment along with interest to be paid monthly for a set period of time. At the end of that period, the principal of the note would be repaid to the investor. He usually asked investors to give him cashier's checks in amounts less than $10,000 to avoid the reporting of currency transactions to the Internal Revenue Service.

In one case, an investor gave Jerome $30,000 in four separate cashier's checks. Jerome produced a $30,000 note, providing for $750 monthly interest payments (that's 30 percent per annum) for a period of two years. The note matured at the end of the two years—but the holder could redeem it at any time, with 24 hours' notice.

To provide himself with some cover, Jerome told investors that The Fund paid him a commission on investments that he arranged. He kept the details of these commissions vague, saying only that they came out of The Fund's end.

In reality, there were no wealthy or successful businessmen. Jerome was paying interest on the notes from the money received from investors and converting some part of the funds received to his own personal use.

He used money from the Ponzi scheme to invest in real estate up and down the California coast. While he made some money from these investments, it wasn't anywhere near enough to generate big profits for his investors.

Jerome was able to keep the scheme going for about two years. (Basically, until the oldest notes started maturing.) A few investors got their money out; but, by the latter part of 1982, The Fund started missing monthly interest payments. Some investors were having difficulty reaching Jerome. In a few cases, he'd failed to return principal amounts at the end of the investment term.

By the end of the year, Jerome's Ponzi scheme had collapsed. Numerous civil lawsuits followed, with burned investors seeking the return of their money plus damages. Between 1983 and 1985, several dozen of these lawsuits resulted in judgments against Jerome. When he didn't pay these damages, criminal charges followed.

In 1986, Jerome was charged with 24 felony counts related to the scheme. He eventually pleaded guilty to three felony counts involving the willful and unlawful taking of money from others. He was sentenced to a prison term of one to three years.

One of the ugly facts that emerged from the investigations: Jerome and a former wife had been sued in the 1960s for fraud connected to the sale of tax shelter investments. The Fund was actually Jerome's *second* failed Ponzi scheme.

Beginning in early 1986, IRS agents attempted to discuss the Ponzi scheme and related income tax matters with Jerome, but he was uncooperative. So, the IRS pieced together a history of The Fund from interviews with investors and local law enforcement authorities—and research into evidence used in Jerome's trials. The difference between funds received and disbursed by Jerome was considered to be taxable income. His total take during the life of the scheme was $1,120,551.

Because the Feds considered the Berenbeims a married couple filing their taxes jointly during Jerome's fraud, they tried to hold Phyllis jointly liable for his debt. At this point, she made her innocent spouse argument.

The earnings of either spouse during marriage are both spouses' community property. However, according to the tax code, the innocent spouse doctrine excludes items of community income from a spouse's taxable income where all of the following four requirements are met:

1) the spouse seeking relief did not file a joint return for any taxable year;

2) the income item omitted from the gross income of the spouse seeking relief is treated as the income of the other spouse;

3) the spouse seeking relief establishes that she did not know of and had no reason to know of such item of community income; and

4) under the facts and circumstances, it is inequitable to include such item of community income in the income of the spouse seeking relief.

To meet this standard, it's not enough to show a lack of knowledge. An innocent spouse must also show that he or she had no *reason* to know about an understatement. In order to do this, he or she must convince a court that a reasonably prudent person—with a comparable level of education and experience and with equal knowledge of the circumstances—would not have known about the wrongdoing.

Jerome had kept Phyllis from knowing about the fraudulent nature of his scheme. And he didn't do this to protect her; he did it because he was stealing from her. Between 1978 and 1983, Phyllis loaned Jerome $76,590 to help him pay some old debts and get his business started. He repaid a few thousand dollars to her directly...but convinced her that he was investing money for her in The Fund.

In 1983, as The Fund was approaching collapse, Phyllis became suspicious because of inquiries from various friends and acquaintances concerning Jerome's failure to make monthly payments. She asked him about The Fund and his other investment activities. He said he was having some problems—but that The Fund was basically sound. She believed him.

She trusted Jerome and permitted him to manage their financial and tax matters. She was prone to accept his explanations without question.

The IRS didn't care how naive the woman was. Its lawyers argued that Phyllis didn't meet the burden of proving all of the necessary elements of an innocent spouse claim. Specifically, the IRS argued that she did have reason to know about Jerome's scheme. Therefore, it was equitable to include one-half of his income in her taxable income calculation.

The tax court ruled that Phyllis had reason to know that Jerome was underreporting the money he made on his real estate investments. She would be responsible for her share of that income—about $42,000. However, it ruled that she did not have reason to know that he was running a Ponzi scheme. So, she was not responsible for any part of that income—over $1 million.

It concluded with a useful observation about one spouse's duty to investigate another:

> *We are cognizant of the marital relationship here and considered whether it would have been reasonable for Phyllis to check with [the IRS] as to whether Jerome had in fact filed [accurately]. Marital relationships are usually based upon mutual trust and such unprecipitated inquiries would not foster a trusting relationship.*

Case Study: Bennett Funding Group

Bennett Funding Group (BFG) was born in 1977, when Edmund "Bud" Bennett started leasing office equipment out of a former gas station in upstate New York. He was the CEO and his wife, Kathleen, was the president. Their children, who were in high school and college, helped out.

BFG quickly dominated the business of originating, purchasing and selling commercial leases of copy machines and other office equipment in its part of the country. For several years during the 1980s, *Inc.* magazine listed BFG as one of America's fastest growing firms.

The Bennetts were financially savvy. They organized groups of leases into portfolios, which they pledged as collateral for bank loans. Cash flow from the portfolios would easily cover principal and interest payments on the loans.

Because BFG made its payments in a timely manner, the banks were willing to loan more money. Usually, a bank would draft a standard loan agreement and then take a file of documents as collateral. The documents included:

- a bill of sale for the equipment;
- an assignment of contract from BFG of all of its interest in the equipment leases;
- a promissory note from BFG ; and
- copies of the original leases, including a description of the leased equipment, as well as the identification of the lessee and a schedule of payments to be made by the lessee.

Bankers were usually satisfied with this paper trail. As the business grew, though, the bankers started to demand more reporting and better performance standards. Most of the banks believed that the equipment-leasing business was so service-intensive that no company could expand beyond a regional base.

So, BFG looked beyond traditional bank financing. Modifying its package slightly, the company started offering the portfolios to individual investors. They were even more eager than the banks to get involved.

BFG would organize a portfolio of 30 photocopy machines leased to a city or federal agency. An investor would then buy a short-term note backed by the income BFG expected to receive on the leases. BFG would offer an interest rate of between 7 percent and 10 percent, depending on the portfolio's size and risk factors. It would make monthly or quarterly distribution payments covering some combination of interest and principal.

Investors were invited to reinvest the distribution payments in new notes. Many did. "Retirees loved it," said one Washington, D.C., stockbroker who sold BFG lease securities. "It was so in demand, there was a waiting list.... They would just keep buying and buying and buying."

Bud Bennett's son Patrick took over day-to-day management of BFG in the early 1990s. The father and son weren't much alike. Bud had few pretenses, preferring to be low-key and cagey; Patrick was slick and aggressive. Bud seemed to have the hard-earned pride of a man who'd built a company from scratch. Patrick seemed to have contempt for BFG's humble origins.

While his title was Chief Financial Officer, Patrick was clearly running the company. He talked about bringing in more professional management to raise BFG's profile. What he actually accomplished was something else entirely. Impatient to grow, he began selling investors millions of dollars of notes backed by questionable office-equipment leases. He kept the notes current with proceeds of later note offerings.

What started out as an aggressive tactic to create some extra capital apparently became a full-fledged Ponzi scheme. Between 1991 and 1996, BFG sold over $422 million of dubious lease-backed notes. Patrick allegedly commingled these proceeds with other company funds, creating a pool of more than $900 million. He transferred that money to a shell corporation—which, in turn, used some of the money to make payments to investors.

He allegedly used the rest of the money to buy a racetrack, a hotel, gambling casinos and a yacht. The titles to these properties were held in the names of individual Bennett family members. Specifically:

- Bud and Kathleen Bennett owned a $600,000 yacht, the 70-foot *Lady Kathleen*. The boat and its owners spent winters in Florida and summers in the Thousand Islands—near where the St. Lawrence River flows out of Lake Ontario.
- Patrick and his brother Michael spent $13 million building the Speculator, a 238-foot gambling showboat which they planned to operate in Mississippi or Louisiana.
- Michael spent more than $60 million buying control of American Gaming Enterprises Ltd., which operated the Gold Shore Casino—a gambling barge in Biloxi, Mississippi.
- Michael also spent about $18 million buying and refurbishing The Hotel Syracuse, an art deco classic in a run-down part of Syracuse.
- Patrick spent several million dollars buying a majority stake in Vernon Downs Racetrack near Syracuse. He spent another $8.5 million to build a Comfort Suites Hotel at the track.

All this was a long way from leasing copier machines to bureaucrats. According to people who worked at BFG, Patrick had never been interested in the core business. Other than racetracks and casinos, his focus had been on syndicating lease portfolios to suckers.

By early 1995, BFG was in deep financial trouble. It was selling $10 million to $15 million each month in lease-backed notes; but it owed between $20 million and $25 million each month in distributions. The company started missing payments. And the greedy investors who'd been its biggest supporters turned into vicious enemies.

In early 1996, the SEC and the U.S. Attorney in Manhattan filed criminal charges against Patrick. The Feds accused him of securities fraud and perjury. He was arrested, then released on $500,000 bail pending trial.

The SEC also sued Patrick and BFG in a civil complaint which alleged the company had been run as a Ponzi scheme. The Feds alleged that the Bennetts sold the same leases to more than one investor and sold other leases that did not exist. They then used money from new investors to pay off earlier investors.

The Bennetts had suspected that they'd been under an SEC investigation for several months. They were prepared with their responses. Lawyers for Michael, Bud and Kathleen Bennett all said that their clients knew nothing about any wrongdoing. "Our position is that Mr. and Mrs. Bennett didn't do anything wrong," said Alan Burstein. "Mr. Bennett turned over financial matters to his son, Patrick."

"Mistakes were made, but they weren't intentional," said Charles Stillman, Patrick's attorney. "We're trying to talk reasonably with the prosecutor to convince him that...there was no criminal intent. Patrick Bennett wasn't looking to cheat anybody [or] steal anybody's money."

In March 1996, BFG and several related operating units filed voluntary Chapter 11 bankruptcy. According to the filing, more than 12,000 investors had invested $674 million with the company.

Patrick, Bud, Kathleen and Michael all resigned their management positions in BFG. Soon after, the bankruptcy court appointed Richard Breeden, a former SEC Chairman, as receiver. "I don't buy for a moment that Patrick did it alone, that the parents and others didn't know," Breeden said. "It was Bud's company, and the employees say nothing happened that he didn't know about."

Their lawyer said the senior Bennetts suffered from multiple ailments that precluded them from traveling to Syracuse to talk to investigators. Breeden remained unsympathetic. He cut off their $15,000-a-month consulting fee, their car and driver and their health benefits.

In June 1996, Breeden filed a $1.65 billion lawsuit to recover the money lost by creditors and punitive damages. $650 million of the damages covered the actual money lost by creditors who invested in equipment leases or loaned money to Bennett companies; $1 billion was to punish the Bennetts. Breeden said:

> *The company was much more than troubled. It was massively insolvent. Apparently, someone decided it was too dull selling leases once, so quite a few were sold to more than one person. [The scheme] was reminiscent of some of the S&L guys who...had to move money around to pay other debts.*

Specifically, Breeden's lawsuit focused on Patrick's Comfort Suites project at the Vernon Downs Racetrack. Breeden claimed that Patrick had improperly taken $8.5 million from lease-backed bonds to fund construction of the hotel. In August 1996, Breeden added BFG's former auditors to the lawsuit—and increased his damage request to $2.2 billion.

Breeden said it had taken 72 accountants and staff members 12,391 hours over four months to piece together the companies' finances. Lawyers spent another 8,723 hours sorting through the wreckage. "It was an accountant's nightmare and a lawyer's nightmare, too," said Mike Sigal, who led the team of lawyers representing Breeden.

As the smoke of a burning business cleared, it became clear that the family involvement applied to all sides. An attorney representing some of BFG's investors admitted, "My whole family was in it, my girl friend was in it for seven figures." In an attempt to excuse the involvement he added, "They didn't think it was a scam. The Bennett family had a good reputation."

CHAPTER 12

Secrecy and Privacy

The Supreme Court Justice Louis Brandeis once wrote: "The right most prized by civilized man is the right to be left alone." This is a noble sentiment that Ponzi schemes often twist on its ear.

In the United States, the law goes a long way to protect people's right to privacy. And that's a good thing. The commitment to privacy has some strange and unintended results, though. One of these is that it allows some people to be overtaken by their impulses for a baser mutation of privacy—secrecy.

Secrecy and privacy may be similar, but they aren't the same. Privacy entails sheltering your own thoughts, acts and possessions from public scrutiny. Secrecy entails sheltering from public scrutiny the fact that you've shared thoughts, acts or possessions with someone.

The social element of sharing private things marks a secret. And, to be sure, money is one of the most common social elements that turns privacy into secrecy. The urge for secrecy gets a strong boost from capitalist systems. There's no doubt that anonymity offers some level of protection. This is why old-line moneyed families used to repeat the mantra: "Foolish names and foolish faces find themselves in public places."

The Foundation for New Era Philanthropy[1] Ponzi scheme that collapsed loudly in 1994 relied on a group of "anonymous donors" who would match charitable contributions filtered through the scheme.

---

1 For a detailed description of the New Era case, see page 235 in Chapter 16.

Several dozen of America's richest and most sophisticated philanthropists gave money to the scheme. They were so familiar with the notion of anonymous giving that they didn't stop to think—and check out the proposition.

The secrecy that money can breed explains many mistakes, eccentricities and moments of bad judgment.

"People are just strange about their money. They delude themselves, so they bullshit everyone else. You know the type—the big-mouth brother-in-law who's always talking about how he bought Microsoft at three. But he never talks about all the money he's lost on crap he bought for 30 or 100," says one federal investigator who has little sympathy for Ponzi investors. "He doesn't talk about the losses because he doesn't think about them. The closest comparison is fishing or gambling in Las Vegas. It's competitive—and very personal."

Bogus Loans Made Behind the Scenes

One of the best examples of how secrecy about money sets people up to be conned is the second mortgage scam that we considered in Chapter 2. A quick recap of how this works:

> *The Ponzi perp approaches Investor A and says that Mutual Acquaintance B is in a cash crunch and needs to take out a second mortgage on his house. The perp explains that Acquaintance B will pay a high interest rate, typically 12 percent or 13 percent, and even a bonus on the loan—if it can be arranged quickly and quietly.*
>
> *Acquaintance B knows nothing about the bogus deal. The perp forges or manipulates information and signatures onto phony documents. These documents are not filed or registered as required by law. The Ponzi perp simply pockets the loan money.*

In these deals, the perp will usually tell an investor that the loan will be blind. That means that the mutual acquaintance won't know who loaned the money. Even if the Ponzi perp is a little questionable, the legitimacy of the mutual acquaintance is often compelling.

For the Ponzi perp, the blind loan makes it less likely that the investor will ever try to contact the mutual acquaintance directly.

The blind loan also makes it easy for the perp to sell a phony mortgage a *second* time. In this situation, the perp tells a second investor that the first needs to get his money back and will sell the mortgage at a discounted price. All of the same terms—including the need for secrecy—apply.

"It's amazing how well this works, even when all the principles know one another. In fact, it usually works even better when they do," says a northern California lawyer who's prosecuted several Ponzi cases. "People who have a certain amount of money and not very much sense will be used to the idea of secrecy in money matters. And they'll put a great deal of unspoken trust in people they consider financial equals. If a crook has the guts to take a chance on this secrecy and trust, he can steal a lot of money."

Secrecy and Trust

The relationship between secrecy and trust sometimes leads to a fundamental logic flaw that makes most pyramids and Ponzi schemes possible. The logic flaw can be explained, roughly, like this: Trust sometimes results in exclusion. Exclusion often results in secrecy. Therefore, secrecy is (always) the result of trust.

You don't have to get out your college philosophy notes to realize a premise that includes *sometimes* can't lead to an affirmative conclusion that includes *always*.

The emphasis that many pyramid marketing schemes put on recruiting friends and family results from the misunderstanding of the link between trust and secrecy. "You've got to understand the temptation," says one pyramid scheme participant. "It's not only to make money. It's also to let the people closest to you—many times, people who think you're a loser—in on a secret for success. *That's* what draws in so many families."

The sadly mistaken idea that redemption comes from sharing secrets fuels the growth of most pyramid marketing schemes. This mistake is built on another notion that's as old as society: Financial success is a secret kept by a few people; and getting rich is a matter of being let in on the secret.

People who achieve financial success know that it comes from a combination of hard work, some good timing and a little luck. People who *haven't* enjoyed financial success are often intimidated by any part of that combination. Their lack of achievement is more easily rationalized by the belief that success is a secret.

Pyramid schemes recognize this weak tendency and play to it. They tell losers that they're right—the winners have a secret. And, by joining the pyramid, you don't have to work hard or have good timing to make money.

Secrecy Attracts Ponzi Perps and Politicians

Political power seems to thrive on secrecy. Again, this is a mutation of trust. In democratic systems, political leaders have the explicitly articulated trust of the people. A majority somewhere voted for them sometime. But the day-to-day workings of democratic politics are mired in things most voters don't see—money and secrecy.

In this way, politics and politicians are drawn to the same combination of money and secrecy that attract Ponzi schemes and their perps.

The blind trust deed scheme works especially well when the mutual acquaintance is a public official who's prohibited by law from knowing the details of his finances. A variation on this premise is what got the Clinton Administration in trouble for illegal fundraising leading up to the 1996 U.S. federal elections.

And there are other political stories that connect with Ponzi schemes more bluntly.

In the early 1980s, San Diego County Supervisor Roger Hedgecock was laying the foundation of a campaign to become Mayor of San

Diego. His prospects looked good, except for one thing: Hedgecock was encountering serious financial difficulties. Concerned about the effect this might have on his political future, he asked several supporters for advice.

One of his supporters suggested that Hedgecock contact Nancy Hoover, an old acquaintance from local politics. Hoover was the girlfriend and business partner of J. David Dominelli[2], who was running a massive San Diego-based Ponzi scheme that claimed to be investing in precious metals and securities. Dominelli was spending hard to buy support within the San Diego political and social establishments.

Hoover invested $120,000 in the political consulting firm of one of Hedgecock's main advisors. Hedgecock also received a number of smaller checks—in the $3,000 to $5,000 range—directly from Dominelli. This money allowed Hedgecock to build the foundation of a political machine.

Between early 1982 and the end of 1983, Dominelli gave Hedgecock and his advisors more than $350,000. This paid for everything from a car phone for Hedgecock to blocks of tickets to Hedgecock fundraisers. On May 3, 1983, Hedgecock was elected Mayor of San Diego.

After he was elected mayor, Hedgecock wanted to make improvements on his home in north San Diego County. He explored several options for financing these improvements, finally deciding that Hoover and Dominelli would buy the house, lease it back to him and pay for the improvements. Contractors started on the work. Then Dominelli's scheme collapsed.

The deal for Hedgecock's house was never completed. The contractors working on the house were never paid. A series of lawsuits followed, which resulted in the details of Hedgecock's fundraising coming to light.

In October 1985, a San Diego jury found Hedgecock guilty on a single count of conspiracy and 12 counts of perjury. The offenses involved violations of local election ordinances and the state laws requiring complete and accurate personal and campaign accounting.

---

2 For a more detailed discussion of Dominelli's scheme, see page 289 in Chapter 20.

Hedgecock appealed the conviction, which was eventually overturned on a technicality having to do with testimony of several prosecution witnesses. By that time, in the late 1980s, he had gone on to become a popular radio talk-show host in San Diego.

Secrecy Turns Critics into Supporters

Investors who are burned in Ponzi schemes should be the most vocal critics—eager to have some vengeance, if not their money back. They rarely are. As often as not, they defend the Ponzi perps who've taken their money. And smart Ponzi perps complete the illogical circuit their investors begin. They imply—though they'll rarely say—that because their schemes involve the secrets of wealth, they must be built on trust. An investor who is inclined to believe this will be receptive to the pitch, however loopy it may be.

When the SEC first investigated AYM Financial, a New Jersey-based precious metals Ponzi scheme, it met resistance from the trader/investors in the company—exactly the people the investigation would have helped. One of the investors said that AYM traders had bought in to more than just the company; they imagined themselves aggressive capitalists—the kind of people that small-minded government bureaucrats disliked by nature. "We were the guys out there doing business. They were regulators trying to stop us," the would-be trader recalls. "Traders live in a black-and-white world. Business is good, regulators are bad. When they call or come around, it's hide-the-ball with your most aggressive work."

The trader/investors at AYM would have been better off talking to the Feds. Their secrecy may have made them feel like princes of commerce, but all it did was prolong and enlarge the scheme—and their losses.

In affinity schemes, reluctance to speak with investigators will often be attributed to cultural issues. In family schemes, it will be chalked up to protection. What it should be chalked up to is embarrassment.

The embarrassment Ponzi investors feel and the reticence that follows are the main reasons perps rarely go to jail. One west coast law enforcement agent estimates that his office hears from fewer than one in 10 pyramid or Ponzi investors who get burned. "People are embarrassed because they know they should have known better. They're worried that they'll seem greedy and stupid—which, to some degree, they will," he says. "They shouldn't feel this way. Ponzi schemes are illegal for a reason."

Because prosecutors have such a hard time getting the cooperation they need to build Ponzi cases, their bosses will usually argue criminal charges aren't a good use of the state's resources. That's why in these situations civil lawsuits often come first, followed later by criminal charges—the opposite of how most legal issues proceed.

The nature of most Ponzi schemes—participants taking advantage of their friends and family members—makes it more difficult to acquire witnesses. "They're not exactly jumping up and down to turn each other in," a Nevada police officer said in the wake of one Ponzi collapse.

But the reluctance occurs in more than just a few specific situations. And it happens too often to be dismissed as the deserved embarrassment of greedy investors with enough money to lose in the first place. The reluctance comes from a deeper impulse. It comes from the desire that most people in a capitalist system have for secrecy. Ponzi perps understand this desire—and the smart ones exploit it.

The impulse toward secrecy serves as a contrast to several good human instincts. On one hand, privacy and individualism are usually good things for society; on the other, extreme secrecy often hides uglier motives.

To an experienced and balanced investor, the urge for secrecy is a logical application of a general sense of caution. It can also be seen as a by-product of trust: To believe in one person or idea completely is, in practice, to believe less...or not at all...in another.

But Ponzi investors aren't always experienced and balanced. They're often inexperienced and excitable—about money in general or the premise of the particular scheme. Excitable people tend toward extreme responses in all things; inexperienced investors will often take secrecy to an extreme.

"The sure sign of a thief, a sucker or an idiot child is that they think everything has to be a big secret," says a world-weary New York money manager. "The first thing they'll do is call me and say they've got a hot piece of information on a stock. Then they'll tell me something that was in the *Wall Street Journal* last Tuesday. The second thing they'll do is call me with another hot tip—multilevel marketing for long-distance [phone service] or some Ponzi scheme to sell ostrich eggs or Lithuanian gold pieces."

His conclusion: There really aren't such things as hot tips that need to be whispered on the QT. Useful information comes in pieces that are too small—on their own—to make or break an investment. Top secret information is usually hype.

Case Study: Colonial Realty

Jonathan Googel and Benjamin Sisti formed Connecticut-based Colonial Realty in the 1960s as a vehicle to sell limited partnerships that invested in property in and around Hartford. For the first 15 or 20 years they were in business, the two boyhood friends seemed to do things legitimately. During the 1980s, though, they engaged in scores of secretive and questionable dealings. The reason: Colonial Realty had become a vast Ponzi scheme.

Googel, Sisti and their investors were joined in their downward spiral by a proven loser named Frank Shuch. By most reckoning, Shuch brought the tendency for heavy larceny to the operation.

Shuch joined Colonial Realty as the result of a relationship between the company and accounting firm Arthur Andersen which had begun in 1975, when Googel and Sisti were introduced to Andersen tax partner Richard McArdle.

McArdle helped Googel and Sisti find investors—although he told them that if Colonial Realty "wanted to play in the big leagues, then it had to pay." Andersen's initial contributions were "unofficial." Colonial Realty was not allowed to put the firm's name on any of the documents it prepared. The accountants said that their involvement was best left a secret.

That came to an end in 1981, when Andersen started formally putting its name on financial documents prepared for Colonial Realty's syndications. In exchange for the expertise, credibility and business contacts that the Andersen name provided to Colonial Realty, Googel and Sisti agreed to hire Shuch, an alleged embezzler who was the brother-in-law of an Andersen partner.

Shuch also wanted his involvement to be kept secret. Toward this shady end, he started a company called Consulting Enterprises. He performed all his work for Colonial and related entities as an employee of Consulting, for which he received in excess of $5.5 million in payments between 1986 and 1990.

Why all the secrecy? Colonial Realty sold limited partnership interests in various real estate properties located primarily in Connecticut. These investments were offered through Private Placement Memoranda (PPMs), pursuant to the exemption in the registration requirements for "privately placed" transactions.

Colonial Realty offered money-back guarantees, minimum returns of 14 percent, and projected overall returns as high as 300 percent. And the company's offering materials contained misrepresentations and omissions about revenues, financial reserves, rental income and cash flow. It wasn't a situation that would stand up to much scrutiny.

The cornerstone of Colonial Realty's marketing system was a secret network of *finders*—lawyers, accountants, insurance agents, real estate agents and stockbrokers who were given fees in return for either recommending people to buy Colonial Realty investments or providing lists of wealthy clients.

Most of the finders were, themselves, investors in Colonial Realty projects. Generally, they were paid $1,500 for each person who bought a $50,000 investment. Most received either checks or credits on their investments; some were paid in cash.

Colonial Realty's head bookkeeper said that Sisti and Googel kept several million dollars of untraceable cash on hand for paying finders' fees.

This aspect of the company's marketing system was kept secret until after the company was forced into bankruptcy in September 1990. Colonial Realty salesmen maintained that the finders did not want it known that they were getting money in return for recommending their clients, relatives or friends make investments. (Many of the payments violated federal securities laws, which prohibit anyone other than registered brokers from being paid commissions.)

In September 1990, involuntary bankruptcy proceedings were filed against Colonial Realty in federal court. Six banks that had loaned money initiated the proceedings. Investors had a total of more than $350 million in limited partnerships at the time.

In October 1990, Googel, Sisti and Shuch were indicted on federal felony charges.

Shuch killed himself in February 1992 by putting a plastic garbage bag over his head. The suicide took place in his $10 million custom-built home.

On May 5, 1993, Googel pleaded guilty to two counts of wire fraud, one count of bank fraud, and one count of attempting to impede the administration of the internal revenue laws. Two weeks later, Sisti pleaded guilty to two counts of bankruptcy fraud, one count of wire fraud, and one count of structuring transactions to evade reporting requirements.

Both men cooperated extensively with prosecutors and the civil attorneys. Under federal sentencing guidelines, Googel and Sisti faced sentences of between two and five years. They hoped their cooperation would convince the sentencing judge to impose even less time.

It didn't. The judge not only concluded that they deserved no leniency but found that the guidelines did not adequately reflect the severity of their crimes. He chastised Googel for recruiting millions in investments even after bankruptcy experts had advised that Colonial Realty was failing. And he concluded that Googel had obstructed justice by attempting to arrange a meeting with a witness being interviewed by federal authorities.

Worse still, as Colonial Realty was collapsing, Googel had transferred millions to relatives. Much of that had been recovered as part of a deal with the bankruptcy trustee; but Googel's family was allowed to keep about $1.25 million in cash and other assets—including a half-million dollar house.

The judge sentenced Googel to nine years in a federal prison camp.

Sisti had been even flashier than Googel. He'd lived in a 52,000-square-foot mansion with a movie theater and shooting range and ordered custom-made multimillion-dollar yachts. At his sentencing hearing, though, Sisti seemed delicate and humble. He spoke in a calm, unimposing voice, telling the judge he was sorry for his crimes and sorry he could not make things right. "I can't change what I did," Sisti said, "but I can change the person who did them. I just hope I live long enough to make it all up to [my family]."

The judge gave him an eight year sentence to work on the change.

The criminal sentences moved the focus to various civil lawsuits. In April 1994, a panel of mediators approved a settlement worth about $100 million. The deal resolved some 3,000 lawsuits, representing most of the civil actions spawned by Colonial Realty's collapse; it bailed out investors who'd not only lost their investments but also owed banks for loans that had paid for limited partnerships. All but $18 million of the $100 million owed by the investors was forgiven by the banks under the settlement.

In exchange for the forgiven debts, the banks reserved the right to collect half of any judgment from Andersen or other defendants.

Two of the legal and accounting firms accused of improprieties by Colonial Realty investors and creditors were also part of the settlement, agreeing to pay a total of $11 million. Admitting no wrongdoing, the law firm of Levy & Droney agreed to pay $10 million and the accounting firm of Kostin Ruffkess & Co., $1.1 million. (The payments were covered by professional liability insurance.)

A few months later, Sisti and Googel reached a settlement with the investor groups that allowed each of their families to keep about $1.1 million in return for assurances that they had fully explained their tangled finances and disclosed all assets.

The perps then turned their burned investors into reluctant allies by helping their lawyers prepare lawsuits against accounting and legal firms that participated in selling Colonial Realty partnerships.

In 1996, a federal appeals court considered the burned investors' claims against Arthur Andersen in detail. They alleged that Andersen had prepared or approved financial projections for the limited partnerships that "bore no relation to reality" and misrepresented the real estate market.

The investors alleged that Andersen "knew that the projections would make an investment in [the limited partnerships] appear economically feasible...notwithstanding the excessive fees charged by the general partners and made the projections, which they knew to be excessive, for the express purpose of distracting the attention of plaintiffs from those fees."

Andersen argued that the language contained in the PPMs concerning the limited scope and inherent uncertainty of the projections prevented reliance on the projections as a matter of law. The court disagreed.

According to Andersen, the investors could not sustain their negligent misrepresentation claims because they failed to allege either that they had a fiduciary relationship with Andersen or that Andersen possessed actual knowledge that the investors would rely on the alleged misrepresentations. The court disagreed.

Because Shuch was merely the "brother of a member's spouse," Andersen argued that he could not have jeopardized its professional independence. Therefore, the firm believed it was not required to disclose Shuch's relationship with its errant employee. The court disagreed.

The burned investors alleged that Andersen broke RICO law because it secretively "sought to place Shuch as an employee of Colonial so as to obtain control of Colonial," that "[t]he dramatic increase in Colonial's business was a direct and proximate result of Andersen's control over the Colonial syndications," and that Googel and Sisti "may not have fully understood" the financial status of their burgeoning operations, while Andersen "knew everything" because it was "[sophisticated] and highly skilled in business, real estate finance and syndication." In short, they claimed that:

> *Andersen created in Colonial an industry giant which Andersen could and did display to other potential clients as an example of the success and prestige which any company could attain if it hired and paid Andersen.*

But the court didn't agree with the investors. It doubted that Arthur Andersen controlled Colonial Realty through Shuch. The investors' lawsuit described Googel and Sisti as "Ponzi Participants," which the court called "an unlikely description for entirely subordinate, dominated toilers in the Ponzi vineyard."

Finally, in May 1996, Arthur Andersen agreed to pay $10.3 million to settle the charges. This brought its total settlement to about $15 million. (After a state investigation in 1993, Andersen had paid $3.5 million in refunds and fines.)

As a result of the various settlements and the bank forgiveness, most of the burned Colonial Realty investors were able to recoup more than half of their losses. Of course, it took them more than five years to get the money back.

CHAPTER 13

Loneliness, Fear and Desperation

White-collar thieves often think they can make up a loss and come to believe they deserve what they are taking. But these rationalizations usually crumble under the weight of anxiety and paranoia.

Pyramid and Ponzi schemes exploit impulses like trust, greed and secrecy. But these schemes are built on darker foundations. For both Ponzi perps and investors, the impulses which get them involved are pretty bleak—usually wrapped around loneliness, fear and desperation.

These factors fit the circumstances. A Ponzi scheme requires a certain amount of fatalism on the part of the perp. The schemes always collapse. When the perps go in, they know there's going to be a reckoning. The battle is to delay the reckoning as long as possible.

Many people find the impulses that motivate crooks more interesting than those that motivate their marks. It's almost a staple of crime novels and magazine stories to portray con men as characters from the psychological and philosophical theories of Friedrich Nietzsche. That is, perverse supermen with a twisted strength for shouldering the weight of their crimes.

The truth is less dramatic. There's no doubt that Ponzi perps are affected by some dark impulses. But they usually aren't supermen. They're more like unexamined people who give in to fairly common weaknesses.

Time and again, in the wake of a collapsed Ponzi scheme, burned investors and participants ask "How could this person sleep at night?" The answer seems to be that, from the perp's perspective, the fraud is usually inevitable.

Perps candid enough to speak truthfully about their deeds will admit that they've always felt like they don't belong—in any group. "It's been like that since I was in school," says one perp who ran several Ponzi schemes in the Midwest, got in legal trouble for two, and then moved to southern California—where he insists his start-up multi-level marketing company is legitimate. "You know how it is—kids gather in cliques. I could get along with just about every clique, hang out with them. But I didn't really belong in any. I'm in my fifties now and it's the same way. I can get along with all kinds of people, but I don't belong with anyone."

To a psychoanalyst, this probably sounds like impostor syndrome—the disabling feeling that a person doesn't rightly deserve his place in any circle, system or organization. Asked if he suffers from impostor syndrome, the talkative perp shrugs. "Maybe. But I'm not a big believer in psychology or dwelling on the past. I focus on the future."

This standard dodge may mark the limit of a criminal's ability for self-examination. The most relevant downside of the impostor syndrome—a shifting code of circumstantial ethics necessary to get along with everybody—is beyond most Ponzi perps. It's too much a part of the charm or charisma that's often the perp's strongest personal asset.

Everyone feels some part the impostor syndrome at some point in his or her life. People deal with the feelings of isolation in different ways. Most well-adjusted people realize that the feelings of an impostor's isolation are a common part of life. Less well-adjusted people are so disturbed by the feelings that they slip down a slope of egocentrism...and into pathological behavior .

This is where the circumstantial ethics exact their price. Dwelling on themselves, these egocentric types can't get past the idea that they are outsiders—and even frauds—within any social or economic circle. From this place, committing an actual fraud is easier than most people would think.

In August 1996, a Florida woman who'd bilked almost 200 investors out of nearly $8 million—and then plotted the murder of the federal judge who put her out of business—was sentenced to more than 24 years in prison. Jan Weeks-Katona, founder of Premier Benefit Capital Trust, had been convicted in December 1994 of fraud, money laundering and conspiracy to commit murder.

Immediately after her conviction, Weeks-Katona started lobbying for easy treatment. She argued that, if she hadn't been medicated during her trial, she could have assisted her attorney. "I'm sure the jury would have found me not guilty if I had been able to do so," she'd later say.

Her sentencing was delayed for more than a year, while she underwent court-ordered psychiatric evaluation and treatment.

In the early 1990s, Weeks-Katona and her son had operated Premier Benefit Capital. Through the company, they sold unregistered securities on the guarantee of a 12 percent return on investments of at least $25,000. Using radio programs and free seminars to attract investors, they quickly amassed millions—mostly from senior citizens.

They spent some of the money buying two extravagant gulf-front homes near Tampa.

But complaints followed as the Ponzi scheme collapsed. The Securities and Exchange Commission sued the company in 1993. U.S. District Judge Steven Merryday promptly ordered a receiver to take over operation of Premier. (The receiver eventually recovered some assets and returned about 40 cents on the dollar to Premier Benefit investors.)

Weeks-Katona, her son and others involved in the company fled to Mexico, where they plotted to kill Merryday and other officials. The group was eventually arrested by Mexican law enforcement officials working with the FBI.

At her sentencing hearing, Weeks-Katona appeared calm and relaxed. But her doctors and her attorney said she still suffered from a combination of mental disorders, which produced "delusions of grandeur and extreme paranoia" that led her to commit her crimes. So, her court-appointed lawyer argued for an unusually light 10-year sentence.

Federal Judge Susan Bucklew agreed that Weeks-Katona was mentally ill but said she had to consider protection of the public. (Bucklew had sentenced Weeks-Katona's son, Jason Spencer Weeks, to 30 years in prison from the same case.) "She feels no responsibility for any of this," Bucklew said. And the judge cited other problematic testimony. Weeks-Katona had said that she hadn't taken medication for her condition in two-and-a-half months. "That's sort of scary," Bucklew concluded, as she rejected the pleas for leniency and sent the perp to jail for a long time.

Stealing Becomes More Natural Than Earning

Another question that burned investors often ask is: "Why did they commit this crime? They could have worked straight and gotten as much money."

This is a natural but flawed assumption. Yes, many Ponzi perps hang around the rich and famous...and seem to work close to legitimate business. But, in most cases, it's their fraud that got them even that close.

With a very loose sense of loyalty or obligation, the Ponzi perp is always susceptible to thieving temptations. That's why so many are repeat offenders. They don't feel the constraints that most people do. Ponzi perps are usually loners by preference, inevitably drawn toward the action or situation that leads to their break with people around them.

This impulse away from others may be connected with the fact that Ponzi schemes have a certain element of class envy to them. Repeatedly, the perp is someone with notably less education or a weaker financial background than the people with whom he or she lives and works.

In this sense, the scheme may be a slightly-thought-out insult to the relatively rich and mighty.

This is the biggest refutation of the hack screenwriters, magazine journalists and commentators who argue that Ponzi perps are Nietzschean supermen. A Ponzi scheme is the tool of a relatively weak criminal. It's indirect, takes awhile to collapse and is nonviolent. And—in the ultimate affront to Nietzsche's machismo—many Ponzi perps offer whining rationalizations for their crimes, when they come to light.

The weakness and feeling of isolation are two reasons that so many Ponzi perps are comfortable going on the lam when their schemes collapse. The huge 1980s Ponzi scheme Lake States Investment Corp. illustrates the full range of a perp's loneliness, fear and desperation.

Beginning in 1984, Lake States founder Thomas Collins began soliciting customers to invest money into a pool which would be used to trade commodity futures.

One problem: Collins was not registered with the CFTC or any other securities regulator and—consequently—could not legally solicit, accept or pool customer funds. He also couldn't trade funds on the commodities market. And Lake States never did any legitimate business as a futures commodity merchant—nor did it operate as a legitimate trading pool. Nevertheless, Collins attracted money like a pro.

The scheme went something like this: Lake States maintained an office in Rolling Meadows, Illinois. Inside the office, most of the commodity pool sellers and other employees could watch electronic commodities tickers and call investors. Collins convinced investors to put their money in his commodity pools by showing them the substantial returns early investors were making—without any reported losses. He showed them account statements that seemed to confirm the promises. Existing investors reported no difficulty in withdrawing money from their pool accounts.

To seal the deal, Lake States salespeople would offer investors "Promissory Notes." They said the notes were a "legitimate way to structure investments to save on commissions."

Most Lake States investors came into the situation inclined to believe the sales pitch. They were often steered there by friends and relatives. "Investors would get great reports every month and would tell their friends," said Art Aufmann, a lawyer who represented about 250 investors in a federal lawsuit against Lake States employees. "People would say, 'Geez, I'm nuts if I don't get into this.'"

Lake States operated as an individual investor, trading commodities in several accounts at Geldermann Inc., a legitimate trading company. Geldermann received commissions on every trade Collins conducted, and thus had an incentive to assist the Lake States fraud.

Geldermann provided Collins with a desk and a phone at the Geldermann booth on the floor of the MidAmerica Commodity Exchange. Geldermann also permitted Collins to write orders on its forms—a task which only its employees should have been allowed to perform. The effect was convincing. It was close enough to legitimacy that hundreds of investors—many of them sophisticated people—believed that Collins was a mover and shaker in his field.

In August 1988, Geldermann's parent company, ConAgra, hired James Fuller as an audit supervisor. Fuller was aware that Collins had skirted various rules of the CFTC and other agencies. He investigated the Lake States accounts and discovered that Geldermann was allowing Collins to transfer funds between accounts improperly and to open joint accounts with investors without proper documentation.

When Fuller informed them about these problems, Geldermann's officers told him to stop investigating Collins.

In October 1989, the CFTC began an investigation of Collins. It subpoenaed Geldermann's records regarding his trading accounts. The Feds asked Geldermann officials to provide copies of account statements and other records associated with Collins and Lake States.

The records showed large deposits into and withdrawals from Lake States accounts. For example, an account held solely in Collins' name showed more than $3,148,000 in deposits and $3,574,000 in withdrawals during the period from January to September of 1989. This wasn't, by itself, illegal. But the big volume of big transactions suggested the growth pattern of a Ponzi scheme.

Collins dealt with the CFTC investigations surprisingly well. Most Ponzi perps fold their operations or start making incriminating mistakes as soon as they know the Feds are watching. Lake States kept its interest payments going—and continued recruiting new investors—for more than four years. Collins made legitimate investments often enough to extend his scheme's life expectancy. "He had quite a few hits," recalls one investor. "It's really too bad he was so desperate that he had to steal. If he'd played it straight, he might have really accomplished something."

But Collins was a thief from the beginning. There was no chance that he could have played it straight. Whatever investment success he had was a happy accident that just borrowed more time.

Lake States reached its breaking point in late 1993. The ill-timed combination of several bad investments and the steady scrutiny of the CFTC put the company in a cash crunch. New investors were getting hard to find.

In early 1994, Lake States investors were complaining that the company wasn't sending out interest checks. Worse still, it was being evasive about withdrawals of *any* kind. Some investors formed a group that filed a series of involuntary bankruptcy petitions against Collins and Lake States.

In June, Collins had his chauffeur drive him to a business meeting in suburban Chicago. He went into the meeting...and didn't come out. A few investors wondered whether he'd been kidnapped or killed. But most guessed—rightly—that he'd simply fled.

For most of Collins' investors, his disappearance meant the loss of a small part of their net worth. But a handful of big investors were wiped out. About a week after Collins was declared missing, a Washington D.C. man who'd invested several million dollars of family money in Lake States hanged himself.

Because it had lasted so long, Lake States had grown to an epic size. In the 10 years between 1984 and 1993, Collins had taken in more than $100 million from almost 500 investors. He returned about $70 million to investors in the form of bogus profits. He lost about $10 million making commodities investments. The rest went to Lake States overhead—and Collins' pockets.

After his disappearance, Collins took his mistress—Kathleen Chambers—to Costa Rica for several months. Collins had met Chambers when she was waiting tables a restaurant outside of Chicago that he liked. The couple rented an ocean-view villa while the collapse of Lake States played out back in the States.

Collins had been planning his escape for months. He had detailed aliases for Chambers and himself. By late 1994, they'd moved to La Jolla, California—a posh suburb north of San Diego. Collins had become Bill O'Mara, a stockbroker from the Midwest who'd gotten rich during the 1980s and then developed a heart condition. On the advice of his doctor, he'd cashed out and moved to the west coast with his girlfriend, Meg.

The couple rented a luxury condo and spent most of their time together. Their most notable outside interest was going to San Diego Padres baseball games. Collins, sporting a graying ponytail, blended in easily with the wealthy refugees from cold climates who live in La Jolla.

The ruse lasted more than two years. But, by the summer of 1996, Collins and Chambers were broke (though she didn't know it). Most of the people involved in the case thought that Collins had disappeared with about $10 million. In fact, he may have only had a few hundred thousand.

Desperate, and lacking the time or focus to start another Ponzi scheme, Collins tried a bank heist. He took a .22 caliber pistol into a Great Western Bank branch in San Diego and ordered a teller to fill a paper bag with cash. While she was doing this, another employee activated a silent alarm.

With only $840 in his bag, Collins got as far as his car. Then the police arrived. Trapped, he put the barrel of the pistol in his mouth and pulled the trigger.

$$\left(\frac{180 \times .0000001}{25 \times 600}\right) = 43.80$$

to \$60

60 − 43.80 = 16.20

73%

48 WITH 3,291.00

= 210.24

Case Study: Bill and Marika Runnells

One of the telling questions is why some people who work for years legitimately suddenly snap and start stealing.

Again, they may have always felt like they were only somewhat legit. This insecurity explains why so many Ponzi perps work so hard to impress people. They are—among other things—social climbers, looking for the excitement and recognition of making big money.

In a few cases, the Ponzi perp actually will progress to a level of legitimacy. Anthony Robbins, Amway, Herbalife and a handful of other seemingly mainstream people or outfits come from backgrounds tinged with allegations of Ponzis and pyramids. Perps may hope that they will be one of the lucky handful that can grow fast enough...or move fast enough...that they attain the level of legitimacy. And, after the schemes crash, the investors confuse their fear of being poor with innocence.

Some people thrive on the fear and desperation that fray the nerves of most Ponzi perps. During the mid-1980s, William and Marika Runnells scammed investors and lenders with a sophisticated Ponzi scheme called Landbank Equity Corporation. The Runnellses started Virginia-based Landbank in 1980. The company made second mortgage loans and then sold pools of the mortgages to investors.

Typically, the investor would not actually take possession of the promissory notes and collect on them from the borrower; instead, the investor would pay Landbank a servicing fee for processing and servicing collection of the loans. In return, Landbank guaranteed timely "pass-through" of principal and interest.

A high school dropout who'd been buying and selling real estate since he was 18, Bill Runnells had a checkered past—including numerous lawsuits and dodged judgments. He was locally notorious for two things: a shaved head and a weakness for high-stakes gambling.

Starting with not much more than a $50,000 line of credit, he built Landbank into one of the largest second-mortgage companies in the nation, with 33 branches in five states up and down the East Coast.

But even the $50,000 line of credit was a stretch for Runnells. The president of the bank that issued the line admitted, "Runnells had not handled his dealings in the real estate industry in an entirely satisfactory manner." The only reason the bank did business with Runnells was that Frank Butler, an early partner in Landbank, had a good reputation in local business circles.

Because Virginia did not regulate second-mortgage lenders in the 1980s, Landbank was able to avoid outside audits and charge interest rates averaging 18 percent and fees of up to 40 percent. Its borrowers accepted the steep terms because they were usually bad credit risks who didn't have many choices. Landbank's advertising slogan was, "When the bank says no, Mrs. Cash says yes."

Charging such high rates, Landbank didn't have much trouble making money. It collected delinquent accounts aggressively. Business was good. So good, in fact, that Landbank was able to secure a seal of approval in 1982 from the Federal National Mortgage Association, a quasi-government agency better know as Fannie Mae.

By meeting the strict requirements of the agency, Landbank gained prestige, and was able to secure insurance on its loans from a California company called Balboa Insurance. The insurance prompted Perpetual American Bank of Washington, D.C., to offer Landbank a $10 million line of credit to make new mortgages. It also allowed Landbank to resell its otherwise risky mortgages to conservative entities like savings and loans, which saw the insurance as a guarantee that any losses would be repaid.

At this point, the scheme had grown large enough that Runnells' shady personal history wasn't an issue. But it should have been. Once the big credit line was in place, Landbank started growing its business recklessly. Misrepresentation was routine.

Though it promised investors that its lending and appraisal practices satisfied Fannie Mae standards, Landbank often loaned money on the basis of informal, "drive-by" appraisals. Landbank would inflate the value of collateral property. Its loan processing people would regularly overstate a borrower's ability to repay. Creditworthiness was—

as one court put it—"a welcome but unnecessary trait" in borrowers. Landbank didn't mind these issues because it made most of its money up front.

This was all more than just aggressive growth. Landbank's practices violated federal truth-in-lending laws in numerous ways. These violations made its loans vulnerable to legal challenge.

Runnells never mentioned any of this. Even though they'd been running Landbank for only a few years, he and his Hungarian-born wife Marika started living a lavish lifestyle. As he explained to some employees, they were "taking some of our chips off the table." They bought a big house, a couple of expensive cars and other symbols of wealth.

Landbank was far from a self-sustaining business, though. There were some major flaws in the scam. The riskiness of privately-backed pools of mortgages forced Landbank to offer high interest rates to investors who could choose less risky government-sponsored mortgage securities. And the company's default rates started creeping up.

"It's hard work to keep these low-quality loans from defaulting," says one Virginia banker familiar with Landbank's story. "When they were small and regional, they spent the time and effort to keep their loans current. After 1982, they grew so fast they couldn't keep up the effort. By that time, though, I don't think they cared."

Landbank made 10,000 mortgages between 1982 and 1985 in Virginia, Maryland, Alabama, South Carolina and Georgia. Within three years, half of its mortgages were in default. Runnells handled the default problem by leaping headlong into a Ponzi scheme. He paid "principal and interest" payments to investors out of fees for new loans, while falsely telling investors and his insurance carrier that default rates were low.

As in all Ponzi schemes, the pyramid could stand only as long as more new money was coming in. As long as it did, Bill Runnells took chips off the table. Unfortunately, he put a lot of the chips on other tables—in Atlantic City and Las Vegas. And he wasn't able to take those chips back.

The pyramid scheme began to unravel in early 1985 when Balboa Insurance alerted Landbank investors that it was considering canceling its mortgage insurance because it suspected Landbank of violating state and federal lending laws.

Balboa Insurance also passed along copies of some of its correspondence with Landbank. In one letter, Balboa complained to Landbank management that appraisals were too high, yielding an artificially low loan-to-equity ratio. In another, Balboa detailed the manner in which Landbank's up-front fees violated the Truth-in-Lending Act (the fees were not included in calculations of annual percentage rates, as the law required). In a third, Landbank urged Balboa to keep its concerns private and not to notify investors.

Landbank responded by informing investors that Balboa Insurance had been replaced as mortgage insurance carrier by an entity called the Insurance Exchange of the Americas (IEA). While Balboa Insurance didn't have the highest financial solvency ratings, IEA wasn't rated at all.

At about the same time, Fannie Mae backed away from Landbank. It cited concerns over the mortgage insurance and rising delinquency and foreclosure numbers. This effectively shut down Landbank's access to new money from investors.

In the fall of 1985, 43.7 percent of Landbank's loans were 30 or more days delinquent, and 29.2 percent were at least 60 days delinquent. Both numbers were exceptionally high. Within six months of Balboa Insurance's first letters to investors, Landbank declared bankruptcy. More than $200 million in investments were left hanging.

Days after taking over, a court-appointed trustee charged that the Runnellses had made off with up to $20 million. They'd been shifting funds through a maze of dummy corporations and made dozens of illegal "insider loans" to purchase land, houses and cars. The bankruptcy proceedings and a wave of civil lawsuits took up most of the next 18 months.

Even as these civil cases proceeded through the courts, Runnells remained desperately flamboyant. He'd taken hundreds of thousands of dollars in cash out of Landbank before it collapsed; and he used this money to support his flashy lifestyle. On one Caribbean gambling trip in January 1986, he lost $40,000 in a few days. In all, he paid bookies and casinos more than $600,000 over a two-year period.

As is often the case, criminal charges took longer to develop than civil charges. But they did finally follow.

Bill Runnells was indicted in March 1988 on 24 counts of tax fraud, bankruptcy fraud, criminal contempt and obstruction of justice. Runnells spoke with his lawyer by phone after the indictment was handed down; the two made arrangements for Runnells to appear at his April 6 arraignment.

He never showed up at the arraignment. Both he and his wife had disappeared. The same grand jury which had indicted Bill Runnells expanded the charges against him and his wife. The second, 74-count indictment charged the couple with wire fraud, bankruptcy fraud, racketeering and obstruction of justice.

The Runnellses eluded authorities for two years. They fled to Southern California where they became hypnotherapists, running clinics to help people lose weight and stop smoking. Runnells called himself Dr. William Austin and operated a company called The Pinnacle Method of America Inc. out of an office in working-class Santa Ana. The couple left California in September 1989, when they learned they were about to be profiled on the television true-crime program *Unsolved Mysteries*. After keeping a low profile for several weeks, they decided to settle down in a suburb of Dallas, Texas.

Runnells answered a classified ad for a job as a hypnotherapist at the Phoenix Centers for Addiction Control in Dallas. He applied for the position under a new alias—Dr. William Allen. He claimed to have a Ph.D. in psychology from...somewhere...in Georgia.

Since a person doesn't have to have a doctorate—or any other degree—to perform hypnosis in Texas, the managers at Phoenix Centers didn't check his background. They hired him part-time. "He was a very good hypnotist, one of our best," said one co-worker. "He was able to hypnotize [customers] and they quit smoking. They were happy and we were happy. He was just a charmer."

He was charming enough to open his own hypnotherapy clinic a few months later, taking many of the Phoenix Centers' clients with him. But he wasn't charming enough to elude the FBI. The Feds tracked him to southern California and—using leads gathered there—eventually tracked Runnells to Dallas.

Runnells answered the door when FBI agents rang the bell at his luxury high-rise apartment in March 1990. He and Marika were arrested.

Prosecutors said the Runnellses "robbed Peter to pay Paul," creating a pyramid scheme that could not survive. "Landbank was nothing but a pyramid of debt...a complex and elaborate scheme to defraud," said assistant U.S. attorney Joseph Fisher.

The Runnellses' son testified that his father instructed him to hide $200,000 in cash taken from the family home after a federal judge had frozen assets of Landbank. "I was to take it to Farmville, [Virginia,] where my great aunts lived, and put it in a family safe," Steven Runnells testified. He said he found another $200,000 in the safe when he deposited the money.

At first, Bill Runnells claimed he had a drinking problem that clouded his memory of Landbank's financial details. When that didn't seem to diminish any of the charges, he tried to raise an insanity defense—claiming that he couldn't control his actions because he was a compulsive gambler. "He says he has no control over anything," said his lawyer, Richard Brydges. "He's taking a position that he didn't do anything wrong because he was out to lunch."

The judge hearing the case rejected the insanity claims. So, Bill and Marika Runnells gradually turned against one another.

He said that, during the worst of the fraud, he'd been semi-retired with the rank of president. Instead, Marika had actually run the business. "Mrs. Runnells is a smart woman. She's a lot smarter than her husband," Brydges argued.

She said it had been Bill who'd launched Landbank and Bill who'd approved all the shaky loans. She'd worked night and day, without pay, to keep the company afloat. The reason Landbank went bankrupt was "not fraud, but poor business decisions, dumb decisions," according to David Bouchard, Marika's attorney.

In two days of testimony, Marika portrayed herself as a competent manager and hard worker who was not able to control the actions of other Landbank officials—including her husband. At one point she broke down, sobbing that his sexual infidelities added to their problems at Landbank. "In early 1983 it was brought to my attention that Bill was seeing someone else and I became very upset," she said.

Bill did not take the stand.

In November 1990, after a nine-week trial, Bill and Marika Runnells were found guilty of 87 and 59 felonies, respectively—including conspiracy, racketeering, tax fraud and obstruction of justice.

In January 1991, they were each sentenced to more than 30 years in prison and fined $500,000.

"I always think about [Runnells] on the lam, in some God-awful place in southern California trying to get housewives to stop smoking," says one Landbank investor...with some satisfaction. "After he'd been a big player in the banking world. It's not romantic. It's pathetic."

PART THREE

Contemporary Variations

CHAPTER 14

Multilevel Marketing

Multilevel marketing—also called *network marketing* or the shorthand MLM—takes an almost evangelistic approach to selling. It's been around for a long time. But, for most of the last fifty years, it's been frowned upon as a sleazy way to do business. This reputation is due, in part, to how much MLM resembles a Ponzi scheme.

In the 1970s, the frowning started to fade though. MLM began gaining credibility in mainstream business circles. From a corporate perspective, the strength of MLM is that it shortcuts the traditional retail distribution mechanism with all of its attendant support costs—marketing, sales, inventory and distribution.

MLM networks can be run and maintained with limited overhead—no expensive offices, large staffs or marketing support, just an inordinate amount of energy and a heavy long-distance phone bill.

Finally, MLM offers companies a level of plausible deniability if any distributor does something illegal or unethical. People who get involved in MLM are not employees of the producing company; they are independent business owners.

Several interlocking trends have contributed to the growth of network marketing, including technology advances, economic changes, job insecurity and the twin desires for financial security and control of one's destiny. (Frankly, some of these trends have also encouraged Ponzi schemes.)

There's no doubt that technology has made MLM more appealing to potential recruits who would otherwise be reluctant to handle the chores of sales, recruiting, inventory, deliveries and recordkeeping. In the age of Windows, these things can be managed in ten minutes a week, using any of numerous $99 software packages.

But the economic motives are more powerful. "We're seeing a much more highly educated group of people coming in," said Neil Offen, president of the Direct Selling Association, an MLM lobbying group. "We're seeing a lot of middle-management executives who've been laid off because of corporate downsizing. The American reality of 'you work hard, play by the rules and your talent will get you to the top' is not true anymore in the corporate world."

But not all of the growth is simple economics. People recruiting MLM distributors know who's most likely to join. "When you're unemployed, you're most vulnerable," said Jim Lyons, a financial investigator for the Florida Attorney General's office.

As experienced managers are downsized or forced to take early retirement, they take with them tidy retirement packages. They also have expanded networks of business acquaintances and friends...and the entrepreneurial determination never to be downsized again.

A caveat: According to the DSA, 90 percent of MLM distributors earn less than $5,000 a year.

Another—bigger—caveat: MLM is a ripe hunting ground for Ponzi perps. The lines of demarcation between legitimate MLM and illegitimate pyramid schemes have always been...and remain...fuzzy.

The Tempting Mechanics of an MLM Program

MLM companies sell products into the distributor system at a discount deep enough to make the products or services inexpensive, compared to competing products. But this usually leaves enough margin to fund the commissions and bonuses that drive the system.

The company will also fund the commissions and bonuses by charging new distributors a nominal amount—usually less than $500—as a franchise fee for joining.

Not only does the MLM distributor receive accumulated commission on the sales made from his or her recruits, but also from the commission on the sales made by each recruit's recruits—and on down the line.

An often-made analogy is to a family tree, with roots extending down six—and sometimes nine or 10—multiple levels. You recruit five distributors, who recruit five distributors, who recruit five distributors....

A few percentage points of override commission on the sales made by everyone below you in the scheme can result in some big monthly sales commissions.

But the fat-check math that drives most MLM schemes is often calculated selectively to make the strongest impression. Consider another, disinterested, calculation: If one person recruits six distributors, each of whom recruits six others, the total number of people in the program is 43 by the third level. It's 9,331 by the fifth. And more than 10 million by the ninth.

That's the exploding hunger of geometric progression. It's the same thing that makes all Ponzi schemes eventually fail.

To overcome the hard numbers, most MLM programs appeal to recruits' hearts rather than their brains. Informational and motivational meetings are one of the most common methods for introducing potential recruits to an MLM program. This is where the evangelism comes into play. The meetings use many of the same motivation devices that religious revival meetings use.

Meetings often include songs and testimonials, stressing dedication to the business. Some companies go further, encouraging their distributors to follow an approved way of life. For some people, "MLM is close to religion," says Thomas Hayes, an expert on multilevel marketing and chairman of the marketing department at Xavier University in Cincinnati. "They want to believe in something. They are looking for a reason to believe in something. And here it is. It says, 'I, too, can be wealthy.'"

Most distributors—particularly at the lower levels—will not make a fortune from the programs. Many of the lower-level distributors sign up simply to buy products at a discounted price. For this reason, the most effective MLM programs are those that distribute products that require continual replenishment—detergent, cosmetics and vitamin supplements.

Because MLM programs are usually regulated at the state level, attorney general and consumer protection agencies from various states will sometimes cooperate in investigating suspicious ones.

In April 1993, attorney generals offices from nine states forced one MLM company, Tennessee-based National Safety Associates, to buy back thousands of water filters from struggling distributors.

The company let distributors recruit others with get-rich-quick promises that delivered garages full of unsold water filters. In a common move, National Safety argued that its distributors—who were independent contractors and not employees—were the ones who fell out of line.

Under the coordinated pressure of several states, National Safety had little choice but to change its policies. The company agreed to buy back 90 percent of products from distributors who wanted to get out within a given period of time.

The company also agreed to monitor that its products were being sold to consumers who actually used them—rather than piling up in distributors' garages. Finally, it agreed to review distributors' promotional activities, checking that claims about products and earnings potential were realistic.

The package of changes followed the standard guidelines recommended by DSA and several other MLM trade groups.

"More people are interested in [MLM] now because of the economy," said Terri Norton, education coordinator for Florida's Division of Consumer Affairs, in 1996. "Maybe one of the couple is out of a job, or there was no cost-of-living raise this year."

She offered this advice: If you go to an MLM presentation, take someone with you who isn't interested in the business and leave your checkbook at home. "You get caught up in the mood and excitement," Norton said. "You sign up right then and there without reading what you're signing. If they're really legitimate and want your business, your money will be just as good later."

Many MLM firms lure participants and investors by telling them they have to sign up right away or they'll lose the opportunity.

A Fast-growing Company Tests the Law's Limits

Utah-based Nu Skin International Inc., was founded in 1985 by Blake Roney, his sister and a childhood friend. The company sells skin care, hair care and nutritional products through an MLM system. Its independent distributors make an initial investment to acquire a distributorship and inventory. Then, they can sell product—keeping about half of the suggested retail price—and recruit other distributors.

For every additional salesperson he or she recruits, a distributor gets 5 percent of that person's wholesale purchases from the company. There are six levels of salespeople in Nu Skin's organizational plan, each named for a precious metal or gem. At the top is the Blue Diamond Executive—who's recruited at least 12 other salespeople directly and draws commissions from at least six downline groups. A Blue Diamond's downline can include up to 15,000 people.

Most companies in the cosmetics business spend heavily on advertising. Nu Skin doesn't—and forbids its distributors from doing so. It relies exclusively on MLM.

In addition to cosmetics and some nutritional products, Nu Skin sells motivational audio tapes to help distributors recruit new salespeople. The tapes, which include subliminal messages encouraging success, are controversial. "This is one of the greatest examples of snake oil currently being sold in the marketplace," said Gerald Rosen, a Seattle psychologist who chaired the American Psychological Association's 1990 task force on self-help products.

"Independent and business consulting firms are calling this the greatest business opportunity in the last 25 years," the narrator of one audiotape says—in a non-subliminal passage. He describes how Nu Skin distributors can earn $168,000 per year by recruiting five people, who recruit five more...and so on. (The numbers assume each recruit sells $100 of Nu Skin product a month—and that 25 percent of the recruits stay with the program a year. Both assumptions are optimistic.)

Roney, Nu Skin's founder, combats the skepticism by giving recruits a cosmic pitch. According to one distributor, he avoids talking about products or the money distributors can make. Instead, he talks about having "harmony in your family life and...high standards and morals."

Of course, Nu Skin distributors also use more traditional recruitment tools—namely, greed. They tell prospects that top distributors can earn commissions of up to $400,000 a month.

Nu Skin doesn't miss many opportunities because a number of key people have experience with aggressive MLM companies. Since Nu Skin's beginning, Roney has been dogged by allegations that he was part of Cambridge Plan International—a notorious MLM company that went bankrupt in the early 1980s. (Cambridge sold diet plans and powdered supplements that went with them. In September 1983, the Food & Drug Administration received reports alleging that seven people had died as a result of the company's 330-calorie-a-day diet. Cambridge shut down soon after.)

Roney was not involved directly with Cambridge. But several people close to him—and involved in Nu Skin—were. The connection, disturbing to some, seems to have worked well for the company. Through the late 1980s and early 1990s, earnings financed a 200,000-square-foot distribution center, a multimillion dollar lab and a 10-story corporate headquarters in Provo.

Early in 1991, Nu Skin hosted 7,500 distributors at the huge Salt Palace Convention Center. The convention theme: Dare to dream. Bill Cosby and former President Ronald Reagan stirred up excitement in the crowd.

But not everyone who worked for Nu Skin shared this enthusiasm. In August 1991, distributor Patricia Arata filed a class action lawsuit in federal court in California. Arata, a widow who lived in rural Gilroy, California, had started selling Nu Skin products part-time in the late 1980s to make some extra money. Instead, she said she'd lost money due to the unscrupulous practices of Nu Skin distributors above her. "Everyone at the top made money," Arata complained. "I lost thousands."

Legally, the crux of her complaint was this:

> *Despite the lip service to "products," Nu Skin is a classic pyramid scheme in which members/distributors focus their efforts on recruiting new distributors rather than on selling products, and must maintain "personal volume" of wholesale purchases in order to remain members of the distribution chain and reap commissions from the efforts of their "downline" distributors....*

Arata's lawyer said the widow had invested $4,000 in Nu Skin products and marketing materials. He guessed that 100,000 other participants—the rest of the class action plaintiffs—had invested at least $75 million.

Nu Skin tried to have the complaint dismissed immediately. When the court wouldn't do that, Nu Skin held settlement discussions with lawyers representing Arata and other class members. In November 1991, a short four months after the suit had been filed, the court approved a settlement.

In one of its responses to Arata's charges, Nu Skin pointed out that she had inaccurately stated that the State of Michigan had issued a cease-and-desist order against Nu Skin. "There has never been such an order," Nu Skin lawyer John Shuff said. "In its seven-year history, no regulatory complaint has ever been filed against Nu Skin."

Shuff was right, technically. But his objection denied a more general truth. The California lawsuit had come during a tough period for Nu Skin. Throughout late 1991 and early 1992, the company was fighting off a number of states agencies—and the Federal Trade Commission—who were investigating its practices. Among these investigations:

- In Michigan, Attorney General Frank Kelley said in reference to Nu Skin: "The emphasis is on the sale of distributorships. The sale of a product is secondary. ...Many people who signed up with the hope of getting rich instead just got basements full of Nu Skin products." His office had fielded complaints from Nu Skin dealers who'd spent thousands of dollars on promotional materials, motivational tapes and Nu Skin products, only to find their neighborhoods saturated with other Nu Skin distributors. (While he didn't issue a cease-and-desist order, Kelley did file a notice of intent to sue Nu Skin.)
- In Pennsylvania, the state Bureau of Consumer Protection sued Nu Skin for operating an illegal pyramid scheme that was focused more on collecting up-front fees from new distributors than selling products. "My [department] began an investigation into allegations that some Nu Skin distributors were promising fantastic financial profits for prospective recruits and using possibly illegal pyramid-scheme tactics," said Pennsylvania Attorney General Ernie Preate Jr.
- In Ohio, Robert Hart, consumer protection assistant to the state attorney general, said his office had investigated concerns that Nu Skin "emphasized sales to distributors over the sale of retail product to people.... Our primary concern was that there was an overwhelming emphasis on getting new distributors into the program. Distributors were stockpiling inventory just to keep their place in the program with no way to sell it."
- In Connecticut, the state filed suit against Nu Skin. Attorney General Richard Blumenthal accused Nu Skin of violating the state's anti-pyramid law by emphasizing recruitment of new distributors rather than the sale of its products to consumers. "We're concerned, especially during difficult economic times, that unsuspecting consumers will be lured into believing the company's claims that they can earn more than $10,000 a month as a Nu Skin distributor," Blumenthal said.

Nu Skin resolved all of the actions without having to go to court or admit any wrongdoing. In exchange, it agreed to make several changes in the way it did business. It rewrote recruiting materials to emphasize the sale of products more and recruitment of other distributors less. It discontinued the requirement that distributors buy set amounts of product to maintain their positions. And, in most of the states, it agreed to pay fines or reimburse agencies for the cost of their investigations.

"Anytime you talk about multilevel marketing, a red flag pops up immediately, and it should," said CEO Roney, acknowledging that some people might draw an inference of guilt from the settlements. He admitted that sales and financial figures reported by multi-level companies and their distributors often "sound too good to be true." But he blamed most of Nu Skin's problems on over-aggressive distributors—who had no direct ties to the company.

Nu Skin's growth leveled off for a year or two in the early 1990s. But it rebounded and doubled its distributor base from 150,000 worldwide in 1992 to 300,000 in 1994. Then there was more trouble.

In 1994, Nu Skin paid $1.23 million to settle charges by the Federal Trade Commission that it exaggerated the effectiveness of its products. Among other things, FTC officials took issue with Nu Skin claims that its Nutriol Hair Fitness Preparation was as effective as the prescription hair-loss drug Minoxidil and that its Face Lift with Activator product was just as effective at removing facial wrinkles as the medication Retin-A.

Again, Nu Skin blamed the problem on rogue distributors—and said it had stopped doing business with about 10 of those involved.

In the same case, the FTC said Nu Skin misled potential distributors about how much they could earn by selling Nu Skin products. Nu Skin promotional materials cited by the FTC had mentioned earnings "in excess of $60,000 to $80,000 their first year" and claimed "a lot of other people" earned as much as $168,000 a year.

In addition to paying the big fine, the company agreed to tell prospective distributors what the average earnings were of all distributors—in

1994, this meant reporting that seven out of 10 distributors cleared an average of about $300 that year.

The Blurred Boundry Between Legal and Illegal

MLM is legal. But some MLM companies press the limits of the law—and become, essentially, illegal pyramid schemes. MLM programs are regularly accused by prosecutors of shady practices, including violating anti-pyramid laws and making false claims about "miracle" products.

Other problems: misrepresentation of potential income and "inventory loading," the practice of encouraging distributors to buy a basement full of products in order to reap a higher sales commission.

Much of that merchandise never gets sold. This practice is illegal in many states, and attorney generals are eagerly investigating complaints. "Every illegal pyramid is an MLM company," said Robert Ward, a Michigan assistant attorney general. "But not every MLM is an illegal pyramid."

Ward says that, in his state, the average multi-level marketer remains in business just 18 to 24 months. This observation is generally true. The turnover rate in MLM sales is high; in most programs, as many people drop out as join up in a given year. Which means, eventually, the MLM is going to run out of distributors.

Jeffrey Babener, an Oregon lawyer who specializes in MLM cases, says that an ordinary person can reasonably expect to make $300 to $1,000 per month from a legitimate program. If he or she works hard at it. He also says that, because MLM relies so heavily on social interaction, the programs work better in some regions than in others: "MLM does not do that well in the Northeast. It does best where people are friendly and are out and about—the Sunbelt, Bible Belt and California."

Still, MLM's ability to defy conventional marketing notions and generate eye-popping revenue attracts unscrupulous marketers and Ponzi perps. It will always be a source of concern for regulatory bodies at state and federal levels whose job it is to protect the unwary buyer from tall stories promising outrageous riches.

One MLM Program Crashes into the Law

Missouri-based Consumer Automotive Resources, Inc. (C.A.R.) was a clear case of an illegal pyramid scheme that tried to pass itself off as a legitimate MLM program. William Herbert and Robert Warren promoted the scam as a program for helping people buy cars inexpensively. In exchange for a steady flow of customers ready to buy, participating car dealers would offer deep discounts and good financing packages. Then, the dealers would pay a 5 percent commission to C.A.R. on the car sales resulting from references it made.

In the early 1990s, C.A.R. was looking for distributors who would—theoretically—earn commissions for locating the people who wanted to buy cars.

Like the worst MLM programs and most Ponzi schemes, C.A.R. was full of jargon and complex commission guidelines. To participate in the program, a distributor (called a "member") created a personal income center (PIC) by completing an application form and paying a $190 enrollment fee. The PIC was "activated" when the member recruited at least one other person in the program. The member earned maximum commissions when he or she recruited two people.

The initial member received a one-time commission of $70 for each person he or she recruited and a "network management commission" of $6 a month for each person enrolled in his or her downline group. C.A.R. executives claimed lamely that these commissions were advances against the 5 percent fees for car sales—rather than for recruiting dupes. (The monthly commissions paid to the members, however, depended only on the number of people enrolled in a downline pay group.)

As unlikely as it seems, the pitch worked. In December 1992, C.A.R.'s membership included approximately 1,400 distributors from 20 states.

C.A.R. offered members various tools for recruiting people. It scripted public informational meetings, provided a video and brochures, and gave distributors pointers for recruiting. However, in more than two years of operation, C.A.R. only sold two cars.

In December 1992, the scheme started running into trouble. The Missouri attorney general sought an order freezing C.A.R.'s assets, charging that it was an illegal pyramid scheme. The state filed for preliminary injunctions against C.A.R., CEO William Herbert and president Robert Warren.

The attorney general's office had used a decoy investigation to discover how the program worked. "We had this guy in there, and the things he saw were amazing," says one investigator involved in the case. "These guys were draining hundreds of dollars out of the poorest people around. They promised new cars—for free or close to it. It was like a lottery. And they were lining up to hand over the two hundred bucks."

The State charged Herbert and Warren with selling the right to participate in a pyramid sales scheme in violation of Missouri law. Under Missouri law, a pyramid sales scheme was defined as:

> *Any plan for the sale or distribution of goods, services or other property wherein a person for a consideration acquires the opportunity to receive a pecuniary benefit, which is not primarily contingent on the volume or quantity of goods, services, or other property sold or distributed for purposes of resale to consumers, and is based upon the inducement of additional persons, by himself or others, regardless of number, to participate in the same plan[.]*

In the spring of 1993, a Missouri court issued a summary judgment granting the attorney general's requests—and effectively closed down the scheme. While it considered the details of the case, the court ordered C.A.R. and its principals to stop selling memberships in the program and from promoting it in any way.

In May 1993, the same court concluded that the C.A.R. program was a pyramid sales scheme. This made its preliminary ruling permanent.

Cautionary Steps

From the Ponzi perp's perspective, there are many things that are appealing about MLM. A couple are psychological.

People who get ripped off by MLM programs are often unwilling to go public. They aren't likely to complain about a scheme full of their friends and relatives. Also, because of the entrepreneurial and patriotic rhetoric that marks recruiting meetings and MLM literature, people often assume that they're to blame if they aren't able to recruit enough people to make money.

To avoid these traps—and others—there are some basic steps anyone considering joining an MLM program should take before signing up:

- Determine how much of a distributor's income comes from sales rather than recruiting other distributors. One common standard is that 70 percent of a distributor's income should come from selling product.
- Ask how many levels of recruits a distributor has to bring in before making money. The geometric progression of recruitment tends to burn out by the third or fourth level.
- Be cautious of large start-up fees. Sleazy MLMs charge as much as they can. Since many states require reporting for franchises that cost more than $500, a lot of MLM's charge $499 to join.
- Get a written guarantee that the company will buy back unsold product. Some state laws require a 90 percent buy-back.
- Resist the temptation to invest just because you know the person selling the program. Most MLM programs rely on recruitment of friends and family. This gives people an unrealistic impression of the company's size and market presence.
- Ask how long it typically takes to get payment from the company. A legitimate MLM company should take no longer than 90 days to pay commissions and bonuses—and good ones will pay even sooner.
- Find out what expenses you'll have to pay. Sleazy MLM programs require that you attend sales conventions at your own expense in order to receive overrides and bonuses.
- Don't believe a promoter who says the venture has been approved by the state attorney general's office or any other regula-

tory agency. These offices don't approve of or endorse *any* business ventures.

In the end, the difference between legit and bogus schemes is simple: an illegal pyramid focuses on recruitment of new members to make money; a legitimate MLM program focuses on selling product.

The problem is that, in the heat of a dramatic recruitment meeting, the difference may be hard to see. "The whole concept of multilevel marketing is that they feed on people's emotions and greed," says Xavier University marketing professor Thomas Hayes. "Especially in hard economic times, people are looking for something easy, something that will make them rich. The only pure guarantee in a multilevel marketing scheme is that you will lose friends."

Case Study: Amway

No company has been investigated—and sued—for being an illegal pyramid scheme more often than Michigan-based Amway Corporation. As a result, Amway has emerged as a kind of dividing line for the legitimacy of multilevel marketing schemes. Its structure and methods have survived legal scrutiny. But any MLM firm that operates beyond the bounds of the Amway model may have trouble with the law.

Amway makes and sells home care products, such as laundry detergent and household cleaners; health and beauty products, such as cosmetics, vitamins and food supplements; "home tech" products, such as air and water treatment systems; and some commercial products, such as janitorial and food service items.

It moves these products and services exclusively through a network of some 300,000 independent distributors.

The company started in 1949. About 10 years later, Jay Van Andel and Richard DeVos—two successful distributors—decided that some of their suppliers were in danger of collapsing and that they should go into the business themselves, making their own products and selling them through the sales organization.

Within five years, they controlled the entire organization. As they grew the business, Van Andel and DeVos decided to look for products which were readily consumable, relatively low-priced, and competitive with those found in retail stores—all of which would lead to repeat sales. This product profile has become standard for MLM programs.

When a person becomes an Amway distributor (typically for an upfront investment of about $150) he or she receives an identification number to use when ordering anything from the company. That number tells Amway everything it needs to know about the distributor, including the identity of upliners—the people who recruited him or her.

Amway distributors generally sell products to friends and neighbors at parties or other informal gatherings. People who join Amway are urged to change their buying habits. One common pitch is: "Every time you buy from a retail outlet, you are sending someone else's kid to college." Newly sponsored distributors—the downliners—normally purchase their products from the distributor who personally sponsored them.

For each sale above a certain minimum, the Amway distributor makes a percentage computed under a graduated schedule. The percentage of sales volume the Amway distributor receives is called the *discount* and averages between 15 percent and 35 percent of the cost of each item sold. One Amway distributor explained the system:

> *Say you become a distributor and order $200 worth of products a month. You'd have a gross income of $66—that's a $60 discount from retail price, plus a $6 commission. Your annualized "income" is $792, nothing to quit the day job over.*
>
> *But if you recruit six people who also order $200 a month, you now are generating monthly group sales of $1,400 for Amway, and a monthly income of $150 for yourself ($90 in commissions, $60 in discounts for products you consume). If your six recruits duplicate themselves four times each, you'll take down $816 a month. If those 24 new recruits duplicate themselves twice, you'll have a network of 78 distributors and a monthly income of $2,138.*

When a distributor recruits a group of downliners that generates a certain level of sales (approximately $15,000 per month for six months during each year), that distributor becomes a "Direct Distributor" and is then entitled to purchase products directly from Amway.

Direct Distributors receive 3 percent of the personal group Business Volume of the Direct Distributors whom they sponsor. At that level both the sponsoring and the sponsored distributors are in the same performance bonus bracket—25 percent. The extra 3 percent is meant to cover recruitment and training costs.

Many observers—including federal regulators—have found the Amway system suspiciously complicated. In March 1975, the FTC issued a complaint against Amway that included five separate counts involving anti-competitive and deceptive practices. The Feds also alleged that Amway promoted the "endless chain" element of its pyramid structure as much or more than it promoted the actual sale of goods or services.

The agency noted that the Amway Career Manual for distributors explained how to recruit distributors by appealing to the financial goals of prospects. The Manual then offered specific questions for recruiters to ask. These included:

- What are some of your dreams? Do you want a new car, a new house, college education for your children?
- Do you want retirement income that will afford you a comfortable standard of living?
- What income do you want six years from now? Are you willing to work hard to get this?
- How much would you like as a continuing income? Would you work for your goal?
- Would you be interested if I could show you a way you can make your dreams come true?

These loaded questions—which are so basic and vague that they beg simplistic answers—are typical of MLM recruitment tactics.

The Feds also argued that Amway fixed prices at which products and services could be sold through its network. They cited one of the company's Rules of Conduct:

> *No distributor shall sell products sold under the Amway label for less than the specified retail price, when making sales to persons who are not distributors, except where commercial discounts are authorized to be given. No distributor shall give a greater discount than that authorized in the appropriate Amway Product Sales Manual.*

The FTC noted that, to enforce this rule, Amway threatened termination of the distributorship to discourage retail price cutting.

Finally, the Feds argued that Amway, even without actual proof of economic failure, was "doomed to failure" and contained an "intolerable potential to deceive." This all stemmed from the alleged fact that Amway would saturate its markets, leaving distributors unable to sell the detergent and household products.

Amway fought back against the FTC charges. It pointed out that its distributorships were not for sale and sponsoring distributors received no profit from the act of sponsoring. "It is only after the sponsored distributor begins to buy products that the sponsoring distributor will receive income," the company argued.

To receive a bonus, distributors had to resell at least 70 percent of the products they purchased each month. And the company's so-called "ten-customer rule" held that distributors could not receive bonuses unless they proved a sale to each of 10 different retail customers during each month.

Amway also pointed out that it had, since its beginning, a policy of buying back any unused marketable products from a distributor whose inventory was not moving or who wished to leave the business. Most illegal pyramids don't do this.

While Amway admitted that it published a suggested retail price list, it denied fixing prices. It claimed:

> *[E]ach Amway distributor is an independent businessman who purchases products from Amway for cash. Title to these products actually passes from the company to the distributor under a purchase and sales agreement. Thus...each buyer has latitude in determining what price he will charge for the product....*

In June 1978, Administrative Law Judge James Timony ruled on the case—and saw things mostly Amway's way. Among his findings:

- In order to recruit an effective sales force, Amway encourages its distributors to sponsor new distributors. This is not, however, a pyramid plan.
- In the Amway system, the incentive to recruit comes from the commission distributors receive on product sales by sponsored distributors in their organizations. But, by several rules, Amway requires that commissions are not paid unless the products are sold to consumers.
- Amway has successfully entered the soap and detergents market because its distributors sell directly to consumers in their homes or businesses, rather than through retail grocery stores.

The Court also found the FTC's charges that Amway lied about how easy it was to make money unfounded. On this count, It concluded:

> *There is no doubt that the Amway Sales and Marketing Plan is designed to catch the interest of a prospective recruit by appealing to material interests.... But the Amway plan also makes clear the idea that work will be involved, and that the material rewards to be gained will depend on the amount and quality of work done.*

The judge gave particular attention to the FTC's allegations that Amway was doomed to failure because it saturated its markets. On this count, he noted:

> *The preponderance of the evidence in the record does not support the allegation of "saturation." Amway is not a "modern-day version of the chain letter." [Its] system does not create the potential for massive deception present in a pyramid distribution scheme.... Unlike the pyramid companies, Amway and its distributors do not make money unless products are sold to consumers.*

In short, Amway was exonerated. All it received from the FTC investigation was a small fine for some misleading promotional and advertising statements. The bad publicity took a toll, though. Some former employees sued the company for brainwashing them; the suits gave life to talk that Amway was a quasi-religious cult. Sales, which had been growing steadily for 30 years, plateaued.

In 1986, just as the company was entering another growth spurt, the FTC took another shot. It fined Amway $100,000 for illegally inflating earnings projections. Rather than drag out this administrative action with a legal challenge, Amway worked out an agreement with the Feds. It changed its business plan brochures to point out that the average monthly income for active distributors was $65. It also stated in bold type that only one in 82 distributors sold enough products to earn $2,138 a month.

Many people remained skeptical about Amway, though.

In 1996, the company ran into some unexpected trouble. Several record labels sued Amway, charging that motivational videotapes produced by some of its top salespeople were sprinkled with pop songs they'd never received permission to use.

The lawsuit, filed by the Recording Industry Association of America, claimed that top Amway distributors sold the tapes to lower-level recruits through the mail or at sales conventions. And the tapes weren't cheap, running up to $25 each. The RIAA lawsuit went on to claim that the copyright violations entitled the injured record companies to at least $11 million in damages.

Some of the tapes mentioned in the lawsuit showed top Amway distributors—called "diamonds" in company jargon—enjoying the big homes and flashy cars Amway sales provided.

Aside from catching the record industry's attention, the tapes bother many regulators. In many cases, the business of promoting the Amway dream is a thriving industry all by itself—and one that more closely resembles an illegal pyramid.

One of the diamonds named in the RIAA lawsuit was Dexter Yager. Yager was a famous character in Amway lore. He came from humble origins, without much formal education, to build a downline network that accounted for as much as a third of Amway's total sales.

(Most people who know Amway readily admit Yager has been as important to the company's growth as either of its founders. Many people in the business call him the "patron saint of multilevel marketing.")

From all of this, Yager made tens of millions of dollars a year in bonuses. And he has many of the quirks of a Ponzi perp. He owns a huge home near Charlotte, North Carolina. He has various Mercedes-Benzes, Rolls-Royces and Jaguars. He boasts about his political connections—having met Ronald Reagan, George Bush and various other pro-business pols.

Of course, Yager is a rarity. He joined a fast-growing MLM firm in its early years. He brought a zeal to selling that would have probably set him apart anywhere. And he has stayed with the venture for most of his working life. In these ways, he is like the investor who bought Microsoft stock at its initial offering. It would be very hard—if not impossible—for a person joining Amway today to replicate Yager's success.

The nature of the system pushes Yager to spread a different message among the Amway faithful. About once a week, at meetings all over North America, he offers motivational speeches to distributors. The talks often run two hours or longer—and have a spontaneous feeling, even if they're well-practiced. He's stoking the fires of his downline troops.

Like many Ponzi perps, Yager makes a big deal about having the courage to dream. He walks his audiences through dream homes; he tells them to dream about owning fancy cars, big boats and personal jets. "I help [downliners] dream," he says. "Most people don't dream enough."

Dexter Yager presses the line of legitimacy that Amway has fought hard to establish. While critics question what they call his "lottery mentality," Yager is not a Ponzi perp. He has the legally-tested Amway guidelines as a frame of reference.

Not all MLM promoters do.

CHAPTER 15

Faith, Religion and New Age Gurus

Multilevel marketing programs and pyramid schemes use the rhetoric and psychology of religious evangelism to recruit and motivate distributors. They do this because many people confuse the *faith* they feel in religious contexts with *trust* of people or institutions.

Some Ponzi perps decide that the rhetoric and psychology isn't enough. They use religion and spirituality explicitly to fleece investors.

Con men using religion as their pitch are nothing new. They trace back, through the novel *Elmer Gantry*, to the time of Christ (who was infuriated by money changers in the Temple)...and even beyond that. But the same social and technology issues that make the 1990s a high time for Ponzi schemes encourage *religious* Ponzi schemes.

The Ponzi Scheme Church of Hakeem

Few religious Ponzi perps can match Hakeem Abdul Rasheed for incorrigibility and sheer gall. Rasheed founded the Church of Hakeem in Oakland, California, as a non-profit religious corporation in March 1977. The Church obtained a tax-exempt status under Internal Revenue Code Section 501(c)(3).

In December 1977, Rasheed held a meeting with about 10 members of the Church and announced the creation of a program he called the "Blessing Plan Covenant." Participation in the Plan was open to anyone who paid a onetime enrollment fee of $25. Upon becoming a member, a person could then make "donations" to the Church—and receive a 400 percent investment return as a "blessing" or dividend.

Rasheed said that the goal of the Plan was to create 10,000 millionaires. He was looking for people who had faith and wanted wealth. In January 1978, a month after his announcement, Rasheed renamed the Plan the "Dare-to-be-Rich Program."

The principal method by which Rasheed promoted the Dare-to-be-Rich Program was a series of "Celebrations." These were meetings conducted personally by Rasheed. At the Celebrations, Rasheed described the Program: become a member of the Church; invest in the Dare-to-be-Rich Program; receive a 400 percent return on investment within a prescribed time period; and become one of the Church's 10,000 millionaires. Rasheed said that the 400 percent return on investment was possible because the Church had "national and international" investments, which generated "tremendous profits" that the Church chose to make available to investing members.

As the membership grew, Rasheed relied increasingly on a small group of staff personnel to solicit the general public by restating the elements of the scheme. By July 1979, the Dare-to-be-Rich Program had grown so large that it required an organized staff which was formally instructed on how to promote the Program.

Rasheed was a big believer in direct mail. The Church printed and mailed recruitment brochures to a wide cross-section of the public. Internally, these brochures were known as "Calendars." They invited the general public to attend Church Celebrations and contained—among other things—the following statement:

> *You Can Turn: $25 into $100 in 70 days, $250 into $1,000 in 90 days, $25,000 into $1,000,000 in 9 months. The Church of Hakeem, Inc. is an international as well as national church function. International and national investments return "Profits" which the church does not choose to keep. So it distributes its "Profits" to its active ministers only. These "Profits" we call an "Increase of God."*

The Church also printed and distributed tickets for free entry to Celebrations, which contained promotional statements of the wealth to be gained through investment in the Dare-to-be-Rich Program.

In fact, Rasheed followed Carlo Ponzi's steps carefully. He paid big profits to early investors with money invested by later ones. He counted on word of mouth to promote his scheme in black communities throughout the Bay Area. Within a few months, the money was coming in faster than the Church could count it.

The scheme only lasted a year—but it was a busy year. During November and December 1978, the Church collected at least $3.6 million through the Dare-to-be-Rich Program. Rasheed poured money into a number of questionable investments, including a Church-related private school, a yacht and Rolls-Royces. He didn't invest in any for-profit businesses, national or international.

On January 17, 1979, Internal Revenue Service agents seized all of the Church of Hakeem's assets and effectively shut down the Dare-to-be-Rich Program. At that point, at least 4,064 people had paid the membership fee and Rasheed had promised total returns of no less than $30.5 million. A flurry of civil and criminal charges followed.

At his criminal trial, Rasheed testified that money in bank accounts seized by the IRS, like all money invested in Church activities of any sort, had been obtained from member donations. He'd told Church members, investors and the IRS that he held this money as a "trustee."

This wasn't exactly true. Rasheed admitted that he'd converted money from the investors in the Church to his own personal use. The Feds had determined that Rasheed had purchased a yacht for $915,000 and transferred $1.5 million into accounts in his name at several local banks. In doing this, he'd ceased to be a trustee (if, in fact, he'd ever been one) and become a thief.

The IRS considers the money thieves steal as income and taxes it, just like legitimate money that working people earn. This was part of the reason the IRS had seized the Church's assets—to collect $1,533,853 it concluded Rasheed owed for 1978.

In February 1980, Rasheed was convicted of six counts of mail fraud arising from his activities in the Church. He was sentenced to 15 years in a federal penitentiary.

In March 1980, the court certified a class action lawsuit in which burned investors could seek money back from Rasheed and what was left of his Church. They were able to proceed with the facts established by the criminal case. They won the case, but neither the church nor Rasheed had any money to collect.

In March 1981, the same federal court which had handled the criminal and civil cases against Rasheed considered a lawsuit the Church investors filed against the IRS. They wanted their yacht back.

One problem: The Feds had already sold the yacht. So, the investors wanted the $915,000 it had been worth when the IRS seized it. The court ruled for them, concluding that:

> *The question before this Court is whether the specific property obtained through the misappropriation of church membership fees and donations by means of a Ponzi or pyramid scheme can be levied upon by the government for the purpose of satisfying the tax obligation arising [from] its passage into Rasheed's possession. We think not.*

The Feds eventually agreed to rebate the money it got for the yacht at auction back to the investors. The IRS was left with a $2.6 judgment against Rasheed—but no way to collect from the bankrupt perp. It was the same position the investors had been in a year earlier.

And the saga wasn't quite over yet. After serving six years of his 15-year sentence in a federal prison, Rasheed was transferred to a San Francisco halfway house to serve the rest of his sentence. In prison, he had been a model inmate; once out, he reverted to his old ways.

In May 1986, Rasheed fled from the halfway house after depositing $178,500 in stolen checks into a Michigan bank account—and then writing more than $20,000 in checks on the bogus deposits. He was captured in San Francisco a short time later.

Back in federal court, Rasheed claimed that he'd merely left the halfway house as scheduled: "I had no intention of doing anything illegal. I was on the square."

A few months later, after a trial in which the jury took 26 minutes to find Rasheed guilty of escaping the halfway house, he was sentenced to an additional five years in prison.

A Slightly More Subtle Approach

There's no doubt that people trust their pastors and people they meet through their churches. Ponzi perps know this—and don't usually hesitate to exploit this presumption of trust.

Exploiting the presumption of trust doesn't require religious piety. It simply plays on the social element of church, which is infused with trust and optimism. This relieves the perp of any direct connection to religion—he or she can simply act like a well-meaning church-goer, who happens to trade silver futures or sell pre-paid phone cards.

Of course, the pitch is always strongest when the person making it is the pastor. More than anyone, he or she benefits from the trust and optimism people feel when they socialize with fellow church-goers.

Robert Tilton, a controversial Texas televangelist who bills himself as the "Pastor to America," exemplifies the issues that arise when the social element of religion meets the mechanics of a Ponzi scheme.

Tilton has a background that suggests a Ponzi perp. A baby-boomer, he acted like James Dean—black leather jacket and minor scrapes with the law—in his Richardson, Texas, high school. Not much of an intellect, he bounced around Texas Tech University and several junior colleges. He talked about studying architecture but ended up working construction.

In the late 1960s, Tilton drifted to Los Angeles. There, he spent most of his free time going to parties and sampling the expanded consciousness of the West Coast drug culture.

On a trip home to Dallas in 1968, he met Martha Ann Phillips. They were married a few months later before a Justice of the Peace. The newlyweds spent their honeymoon dabbling in the just-starting New Age movement in and around Santa Barbara, California.

By the summer of 1969, the Tiltons had moved back to Dallas. One night, two evangelical "Jesus freaks" knocked on their door. Tilton said he and his wife were "transformed" when one of the young men said, "Come with me, and I'll make you a fisher of men."

In 1974, after Tilton had been able to put away some money from working for a Dallas home builder, the couple decided to become itinerant evangelists. They sold almost everything they owned, bought a used travel trailer and a secondhand gospel tent. They hit the road with their two young children.

The family spent time on the revival-meeting circuit, preaching in small towns from north Florida to east Texas. After two years on the road, the Tiltons settled in Houston. There, Tilton worked with John Osteen, the pastor of a 7,000-member fundamentalist church. He still worked an occasional construction job to make ends meet.

In early 1976, Tilton had a "revelation." He'd preach a message that combined conservative Christianity, New Age spirituality and entrepreneurial wealth-building. He went back to Dallas to start the Word of Faith Family Church—which was some leased space in a former YMCA building in suburban Farmers Branch. Word spread about "Brother Bob" and his unusual theology of prosperity.

Tilton encouraged his flock to follow his advice for making money in multilevel marketing and other bootstrap operations. This harkened back to early Protestant America, when material success was supposed to reflect God's favor. Word of Faith's annual budget jumped from about $27,000 in 1976 to $250,000 in 1977, $750,000 in 1978 and $1.8 million in 1980.

Like many pyramid schemes, Tilton's investment pitches tend to emphasize simplicity and profitability rather than the details of any particular business or market. In the mid-1980s, he moved his ministry to modern pulpit—a television show called *Success-N-Life*.

Among his sources of inspiration, Tilton said, was TV real-estate pitchman and alleged Ponzi perp Dave Del Dotto. Rather than just talking about the righteousness of worldly success, Tilton started offering viewers specific stories of people who'd made it. "Sure, some people think the TV shows are kind of exaggerated," says one supporter. "But you've got to realize who he's trying to reach: the down-and-out, the lowest of the low, the most desperate."

In the mid-1980s, Word of Faith considered $6 million to be a very good year. Six years later, annual receipts exceeded $100 million and the ministry had 850 employees. Tilton's annual salary was estimated at more than $1 million.

The Tiltons claimed to have 8,000 members in their church. But, more importantly, they received 220,000 letters a month from people who watched their television program. No longer a struggling start-up, *Success-N-Life* was carried nationally on 212 television stations. The show was seen in an average of 199,000 households each day.

But Tilton's rapid growth and aggressive pro-business proselytizing had led to some disgruntled investors and attracted the attention of the regulators. In late 1991, Texas authorities told Tilton that his Word of Faith Family Church & World Outreach Center was being investigated on charges of consumer fraud. The state attorney general was seeking a court order to seize Tilton's financial records...and was sharing his information with federal investigators.

In November 1991, the television news magazine *Prime-Time Live* aired a story that raised allegations of mail fraud in Tilton's ministry. The news show portrayed him as a huckster of dubious pyramid schemes. Brother Bob angrily denied the charges and dismissed the news media in general as "agents of the devil."

Criticisms about Tilton's lavish lifestyle seemed to unnerve him. He and his wife stopped wearing their Rolex watches and driving their Mercedes-Benzes. But their efforts came a little too late to quiet their critics. "Tilton, in terms of just being an outright sham...is just awful. And he may be the only [television preacher] I've ever said this about," said Jeff Hadden, a professor of sociology at the University of Virginia. "If Tilton believes himself, he has created the greatest act of self-deception of all of them."

J.C. Joyce, a Tulsa lawyer who had become Tilton's main spokesman, responded to Hadden harshly: "I guarantee you he has never set foot in Robert Tilton's church. It doesn't take any giant to critique something. Any fool can do it."

Declining to say how much money Word of Faith brought in annually, Joyce said, "The church pays every single obligation it has on time. That's the only thing that's important. It doesn't make any difference whether the church is making $2,000 or $100 million or $125 million.... All the man wants is to be left alone to preach."

A New Age Prophet Battles Ponzi Complaints

There are many parts of America, and the rest of the word, where traditional religion doesn't have much influence. Even in these places, though, there's the need for some framework of spiritual thought. Enter the New Age movement, which combines watered-down psychology with the softest elements of religion and mysticism and adds a dash of occult superstition. The result is usually an outlook on life that avoids guilt and emphasizes physical and emotional comfort.

Many people dismiss the New Age movement as a ridiculous product of West Coast flakiness. But it does create a religious-like trust in some. Ponzi perps know this.

In January 1995, the White House confirmed that Anthony Robbins, a California-based motivational speaker and New Age guru, was summoned to the presidential retreat at Camp David, Maryland, for a consultation with Bill Clinton.

The meeting became a subject of derision in Washington. "The president has had a lot of individuals come up and visit and talk with him at Camp David," said a White House spokesman, trying to downplay the meeting's significance. "Robbins is merely the latest on the list."

Robbins Research International, the guru's company, was a little coy in its response. A spokeswoman said: "Tony has a consistent policy. Any meetings he conducts, particularly with President Clinton, are private matters. They're privileged, and he does not provide details."

This response implied that the meetings with Clinton were regular occurrences.

The Camp David meeting was a rite of passage to legitimacy for Robbins, whose background was tarred with allegations that he was just a particularly glib (and, at 6'8", particularly tall) Ponzi perp.

Robbins, who refers to himself as a "peak-performance consultant," has often said his life's work is helping people with "image problems realize their full potential." He made millions of dollars from selling franchises that marketed his positive-thinking seminars. The business was lucrative; but it brought him legal troubles from disgruntled franchisees. Most of these former business associates made the same—or at least a similar—complaint: breach of contract or fraud.

Many individual suits were filed in 1991 and 1992. Some franchisees charged that Robbins violated exclusivity rights given to franchisees in a particular region.

Some of these suits took these complaints a step farther and alleged that Robbins was running a Ponzi scheme. They claimed that Robbins' California-based holding company was flooding the market with new franchises, effectively guaranteeing that existing franchises would never meet the profit levels originally promised.

In one suit—which was eventually settled—Dallas, Texas, franchisee Larry Sergeant charged Robbins with violating his exclusivity rights in northern Texas and running a Ponzi scheme. Sergeant claimed that Robbins' franchise delivered no goods or services, even though it had taken his $20,000.

According to Sergeant, Robbins set out to make money, not by selling the product in question (video seminars) but by attracting new investors (franchisees). Sergeant claimed that only Robbins could profit from the scheme. He and other investors criticized the video and audio tapes they'd received as "useless sales pitches."

As a group, they charged that the product not only lacked substance and value, but the franchise plan was doomed to fail since franchisees did not receive the exclusivity promised them, nor any marketing or advertising backing from Robbins Research International. Sergeant told one newspaper:

> *Tony Robbins has made an art form out of stretching the truth, amplifying things, painting incredibly vivid pictures in three dimensions with you in them—with a smile on your face, your favorite music playing, seeing your favorite colors.... But sooner or later, he (cheats) everybody he does business with. And the thing that scares me is, he may get away with it.*

While Robbins never lost a suit at trial, he settled many. By 1993, he had stopped selling franchises for video seminars. Unfortunately for Robbins, federal investigators also wanted a piece of him.

In 1995, Robbins settled charges by the Federal Trade Commission alleging that he had violated federal franchise laws. While denying any wrongdoing, Robbins paid a fine and fees of more than $221,000. He indicated that settlement was simply "the most prudent and efficient way to resolve this dispute with the FTC."

That was probably true. According to the FTC, Robbins Research International sold franchises that granted the right to run self-help seminars featuring Robbins' videotapes, *Unlimited Power* and *Power to Influence*. The franchises cost between $5,000 and $90,000, depending on the territory they covered.

The FTC alleged that financial information provided by Robbins and his company misled investors, who never made the kind of profits mentioned in Robbins' recruitment materials. The Feds explained that Robbins and his company told franchisees that in a given month they could make between $6,250 and $25,000 from presenting between 25 to 100 seminars. "Few, if any, franchisees have been able to sell that many seminars or make these earnings," the FTC said.

Case Study: Sell America Scams a West Virginia Church

In 1990, the United States Corps of Engineers determined that a church building owned by the First Assembly of God in Matewan,

West Virginia, was located on an unprotectable flood plain. The Corps wanted to use the Church property to complete a flood-wall project along the Tug Fork of the Big Sandy River. It condemned the building and compensated the Matewan Church with a $375,000 lump-sum payment.

The Matewan Church paid off its existing debts with the proceeds and deposited the remaining $200,000 in the Matewan National Bank pending the construction of a new church building.

The Matewan Church needed a building site for the new church. It enlisted the aid of the Reverend Gordon Shinn, who was a pastor of the Heritage Assembly of God in nearby Dublin, Virginia. Shinn had construction and engineering experience.

While looking for suitable real estate, Shinn visited and "fellowshipped" with the Matewan congregation. About this time, he learned that church leaders were dissatisfied with the interest rate they were earning on the $200,000 at the Matewan National Bank. The leaders asked Shinn to help them find a better return.

At this point, the trouble started. Shinn accepted the assignment to find a better rate of return. He had no financial background, so he turned to acquaintances who did. After talking with several of these contacts, Shinn was referred to a Kentuckian named John Holtzclaw, who—by star-crossed circumstance—was at the time involved in a Ponzi investment scheme operating under the name Sell America.

Sell America was an Alabama corporation involved in various bogus multilevel marketing programs.

Over the course of several weeks, Shinn had many conversations with Holtzclaw and several of his associates. According to Shinn, Holtzclaw spun a convincing tale of the golden opportunities awaiting those who would participate in the Sell America program.

Shinn was dazzled. At a February 14, 1991 meeting with the Board of Trustees of the Matewan Church, he relayed Holtzclaw's big talk of riches without risk.

Shinn arranged another meeting with the Board for a few nights later to complete the deal. At the second meeting, Holtzclaw and his cronies made a presentation that included an agreement authorizing them to carry away the money for an "investment" in the Sell America program. Shinn did his part to close the deal. He would later testify, shamelessly:

> *I informed the board of trustees that they dealt with gold-minted coins, not with mines or speculation.... I informed them in my presentation that the investment was risk-free. I told them, in explanation of investments, that it was similar to buying a piece of pie. A restaurant buys a pie for, say, two dollars...and sells each piece for two dollars apiece. And that's how [Sell America] generated profits. They buy in large volume and then sell the individual pieces.*
>
> *I also included a river analogy where a stream starts quite small but as tributaries are added to it, it becomes larger and more powerful. And for investors in firms like Sell America, each tributary added to the size of their buying power. In other words, the size of the river would grow as more tributaries joined it.*

None of the Board members remembered any discussion of rivers, tributaries or pieces of pie. A few remembered that four professionals and a preacher presented a "risk-free" investment that would yield an 18 percent return—and that one of Holtzclaw's cronies flashed a few gold coins. (Of course, since the members proceeded to lose Church money in a fool-hearty investment, they had reason to claim sketchy memories.)

Shinn said that Holtzclaw and his crew gave every person attending the second Board meeting a Sell America brochure with gold coins on the front of it. The brochure described the scheme's "Unitary Marketing Plan" as follows:

> *You start with an initial down payment of as little as $60. As you sell Gold Eagle coin purchase agreements, you can use the commissions you earn to complete your own purchase agreements. Upon completion of each agreement you can receive the coins or, if you choose, have the value of the coins applied toward the initial payment required for the*

next higher denomination purchase agreement. Of course, your earnings are based solely upon your own efforts and abilities.

Holtzclaw stated that there would be very little risk involved because the "money would be in gold coins or be in a federally audited trust fund." However, he never explained what *federally audited* was supposed to mean. He also said that gold was a solid investment because its price always paralleled the price of bread. (This may sound convincingly biblical, but it isn't solid economics.)

Like a character from a Damon Runyon story, one of Holtzclaw's cronies then proceeded to hand around a gold coin and say, "This is what you're investing in and that's your security right there."

All of this meant very little. The scheme wasn't about gold, it was about recruiting other suckers. And it was destined to fail. Recruiting four investors at x dollars each in order to receive a commission of 3x dollars is a rotten deal for the participant—and a capital cost so high that the company isn't likely to have enough money to do anything but slosh proceeds around.

As one lawyer noted: "The Sell America deal could only appeal to a complete cement-head." The Board of the Matewan Church may not have had cement heads; but it did have blind trust. The church secretary was dispatched to get a check. The agreement was signed. And the $200,000 left Matewan in the hands of Shinn and Holtzclaw.

Shinn, Holtzclaw and their cronies cashed the check and wired the money to Alabama in payment for the bogus "gold contracts." They took large fees for landing the big check. Finally aware of its folly, the Matewan Church sued everyone involved in the scam. The suits, filed in stages during February and March 1996, alleged that no gold coins were ever purchased. As one court dryly noted:

The Church lost all of its money. The congregation was shocked. The trustees felt guilty. The pyramid pharaohs in Alabama were prosecuted...and received light sentences.

Criminal charges followed. Shinn, Holtzclaw and several associates were charged with conspiracy, interstate transportation of money taken by fraud, fraudulent sale of securities and fraudulent purchase of securities. Each faced up to 30 years in prison and a fine of up to $1.5 million if convicted of all charges.

Shinn quickly cooperated with federal prosecutors. Holtzclaw and his three cronies were all convicted at trial. But the January 1997 federal court decision *United States of America v. John Holtzclaw, et al.* overturned those guilty verdicts. It said—in plain language—that greedy investors are not victims.

The critical issue in the decision was whether the pyramid scheme sold by Shinn and Holtzclaw was an "investment contract" and, thus, a security. The prosecutors, arguing that the scheme *was* an investment contract, asked the court to limit its consideration to the statements made by Shinn at a the second Board meeting. They argued that these promises were a "security" under federal law.

The court disagreed. It had to look further and analyze the transaction "on the basis of the content of the instruments in question, the purposes intended to be served, and the factual setting as a whole."

In fine print, the Sell America brochure stated that what was being purchased by investors was not gold coins at ridiculously inflated prices but the *idea* that investors could make money by doing unto others what had been done unto them.

The court concluded that no reasonable juror could conclude that the substance of the transaction was anything other than a pyramid scheme. So, the case did not involve a security. Accordingly, the court overturned the convictions against Holtzclaw and his cronies.

In the wake of the federal court's ruling, Cynthia Rife—the secretary-treasurer of the Matewan Church—said the 70-member congregation had lost all of its money and was deeply in debt. "Several members and Pastor Thomas Larinson signed personal notes to pay the vendors. We now have a new building, but it's not paid for and it will be a while before the notes can be paid," she complained.

CHAPTER 16

Charities and Not-for-profit Organizations

Religion and spirituality may be fonts of trust for some; but, in a secular age, other institutions have taken over as the most trustworthy in many people's lives. For these people, involvement in charities and not-for-profit (NFP) organizations offer the feelings of camaraderie, reflection and renewal that—in earlier times—religion offered.

The Ponzi perps haven't missed this trend. As a result, charities and NFPs have been the scenes of some dramatic Ponzi schemes in the 1980s and 1990s.

In many NFPs, management is granted considerable autonomy. These managers often act as the de facto owners of their organizations, accountable to no one or to a board of trustees or directors appointed by management in the first place. This loophole of accountability can come into tight focus when economic realities force an NFP to act entrepreneurially.

Most NFPs derive their revenues from a combination of endowments and current fundraising. As the segment has become more professional, fundraising has become more scientific—even small, local charities are usually pretty sophisticated about building donor lists and scheduling fundraising drives.

With the fundraising done well, the remaining issue is how the endowment is managed. This is where the Ponzi perp will try to enter the equation.

At a time of time of intense competition for resources and pressure to provide more programs, organizations often become more aggressive with their investment strategies. They become vulnerable to promises of higher returns and the willingness to assume more risk.

How a Ponzi Perp Played on NFP Trust

California-based United Grocer's Clearinghouse was a Ponzi scheme that marketed itself to naive investors by affiliating itself with charities and NFPs. In the end, the investors, charities and NFPs were all in the same boat; they'd been fleeced in a not-so-creative Ponzi scam.

The pitch was pretty simple. UGC printed coupon books that provided deep discounts and free samples of consumer dry goods. Consumers could purchase family-size packages of things like breakfast cereal and coffee by mail from UGC for less than a dollar per item.

The company claimed it made its money from advertisements that other companies paid to have mailed along with the cereal and coffee. To market the coupon books, UGC enlisted charities and NFPs like church groups or Scout troops. The NFPs would buy the coupon books for between $10 and $15 each and then sell them to supporters for $30 each. Each book had 30 coupons, so consumers could save between $30 and $60 with each book they used.

At least that was how it was *supposed* to work.

UGC opened its doors during the summer of 1995. In less than a year, it had sold more 200,000 coupon books and taken in about $3 million. However, while UGC was growing through word-of-mouth in charitable organization circles, complaints from consumers slowly started trickling into the offices of consumer protection advocates throughout the western U.S.

Initially, consumers were able to redeem coupons for the merchandise. UGC claimed that it would send the cereal or coffee within one day of receiving coupons, but it actually took up to eight weeks. "The reason was simple," recalls one investigator who looked into UGC's operations. "[They] staked a little cash up front to buy some cereal and coffee. Then, they only spent a little of their cash flow to buy more. They couldn't ever catch up because they were running behind from the beginning."

The delays caused bigger problems. In order to redeem UGC coupons, consumers were supposed to contact the company at its Costa Mesa, California, headquarters. But, if consumers contacted the manufacturers whose products were included in the UGC coupon books, those companies denied any connection to—or even knowledge of—UGC.

In early 1996, the California Attorney General's office began an investigation of UGC. In March, Attorney General Dan Lungren announced a lawsuit against UGC. Lungren's office based its charges on simple math: UGC had sold more than 210,00 books of 30 coupons each; this meant more than 6.3 million coupons were in circulation. UGC executives disputed the number as too high—but were unable to say how many had actually been sold.

UGC earned 40 cents per coupon from advertising sales but spent $7 to buy and ship each box of cereal. This meant that, if even one in four of the circulated coupons were returned at once, UGC would need more than $10 million to ship product to consumers.

Since the company had almost no financial resources to cover this kind of cost, the lawsuit concluded that UGC was a Ponzi scheme that would leave "hundreds of thousands of consumers with worthless coupons and many coupon book distributors with a supply of worthless coupons."

The lawsuit asked for $2 million in civil penalties and restitution for consumers affected by the scheme. In addition, it asked for an injunction prohibiting the company from further violations of the California Consumer Protection Law.

UGC president Steven Lee started out defending his company's practices vigorously...maybe a little *too* vigorously: "All of this talk of Ponzi schemes, a house of cards, fraud...is completely incorrect. This is not a fraud and nobody's being ripped off."

But this aggressive tactic didn't last long. In an April meeting with deputies from the attorney general's office, UGC agreed to a preliminary injunction, which allowed it to remain in business but prohibited it from selling any new distributorships without the appropriate registration. The injunction also prohibited the company from making any further misrepresentations.

UGC suspended its California operations a few weeks later, blaming its problems on media attention to the lawsuit. Telephone calls to the company were answered with a recorded message that told UGC coupon holders that they'd soon be able to use the coupons to get discounts on name-brand pantyhose. The recorded message concluded, lamely: "Both the attorney general's filing and unfavorable media coverage have had a devastating effect on UGC's ability to generate new revenues and to operate its day-to-day business."

The message went on to say that company management had tried to restructure but "could not overcome the stigma that was created by the negative publicity heaped on UGC by the media back in March and April of this year."

Word of the state attorney general's suit stunned coupon holders and officials at NFPs and schools that had used UGC coupons.

Southern California's Irvine Education Foundation, which ran a fund-raising event in the fall of 1995, was one of the first big groups to use UGC's coupon books. IEF Executive Director Elizabeth Thomas said that her group had netted about $15,000 from a fund-raising drive in late 1995. It was considering a rebate to everyone who'd bought books.

At C.H. Taylor Elementary School in West Valley City, Utah, students had sold 200 coupon books valued at $6,000. According to school principal Orwin Draney: "Of that, $2,000 was for us and $4,000 went to [UGC]." He was hoping to offer some other service in place of the coupons.

By August, UGC's recorded announcement had changed from whining about the attorney general to saying that it had begun a liquidation under Chapter 7 of the Bankruptcy Code.

Most of the NFPs that had sold UGC coupons felt liable for returning money to supporters—though they weren't, legally.

Albert Sheldon, an assistant attorney general in California, explained that people who'd bought coupons were creditors. They would receive notice of UGC's bankruptcy when it was filed. But they would be standing in a long line of creditors—headed by Federal Express, which claimed more than $400,000 in unpaid delivery bills. "There really isn't much [coupon holders] can do," Sheldon said. "Our investigation has led us to believe there aren't any huge sums of money lying around to make restitution."

Using the NFP Structure to Build a Ponzi Scheme

An even more creative approach is to set up an NFP as a vehicle for Ponzi fraud. A perp who starts a "nonprofit" can take advantage of the presumption of goodwill that many people feel toward the things. And, in some cases, it's not only *people* who make the mistaken presumption...it's sometimes banks or governments that do.

Lee Sutliffe exploited this goodwill with a Missouri-based NFP called First Humanics Corporation (FHC). FHC turned out to be a Ponzi scheme—and serves as a good illustration of the mechanics of an NFP fraud.

The company was incorporated in the 1970s as Faith Evangelistic Mission Corporation, a tax-exempt NFP which was intended to own and operate church-affiliated nursing homes in the Midwest. In July 1984, Sutliffe gained control of the company and changed its name to First Humanics. He used FHC's tax-exempt status to issue so-called "Section 103 bonds."

The interest paid by these bonds is often high and always exempt from federal income tax. The bonds, which aren't registered or rated like corporate bonds, are usually issued by local governments; but NFPs that provide public services can issue them, too.

Between 1984 and 1987, FHC acquired 21 nursing homes and paid for the purchases by issuing a total of over $80 million in Section 103 bonds. Sutliffe—a Kansas City financier with a long history of troubled bond deals—treated the municipal bond market as his sucker investor, selling it round after round of new bonds pledged against the same 21 nursing homes. "He knew underwriters all over the county and bond lawyers," said one former business associate. "He was familiar with the bond industry."

Sutliffe shrouded his questionable deals in a cloak of legitimacy by hiring top-flight accounting firms to give advice. From 1984 until 1986, Deloitte & Touche provided financial forecasts and feasibility studies in connection with FHC's bond issues. But, as the scheme grew, a new accounting firm was brought in. Starting in 1986, Price Waterhouse advised FHC on its bond issues.

An important note: Neither Deloitte & Touche nor Price Waterhouse audited FHC's finances. They were merely brought in to do consulting work—and lend their names.

In 1987, FHC ran into problems. The Illinois Department of Public Health reported substandard conditions at some of its nursing homes. Among other things, state inspectors found untended elderly patients tied to wheelchairs for hours at a time. Daily food budgets at some of the homes had been cut to as little as $2.15 per day per patient.

In the next 18 months, FHC's nursing homes saw an exodus of residents. While this was happening, the company moved deeper into its Ponzi scheme. It raided the proceeds from each of several new bond offerings to pay the holders of previously issued bonds. This kept existing, troubled nursing homes from financial failure.

But the scheme couldn't last forever. In the fall of 1989, the company defaulted on the bonds connected with one of its nursing homes. Sutliffe insisted that the default was a technicality: "The bank just screwed up and paid more money to the nursing home instead of covering the bond debt service first."

Within a few weeks, though, anxious bondholders had forced FHC to file a petition for relief under Chapter 11 of the Bankruptcy Code. After the filing, Sutliffe's story changed. He blamed the bankruptcy on inconsistent Medicaid and Medicare reimbursements that forced the outside management company FHC had contracted to run the nursing homes to shift funds from financially healthy locations to those suffering cash flow problems.

The bondholders didn't buy this argument. In court papers, they claimed that FHC "was ever falling behind on its debt service and other obligations, was ever short of adequate cash flow and working capital, and was having to make up such shortfalls by borrowing revenues from other projects and by closing more and later bond-financed deals."

By September 1989, FHC had sold $82 million of bonds against assets worth no more than $30 million. And the $82 million couldn't be accounted for fully. FHC had spent only $54 million to purchase the 21 nursing homes. As the bankruptcy proceeded—and a criminal investigation began—the trail of the missing money emerged:

- FHC had used two separate corporations, Zandlo and Associates Inc. and Shoreline Design Inc., to certify falsely that repairs had been made to nursing homes it acquired. Both corporations were owned by Sutliffe's girlfriend, Carol Zandlo. She received fees of between $19,000 and $30,000 for each project.
- Sutliffe's daughter, who served on the FHC board of directors, also worked for a company called Premiere Development—which identified potential nursing homes for acquisition. Premiere Development had received fees from the bond offerings.
- Sutliffe, as "developer" of the nursing home deals and bond offerings, received fees ranging from $100,000 to $300,000 from each offering.

Like any NFP bankruptcy, FHC's case was a tough one. NFPs don't have owners in the traditional sense, so finding liable parties is difficult. Sutliffe, who never held an executive position with FHC, said his involvement with the company was limited to consulting on potential acquisitions and financing opportunities. Several months into the bankruptcy proceeding, Sutliffe told a local newspaper: "If I went back and billed First Humanics for all of the money and expenses and so forth that I have incurred on their behalf, I probably would be the number one unsecured creditor."

But he didn't stick around to collect. By the end of 1990, Sutliffe and Zandlo were living in Fort Meyers, Florida, aboard a yacht they named *Vagabond II*.

In the meantime, the wheels of justice ground slowly. By February 1991, after months of delays and dozens of reorganization proposals, a federal bankruptcy court judge approved a plan that gave FHC bondholders control over 15 of the company's 21 nursing homes. (Of the remaining six homes, one had already been sold, another turned over to an institutional investor, and the rest would be sold by the FHC bankruptcy estate to pay bills.)

In March 1993, Sutliffe pleaded guilty to one count of mail fraud in connection with criminal charges brought by the Justice Department over the bond offerings. He was sentenced to serve 15 months in prison and to pay $1 million in restitution.

Under the plea agreement, Sutliffe confessed that he had "obtained money and property from investors and trustee banks by means of false and fraudulent pretenses, representations and promises, well knowing at the time that the...promises were and would be false and fraudulent when made."

As part of the same settlement, other FHC defendants—including Deloitte & Touche and Price Waterhouse—settled for about $45 million. "The assumptions that were used to generate the feasibility studies were unrealistic and Touche knew they were," said David Donaldson, an attorney for some FHC bondholders. "Price Waterhouse had even more reason to know there were problems because they came later on."

Later, the trustee running what was left of FHC tried to squeeze some more money out of Deloitte & Touche and Price Waterhouse. He claimed that the accounting firms had been negligent in relying on financial information from Sutliffe.

But, in a December 1995 decision, a federal court in Kansas City ruled that FHC couldn't seek damages against the accounting firms because "a participant in a fraud cannot also be a victim entitled to recover damages, for he cannot have relied on the truth of the fraudulent representations, and such reliance is an essential element in a case of fraud."

The court went on to make a legally important distinction:

> *Sutliffe and his hand-picked company insiders did not loot FHC, but used FHC for the purpose of committing a fraud against outsiders, in this case the municipal bond purchasers.... FHC benefited from Sutliffe's activities. It prolonged its life as a corporation through the machinations of Sutliffe and had some $30 million in assets at the time of confirmation of its bankruptcy plan.... Driving a corporation into bankruptcy is not to be equated with looting that corporation.*

Even though he lost the case, the FHC trustee did have one legitimate point. Like most Ponzi perps, Sutliffe had had a long history of run-ins with the law. The accounting firms—or *someone* connected to the FHC bond offerings—could have looked up Sutliffe's background. But, then again, they were inclined to trust the NFP. That's why it was such a successful scam.

Case Study: The Foundation for New Era Philanthropy

FHC was unusual, in that it used an NFP financing mechanism to commit fraud. Most NFP Ponzis play on misplaced idealism.

Hundreds of non-profit groups, philanthropists like Lawrence Rockefeller and prestigious organizations like the Philadelphia Orchestra were duped by a structurally simple Ponzi scheme called the Foundation for New Era Philanthropy.

New Era stands out as a shining example of how well-suited the non-profit sector is for buying into Ponzi schemes. The Pennsylvania-based scheme was started, as a tax-exempt charity, in 1989. Founder John G. Bennett[1] solicited contributions from a variety of nonprofit orga-

1 This Bennett is no relation to the family of Ponzi perps in New York who ran the equipment-leasing scam Bennett Funding Group. (At least none that either side will admit.)

nizations. He said that New Era had assembled a small group of anonymous donors that would match the funds that participants deposited with New Era for three to six months.

Bennett described the process as a hard-headed approach to charitable fund-raising. If the non-profits were willing "to put your money to work" with New Era, it would reward the investment with huge returns. Exactly what "work" the money was doing was never explained. Most of the investors assumed it was some sort of charity.

In most situations, this kind of offer would be laughed off as too weird and too sketchy to be taken seriously. But the non-profit world is insular and trusting. Bennett knew a few key people in the Philadelphia non-profit world; these contacts gave him credibility.

Large and experienced entities fell for New Era's pitch. Among the investors: the University of Pennsylvania, Harvard University, Princeton University, the Nature Conservancy, several foundations controlled by former U.S. Treasury Secretary William E. Simon and foundations controlled by mutual fund guru Peter Lynch.

Bennett played on the close quarters of NFP circles. He encouraged prospective investors to talk with the early participants. They were usually impressed with the stature of these players. The phone calls almost always sealed the deal. All the while, Bennett pocketed millions. The one-time high school chemistry teacher entertained highbrows at his Main Line home, drove a big Mercedes, traveled to Caribbean resorts and dressed...expensively.

The first groups to invest money with New Era did, of course, double their returns. About 600 charities and non-profits invested about $350 million in New Era between 1989 and 1995.

Albert Meyer, an accounting professor at Spring Arbor College in Michigan, burst the balloon. He was suspicious of New Era's big promises and vague explanations. Meyer contacted the American Institute of Certified Public Accountants (AICPA) and explained why he thought New Era was a Ponzi scheme. When he concluded the AICPA hadn't moved decisively, Meyer contacted the SEC.

SEC investigators examined New Era's structure and finances and realized that Meyer might be right. The Feds contacted several banks and brokerages doing business with New Era.

The downward spiral accelerated when Prudential Securities demanded immediate repayment of a $44.9 million margin loan that Bennett had personally guaranteed. When he didn't pay off the loan in a timely manner, Prudential sued Bennett and New Era. That suit opened the floodgates of trouble.

In May 1995, New Era sought bankruptcy protection. At a tearful meeting with New Era staffers, Bennett admitted the anonymous donors had never existed.

The Chapter 11 reorganization filing was quickly converted to a Chapter 7 liquidation. In June 1995, New Era's creditors held a meeting in Philadelphia, where an interim trustee told them that the net losses totaled about $107 million and that the shortfall eventually could be around $41 million.

The interim trustee claimed that 163 investors were owed money and 74 investors had taken out net profits at the point New Era declared bankruptcy. He wanted the winners to give back the money so that other creditors could recoup some of their losses. He was ousted days later by a committee of creditors and investors frustrated with what it considered slow response. The committee voted in Arlin M. Adams, a former federal judge in Philadelphia, as trustee.

By September 1995, hundreds of New Era investors had filed more than $725 million in claims, many seeking not only the money they lost but also the promised returns on their investments. New Era's bankruptcy estate had about $31 million in cash assets. So, there were going to be a lot of unhappy people.

In October 1995, Bennett released a videotape that contained his first detailed comments since New Era had declared bankruptcy. Apparently speaking with the aid of a teleprompter, Bennett apologized for the pain and suffering he had caused. "Please hear me when I say I never intended to hurt any one of you," he said. "I know that I've done that, however. And I'm so sorry."

He said that his shortcomings as a manager played a role in New Era's failure.

> *Management was never my talent. Administration was never my expertise. But the responsibility rests with the chief executive, so the buck stops here.... I was at the helm when the ship sank and I should have long before attacked those weaknesses and paid attention to other needed areas of responsibility. Did I ever intentionally set out to hurt anyone? No. My professional life has been motivated toward helping people, not hurting them.*

But Bennett whined that he couldn't provide any details about his personal role until his attorneys had more time to review New Era's documents. "I'll be in touch with you as soon as the facts can be disclosed," he said. His investors weren't looking forward to that; but Ponzi perps often have an egocentric need to explain themselves. ("For some of these people, the confession is a thrill," says one federal agent. "It's part of the drama.")

In January 1996, Adams—the new trustee—filed for court approval of a settlement under which Bennett would turn over about $1.2 million from a house, car, stocks, retirement savings and other sources. Bennett described these things as "literally all of my assets."

One attorney representing some New Era investors was ambivalent about the settlement: "On the one hand, [we're] pleased with the job the trustee has done in capturing most of Bennett's available assets. On the other hand, the assets captured pale in comparison to the extraordinary damage done to nonprofits."

Adams and a group of more than 30 investors then sued Prudential for $90 million, alleging the brokerage firm was a "co-conspirator" in the New Era fraud. "Prudential's involvement in the Ponzi scheme not only legitimized the venture to the charitable community, but was the crucial element that enabled Bennett and New Era to overcome any skeptics," the lawsuit said. Prudential and Bennett "privately agreed to release the money directly to Bennett and New Era to use as they saw fit."

The suit claimed that Bennett established a toll-free telephone number staffed by Prudential employees, who took calls from investors with questions about accounts. Prudential told investors their funds were being held safely in escrow accounts when New Era was actually using the money to pay off early participants.

Finally, the lawsuit argued that Prudential made more than $740,000 in interest from millions of dollars in loans. "Prudential knew, should have known, or had a reasonable basis to suspect that New Era was operating...a scheme to defraud its creditors," the suit said.

Charles Perkins, a spokesman for Prudential, said:

> *I sympathize with the charities that have invested their people's money with the foundation. They were victimized. They were victimized in a very sophisticated scheme that took in some of the most sophisticated financial investors in the country, people like Lawrence Rockefeller and William Simon, but I think that they should be directing their anger at the people who are responsible, which is the foundation and Jack Bennett.*

In August 1996, the bankruptcy judge presiding over the New Era case approved a partial settlement—with the understanding that the lawsuit against Prudential would continue. The brokerage began negotiating a settlement.

In March 1997, facing 82 criminal counts of fraud, filing false tax returns and related offenses, Bennett pleaded *nolo contendere* and turned his focus toward convincing the federal judge hearing his case to be lenient.

In an ill-advised move, he tried to argue that, having grown up in povery with an alcoholic father, he had a delusional mental disorder which limited his responsibility for his actions. Aside from outraging burned New Era investors, this tactic had little effect.

In September, he was sentenced to 12 years in prison.

This satisfied some of participants. As one group had written the court: "...the tremendous negative impact of Mr. Bennett's actions on hundreds of non-profit organizations...and on the image of those associated with philanthropy in general warrants severe punishment."

Contrary to this sentiment, some of the most observant of the people affected by the New Era debacle doubted that the non-profit sector would recognize another Ponzi scheme—if it were executed as carefully as New Era.

"It's hard to say what everybody learned," said Kathryn Coates of the Greater Philadelphia Cultural Alliance. "There weren't any groups that participated in this that didn't check [Bennett] out thoroughly. So I don't know what's changed. What else do you do? The only recourse is that, if you feel nervous about something, don't do it."

In the wake of New Era's collapse, the Pennsylvania Joint State Government Commission considered changing state laws regulating NFPs. But it concluded...rightly...that the laws weren't the problem:

> *[New Era] continued as long as it did due to the combination of its ostensible performance as promised, exceptional references, inadequate regulatory and enforcement efforts, and careless practices by boards of directors or some of the contributors....*

CHAPTER 17

www.ponzischeme.com

The Internet is undoubtedly a commercial marketplace, which means it attracts gamblers, hustlers, Ponzi perps and other crooks.

"We are seeing a number of pyramid schemes taking to the Internet," says Andrew Kandel of the New York State Attorney General's Office. "One of the reasons this poses a particular problem for regulators is that they can reach an increasingly large number of people." In an effort to mitigate the problem, "[We've] established an Internet surveillance program," he added.

For most of the people who turn to the Internet for business or personal reasons, it is a useful tool for sending and collecting information. Some people get more intensely involved, however, spending long hours communicating with other people.

This split approach to Internet use is part of the reason that the thing has been such a challenge to businesses looking for commercial applications. The technology exists to buy and sell just about everything on the net. But some people still don't trust it enough to use it to the full capacity.

"The comparison you keep hearing is to VCRs," says an executive for a big West Coast Internet access provider. "Though a lot of people in this business don't like the comparison."

What he's talking about is the familiar—and partly true—story that the application which made video cassette machines truly household appliances was pornography. In other words, the desire to watch dirty movies on tape (at home, rather than in a seedy theater) drove the first wave of consumer VCR purchases.

For the Internet, two vulgar applications are driving the fullest technological uses of on-line commerce. One is, as with VCRs, sex. Pornography (usually still photos) and on-line sex talk are big applications on the net. The other is get-rich-quick schemes, most of which are simple variations on the basic Ponzi premise.

Through the mid-1990s, two key characteristics of the Internet have acted as partial checks on fraud. Unfortunately, both of these checks may weaken over time.

First, Ponzi perps who use traditional media (telemarketing, direct mail, MLM) seek out investors aggressively. Perps on the Internet make offers on their websites—and then wait for consumers to find them—clearly, a much slower way of reaching people. This check is likely to weaken as so-called "push technology" makes it easier to send junk mail on the net.

Second, most users remain reluctant to give out their credit card numbers and other personal financial information over the Internet. This check is starting to weaken as legitimate businesses refine transaction security and people have a higher level of general comfort with the system.

Trust Is a Difficult Issue

While many investors know the Internet contains a wealth of investment information, they often don't know how to find what they're looking for and have no way of knowing whether the information is reliable when they *do* find it.

Overall, few people—only about one in eight—say they would invest money based on anything they read or heard on the Internet. But, according to a 1996 survey by Massachusetts-based Dalbar Associates, demographic groups that use the Internet the most trust what they read on it more. And another factor troubles many regulators. Heavy users of the Internet share a libertarian, frontier mentality that is conducive to investment frauds.

And more than a third of people under 35 years old—Generation Xers—told the Dalbar survey that they considered the Internet a reliable source of investment information. This level of trust is music to Ponzi perps' ears. From a crook's perspective, there are suckers born every time a new person goes on-line. And more are going on-line all the time.

In 1995, about 40 million people used the Internet at least once in a while. That number was only a hint at what could be, though. Some marketers were predicting that by the new millennium, the number could be several hundred million.

The SEC has dedicated an entire unit to investigate and prosecute on-line investment fraud and is stepping up its own on-line presence to raise consumer awareness and access to the agency.

"It's becoming a bigger and bigger problem," says John Stark, who oversees Internet fraud for the SEC. "But they're just the same old swindles with a new medium.... These [perps] are not like hackers, who can be difficult to track down. As long as they're located in the U.S., it's no different from any other fraud case. They need to advertise to lure victims, which means they need to post a phone number or an address or a post office box."

Interestingly, Internet regulars don't yet seem to have developed the shame that shuts up burned Ponzi investors in other environments. The SEC has been surprised by the amount of information some web users are willing to disclose about themselves and their experiences.

"This is a very sophisticated group of self-policing individuals, and they're willing to identify themselves to help us because they don't like fraud," Stark says.

He tells the story of one group of crooks that not only created a professional-looking website, it even created links to bogus investment newsletters that touted the offering as a good investment. Some of the people conned by the set-up showed a refreshing outrage at having been ripped off.

Cyberspace Ponzi Perps Learn Quickly

Jeff Herig, a computer evidence analyst for the Florida Department of Law Enforcement, says: "The time it takes for criminals to learn a new way of beating the system is compressed down considerably from what it used to be. It used to be year to year that criminals would find a new hole to get through. Now a new way to beat the system is being developed from month to month."

In the early stages of the Internet, much of the financial fraud was based on hyping stocks. "When we see a stock fluctuating wildly, we go into the chat room and take a look at what's being said," explained Mike Robinson, spokesman for NASDR, an independent regulatory arm of the National Association of Securities Dealers (www.nasd.com).

But, as more people logged on and technology advanced, the Ponzi perps started getting active.

Internet Fraud Watch (www.fraud.org), a project of the National Consumers League, was launched in the mid-1990s to discourage on-line fraud before it gets a hold in the workplace. "Our website alone has received more than 300,000 visits from consumers and averaged 25,000 hits a week," said NCL president Linda Golodner.

Cleo Manuel, an Internet fraud specialist with NCL, offers an explanation for all the interest:

> *The Internet is the new frontier. For con artists, it's the natural next step. It's the evolution of fraud. People see a sense of credibility when they see something on the 'net because they trust the technology and trust the people on there. It's a new marketplace and people need to be as careful there as they are in other marketplaces.*

The Wild West of Fraudulent Schemes

"Cyberspace is a new frontier for advertising and marketing," said Jodie Bernstein, director of the FTC's Bureau of Consumer Protection. "But the Internet will not achieve its commercial potential if this new frontier becomes the Wild West of fraudulent schemes."

Ponzi schemes crop up all the time. "It's interesting that over the years, the scams remain the same," says William McLucas, director of the SEC's enforcement division. "It's just the pitch that changes."

The Internet combines various attributes of publishing, broadcasting, public space and private commerce. This melange confounds many legal theorists—to say nothing of law enforcement officials.

Among the specific issues that perplex law enforcement agents:

- the distinction between advertising and fact (and what this means for free speech) on the Internet;
- the liability of Internet Service Providers for fraud committed through their networks; and
- what constitutes a "clear and conspicuous" on-line consumer-alert warning.

At the state level, some regulators are more aggressive about Internet Ponzi schemes than others. Larry Cook, director of the enforcement division of the Kansas Securities Commission, explains that his agency looks at three kinds of Internet frauds:

> *You have the scams, you have the misinformed who need to find legal advice in putting together an offering to solicit investors, and then you have the pie-in-the-sky people who are not necessarily [Ponzi perps], but they don't have a clue how to run a business.*

The dilemma for regulators and law enforcement officials: It's an impossible task to monitor every investment-related posting in the dozens of chat rooms, news groups, bulletin boards and Web pages on the net.

The SEC and the North American Securities Administrators Association have set up informal Internet surveillance programs, often cruising around user groups and examining the messages posted there. But this is—at best—a random sampling process.

The SEC admits there's no way of knowing how many scams are operating on-line, so there's no way to know for sure whether the fraudulent offers are increasing or decreasing. The only thing the regulators do know is that complaints are rising as Internet use increases.

SEC regulators say that Ponzi-type fraud is well-suited for the world of on-line computing, because a perp can easily send messages to thousands of people with the touch of a button. One example: An ad titled "How to Make Big Money From Your Home Computer," in which a promoter claimed investors could turn $5 into $60,000 in three to six weeks, was sent to thousands of Internet users in a few days in 1996. The pitch was a crude six-level pyramid scheme.

MLM on the WWW

Multilevel marketing programs—both legit and not—abound on the Internet.

The Health Club Network, which called itself "A Price Club for Health," used the Internet to accomplish the near-impossible. It combined sex and multilevel marketing. The company claimed that Internet users would get a special discount of 60 percent off the price of products and make money 24 hours a day, "even while you're sleeping!" Among Health Club Network's products: Passion Tonic, which was supposed to improve orgasms, overcome female frigidity and male impotence and release libidos. Though perhaps not in that order.

For Ponzi perps, the advantages of plying their trade on the World Wide Web are many. For a few hundred dollars—and sometimes less—their scams are delivered straight into a person's home or business with all the polish of a Fortune 500 company.

California-based Dennis Enterprises told Internet users that its system of auto-responders could send out 10,000 e-mail messages a day for a single client. For an up-front fee of between $12 and $200, an aggressive Internet MLM entrepreneur could send out over three-and-a-half million e-mails a year. This electronic version of junk mail is what on-line enthusiasts call "spamming."

But one user's spam is another's filet mignon. With just a tenth-of-1 percent response rate, the e-mail barrage would mean 3,500 sales.

The Dennis Enterprises pitch was for selling computer hardware, peripherals...and even the company's own e-mail services. But some MLM programs don't seem to care much about *what* they're selling.

In general, Ponzi perps would rather focus on the size and shape of the pyramid—and the money at the top—than pestering details like product line specs. That's why so many Internet Ponzi schemes involve surprisingly low-tech pitches.

Fortuna Alliance was an alleged pyramid scheme based on the Fibonacci numbers sequence (each number is the sum of the two preceding numbers). Fortuna—which started in Washington state and quickly spread through the Pacific Coast—promised investors profits of up to $5,000 instantly.

According to the FTC, Fortuna separated more than $6 million from roughly 17,000 members and diverted at least $3.5 million to a bank in the Caribbean.

Some Simple Issues Persist

However an investment is promoted—in person, by mail, telephone or over the Internet—the SEC recommends that an investor ask the following questions before plunging in:

- Is the investment registered with the SEC and state securities regulators—or is it subject to an exemption?
- Are the people pitching the investment registered with the securities regulators? If so, is there a record of any complaints against them?

- Who is running the company? What experience do they have? Also, how long has the company been in business?
- How liquid is the investment? Can an investor sell his or her position easily—without paying unusual penalties or premiums?
- What level of detail does the company offer about itself in promotional literature? Also, does it make reviewed or audited financial statements available to investors?

Generally, if the answers to these questions are *no*, *not yet*, *it's unclear* or *no one else in the business does that*, you should steer clear of the investment.

A note: There are many legitimate start-up companies that are using the Internet to raise development capital inexpensively. But, these companies tend to talk about themselves to a fault. They'll usually post detailed biographies of principals, business plans (even if these are largely prospective) and information on money raised to date.

Be careful of any investment opportunity offered over the Internet that's in any way vague about the people involved or how money raised will be spent. According to Russell Damtoft, an assistant regional director in the FTC's Chicago office, "Most of the scams on the net are old wine in new bottles. They're Ponzi schemes, credit-repair scams, vacation frauds."

There are no laws specifically governing Internet use, so states are trying to use their laws to root out cyberspace hucksters who promote get-rich schemes, phony health cures and other scams. In 1996, Minnesota Attorney General Hubert Humphrey III became the nation's first to file consumer fraud complaints against Internet firms. One involved a pyramid scheme that promised participants $157,900 in tax-free income. Illinois Attorney General Jim Ryan, an established Ponzi scheme buster, described the Internet as an "unregulated and unmonitored territory where scam artists and other lawbreakers roam freely."

Jim Jacobson, special assistant attorney general in the consumer division, said the state isn't interested in regulating everything on the Internet, or in stifling free speech. "All we're talking about here is exercising our normal powers to protect the public from fraud and false advertising in commercial activity," he said.

Case Study: Western Executive Group

In October 1996, a federal judge issued a temporary restraining order against two Nevada companies for running an ATM investment Ponzi scheme that used an Internet website as part of its pitch for investment dollars.

U.S. District Judge George King froze the assets of Cash Systems USA Inc. and Western Executive Group Inc. (WEG). The SEC had asked for a court order to stop the two related companies from selling investor contracts for ATMs.

The suit, filed in federal court in Los Angeles, was one of the first SEC actions to implicate an Internet website with a Ponzi scheme. It was also one of the first to involve the newly deregulated ATM machines. A 1995 deregulation rule had allowed individuals to own the machines; until then, only banks and other financial institutions had been allowed to own them. "As of late 1995, you saw ATMs only at banks," said SEC spokeswoman Lisa Gok. "They had to be affiliated with a bank. Then there was deregulation and now you see these freestanding ATMs at even convenience stores."

The SEC claimed that WEG offered investors ownership in a freestanding ATM for up to $24,000, promising returns of 17 percent to 20 percent each year for five years. Between September 1995 and October 1996, more than 130 investors bought WEG cash machines for $23,950 each and immediately leased them back to Cash Systems for placement in retail locations. The investors poured more than $3.5 million into WEG. The company returned about $815,000 in lease payments. But the SEC claimed this came from proceeds generated by new investors.

Most of the investment pitches were made by telephone salespeople. In typical Ponzi scheme fashion, WEG also held what it called "private investment seminars" and did mass mailings to potential investors. The company singled out retirement-age investors as targets.

"All of these schemes tend to hit the retirement communities quite hard," one SEC source said.

Adding a high-tech twist, WEG set up an Internet site to display pictures of the ATMs it deployed, as well as other promotional materials. Potential WEG investors were encouraged to visit the Internet site and "see for themselves" what the machines looked like and how the WEG program worked. Many people took the advice—and foolishly considered the material in the Internet site independent verification of what the telemarketers pitched over the phone.

"It was really kind of sad. You had a lot of these older folks saying they'd investigated [WEG] on the Internet, when all they'd done was have someone download promo material from the company's own website," said one SEC source.

The SEC argued that, in return for the $3.5 million in investment dollars, WEG signed contracts to purchase 228 terminals. In fact, the company only purchased 119 machines and placed 41, most of them in retail locations in Florida. And only two of the machines in operation made enough money to cover expenses.

While the company's promotional materials had mentioned potential transaction volumes of 100 transactions per day and a break-even point of 25 daily transactions, some of the terminals were registering as few as eight transactions per day. As a result, WEG "had to resort to paying investors with new investor money," said James Howell, a litigator in the SEC's Los Angeles office.

In the same order that shut down WEG, Judge King also froze the assets of four Cash Systems and WEG executives. These people were: Charles Rietz of Mesa, Arizona; Robert Parrish of Gilmer, Texas; Robert Struth and Stephen Edgel of southern California.

Rietz had a long history of trouble with the law. In 1978, he had been enjoined from selling securities by the SEC for fraud allegations in an offering of investment contracts. (He'd tried the "it's not an investment" argument then, too.) In 1982, he'd paid a fine to the Commodity Futures Trading Commission for running what one CFTC investigator said was "pretty much a Ponzi scheme."

Edgel denied that Cash Systems and WEG were a Ponzi scheme. "We vigorously deny each and every allegation of the SEC's complaint," he said. "We deny that the investment is a security—we have two qualified securities attorneys who say it is not a security. It is our opinion that the SEC has no jurisdiction in the matter."

The Feds weren't impressed. "We were able to stop this offering at a point when it was still growing," said one SEC lawyer. "A lot of times you only catch these schemes after they collapse."

PART FOUR

What to Do if You've Been Scammed

CHAPTER 18

Make Friends with the Regulators

Ponzi schemes are investigated and prosecuted by various local authorities and federal regulators. In 1995 alone, the Securities and Exchange Commission prosecuted 24 Ponzi-inspired frauds, each of them multimillion dollar rip-offs.

In a related market, the Commodity Futures Trading Commission (CFTC) and the National Futures Association (NFA) oversee commodities trading. These groups serve as a good model of a regulatory system that deals with a fair number of Ponzi schemes.

Although the CFTC does not place stringent requirements on those who trade their own funds in the market, it does require anyone who handles customer funds to register with the NFA, the self-regulating body of the commodity futures market.

Anyone who accepts orders, money or securities for the purpose of making a purchase or sale of a commodity futures contract must register as a futures commission merchant (FCM). Anyone who operates a "commodity pool" of third-party funds in order to buy and sell commodity futures contracts is required to register with the NFA as a commodity pool operator (CPO).

Direct participation in trading is not required to fall under the purview of the CFTC. Anyone who advises others—for a fee—about trading futures contracts must register as commodity trading advisors (CTA). Anyone who solicits orders or customers on behalf of a FCM, CPO or CTA must register as an associated person (AP).

The law also offers a higher level of protection for what it calls "vulnerable victims." A Ponzi perp who steals from such investors—and gets caught—faces harsher punishment than the average crook.

In this regulatory sense, *vulnerable* means a person whose "age, physical or mental condition" makes him or her weak. Of those three terms, *age* is the most difficult to define. The government has identified investors who are over 50 as "elderly" individuals...and vulnerable victims due to their age and their special financial needs.

But this definition is somewhat vague. As one court, when sorting through a collapsed Ponzi scheme, wrote: "it is logical to assume the intended victims of *any* premeditated offense will be selected because something in his or her persona or circumstances will make successful the intended criminal act."

The Federal Government's Ponzi-fighting Tools

Rule 9(b) of the Federal Rules of Civil Procedure outlines the requirements for making fraud claims. The fraud allegations in the complaint must be specific enough to allow the defendant "a reasonable opportunity to answer the complaint."

In order to satisfy the Rule 9(b) pleading requirement for fraud, most courts require that the person making the charges state:

- precisely what statements were made in what documents or oral representations or what omissions were made,
- the time and place of each statement and the person responsible for making (or, in the case of omissions, not making) it,
- the context of such statements and the manner in which they misled the investors, and
- what the perps obtained as a consequence of the fraud.

When the charge is based on an offering memorandum or other document, these requirements are "somewhat relaxed." The document satisfies the time, place and content requirement of Rule 9(b). If you don't have a document, the charges will be difficult to establish.

In a similar vein, Section 10b-5 of the federal Securities Act prohibits fraudulent activities in connection with the purchase or sale of securities, whether or not those securities are registered. (This is important in cases involving Ponzi schemes, because the investments usually *aren't* registered as securities.) Specifically, Rule 10b-5 states:

> *It shall be unlawful for any person, ...by use of the mails or instrumentality of interstate commerce...or of any facility of any national securities exchange, 1) to employ any device, scheme or artifice to defraud; 2) to make any untrue statement of material fact necessary in order to make the statements made, in light of the circumstances under which they were made, not misleading; or 3) to engage in any act, practice or course of business which operates or would operate as a fraud or deceit upon any person....*

To elaborate this point further, section 12(2) of the Securities Act of 1933 provides that:

> *Any person who...offers or sells a security...by means of a prospectus or oral communication, which includes an untrue statement of a material fact or omits to state a material fact...and who shall not sustain the burden of proof that he did not know, and in the exercise of reasonable care could not have known, of such untruth or omission, shall be liable to the person purchasing such securities from him....*

There are limits to how these various rules can be applied. As one court has noted, "Congress did not intend the securities laws to be a broad federal remedy for all fraud." However, the Securities and Exchange Act covers not only the enumerated instruments but also "many types of instruments that in our commercial world fall within the ordinary concept of a security." This generally includes private placement debt, participation notes, investment contracts and other familiar Ponzi tools.

How State Regulators Fight Ponzi Perps

The Feds aren't the only regulators who battle Ponzi perps. State attorneys general and consumer protection groups have specific laws that they can use to shut down Ponzi schemes. One example: New

York State General Business Law prohibits "chain distributor schemes" which are defined as:

> *a sales device whereby a person, upon condition that he make an investment, is granted a... right to... recruit for profit... one or more additional persons who are also granted such... right upon condition of making an investment and may further perpetuate the chain of persons who are granted such... right.*

Another example: Under Texas law, a person who runs a pyramid scheme violates the Texas Deceptive Trade Practices and Consumer Protection Act, or may be convicted of a state jail felony.

And then there's Illinois, which takes a noticeably hard line against Ponzi schemes.

Kevin Trudeau said he was an entrepreneur trying to build value—and start companies—at the grass-roots level. Regulators in half a dozen Midwestern states said he was a Ponzi perp who moved from pitch to pitch, leaving burned investors in his wake. In the mid-1990s, Illinois led an investigation into Trudeau's operations.

Trudeau fit the profile of a Ponzi perp. A convicted felon who had served two years in prison for credit-card fraud in the early 1990s, he had a personal history littered with troubles like a larceny conviction and personal bankruptcy.

When he got out of prison in 1992, Trudeau started an eponymous multilevel marketing company which used vitamins and food products made by a Texas-based company called Nutrition for Life as its premise. But Trudeau Marketing Group's focus was on recruiting distributors more than selling vitamins.

Trudeau also sold self-help and motivational tapes from a related company called Nightingale Conant.

Nutrition for Life president David Bertrand tried to distance his company from Trudeau, referring to Trudeau as just one of several distributors the company used. He argued that none of his distributors were pyramid schemes. "You don't have to sign anybody up to make money," Bertrand said.

But Trudeau was clearly a big part of Nutrition for Life's growth. About one-third of the vitamin company's 82,000-person salesforce had been brought on board by Trudeau—who remained a handsomely-compensated independent contractor. In an advertising campaign that aired on syndicated television and radio shows, he promised investors big money for recruiting new members into his program.

Trudeau encouraged his distributors to recruit others to become so-called "instant executives." The phrase itself suggested an illegal pyramid scheme to investigators. One Illinois lawyer said, "Unless you're rolling out of Harvard Business School with honors, you don't usually become an executive instantly anywhere. And these guys weren't dealing with a lot of Harvard grads."

Regulators at both the federal and state level were watching Trudeau. Among the challenges his company faced: Two people associated with the marketing operation were also convicted felons. They'd met Trudeau in a federal prison in California.

On a simpler business point, many of the regulators believed that—regardless of Trudeau's background—relying so heavily on one distributor could spell serious trouble for Nutrition for Life.

The SEC wanted to know how Nutrition For Life recruited its distributors. Investigations on the state level were more aggressive. Illinois Attorney General Jim Ryan made a particularly pointed effort; part of a lawsuit he filed against Trudeau cited a state law that required anyone who sold marketing plans for $500 or more to register with the state and disclose any criminal convictions. The Instant Executive program required participants to buy a $35 Nutrition for Life distributor kit, $1,000 worth of products and allow automatic credit card or checking account debits of $135 a month for new products.

The lawsuit made numerous technical points; in layman's terms, Ryan had accused Trudeau of running an illegal pyramid scheme.

In April 1996, Trudeau agreed to a temporary restraining order prohibiting him from recruiting instant executives until Ryan's lawsuit was resolved. As part of the settlement with Ryan's office, Nutrition for Life would no longer use Trudeau's "instant executive" designation. "The confusion was that some people did not realize that to be in Nutrition for Life, the only requirement was to purchase a $35 sales kit," Bertrand said.

But the agreement would hurt. Since Trudeau had become involved with the company, the Instant Executive program had accounted for well over half the company's revenue.

Close to a hundred of Trudeau's distributors packed a courtroom in Chicago to hear the details of the temporary restraining order being hammered out. The distributors drew an early rebuke from the court when they responded angrily to the state's description of the program as a pyramid scheme.

Trudeau's lawyer claimed that Trudeau Marketing Group was only a "shell corporation" that didn't transact business. "It is therefore incapable of being a pyramid sales scheme," he argued. However, the addled argument didn't accomplish very much.

Even though he agreed to the temporary court order, Trudeau insisted that: "the allegations are 100 percent totally untrue." In messages on the Internet, Trudeau wrote, "There was NO HEARING before the court!!!!!" and "The court DID NOT rule that anyone is running an illegal anything!" And, technically, he was right.

He put a positive spin on the changes in his marketing plan: "We encourage all distributors to continue selling Nutrition for Life products and recruiting others to do so." As to whether they should continue to recruit for the costly Instant Executive program, he said, "that issue is one we are working out."

At the same time the Illinois agreement was being worked out, the State of Michigan issued a cease-and-desist order barring Trudeau from recruiting any more of its residents as Instant Executive distributors.

The Michigan order was issued after months of negotiations failed to resolve the state's complaints, according to Bob Ward, an assistant attorney general. The order restricted Trudeau from doing anything other than selling Nutrition For Life products in the state. Ward said that effectively shut him down, because "I'm not convinced there are any retail sales in Trudeau's program."

A few months later, in July 1996, Illinois and seven other states entered an agreement with Trudeau that essentially applied the terms of the Illinois agreement to the other states. The multistate deal also required Trudeau and Nutrition for Life to pay a total of $185,000 to reimburse states for the cost of their investigations.

The agreement meant the Instant Executive Program was abolished. Compensation in the Trudeau Marketing program would be based on sales rather than on recruitment. To receive a commission, an executive distributor would be required to make five verifiable sales each month. "[The agreement] provides a significant new layer of disclosure that gives participants a clear picture of how the program works and a realistic estimate of income possibilities," Ryan said.

Trudeau had a different take on the outcome. "With the legal issue resolved, I can now focus my full energies and marketing expertise in helping thousands of people achieve financial freedom through a home-based business of their own," he said. He claimed that the agreement resolved the legal issues "without any determination of wrongdoing." Again, this was technically true—but it missed the larger point made by the settlement.

Trudeau wasn't long on nuance. In the wake of the Instant Executive settlement, he celebrated the end to the legal skirmishes by throwing a party for employees and investors at Chicago's Bismarck Hotel. He said he was about to begin "the largest advertising and marketing campaign in multilevel marketing history!"

A State Regulator Forces Some Repayments

Law enforcement agencies don't usually concentrate their efforts on making burned Ponzi investors whole. But, state agencies will often do more than the Feds to help the people who their lose money recover at least some of it.

In late 1986, an woman named Lynn Ridenhour introduced what she called an MLM program to residents of Topeka, Kansas. The program was called the Top Flight Success System (TFSS). It was marketed by Ridenhour on behalf of Products Management Corporation (PMC). TFSS participants joined the program by paying a $1,500 entry fee. The $1,500 entry fee was paid in two checks: One check for $1,250 was made payable to TFSS; the second check for $250 was made payable to PMC. The check made payable to TFSS was deposited into a TFSS account, and the money was eventually paid to participants. PMC kept its check.

Payment of the fee entitled the participant to have his or her name placed on a chart in an entry level position as a *passenger*. The charts consisted of four levels organized in a pyramid fashion. At the base of the pyramid were eight passengers. Above this—in ascending order—were four *crewmen*, two *co-pilots* and one *pilot* at the top.

Once eight passengers paid their money (or, as Ridenhour called it, "boarded the airplane"), the pilot cashed out for $10,000. The remaining participants split into two new pyramids with everyone advancing one level. Each new airplane then recruited eight new passengers—at which point, the pyramids multiplied again. Theoretically, the process continued ad infinitum. Participants were encouraged to re-enter the TFSS system multiple times. Many did.

In addition to the pyramid scheme, TFSS ostensibly marketed two products:

- a Top Flight Vacation Card, which entitled the holder to use of a recreational facility near Missouri's Lake of the Ozarks (to be developed later by a subsidiary of PMC) for 20 weeks a year for five years; and
- a set of motivational tapes.

As a court would later note, "The value of these products was insignificant in comparison to the value of the $1,500 entry fee."

In the Topeka area, some 250 passengers joined the TFSS scheme. As the program was originally structured, PMC maintained investor charts and kept track of the placement of passengers' names and their movement on the various charts. However, as the scheme grew, these arrangements broke down. Individual participants kept track of the charts; checks were endorsed over for direct payment to the pilots.

But TFSS had the same fatal problem all Ponzi schemes share. As it operated, its demand for passengers increased exponentially. During the summer of 1988, the scheme collapsed. That October, Ridenhour pleaded *nolo contendere* to selling unregistered securities, was placed on probation and ordered to pay $10,000.

In late 1988, the Kansas Securities Commissioner's office sued Ridenhour's colleagues for operating an illegal pyramid scheme. The Commission sought a mandatory injunction, the disgorgement of profits, the appointment of a receiver, and the production of records to allow an accounting.

The court ruled for the Commissioner and ordered TFSS and PMC to cease operations. The companies filed an appeal, which resulted in the 1991 Kansas Supreme Court decision *Mays v. Ridenhour, et al.*

The state's high court considered several issues, including whether the TFSS investments were securities, the status of Ridenhour and her colleagues within the scheme, and whether intent to defraud must be established in order to determine liability. The court concluded:

> *[T]hese defendants have unjustly enriched themselves at the expense of others through the acceptance of proceeds from the unlawful sale of securities. Even though defendants did not actively solicit or recruit, they relied upon others to do this and accepted the benefits of these unlawful acts. The Commissioner argues that it is ironic that defendants could receive and retain sale proceeds but bear no responsibility or accountability for the unlawfulness of the sales. We adopt the "but for" or proximate cause test. Thus, for an individual to be liable for the injury, all that must be established is that the injury flowed directly and proximately from the actions of the person sought to be held viable.*

The court upheld the trial court's decision requiring 10 people who participated in the scheme to pay back about $60,000 to other investors. "This allows us the ability to require the repayment of profits," said Securities Commissioner Jim Parrish. "We needed an opinion like this.... It's going to strengthen the law in that regard."

Case Study: The Feds Versus William Kennedy

Several regulatory agencies cooperated to bring a big Ponzi scheme known as Western Monetary Consultants, Inc. (WMC) to justice.

WMC was founded in 1979 by William R. Kennedy, a Colorado businessman (no relation to the Massachusetts Kennedys) who used a variety of pitches—including supposed political affiliations—to sell WMC investments.

Kennedy was "quite an intelligent guy, very aggressive, always," said Willard Walker, a Colorado stockbroker. "He was a by-God, sort of a bull-like guy who did get a lot done." But Kennedy's ego and sense of urgency were his undoing. Walker recalled advising him not to run for Congress against a popular incumbent in the late 1970s.

Kennedy ran, anyway. But his bid for the congressional seat didn't get as far as the party primary. "He has an ego like the Graf Zeppelin," Walker said. And a destiny like the Hindenburg.

WMC promoted itself as a wholesale distributor of precious metals and coins. In fact, it wasn't anything like what most merchants would call a wholesaler. It sold precious metals to the public over the phone and, beginning in about 1984, at what it called "investment seminars" or "war colleges."

The seminars were Kennedy's forte. He targeted wealthy, older investors with conservative political and religious beliefs. And he paid out-of-work right-wing politicians top dollar to deliver speeches on geopolitical topics. Speakers at the seminars would warn of the "imminent collapse of the global economy and the possibility that common currency and standard securities would become worthless," one lawyer for disgruntled investors said.

These speeches were designed to convince listeners that world events justified investment in precious metals as a hedge against inflation and political instability. Jules Diamond, a retired executive from a big liquor company, invested after spending three days at an all-expense-paid war college seminar. Kennedy recommended that Diamond put his money in silver to hedge against a collapse of the commercial banking system. "It all seemed so reputable. It didn't dawn on me to check it out independently," Diamond said.

When an investor agreed to purchase precious metals from WMC, an employee would quote the investor an approximate price. The employee would then contact the WMC trading department, which would locate the best price for the metal from a network of dealers. The employee would then inform the investor of the exact, or "locked-in," price. The investor would then transfer funds to WMC. Investors bought the metals with either cash or through cash down-payments coupled with bank loans arranged by WMC.

There was one complication: If WMC did not provide the dealer with the locked-in purchase price within 48 hours of ordering, the dealer usually nullified the contract with WMC. This meant WMC had to reorder at a new price, which could be higher or lower than the investor's quoted price.

At some point about 1984, WMC began delaying purchases in the hope of making money on the difference between locked-in prices and actual prices paid. Word of WMC's questionable practices reached the CFTC pretty quickly—certainly by 1986. But the commodities regulators didn't have enough evidence to take any action.

Once the delays started and no regulators responded, Kennedy seemed to conclude that WMC could collect both buy and sell commissions for metals that were never actually bought or sold. Instead, he diverted much of the investor money to other uses. Among these:

- a 6,000-square-foot Colorado home with an indoor basketball court and other amenities;
- several luxury cars, including the obligatory Mercedes-Benz;

- the purchase of and payment of expenses necessary to run *Conservative Digest* magazine;
- the purchase, refurbishment and transport of a helicopter for Nicaraguan "Contra" counter-revolutionaries.

Ownership of the magazine and the support of the Contras gave Kennedy access to higher-profile politicians, including Ronald Reagan, George Bush, Oliver North and Jerry Falwell. This increased the star-quality of the speakers at WMC's seminars. The magazine's mailing list also provided Kennedy with a ready source of potential investors for his seminars.

Between 1984 and 1987, WMC increased its sales rapidly and began to experience serious cash shortages. Nevertheless, Kennedy continued to promote sales to new investors, without telling them that WMC was between $10 million and $13 million behind in filling orders.

If the precious metals market had been moving downward during the mid-1980s, WMC's delays would have been profitable. But the market was moving upward during the height of the deception. So, the delays were increasing the obligations WMC owed its investors. Kennedy's plan for dealing with the chronic problem: Sell more contracts and fulfill old orders with new money. Hello, Ponzi scheme.

In March 1988, Kennedy sent letters to WMC's clients which blamed the failure to fill client orders on the tremendous growth of the business and the pressures this put on his overworked staff. At this point, the federal regulators were working with the Denver U.S. Attorney's office and local law enforcement agencies to build the case again Kennedy and WMC.

Later that month, WMC's cash shortages were so great that it filed for Chapter 11 bankruptcy protection, listing over 600 creditors from whom WMC had received over $18 million in orders that remained unfilled. The market value of these unfilled orders at the time of the bankruptcy was more than $37 million.

WMC moved to San Diego and continued to operate for a while under a court-approved reorganization plan. "Building a criminal case was still going to be difficult," said one federal regulator. "We had a team of people from the FBI, CFTC, SEC and the U.S. Attorney's office. So many Ponzi crooks get away.... We were determined not to miss the chance to nail this guy."

In July of 1992, after a five-year investigation of WMC's practices, the government indicted Kennedy and numerous employees on charges of racketeering, mail fraud, wire fraud and money laundering. Kennedy himself was charged with 109 separate criminal counts related to operating "a Ponzi scheme in the unregulated sale of precious metals."

Because Kennedy was broke (he and his wife had declared personal bankruptcy in 1990), the court appointed a lawyer to defend him. At trial, the government relied in part on the testimony of Douglas Campbell, from the National Futures Association, as an expert on precious metals and commodity markets. Campbell concluded from reviewing WMC's records that WMC had not purchased enough metal to cover its obligations to numerous investors and had lost money speculating in metals futures trading.

The centerpiece of Kennedy's defense was that he lacked the criminal intent necessary to be convicted of the charges. He admitted that his poor business judgment had caused investors to lose millions—but had never intended to defraud anyone. Kennedy's lawyer called him an "eternal optimist, too inept and untrained to see what was going on under his own nose."

The jury didn't believe Kennedy's stupidity defense. In fact, while it acquitted most of his co-defendants, the jury convicted Kennedy on the most serious charges.

The judge ordered Kennedy taken into custody, noting that because his family lived in San Diego the felon was a flight risk. In January 1994, Kennedy was sentenced to 20 years in prison by U.S. District Judge Lewis Babcock. "His victims were elderly, trusting," Babcock said. "They invested retirement funds, the fruits of lifelong labors." Babcock also ordered Kennedy to complete three years of supervised release after his prison term. Because Kennedy had been declared indigent, Babcock waived $18.5 million in restitution and $750,000 in fines.

Kennedy's attorney had tried to lessen the sentence by arguing that the felon would be targeted for attacks in prison because he was "a formerly rich, white, Republican conservative who had every advantage the other inmates never had."

Babcock wasn't moved. Kennedy never acknowledged that he had intentionally defrauded investors. But he did make a tearful statement after the sentence was announced. Among his conclusions:

> *Whether I agree with the jury's decision or not, in operating the company I was reckless and arrogant. And I've caused a lot of pain.... I hope some day to clear my name and pay these people back. I know this sounds crazy under these circumstances, but this is my heart.... I don't want my children to be bitter toward this country or this system because of what has happened to me.*

One of the lawyers who worked on the case noted, "It's not surprising that this guy was a crook. He was a major egomaniac. The court's sending him to prison for 20 years and all he can talk about is how he's really a stand-up guy. But look at how he said it. *I* this, *I* that. Me. My."

CHAPTER 19

Go After the People Who Got Money Out

It's difficult to define the relationships of the parties involved in a Ponzi scheme by traditional legal or business principles. Many of the most distinguishing features of a Ponzi scheme have little to do with either business or law.

One the most painful parts of being burned as an investor in a Ponzi scheme is the conclusion that you've been taken advantage of by someone that you thought was a compelling entrepreneur or reliable advisor—but turned out to be a smarmy crook.

Prosecuting the perp after a Ponzi scheme has crashed is usually tough. *Locating* the perp can be difficult. And, even if you do manage to find the person, he or she is usually broke—so collecting a judgment is practically impossible. But there are some things a burned investor can do to achieve some degree of either personal satisfaction or financial reimbursement.

A piece of strategic advice: If you're a burned Ponzi investor, you'll probably have to go after the perps for personal satisfaction and then set your sights on fellow investors and the lawyers or accountants who advised the perps for monetary satisfaction.

Investors Turn on Each Other

The twenty-three-year litigation resulting from the ill-fated Home-Stake Production Co.—discussed earlier in Chapter 5—involved one of the biggest and most protracted Ponzi scheme legal battles in American history.

In the early 1950s, Robert Trippet organized Home-Stake to develop oil and gas properties. He raised capital by selling percentage interests to investors through private placements. From 1964 to 1972, Home-Stake organized separate annual programs, units in which were registered as securities with the SEC.

Trippet told investors that each of the programs was organized to develop a particular oil and gas property or properties in the Midwest, California or Venezuela. Like most Ponzi perps, Trippet tailored Home-Stake's pitch to each individual investor's needs.

At first, the operation seemed successful. Quarterly progress reports indicated that substantial oil was being produced. In fact, very little oil was being produced. Payments to early investors came from money raised from later investors. Still, there were some investors who complained that their returns weren't what they'd expected. Home-Stake paid substantial sums of money to hush these unhappy investors.

Shortly afterward, the fabric that held Home-Stake together began to fray. Despite the settlements, word began to circulate that Home-Stake was crooked. Disgruntled investors started turning on each other—which didn't result in much that was good for anyone. "I just remember feeling like I'd been played for a fool," says one Home-Stake investor. "I was angry. I didn't like the idea that a few people with connections were getting their money out while I was just some schmuck stuck in a scam that was heading for the toilet."

In fact, the early settlements had little to do with "connections." But there was so much brewing discord that the facts hardly mattered.

In March 1973, two investors who were dissatisfied with their returns and one who'd been told that the IRS was going to disallow Home-Stake tax deductions filed a lawsuit in California. Six months later, Home-Stake filed for bankruptcy in Oklahoma. A flood of lawsuits from angry investors followed the filing. The various civil cases were combined into one big action.

The Ponzi scheme wasn't giving rise only to civil liability. In December 1974, a grand jury in Los Angeles returned criminal indictments against 13 officers and associates of Home-Stake for violations of the securities and income tax laws. So, the legal fallout of the Home-Stake collapse followed two separate tracks. Both are worth a look.

In the civil lawsuit, *Anixter v. Home-Stake Production Company, et al.*, the investors claimed that the funds collected by Home-Stake through the securities offerings were not segregated for use in developing particular oil properties—as Trippet had said they would be. Instead, the investors said money was commingled with the general funds of Home-Stake and paid out in the form of bogus profits. As is often the case with Ponzi schemes, Home-Stake was running out of money from the beginning. Since there was no real profit from oil operations, each succeeding year generated less bogus profit. So, some investors were paid with money from other investors. And the second group was angry.

Despite internal discord, the various civil complaints were certified as a single class action suit in 1976—three years after the first suits had been filed.

In the criminal case, Trippet and Home-Stake executives Harry Fitzgerald and Frank Sims were charged in a 10-count indictment with defrauding investors of almost $100 million. In May 1976, they pleaded no contest to charges of mail fraud and conspiracy. The three men spent one night in jail and received probation. Trippet paid a mere $19,000 fine, even though he was widely described as the "mastermind" behind "one of America's greatest Ponzi schemes." (Later in 1976, Norman Cross—who had been Home-Stake's auditor—became the only person to go to trial on criminal fraud and conspiracy charges related to Home-Stake. He was acquitted.)

Meanwhile, the civil lawsuits continued to churn along. During the early 1980s, more than $20 million in claims against Home-Stake were settled by insurance companies for several of the law firms that had advised Trippet and his colleagues.

According to William Wineberg, a San Francisco attorney who filed the original lawsuit in the case, collection efforts concentrated on the insurance companies that provided liability coverage for Home-

Stake's accounting firm, Cross & Co., and law firm, the defunct Kothe & Eagleton of Tulsa.

In February 1991, attorneys for three insurance companies asked the court to reconsider its ruling. The insurance companies—Continental Casualty Co., American Home Assurance Co. and Federal Insurance Co.—were liable for $56 million of the total $132 million judgment. And that number could increase to more than $74 million as post-judgment interest mounted during the appeals process.

The court ruled that it "found no just reason for delay in entering the judgment." So, the insurance lawyers appealed.

In 1994—six years after the initial class-action verdict—the U.S. Supreme Court ruled in another case that federal securities law does not permit a plaintiff in a civil lawsuit to make an aiding-and-abetting claim. The court concluded that this issue, common to Ponzi scheme lawsuits, was more appropriately addressed in criminal court.

The Home-Stake class-action case, which was a civil action, had made an aiding-and-abetting claim. The appellate court hearing the defendants' appeal was bound by the Supreme Court's new precedent. Accordingly, in January 1996, the Tenth Circuit Court decided to send the case back—again—for re-trial.

Norman Cross' longtime attorney, B. Hayden Crawford, who had been with the case since September 1973, said that "we feel the decision is correct and do not anticipate it will be changed." He said he was "anxious for a re-trial" even after almost 23 years.

Likewise, the lawsuit has been a long road for wealthy investors who lost large amounts of money, another investor attorney said. "Many of the original investors are dead, so we are dealing with their children and grandchildren."

This was part of the reason the parties were willing to settle. And they did so in 1996. According to lawyers familiar with the case, the amount of the settlement was close to the $56 million due from the three insurance companies.

Who Can Keep Ponzi Money?

Forget all the jokes you've heard about the definition of *chutzpah*. Few people are as brash as Ponzi perps (and those near or dear to them) determined to keep the money they've taken from trusting investors. Like case studies in a psychology textbook, these people will often convince themselves that the money is rightly theirs.

Luckily, the law—or at least the part of the law that deals with fraud—doesn't put much stock in psychology. The 1995 federal appeals court case *Scholes v. Lehmann* dealt with some complicated issues of who can pursue whom in the wake of a collapsed Ponzi scheme. In the case, the receiver for several companies ruined by a Ponzi perp brought fraudulent conveyance actions against one of the investors, the perp's former spouse and several religious organizations. All of these people or groups had received funds from the ruined companies.

The court of appeals ruled that the receiver had standing to assert the fraudulent conveyance claims. The people who'd received money from the scheme argued that the receiver was not really suing on behalf of the companies but on behalf of the investors who had invested in the corporations. They argued that a receiver cannot sue on behalf of the creditors of the entity in receivership.

To sum up their argument, they asked the following question: How can allegedly fraudulent conveyances hurt the instrument—namely, the company—through which the Ponzi scheme was operated?

Judge Richard Posner provided the following answer:

> *The corporations, [the perp's] robotic tools, were nevertheless...separate legal entities with rights and duties. They received money from unsuspecting, if perhaps greedy and foolish, investors. That money should have been used for the stated purpose..., which was to trade commodities.... The three sets of transfers removed assets from the corporations for an unauthorized purpose and by doing so injured the corporations. Thus, it is the removal of assets that damaged the debtor, and the trustee has standing to sue for this type of injury.*

So, the people who'd received money from the scheme could be forced to give it back.

In vivid language, Posner went on to explain: The appointment of the receiver removed the wrongdoer from the scene. The corporations were no longer the perp's evil zombies. Freed from his spell they became entitled to the return of the money—for the benefit of the unsuspecting investors—that the perp had made the corporations divert for unauthorized purposes.

Civil RICO Claims

Because Ponzi schemes follow patterns of fraud and theft, many angry investors pursuing perps will try to press lawsuits which cite the Racketeer and Corrupt Organizations Act of 1970 (RICO). These can get very complicated.

A RICO claim must include seven constituent elements, namely:

> 1) that the defendant 2) through the commission of two or more acts 3) constituting a "pattern" 4) of "racketeering activity" 5) directly or indirectly...participates in 6) an "enterprise" 7) the activities of which affect interstate or foreign commerce.

One strength of a RICO claim is that it allows triple damages; one problem is that it can be tough to make. When investors allege predicate acts of fraud as the basis of their RICO complaint (which is always so in Ponzi scheme cases), they must plead injury and causation with particularity. This means the person making the claim has to show a direct causal link between his injury and specific acts of mail or wire fraud. To state a claim of mail fraud or wire fraud, a complaint must allege:

> 1) a scheme or artifice to defraud or to obtain money by means of false pretenses, representations, or promises;
>
> 2) use of the mail for the purpose of executing the scheme; and
>
> 3) a specific intent to defraud either by devising, participating in, or abetting the scheme.

And then, these charges have to be linked back to specific losses suffered by the people making the RICO claim.

Another difficulty in making a civil RICO claim is that the person doing so has to have exhausted other avenues of recouping lost investments. A federal court in New York put this point plainly:

> *a plaintiff who claims that a debt is uncollectible because of the defendant's conduct can only pursue the RICO treble damages remedy after his contractual rights to payment have been frustrated.... Until plaintiffs can demonstrate that the orthodox methods of recovery have failed them, and that defendants' acts of racketeering have in fact caused them a loss, they should not be entitled to treble damages under* RICO.

Finally, a loss claimed in a civil RICO suit can't be speculative in nature. It must be definable on a factual basis—even if only approximately definable.

Burned Investors vs. Angry Creditors

When burned investors try to get their money back from other investors who got their money out, some pretty arcane parts of the law come into play. Chief among these: Passage of title.

In legal terms, a *sale* is defined as the "passing of title from the seller to the buyer for a price." The passing of title to goods cannot occur before goods are identified in a contract. After this identification, title can pass in any manner and on any conditions explicitly agreed upon by the buying and selling parties. During the interval between the time the goods are identified in the contract and title passes, the buyer has a "special property" in the goods.

In the absence of explicit agreement, title passes to the buyer when and where "the seller completes his performance with reference to the physical delivery of the goods." When people were talking about bolts of fabric or barrels of rum, these distinctions were easy enough to understand and apply. When people are talking about investments in securities, things can get a little fuzzy.

The relationship between a creditor and the Ponzi scheme company is usually pretty clear. The relationship between an investor or distributor and the company is more problematic—and determined in many cases by how title to goods has passed. In short, this issue deals with who owned the investment capital, who owned the assets of the enterprise and when these items exchanged hands.

This distinction often comes into play when commercial creditors of a Ponzi scheme company are battling with investors for who should come first in the resolution. It's especially important when the Ponzi scheme involves multiple levels of salespeople or distributors. The result can be a complicated hash of people trying to take whatever money or goods are left when the scheme collapses.

One often-used tool for clearing up the complication is the so-called "dominion" or "control" test. This standard requires "dominion over the money or other asset, the right to put the money [or asset] to one's own purposes" such as to "invest in lottery tickets or uranium stocks." On this issue, one court has written:

> *Logic and equity require that ordinary market-price sales by retail merchants acting in good faith not be contorted beyond commercial practice for the purpose of expanding the merchant's status as a captive risk taker.*

So long as a merchant has no reason to suspect a customer's Ponzi scheme or other skullduggery, sales made under ordinary commercial terms will usually be viewed as legitimate transactions between merchant and customer. Simply because burned investors claim they are "owed money too," they can't nullify the honest debts of dishonest companies.

Claiming Fraudulent Transfers

In the wake of a collapsed Ponzi scheme, people will rush to claim "fraudulent transfer" in the hope of getting some of their money back. However, the circumstances that support a fraudulent transfer are more limited than most people think. A major source of misunderstanding is that the word "fraudulent" has such pejorative connotations that it becomes difficult for most people to think dispassionately about it.

According to federal law, fraudulent transfers are subdivided into *actually fraudulent transfers* and *constructively fraudulent transfers*. The key distinction between these two types is the intent of the transferrers. Intent is essential to actually fraudulent transfers; it's immaterial to constructively fraudulent transfers.

Bankruptcy law, which controls many of the elements of fraudulent transfer, states that a court or court-appointed trustee may:

> *avoid any transfer of an interest of the [bankrupt Ponzi company] that was made or incurred on or within one year before the date of the [scheme's collapse].*

This goes for deals with creditors as well as deals with investors. However, in order to nullify the transfer, the court has to show that the perp did one of three things:

1) made the transfer or incurred the obligation with intent to hinder, delay, or defraud any entity to which the company was or became indebted;
2) received less than a reasonably equivalent value in exchange for such transfer or obligation; or
3) became insolvent or intended to incur debts that would be beyond its ability to pay as a result of the deal.

(The first activity constitutes an actually fraudulent transfer; either the second or third constitute a constructively fraudulent transfer.)

These activities are relatively difficult to prove in connection with an honest corporate debt. It's another reason courts don't often nullify deals with creditors.

On the other hand, the three standards—particularly the first and third—do fit many of scenarios offered to Ponzi investors. So, courts use the fraudulent transfer theory more often to force investors who took money out of a Ponzi scheme in its last year to give it back.

There are other legal complications. A court can find a transfer fraudulent but choose not to nullify it. And, even if a court *does* nullify a transfer, it can choose not to force any judgment against the transferees. The fraudulent transfer statutes provide carefully crafted remedies and limitations on remedies.

Not every transferee is liable; for example, subsequent good faith transferees often have no liability.

Many courts dealing with these issues cite the 1985 federal court decision *Johnson v. Studholme* as a standard of basic fairness. In the wake of a failed Ponzi scheme, the receiver filed lawsuits against all those investors who had received amounts in excess of their contributions (not just within the previous year).

The *Johnson* court ruled that the investors had given value for the profits they'd received and, so, had not received fraudulent conveyances. The court held that the capital contributions made by the investors and the risk that they could lose all or part of it had been the value provided.

"Unjust Enrichment" and Other Notions of Fairness

Many state have laws which prohibit "unjust enrichment"—or some similar activity. For example: To prevail on a cause of action in Illinois based on a theory of unjust enrichment, a burned investor must prove that the Ponzi perp has unjustly retained a benefit to the investor's detriment—and that the perp's retention of the benefit violates the principles of justice, equity, and good conscience.

Because of their broad language, these laws can be a useful tool for going after people who've taken money out of Ponzi schemes. However, these claims are distinct from fraudulent conveyance and have to be made separately.

In one Illinois case, the receiver sifting through the wreckage of a commodities investment Ponzi scheme filed a suit which argued that fairness required a redistribution of the effects of the scheme "by recovering from those who received more than their investments and paying those who participated in the fraudulent investment schemes."

However, to decide the question of fairness, the court noted it had to keep in mind whom the parties represent. It wrote:

> *The Receiver does not assert the rights or claims of any investors. Rather, the plaintiff stands in the shoes of [the Ponzi perp] and the various receivership entities. So, when asserting his equity claim, the Receiver cannot personally raise those equitable considerations of the later investors that lost their money.*

The companies which were the "receivership entities" had been established to perpetrate fraud. So, to the extent that the receiver sought recovery in equity on behalf of the companies, "it is difficult to imagine a less deserving entity."

The defendants in the case were "innocent investors" who had accepted their payments as legitimate returns on their investments. The court noted that the receiver had made no allegation that the defendants committed fraud or participated in the Ponzi scheme. "The evidence therefore supports the proposition that the defendants received these conveyances in good faith," the court concluded.

If the investors had cited the "unjust enrichment" language in a suit against the receiver, the court might have been more inclined to agree.

The "Special Status" of Ponzi Schemes

Transfers made as part of Ponzi schemes have achieved a special status in fraudulent transfer law. Proof of a Ponzi scheme is sufficient to establish the perp's intent to defraud creditors for purposes of actually fraudulent transfers. As one federal appeals court noted:

> *The fraud consists of funneling proceeds received from new investors to previous investors in the guise of profits from the alleged business venture, thereby cultivating an illusion that a legitimate profit-making business opportunity exists and inducing further investment.*

Smart Ponzi perps—or merchants who've dealt with perps—faced with fraudulent transfer claims from angry investors will usually make a so-called "good faith defense." Basically, they will claim that they entered the business honestly and that whatever trouble followed was simply the unpredictable course of business.

Legally, the good faith claim places the burden of proof on the person making it. The main stumbling block: A person lacks the good faith essential to the defense if he or she possessed enough knowledge of the facts to lead a "reasonable person" to inquire further about the transaction.

Reasonable person standards can be complicated. But one court considering a collapsed Ponzi scheme offered this common-sense guideline: "some facts suggest the presence of others to which a transferee may not safely turn a blind eye."

A Ponzi perp who's able to sustain the good-faith defense avoids claims of actually fraudulent transfer. The easiest way to avoid claims of constructively fraudulent transfer is to show that disputed deals involved reasonably equivalent value.

Reasonably equivalent value can be established in a number of ways. Two of the simplest: to show that the sale was made in a retail environment and to enlist a recognized expert to broker the sale. This is why smart Ponzi perps will be finicky sellers—it gives them credibility in the moment and deniability later.

Case Study: Stanley Cohen's Bogus Benzes

Going after people who get money out of a Ponzi scheme can be difficult—especially if the people are vendors or creditors rather than investors. One colorful car scheme shows why this is.

Ponzi perps love driving Mercedes Benzes. Once in a while, a perp will try to make money from this passion. Stanley Cohen concocted a not very clever, I-can-get-it-for-you-wholesale Ponzi scheme in which he accepted money from prospective buyers of premium cars and used it to buy the things at full retail. Because he was losing money—in some cases, quite a bit—on each sale, the scheme headed for collapse more quickly than most.

Cohen's investors were entertainment industry figures whom he reckoned were greedy enough to want the most expensive cars on the road...and not quite rich enough to afford them. There is no shortage of people like that in Hollywood.

Cohen would explain that he could get a Mercedes-Benz 500SL for $80,000, even though the car had a retail sticker price of almost $115,000. He claimed that he had some heavy connections in the auto industry; but he remained vague about details. If a person wanted the hard-to-get model cheaply, he or she had to give Cohen the $80,000 quickly, in cash and up front. And no questions asked.

As in all Ponzi schemes, this promise was too good to be true. Several people would each pay Cohen $80,000. Cohen would then go to a dealer, say that he was an agent for some Hollywood high-roller, sign contracts to purchase as many vehicles as his funds allowed, and write checks for the full $114,500 for each vehicle.

The dealer, confirming that Cohen had sufficient funds on deposit to honor the check but not otherwise investigating Cohen's bona fides, would prepare the cars for delivery. Cohen would then tell the dealer to whom to deliver (and place in title on) the vehicles.

Neither the numbers of vehicles involved nor the method of payment were, in the experience of the dealers, extraordinary. However, if the dealers had investigated Cohen's creditworthiness in greater detail, they would have discovered that he had a checkered financial past—including at least one previous personal bankruptcy and involvement in financial frauds dating back to the 1940s.

Since Cohen was losing $34,500 per vehicle (or more, because he was also taking money for himself), the number of cars he bought was always lower than the number of people who'd paid him $80,000. Other people's payments were used to make up the shortfall.

Cohen was no stranger to financial frauds. He knew that as he continued to buy high and sell low with the funds provided by the scheme participants that it was doomed to collapse. He knew that his "investors" were his creditors because he owed them either a vehicle or their money back. And he knew that when it collapsed there would be no vehicle and no money left for refunds.

The inevitable collapse landed Cohen in prison and left a number of burned customers—they didn't think of themselves as scheme participants—who'd paid Cohen money and received nothing.

The trustee who took over the pieces of Cohen's operation sued the scheme participants (that's what they were, no matter what they considered themselves) who'd taken possession of the cars and the dealers who'd gotten full retail price. He argued that a federal court should void all seventeen sales because they were fraudulent transfers.

The bankruptcy estate would recoup the difference between the price Cohen paid and the amount paid to Cohen by the scheme participants to whom the goods were transferred.

The trustee's theory was that the act of delivering $114,500 vehicles to people who had paid Cohen $80,000 was a transfer distinct from the $114,500 purchase at the dealer.

This second transfer gave Cohen value only to the extent of extinguishing his $80,000 refund obligation to the person who took delivery. So, this did not qualify for the Bankruptcy Code safe harbor that protects transferees, including merchants, to the extent value is given in good faith "to the debtor."

Seven of the deals had taken place within one year before Cohen filed bankruptcy, so the federal Bankruptcy Code gave the court the power to reverse them. California law and the Uniform Fraudulent Transfer Act (UFTA), which expanded the trustee's range of options under so-called "strong arm" authority, allowed the court to reverse the other 10 deals.

However, the court chose not to reverse these sales—even though the various laws would have allowed it. It disagreed with the trustee's theory, concluding instead that there were no fraudulent transfers because Cohen had received value from the dealers equal to the retail price that he paid.

The trustee appealed. The 1996 federal appeals court decision *In re Stanley Mark Cohen* considered the appeal. In that decision, a Bankruptcy Appellate Panel considered the technical details of the trustee's argument and held that:

> *The Bankruptcy Code makes [Cohen's] purchases from the merchants fraudulent transfers because [he] intended to hinder, delay, or defraud creditors when purchasing goods that were central to the Ponzi scheme. But the merchants have no ensuing liability because they qualify for the safe harbor that shelters transferees who give full value to the debtor in good faith.*
>
> UFTA, *in contrast, makes the transfers not avoidable against the merchants because, although they were made with actual intent to hinder, delay, or defraud creditors, the merchants took debtor's money in good faith for a reasonably equivalent value.*

Under this concept, Cohen's payment in full with checks that his bank honored limited any further duty the Mercedes dealers had. Cohen had what is known as "equitable title" in the cars.

When the lucky scheme participants received their cars, a separate transfer occurred—in this case, Cohen handed his equitable title in the cars to the participants.

Evidence that the bankruptcy court considered had established that Cohen had the requisite intent to hinder, delay, or defraud creditors when he'd purchased vehicles in furtherance of his Ponzi scheme. So, the transfers were actually fraudulent. However, that didn't answer everything.

The differences between the Bankruptcy Code and UFTA forced divergent analyses of the avoidability of Cohen's transactions.

The seven vehicles purchased during the year before bankruptcy could be considered fraudulent transfers under the Bankrupcty Code. Under UFTA, though, the other 10 transfers could not be avoided because the dealers operated in "good faith and for a reasonably equivalent value" when they sold for a market price.

The appeals board upheld the bankruptcy court's decision in favor of the dealers. It concluded:

> *None of the transfers are avoidable under the Uniform Fraudulent Transfer Act because the dealers took Cohen's money in good faith for reasonably equivalent value. Although some of the transfers are avoidable under Bankruptcy Code, the dealers qualify for the safe harbor demarked by good faith and value given to the debtor and are entitled to retain the money they received.*

The trustee would have to look elsewhere for deep pockets.

Long story short: Cohen may have been stealing money from some of the scheme participants; but that didn't mean the trustee could go after the dealers. *They* had operated in good faith. And they were probably the only characters in the story who had.

CHAPTER 20

Go After the Lawyers and Accountants

Trusting someone who turned out to be a smarmy crook is bad enough. What's even worse is realizing that a bunch of smarmy lawyers and CPAs ran up big fees advising the crooks, got paid and then claimed that they didn't know what was going on the whole time.

This is why the second lawsuit filed by most burned Ponzi investors is against any yuppie scum who advised in the scam. Even though it's usually the second suit filed, it's usually the most successful. Why? Lawyers and CPAs have professional liability insurance.

In March 1993, a top-notch law firm found itself in legal hot water over work it did for Stockbridge Funding Corp., the New York mortgage-brokerage business that turned out to be a Ponzi scheme preying on Eastern European immigrants.

Court-appointed trustee David Kittay who was charged with liquidating what was left of Stockbridge claimed that New York-based Battle Fowler, the law firm which had advised Stockbridge's management during its thieving heyday, should be held responsible for the $33 million that hundreds of investors lost. Kittay argued that the 95-lawyer firm "aided and abetted" the fraud by "drafting, editing and supervising illegal and fraudulent advertising" placed in newspapers geared toward Eastern European immigrants.

Battle Fowler answered that it had been unaware of any wrongdoing. Spokesmen for the law firm said it had tried to ensure that Stockbridge abided by the law—but that its efforts had been sabotaged by Stockbridge's owners. "There's not a scintilla of evidence that any of the lawyers at Battle Fowler knew what these characters were doing. They didn't know what these crooks were doing any more than anyone else [did]," the lawyers' lawyer said.

Battle Fowler's attorney said Kittay's suit was a creative—but unjustifiable—attempt to search for deep pockets to repay burned investors. If anything, he said, Stockbridge owed Battle Fowler money. The law firm had only been paid $50,000 for the legal work it did; it was still owed another $40,000.

Apparently, Battle Fowler went too far in fighting Kittay's claim. In an order, the judge presiding over the early stages of the dispute rebuked Battle Fowler's lawyers for attempting to "terrorize" immigrant investors by sending out notices demanding that they bring immigration documents with them for pretrial questioning.

The pushy approach didn't work. Battle Fowler ended up settling with Kittay in exchange for a quiet end to the suit.

The RICO Connection

Generally, the legal rule is that companies that were part of Ponzi schemes can't sue under The Racketeer Influenced and Corrupt Organizations Act (RICO). Only investors can. However, this leads to an inherent conflict: the receiver's primary responsibility is to the corporation—not the burned investors.

This means that receivers aren't usually good advocates for what most people would consider *justice* in the wake of a Ponzi scheme. Their proper role is to liquidate whatever assets are left as quickly and cost-effectively as possible.

The 1995 federal appeals court decision *Hirsch v. Arthur Andersen & Co.* illustrates why receivers in Ponzi cases have so much trouble going after lawyers and accountants.

In *Hirsch* (which was one of many legal spin-offs of the massive Colonial Realty[1] scheme), the receiver sued Colonial's accountant—Arthur Andersen—alleging, among other things, violations of the

[1] For more on Colonial Realty see Chapter 12, page 170.

RICO Act. He argued that Colonial participated with Andersen in fraudulently issuing memoranda to induce individuals to invest in bogus limited partnerships.

The bulk of the receiver's complaint alleged a scheme to defraud investors; but the only alleged damage to the Ponzi company was the generation of some unpaid accounting bills. The accused accounting firm argued that the receiver lacked legal standing because the claims "really" belonged to the scheme's investors and that any claims the companies might make were prohibited by virtue of their own participation in the fraudulent scheme.

The court ruled that the receiver hadn't alleged any distinct way in which the companies were damaged by the wrongdoing of the CPAs. It dismissed the claims and went on to explain that, because the receiver had alleged that the injury to the companies was coextensive with the injury to the investors, "the trustee has done no more than cast the [companies] as collection agents for the [investors]."

If—as the court suspected—the facts of the complaint suggested that the claims actually belonged to the investors, "a blanket allegation of damage to the debtors will not confer standing on the [receiver]." (The investors had already filed separate lawsuits against the law and accounting firms.)

The appeals court, affirming the lower court ruling, noted that the claim against the accounting firm relied on the distribution of misleading memoranda to investors. So, only the individual limited partners could make the claims against Andersen.

Unfortunately, there are exceptions that confuse matters by suggesting that a receiver *can* sometimes go after professionals on behalf of investors. The 1988 federal appeals court decision *Regan v. Vinick & Young* offered an example. In the case, a Ponzi scheme bought and sold rare coins for its customers—but the principals stole significant assets from the company, which eventually led to its collapse.

A court-appointed trustee sued the company's accountant and auditor for certifying reports which summarized rare coin transactions.

His complaint alleged negligence, breach of contract, negligent misrepresentation, and unfair and deceptive acts or practices. The damages sought included: the cost of the accountant's services, the misappropriation of assets by the company's principals, certain sales commissions paid by the company, the costs of its bankruptcy filing and an $11.8 million fine from the FTC.

The accountants argued that the claims filed by the trustee belonged only to investors, a group the trustee did not represent. The court disagreed, ruling:

> *The trustee steps into the shoes of the [failed company] for the purposes of asserting or maintaining its causes of action, which become property of the estate. [Any] confusion may stem from the trustee's repeated assertions that the accountant's wrongdoing caused [investors] to lose money. This emphasis...appears to result from the $11.8 million claim filed on their behalf...and from the concern that the estate may be held jointly and severally liable with the accountant in any eventual actions.*

So, these concerns were legitimate. The trustee could go after the accountants. If he won, the money would go into the company's bankruptcy estate and—all would hope—eventually to the investors.

Lawyers and accountants can't just take money from Ponzi perps without asking any questions about its origins. As one federal court has written:

> *The court's ruling in no way condones the acts of an attorney who blindly handles substantial sums of money for a client with no inquiry into its source if the attorney has reason to suspect the legality of the origins of the funds or if the attorney has reason to suspect his or her client's right to ownership of those funds. The attorney is clearly subject to disciplinary sanctions according to ABA [guidelines]. Moreover, he or she may be liable under conspiracy or aiding and abetting theories, or even under other theories not pled by plaintiff.*

The American Bar Association guidelines were designed to prevent lawyers from playing stupid when advising drug dealers. They apply equally well to lawyers playing stupid when advising Ponzi perps.

The civil conspiracy angle mentioned by the court might make sense in some situations. Burned investors stand on stronger legal ground if they allege a conspiracy existed between lawyers or accountants and the Ponzi perps. The problem here: While the *theory* of a conspiracy makes a better argument, it requires a lot more evidence than a negligence claim.

It's a short step from alleging a civil conspiracy to alleging an organized crime operation under RICO (and triple damages). However, the federal courts severely limit RICO's applicability to lawyers or accountants. In its 1993 decision *Reves v. Ernst & Young*, the Supreme Court explained the RICO restrictions.

The defendants in *Reves* were accountants who drafted misleading financial statements and were subsequently sued for both securities fraud and RICO violations. A jury found that the accountants had engaged in securities fraud; but the U.S. Supreme Court upheld the dismissal of the RICO claim, holding that the mere drafting of statements based on information supplied by the perp did not constitute sufficient participation in the operation or management of the enterprise. So, even if the accountants had engaged in intentional fraud, they could not be held liable under RICO.

In short, the Supreme Court ruled that lawyers or accountants do not incur RICO liability for the traditional functions of providing professional advice and services. It ruled that in order to be liable under RICO, an outside professional must have "participated in the operation or management of the enterprise itself" and must have played "some part in directing the enterprise's affairs."

Some courts have given the matter some leeway. In the 1994 decision *Friedman v. Hartmann*, a federal court in New York ruled:

> *[I]t will not always be reasonable to expect that when a defrauded plaintiff frames his complaint, he will have available sufficient factual information regarding the inner workings of a RICO enterprise to determine whether an attorney was merely "substantially involved" in the RICO enterprise or participated in the "operation or management" of the enterprise.*

But other courts, citing the *Reves* decision, have dismissed RICO claims without giving plaintiffs an opportunity to conduct discovery.

Establishing Fiduciary Duty—to the Investors

In order to make a claim of professional negligence or breach of fiduciary duty, a burned investor has to show that the lawyer or accountant owed some direct fiduciary duty. This usually isn't the case, since the professionals are hired by the company—and owe their duty to *it*.

This guideline stems back at least to a 1930s decision written by federal judge (and later U.S. Supreme Court Justice) Benjamin Cardozo which held that an accounting firm owes a duty of due care only to those in "privity of contract" with it or to "those whose use of its services was the end and aim of the transaction."

This is still generally the law on the duty. However, the duty of accountants in some states has been expanded to include reasonably foreseeable reliance provided it lies "within the contemplation of the parties to the accounting retainer." The 1985 New York Court of Appeals decision *Credit Alliance v. Arthur Andersen & Co.* also created a test which can expand Cardozo's limits. The court ruled:

> *Before accountants may be held liable in negligence to noncontractual parties who rely to their detriment on inaccurate financial reports, certain prerequisites must be satisfied:*
>
> *1) the accountants must have been aware that the financial reports were to be used for a particular purpose or purposes;*
>
> *2) in the furtherance of which a known party or parties was intended to rely; and*
>
> *3) there must have been some conduct on the part of the accountants linking them to that party or parties....*

This so-called "Credit Alliance test" usually requires some evidence of a "nexus between the [professionals] and the third parties to verify the [professionals'] knowledge of the third party's reliance."

The 1988 New York case *Crossland Savings v. Rockwood Insurance Co.* involved a bank that loaned money to a crook in large part because the crook's lawyer wrote several opinion letters attesting—wrongly—to the crook's financial viability.

After the scheme collapsed, the bank sued the lawyer's professional liability insurance company. The insurance company didn't want to pay; it argued that the circumstances didn't meet the Credit Alliance test. The court agreed with the bank: "When a lawyer at the direction of her client prepares an opinion letter which is addressed to the third party [namely, the bank] or which expressly invites the third party's reliance, she engages in a form of limited representation."

Under such circumstances, the "opinion letters do not constitute advice to a client, but rather were written at the client's express request for use by third parties."

Misrepresentations and Omissions

Under Securities and Exchange Act Rule 10b-5, burned investors can go after lawyers and accountants, alleging liability for either "material misrepresentations" or "omitting to state a material fact necessary to render the statements made not misleading."

The first of these charges, misrepresentation, is easy to articulate in legal theory but difficult to prove. A burned investor has to establish that the lawyer or accountant affirmatively stated something untrue about the scheme or its perps. Most professionals—even determinedly crooked ones—can manipulate language enough to avoid this direct connection.

This is why the prospectuses for Ponzi investments will often include critical boilerplate language stating that the securities are not traded on any securities exchange, not approved by the SEC or both.

If the burned investor can establish that the lawyer or accountant has affirmatively made false statements, the investor "must demonstrate that he or she relied on the misrepresentation when entering the transaction that caused him or her economic harm."

A charge of aiding-and-abetting liability against a lawyer under Rule 10(b) is especially tough to prove if there was no fiduciary relationship between the lawyer and the investor. In such a situation, the investor has to argue that the lawyer display an "actual intent to aid in [the] primary fraud" instead of mere "recklessness."

The 1988 federal appeals court decision *First Interstate Bank v. Chapman & Cutler* dealt with a case in which the defendant—a law firm—had allegedly made misstatements in connection with an initial bond offering to finance a nursing home. In a "classic Ponzi scheme," the proceeds of subsequent bond offerings were used to repay the initial offering.

First Interstate Bank, representing a group of burned investors, argued that "the subsequent bond issues were the inevitable result of the defendants' need to acquire funds to avoid defaulting on the [initial] issue." It also argued, that but for the law firm's misleading statements, it would have avoided the investment. These arguments worked at trial but were eventually reversed.

The appeals court dismissed the bank's charges and ruled that "something more than but-for causation is required." It concluded that while the issuance of the bonds might have been foreseeable, the misuse of the bond proceeds "constitute[d] a superseding event" and, therefore, the attorneys were not liable.

The second charge, omission, is more difficult to articulate. To begin, a burned investor has to show that the lawyer or accountant had a specific fiduciary duty or "other relation of trust" to the investors. (This usually isn't the case, any duty they have usually goes to the company that is paying their bills.)

As the U.S. Supreme Court explicitly stated in its *Central Bank* decision, "[w]hen an allegation of fraud is based upon nondisclosure, there can be no fraud absent a duty to speak."

There's a slight benefit to this more difficult standard. If a burned investor can establish that a lawyer or accountant has made a material omission, positive proof of reliance is not necessary if the investor can show that (1) the withheld facts were material, and (2) defendant had a duty to disclose the facts. The two charges are often so closely linked that both—or either—can be made by a burned investor. For that reason, many make both claims. The courts are left to sort through somewhat confusing law and absolutely confusing facts.

As one court noted: "Like standing dominoes, however, one misrepresentation in a financial statement can cause subsequent statements to fall into inaccuracy and distortion when considered by themselves or compared with previous statements."

In the end, the courts themselves aren't clear about the distinctions between *misrepresentations* and *omissions*. In the federal appeals court decision *Little v. First-California Company*, the court stated:

> *The categories of "omission" and "misrepresentation" are not mutually exclusive. All misrepresentations are also non-disclosures, at least to the extent that there is failure to disclose which facts in the representation are not true. Thus, the failure to report an expense item on an income statement, when such a failure is material, ...can be characterized as (a) an omission of a material expense item, (b) a misrepresentation of income, or (c) both.*

One of the issues that kept the Home-Stake Mining Ponzi scheme in the courts for more than 20 years was whether its lawyers could be held liable. Even the question was complicated. One of the appeals courts asked whether the lawyers:

> *aided and abetted the fraudulent conduct...in the preparation of registration statements...either with actual knowledge as attorneys of the misrepresentations and the omission of material facts set forth in the registration statements and prospectuses in which their names appeared, with their consent, or, in the alternative, under circumstances where in the due exercise of their professional responsibilities these attorneys should have known of such....*

The answer, in either case, turned out to be "yes." The professional liability insurance companies for several of the firms settled with the burned investors to make the case go away.

How Two Young Ponzi Perps Conned Lots of Accountants

Barry Minkow was a decade-of-greed oddity who started an unlikely company—it cleaned rugs—when he was 16 and crashed before he was 25. His company, called ZZZZ Best Carpet Cleaning, was nothing more than a particularly aggressive Ponzi scheme. But it stands as a testament to how easily greedy professionals can be convinced to lend an air of legitimacy to a bogus enterprise.

ZZZZ Best started out cleaning carpets in people's homes in the suburban San Fernando Valley, north of Los Angeles. For a short time, it was a legitimate business—driven by Minkow's cloying boyish chutzpah. In the mid 1980s, Minkow started talking about big contracts he was signing to clean carpets for L.A.'s biggest companies and for insurance companies rehabilitating fire-damaged buildings.

The high-margin insurance work was all fiction. Minkow and a handful of advisers (some of whom had organized crime connections) borrowed money from loan sharks, repaid it with money borrowed from investors and sloshed the whole thing around several corporate bank accounts to make ZZZZ Best look bigger than it was.

The company expanded its Ponzi scheme by selling shares to the public (at one point, it had a market capitalization of more than $200 million). This is where the craven accountants came into play.

Mark Morze, the financial architect of the ZZZZ Best scam, said the insurance restoration division was a good example of how accountants are willing to be misled about a scam. "No one ever checked those receivables. Not the auditors. No one. Think about that. If you were having construction done on your home, you'd check the contractor's references and you'd ask about licenses and maybe whether the company's employees were bonded."

The accountants' unwillingness to do basic, "shoe leather" investigation allowed Minkow and Morze to move a few million dollars through dozens of accounts and make the company look like it was worth hundreds of millions of dollars. By learning a little accounting jargon and focusing on winning CPAs over "as friends," Minkow and Morze were able to win professional support in the due diligence process that was required before the stock offering. "We tried to befriend the auditors, to get them to look at us as people, and not just credits and debits," Minkow said.

He also made sure ZZZZ Best paid its lawyers and accountants well...and on time.

Basically, Minkow said ZZZZ Best's auditors—a predecessor of the accounting firm Ernst & Young—never took the time to learn the details of the business. If the auditors had known anything about insurance restoration work, they would have caught the fraud easily.

The ride didn't last long after the offering. By the middle of 1987, the ZZZZ Best empire collapsed under the weight of its lies. After the deluge, more than a dozen people were indicted. Everyone except Minkow reached plea bargains with the prosecutors; the boy wonder decided to take his chances with a jury.

The jury found Minkow guilty of 57 counts of stock fraud, bank fraud, mail fraud and tax evasion. In March 1989, Minkow was sentenced to 25 years in prison and ordered to pay burned ZZZZ Best investors $26 million in restitution from future earnings. "You're dangerous, because you have this gift of gab, this ability to communicate," the judge said, as he sentenced Minkow. "You don't have a conscience."

Case Study: J. David & Company

One of southern California's biggest Ponzi schemes—and that's saying something—was resolved fairly well for burned investors because of a law firm that was held liable for its bad advice.

In the late 1970s, Jerry Dominelli was a stockbroker working at conservative Bache and Company in San Diego, California. In 1980, Dominelli left Bache with Nancy Hoover, a co-worker with whom he was having an extramarital affair. The two formed J. David and Company, the centerpiece of several related investment vehicles. They set up offices in the ritzy La Jolla area to sell tax shelters, manage investors' money and trade foreign currency.

The people who bought into the scheme were told that their money was going to be used to trade foreign currencies through a far-off tax haven, the Caribbean island Montserrat.

Hoover used political connections that she had in the San Diego area to lend an atmosphere of legitimacy to the operation. "I just didn't believe Nancy Hoover could be involved in a scam," one investor said. "I made an error in judgment." Indeed he did. The entire J. David business was a fraud. Dominelli didn't trade foreign currency; he just paid off old investors with money from new ones.

And many of J. David's investors were on the shady side from the beginning. "These people all suspected Dominelli was laundering money...or something," says one lawyer familiar with the scheme. "His story never made sense. Really, all he was doing was promising big, tax-free profits. And winking the whole time. Anyone could see this was too good to be true."

Many of the investors figured they'd keep their money in for a short time—a few months or so—and then pull out. This was a textbook example of the greater fool theory. And, for a short time, there were enough greater fools that some San Diego high-rollers came away from J. David with fat profits. Word of these early wins attracted money from people with more greed than brains.

At the height of J. David's success in the early 1980s, the scheme was attracting hundreds of thousands of dollars a week. Dominelli and Hoover divorced their spouses, moved in together and vied for prominence among San Diego's financial and political elite.

By early 1984, Dominelli's business empire was heading toward trouble. The buzz in the moneyed circles of La Jolla and Del Mar had changed from hushed awe about his success to world-weary recognition of a Ponzi scheme. Once the high-rollers pulled out, Dominelli and Hoover were left with hundreds of smaller investors. This created logistical problems that the couple couldn't manage. J. David checks were being returned routinely because of insufficient funds in the company's checking accounts. At this point, even the smaller investors started to figure out what was happening.

On February 13, 1984, involuntary bankruptcy petitions were filed against Dominelli, J. David and several related entities. Louis Metzger, a retired Marine Corps general, was named trustee to oversee the liquidation. A few weeks later, Dominelli was jailed for refusing to give up J. David assets. He was released, after agreeing to cooperate with authorities investigating the collapse of the scheme.

Beginning about May of 1984—and lasting almost ten years—several groups of burned J. David investors started bickering over which of their groups was most legitimate, who should represent them, and how the liquidation should be handled. After sorting through the disagreements, the trustee recognized investor claims of about $112 million in the bankruptcy action. However, none of the investors could be paid until money was recovered and creditors were repaid.

In March 1985, Dominelli pleaded guilty to stripping investors of $80 million through his Ponzi scheme. Although he'd made sophisticated promises, his actions were simple. He did little, if any, shelter-building or currency trading for his 1,500 investors. He simply paid early investors with money from later ones. A federal court sentenced Dominelli to 20 years in prison.

Dominelli suffered a stroke early in his sentence, while talking with Hoover by phone from jail. Not long after, Hoover married a wealthy man from central California who invested $2 million in her defense. She was eventually sentenced to 10 years in prison but served only 30 months because she cooperated with government investigators.

By early 1988, about $30 million had been recovered. The main source of this money had been the sale of company assets, including artwork, horses, several airplanes and cars. (One of the cars was a 1956 Gullwing Mercedes-Benz that brought $117,000.)

Of this money, about $8.4 million was used to repay secured debts. About $5.4 million was paid to lawyers, accountants and other professionals involved in the case. Another $1.5 million went to administrative costs and related fees. That left a little less than $15 million which would eventually go to investors and unsecured creditors. The trustee planned to keep that money until he'd explored settlements of various claims he had made against lawyers and accountants who'd advised J. David during its criminal heyday.

Allan Frostrom (who started out as Metzger's assistant) completed the J. David bankruptcy proceeding in late 1993. Despite their complaints, the investors did pretty well—most got back about 82 cents on the dollar. Of this amount, about 20 cents came from liquidating company assets and 62 cents came from lawsuits against law firms and accountants. Most of the professional liability money came from the law firm of Rogers & Wells, which paid $40 million to make a flurry of J. David-related lawsuits go away.

One lawyer who represented some burned J. David investors said that the Rogers & Wells settlement was more than should be expected in the wake of a fallen Ponzi scheme:

> *That firm was looking at some major liability. There were boxes full of smoking guns showing that [its] lawyers had signed off on contracts and other documents they knew—or should have known—were bogus. Maybe they were just stupid. But there were so many documents that the stupid defense was going to be hard to make....*

Rogers & Wells restructured its partnership after the J. David settlements. But one person who was with the firm at the time said it—like most J. David investors—was fooled by Dominelli and Hoover's local prominence. For lawyers, that's an expensive mistake.

CHAPTER 21

Go After Banks and Financiers

After greedy lawyers and accountants, the next best place to turn for some recovery is the financial sector. A burned investor will sometimes have success suing the banks, brokerages and institutional financial supporters that help Ponzi schemes flourish. (Often, burned investors will turn to the finance people first. That's a mistake. Professionals are usually insured against bad advice. And—regardless of what the law says—professionals are usually more culpable.)

A burned Ponzi investor can almost always make a couple of charges against banks and financial institutions. The first is the same charge that works for lawyers and accountants—namely, that these outsiders materially supported the fraud by making misstatements or omissions that led the greedy naifs to invest. The second charge is that banks, by supporting the Ponzi scheme aggressively, became promoters of the fraud. All things being equal, this charge is easier to make against institutions than individuals—though an investor *can* make it against either group.

Finally, the burned investor can charge that the bank or financial institution actually participated in the scheme. This charge is usually made against brokerages and financial marketing companies...but sometimes it works for banks.

Some angry investors try to implicate a bank simply because it allowed a Ponzi perp to keep a checking account in one of its branches—and cashed the investors' checks. This argument almost never works. Banks have a long history of court decisions on their side, which says that they're not responsible when customers use their accounts to perpetrate crimes.

One example of a pro-bank ruling sums up this defense:

> *Banks handle a high volume of transactions and cannot be required to supervise the checking account activity of their customers, nor should they be potentially liable for the fraudulent activities of their customers.*

And another elaborates:

> *Facts which warrant suspicion would not necessarily cause the bank to know, or have reasonable cause to know, that the Ponzi [perp] was bankrupt, or that he was a swindler. Banks are under no duty at law to warn the investing public as to the financial condition of their depositors. Investors may be assumed to keep themselves reasonably informed as to the financial capacity of persons with whom they are dealing in their investments."*

Key Standards of Bank Culpability

In the 1988 federal appeals court decision *Williams v. California 1st Bank*, the Ponzi company—a distributor of Mexican seafood—sold investment contracts to individual investors, with a bank serving as the depository.

After the investment program collapsed, the trustee sued the bank on behalf of the estate and the investors, alleging securities law violations arising out of the bank's involvement in the scheme. Since the trustee and the estate would recoup only administrative costs from a favorable judgment, and the investors would receive the bulk of any recovery, the court noted that the "investors plainly remain the real parties in interest in these actions."

As a result, the court held that the trustee lacked standing because the money was owed to the investors, not the estate. The appeals court held that the investors, and not the trustee representing the distributorship, had standing to sue for the loss. In reaching this conclusion, the court noted that because the seafood company and the bank were—effectively—partners in committing the fraud, the bankrupt company had no claim against the bank.

Of course, a burned investor *could* pursue a claim. But even the burned investor will run into some problems. The Supreme Court's 1994 decision *Central Bank of Denver v. First Interstate Bank of Denver* restricted the degree to which aiding-and-abetting liability can be applied to banks and financial institutions that assist Ponzi schemes.

In that case, burned investors sued a trustee on the theory that it aided and abetted Rule 10(b) violations by "recklessly ignoring its oversight duties." Ruling that the claim could not stand, the Supreme Court found that Rule 10(b) "prohibits only the making of a material misstatement (or omission) or the commission of a manipulative act.... The proscription does not include giving aid to a person who commits a manipulative or deceptive act."

While the *Central Bank* decision severely curbed actions against secondary actors, the court admitted that such actors are not "always free from liability under the securities acts." Specifically, it wrote:

> *Any person or entity, including a lawyer, accountant, or bank, who employs a manipulative device or makes a material misstatement (or omission) on which a purchaser or seller of securities relies may be liable as a primary violator....*

So, a burned investor has to prove that the bank—or its personnel—were actively involved in promoting the scheme. Of course, the relationship between a Ponzi perp and his bank isn't always clear. Many perps use unwitting banks—or groups of banks—to create whole systems of bogus transactions intended to hide their tracks. The bank's liability may *seem* larger here; but it can be even harder to prove.

When Banks Become Promoters

In his 1914 book *Other People's Money*, which studied the concentration of power among New York investment bankers, future Supreme Court Justice Louis Brandeis wrote:

> *[T]his enlargement of their legitimate field of operations did not satisfy investment bankers.... They became promoters, or allied themselves with promoters.*

The Securities Act of 1933 was influenced by Brandeis's book. As one congressman put it, "The American investor was relying upon the bankers, since faith in the bankers was virtually the only measuring rod for the investor. How certain bankers and brokers have breached that faith is part of this whole sordid story."

When this line is crossed—which it still sometimes is—banks can be held liable for Ponzi scheme damages. That's exactly what happened in the Great Rings Estate Limited Partnership scheme.

Great Rings was a distant relative of the infamous—and much larger—Colonial Realty pyramid scheme that shook Connecticut money circles in the late 1980s. One of Colonial's most successful salesmen was Kenneth Zak. In early 1988, after studying with master Ponzi perps at Colonial, Zak left to strike out on his own.

What he found was Great Rings, which had been started as a limited partnership among several experienced real estate developers. The stated purpose of Great Rings was to purchase four parcels of unimproved land on Great Rings Road in Newtown, Connecticut, upgrade their zoning, and prepare single-family home sites which would then be resold at a profit.

Zak—who had no experience in developing raw acreage—didn't care what the stated purpose of the vehicle was. To him, it was a method of raising money. He and the founding general partners agreed on an unusual method of financing. Great Rings would solicit investments in the form of limited partnerships. Investors would borrow the entire purchase price of their shares ($50,000 each) from a bank. Their notes would be directly payable to the bank. The partnership would guarantee a return at 8 percent per annum to the investors, to offset the interest on the notes to the bank.

Zak claimed that, in two years, Great Rings would have sufficient funds to pay off the principal—and still have many of the parcels left to sell. So, the general partners would raise millions and the investors would never pay a dime out of their own pockets.

The scheme, while not inherently unlawful, contained a substantial Ponzi element from the very beginning. The raw acreage could not produce income until it was developed and resold, so the only conceivable source of the 8 percent annual return was money from new investors. This aspect of the enterprise was not mentioned in any of the promotional literature or legal filings produced by Great Rings.

The success of the scheme rested on persuading a bank to go along. Zak approached Connecticut National Bank (CNB). In January 1989, he met twice with Neal Fitzpatrick, then a senior vice-president and regional manager of CNB. The first meeting was at Fitzpatrick's office, and the second was at a Super Bowl party at Zak's home.

Fitzpatrick also met with the other general partners of Great Rings. He agreed that, if the general partners would refer potential investors to CNB, the bank would loan money to those investors that it deemed even minimally qualified. "The bank was dying to get money out there working," recalls one of the investors. "The minimal qualifications were that the leads could fog a mirror.

Fitzpatrick contacted two other regional managers of CNB— in Hartford and in Waterbury—who also agreed to go along. The bankers reached a detailed agreement with Zak that each investor's loan was to be in the amount of $50,000 (the purchase price of a Great Rings limited partnership share) with an informal maturity date two years later and with interest set at 1 percent over prime.

The terms were tailored to fit the needs of the Great Rings partners exactly. CNB presented the same terms to every potential investor, with no negotiation on the investor's part. CNB's willingness to make these loans was an enormous selling point for Zak.

Great Rings filed the appropriate paperwork to exempt its limited partnership shares from the registration requirements of the Securities Act of 1933. Its argument was that the limited partnerships didn't qualify as a public offering under Rule 506 of the Act.

Rule 506 exempts transactions involving no more than 35 purchasers of securities. In calculating the number of purchasers under the Rule, "accredited investors" are not counted. An "accredited investor" is a person with a net worth—together with his or her spouse—over $1 million or an income over $200,000 a year in each of the two previous years.

Rule 506 also requires that each purchaser who is not an accredited investor have "such knowledge and experience in financial and business matters that he is capable of evaluating the merits and risks of the prospective investment." Great Rings marketing materials stated:

> *Units will be sold only to persons that the General Partners reasonably believe to satisfy the definition of an "accredited investor" under...the Securities Act.*

So, Great Rings was supposed to be a rich person's deal.

Sometimes Warnings Tease Greater Interest

The various disclaimers included in the marketing materials acted like catnip to greedy strivers of middle-class means. With the marketing pieces circulating around central Connecticut, many people would know that anyone involved in Great Rings had to be rich by the SEC's reckoning. So, investing in the deal was something like leasing a Mercedes. It was a sign you had made it.

Of course, Zak didn't actually follow the disclaimers. He sold Great Rings limited partnership units to accredited and nonaccredited investors alike. And, with CNB rubber-stamping loan applications, a lot of people who wouldn't normally have $50,000 in cash to invest were able to get involved. As one court later noted:

> *The evidence is overwhelming that [Great Rings] solved this problem by ...wholesale forgery. When an investor signed his subscription agreement, he was told what to fill in and not fill in. It would not be completed in full. [Great Rings' staff] would then fill in some cooked up figures on the balance sheet so that the investor's income and net worth would be sufficiently inflated to make him accredited.*

The Great Rings promoters focused their efforts in Waterbury on the city's Republican Party establishment. This was a middle-class crowd...with aspirations for bigger things.

More than 40 investors ultimately joined Great Rings, contributing more than $2 million. Monthly payments to cover the interest payments on the CNB loans started in September 1988. They continued for about a year until the fall of 1989. At that point, the money stopped coming—and explanations were in exceedingly short supply. Only one thing was certain: CNB still expected to be paid.

By this time, Zak had left Great Rings. The money that the company had raised was gone. The partnership had acquired two relatively small parcels of land, totaling 10 lots; and even these parcels were eventually foreclosed on by CNB.

The lawsuits started in early 1990. Angry investors sued every person and entity connected to Great Rings—the company itself, Zak, the other general partners and CNB. The bank turned around and sued many of the investors, holding them personally liable for loans taken against the worthless Great Rings partnership units.

One of the most important ruling on these cases was the 1993 Connecticut state court decision *Connecticut National Bank v. Robert A. Giacomi et al.* Clearly astounded by CNB's actions, the court wrote:

> *Bankers are regarded in popular folklore as shrewd, tightfisted individuals, unwilling to lend money to anyone unable to prove that he doesn't need the money in the first place. This case involves bankers of a very different description.... [CNB] made a deal with the promoters of a speculative real estate scheme to give unsecured loans to the investors in that scheme. [R]ather than employing the traditional close scrutiny of a lending bank, it dished out loans to investors it had never seen with a cursory abandon that left the recipients slack-jawed with astonishment.*

Of course, there's no law against loaning money with cursory abandon. But the court was troubled by the shady histories of people like Kenneth Zak. It went on to write:

> *The promoters here were, essentially, common criminals, who engaged in numerous acts of fraud, forgery, and outright theft of the invested funds. The bank openly allied itself with the promoters and, in effect, became a promoter. ...[T]he general atmosphere of fraud and betrayal in this case [and] the fact that no satisfactory accounting of funds has ever been made...irresistibly lead to the conclusion that the investors' money was simply stolen.*

The court acknowledged that some of the investors had criminal backgrounds themselves—and may have been looking for an easy profit from a sleazy deal. But the argument against CNB—namely, that the bank was a part of the scheme—held up. CNB was in trouble.

The court cited Learned Hand's statement that, in order to be held as an aider-and-abettor, a person or entity must "associate himself with the venture, participate in it as something that he wishes to bring about, [and] seek by his action to make it succeed."

CNB associated itself with the venture, participated in it as something it wished to bring about, and sought by its actions to make it succeed. Its involvement was "affirmative, substantial and wrongful." The court concluded that CNB should not be permitted to recover against the investors. "In a case like this, when the bank went out of its way to act as bait, it cannot complain that the fish were eager to bite."

When Stockbrokers Push People into Ponzi Schemes

More often than banks, stock brokerages will end up promoting Ponzi schemes. But stock brokerages aren't always linked so closely with the investments they sell; the key to establishing a brokerage's liability is proving that it was a "control person." The 1992 federal appeals court decision *Harrison v. Dean Witter Reynolds* held one brokerage liable on these grounds.

The Ponzi perps in the case had used Dean Witter's office space, telephone services and employee trading accounts in order to perpetuate their scheme. The local management failed to enforce Dean Witter's own rules to prevent such fraudulent practices.

The same appeals court later upheld a jury finding of liability in a related case, based on the brokerage firm's:

> *failure to detect and halt its employees' fraudulent activities, the complete lack of supervision over their abnormal trading activities, and the firm's refusal to investigate the obvious rule violations committed by its agents.*

In that later decision, the court noted the existence of :

> *[S]ufficient evidence for a reasonable jury to determine that had Dean Witter not shut its eyes to the various fraud signs available to it, as it did, the whole scheme could have been detected and shut down by Dean Witter far earlier than when it collapsed.*

The problem with the investment world is that it mixes conservative vehicles with high-risk ones, often in close quarters. Few brokerage firms investigate all of the investments they sell—and they don't make false promises about doing so. A New York lawyer who sits on arbitration panels that hear investment disputes lays out the terms:

> *As long as the stock brokerage isn't dumping worthless stock that it owns or coercing a person to make an investment he's said he doesn't want to, the operating rule is "Buyer beware." It's really hard to find a broker liable for a client's losses. Whether or not they should, the rules assume an investor knows what he's doing.*

As a result, some of the most egregious schemes are able to market themselves through legitimate brokerages.

In April 1989, Thomas Mullens started Omni Capital Group in Boca Raton, Florida. He employed commissioned salespeople, secretaries and receptionists for the corporate office in Boca Raton and sales offices in New Jersey, California and Ohio.

Omni Capital sold loosely-defined "investment opportunities" in the form of shares, contract rights and participation rights in limited partnerships. Mullens told investors the limited partnerships were formed to buy and sell small, privately held companies for a profit. He published promotional materials claiming he'd sold 22 companies and his investors had averaged 24 percent annual returns.

In reality, Omni Capital was a Ponzi scheme. Mullens and his staff were able to convince about 150 greedy people to invest some $27 million in the scheme between 1988 and 1992. The investors, mostly elderly retirees, were promised annual returns of at least 15 percent on their investments. (But Mullens promised *some* investors returns of up to 15 percent *each quarter.*) "He customized his deals. If he needed money he'd promise you any interest rate," said Thomas Tew, a Miami lawyer who worked on the case. This is a familiar theme.

To keep investors involved as long as possible, Mullens spent some of the money on false account statements reflecting annual rates of return of 20 percent to 30 percent. As with the typical Ponzi scheme, he used some of the contributions from later investors to pay off returns promised to earlier investors, thus convincing at least some people that Omni Capital was a successful enterprise.

Mullens spent some of the fraudulently acquired money on symbols of success: a million-dollar home, an airplane, country club memberships, glossy brochures full of empty boasts about Omni Capital and elegantly detailed offices.

The scheme began to totter in 1991. First, the SEC began an investigation based on promises Mullens was making. In the course of that investigation, a group of Omni Capital employees learned that Mullens was a twice-convicted felon who'd spent three years in prison in the 1970s for operating a pyramid scheme in New Jersey.

Some of these employees had invested money with Omni Capital. They demanded refunds, and Mullens paid them about $1 million, buying himself a little more time. But the collapse came quickly in April 1992 when word of the SEC investigation leaked to the local press—and investors rushed to liquidate their holdings. Omni Capital repaid about $4 million and then filed bankruptcy in May.

Using Omni Capital's books and bank records, the bankruptcy trustee was able to trace all but about $7 million of the funds invested with

Mullens. Of course, this didn't mean the trustee could *recover* the money. About $15 million was lost.

In October 1992, federal prosecutors charged Mullens with dozens of counts of conducting financial transactions to promote a fraud, conducting monetary transactions with its proceeds and criminal conspiracy. A few months later, Mullens pleaded guilty to 47 criminal counts of defrauding investors and admitted that Omni Capital was a pyramid scheme with no tangible operations. A federal court in Miami sentenced Mullens to 35 years of in prison and ordered him to pay $27 million in restitution.

Many investors suspected that Mullens had diverted several million dollars to foreign bank accounts, but these suspicions couldn't be supported by facts. So, investors had to look elsewhere.

Mullens said that believed the people who sold partnership units had known that he'd run pyramid schemes in the past. That testimony set the stage for suits against the salesmen, including stockbrokers who referred clients to Omni Capital—in exchange for cash payments.

In April 1993, three Miami-area Prudential Securities stockbrokers were accused of taking money from Mullens to steer their clients into Omni Capital. Two separate suits filed in federal court claimed that the Prudential stockbrokers helped Mullens raise at least $15 million. (Both suits named Prudential—with its deep pockets—as a co-defendant.) Burned investors said they were told that Omni Capital was a conservative investment that Prudential employees bought for their own families.

One of the brokers had boasted that he'd raised $8 million for Omni Capital—for which he received more than $500,000 in commissions—during the 18 months prior to the scheme's collapse.

To connect Prudential to the misdeeds, the suits claimed that Prudential supervisors were aware the brokers were selling Omni Capital to clients and that neither Prudential nor its brokers did any due diligence to verify claims Mullens made in a prospectus. One lawyer for the burned investors said Prudential should be held responsible for allowing brokers to recommend investments that were not screened by management and to accept money from an outside source.

Prudential Securities spokesman William Ahearn insisted his firm never had a relationship with Omni Capital. "Anyone who invested with Omni did so directly with that company," he said. "They made the check out to Omni, there was no solicitation by us formally."

Ahearn said that the stockbrokers who took money from Omni Capital did so only after leaving Prudential. Still, Prudential settled with the shareholders.

"The main lesson in the [Omni Capital] case is that some deals are just so sleazy the bankers and brokers will pay money so that they aren't associated with them," says one lawyer familiar with the Prudential case. "And you might think that these deals are rare. But every office of every brokerage in the country has at least one that it's peddling right now."

Financial institutions get involved in Ponzi schemes because of two weaknesses which they share with many investors. First, they are drawn to strong profit-and-loss statements, which—in the early stages and with some manipulation—Ponzi schemes can have. Second, they operate in competitive arenas, so their decision-makers are often nervous about missing opportunities.

Together, these traits lead many insitutions to reach what one banker calls "false positives." Sometimes these miscues are foreign countries; sometimes they're local Ponzi schemes. All financial institutions have their share.

Case Study: Towers Financial Uses Duff & Phelps

Steven Hoffenberg's Towers Financial was a false positive. Hoffenberg dropped out of the City College of New York in the late 1960s to go into business. While he had no particular passion for any one line of work, he was a good negotiator. In a few years, he was buying small businesses in the New York area and reselling them to bigger competitors at decent profits.

In the early 1980s, Hoffenberg stumbled onto the business that suited him best: debt collection. He started a company that specialized in collections, receivables purchasing and factoring. These are activities that make most people—even most business people—flinch. They're the hardest, ugliest part of commerce.

Hoffenberg, with his facile knowledge of financial terms and aggressive, Brooklyn-bred personality *seemed* like the perfect person to handle the ugly work. Within a few years, Towers Financial operated through a number of subsidiaries, the largest of which were:

- Towers Credit Corporation, which purchased commercial accounts receivable and tried to collect them for its own account;
- Towers Collection Services, which collected past-due accounts receivable for third parties on a contingency basis; and
- Towers Healthcare Receivables Funding Corporation, which was involved in factoring health care receivables.

The last subsidiary was the most promising. In the late 1980s, Hoffenberg had gotten into lending money against accounts receivable of financially strapped health care providers. Towers would purchase the receivables—bills owed to hospitals and nursing homes by Medicare, Medicaid and private insurance companies—at a discount from face value.

The genius of the business was that Hoffenberg convinced the cash-strapped hospitals to give him financing (though they may not have realized this was what they were doing). He'd pay half the cash right away and the another 40 percent or 45 percent after he'd collected the receivables.

The collection cycle usually took 30 to 90 days, so Towers was earning an annual return on its money of anywhere from 20 percent to 60 percent. Many of the hospitals paid the premium without complaint. One former finance executive at a New Jersey hospital said, "I needed the cash, and I didn't care what I paid."

Hoffenberg ran into some trouble in 1988, when the Securities Exchange Commission discovered that Towers had violated federal securities law by selling $37 million worth of unregistered bonds. But the SEC agreed to close its investigation in exchange for a consent decree which required, among other things, that Towers make a refund offer to the holders of the bonds.

Towers made the offer—but couched it in such vague terms that only a small percentage of the bondholders took advantage of the chance to get their money back. The company only refunded $440,000 of more than $30 million it had received from the notes in question. As one court would later observe:

> *Had a substantial majority of these noteholders reclaimed their investments, Towers, thus being deprived of funds to pay interest on its other notes, would have been forced to default. The Ponzi scheme would then have been over.*

But they didn't...and it wasn't.

Hoffenberg treated his own employees in much the same way he treated investors. He compartmentalized his company, assigning narrow duties to each manager so that only a few people—and maybe only Hoffenberg himself—knew how Towers really worked.

And there was a lot of expensive bluster. Towers Financial's corporate offices in Manhattan were decorated with tasteful furniture, plush carpeting and oil paintings. It looked like a prestigious old-line law firm. The image of respectability helped Hoffenberg carry out his five-year growth plan, fueled by repeated note and bond offerings.

Most of the notes were distributed by some 240 small regional broker-dealers, while the bonds were privately placed by Towers itself. In its Offering Memoranda, which paved the way for the various bond offerings, Towers stated that it had developed a remarkably profitable operation. The fat profits allowed it to pay fantastic interest rates.

Between February 1989 and March 1993, Towers sold over $245 million of bonds to more than 3,500 investors in 40 states. The money raised from these offerings was supposed to go to buying high-quality accounts receivable that the company could collect easily.

Hoffenberg didn't buy many accounts receivable. And, when he did, he bough low-quality, uncollectable ones for pennies on the dollar. He'd then claim the crap was worth 95 percent of face value.

Another trick he used was to sign deals with corporate clients under which Towers would collect bills which remained the client's property. He'd then enter these bills on Towers Financial's books like accounts receivable his company had purchased.

Towers' Annual Reports for 1988, 1989 and 1990 stated that the company expected to collect 30 percent of all collection receivables as "fees." It never kept anything like that amount.

From 1988 through March 1993, Towers generated almost $400 million in losses—though these losses didn't show up in any of the company's financial reports. Hoffenberg was keeping the company operating by misallocating the infusions of cash provided by the bond offerings. He papered over the losses with phony financial reports presenting an upward trend in earnings. Between 1988 and 1992 profits appeared to rise dramatically, from around $4 million to $17 million; in fact, losses were more than tripling in this period, to almost $96 million in 1992.

Overstating receivables resulted in a reported $25.5 million in shareholders' equity in 1992; in reality, equity was negative $242.4 million. Reinforcing the illusion of prosperity were slickly produced annual reports. People believed the lies.

Hoffenberg lived in a Long Island mansion—complete with a pool, tennis court and private beach. For weekends, he kept a home in Boca Raton. When he needed to drive somewhere, he hopped in one of three Mercedes. In 1993, he tried to buy the *New York Post*. But trouble was looming. When SEC investigators learned about Hoffenberg's efforts to buy the *Post*, they accelerated their inquiry.

In early 1993, bondholder trustee Shawmut Bank began making noises. It had just received the company's fiscal 1992 annual report (six months after the end of the fiscal year) and found what seemed to be indications that Towers had violated the terms of its various loans. Worse still, Towers wasn't forthcoming about whether the "possible events of default had been cured."

Shawmut declared the health care bonds in default and refused to release any more of the bond-issue proceeds for lending to health care providers. That created a huge problem for Towers: It had already sent money to health care providers after purchasing the receivables backing the bond proceeds at Shawmut.

Once the money from Towers stopped coming, many providers simply kept the insurance payments. As a result, Towers Financial's cash flow slowed to a trickle. Realizing his time was running out, Hoffenberg tried to cover his tracks. One attorney would later discover a $6,400 claim against Towers from the Mobile Shredding Corp. of New York that covered work during the last months of 1992. Mobile had shredded 10 tons of Towers documents.

In February 1993, the SEC filed a lawsuit in New York federal court, charging Hoffenberg with securities fraud and demanding the appointment of an SEC trustee to run the company. Towers filed for bankruptcy protection a few days later.

In March 1993, Alan Cohen—a New York-based workout consultant—was appointed trustee. When he arrived at Towers Financial's offices, Cohen found Hoffenberg there, still trying to hang on to his control of the company. "I suggested to him that it would probably be better if he didn't come around anymore," said Cohen.

The federal lawsuit charged that Hoffenberg never intended to do anything with money taken from gullible investors except "apply it to [his] own purposes and use it for the payment of interest owing to other investors." According the U.S. attorney, "Unbeknownst to the investors, the source of the interest they received on the Notes was the principal paid by later Note investors."

That's a succinct definition of *Ponzi scheme*.

During its heyday, Towers had referred skeptical investors to Duff & Phelps, a financial credit rating agency which "would provide independent verification and corroboration regarding the creditworthiness of [Towers Financial] and...confirm the positive statements [it] had made." Duff & Phelps claimed it used what it called a "shadow rating" of Towers Financial. Its staff told a number of investors that it "had conducted extensive due diligence investigations prior to assigning ratings to the bonds."

Burned investors eventually sued Duff & Phelps, claiming that it had known that the false information would be used in investment decisions. They said: "At all times Duff & Phelps knew that the false assurances and information it was providing would be...used by the brokers and their clients...to evaluate whether to purchase and/or maintain investments in [Towers Financial]."

The January 1996 federal court decision *Shain v. Duff & Phelps Credit Rating Company* considered the complaints against the rating company. The case had been brought by Myron Shain, who'd invested $200,000 in Towers notes, on behalf of himself and a class of similarly situated suckers.

The gist of Shain's complaint was that "Duff & Phelps actively foisted a uniform and consistent set of misrepresentations and omissions on the Duff & Phelps Class via the Class Brokers who reiterated them to, or relied on them for, the Class."

Beginning in or about July 1990, "in an effort to lend additional credibility and respectability to its operations, Towers [Financial] hired Duff & Phelps to rate the Towers Bonds." According to Shain, the relationship between Towers Financial, and Duff & Phelps soon became "symbiotic." Towers paid Duff & Phelps fees and Duff & Phelps helped Towers promote itself to the investment community.

Duff & Phelps had never directly solicited Shain or other individual investors. Instead, Shain argued, the firm had "solicited" the sale of Towers notes to the investors by communicating with brokers.

The court ruled that Shain's theory that Duff & Phelps "solicited" investors through brokers was too convoluted to work. It wrote: "the district court decisions in this circuit consistently have held that persons are not liable...for solicitation unless they directly or personally solicit the buyer."

In April 1995, Hoffenberg pleaded guilty to running an investment scam, fraudulently selling notes and bonds to investors and using some of the proceeds to pay interest owed earlier investors. A year later, he asked to withdraw his guilty plea because he had been suffering from mental illness. A federal judge ordered psychiatric tests.

In March 1997, Hoffenberg was sentenced to 20 years in prison. District Judge Robert Sweet also ordered him to pay $463 million in restitution and a fine of $1 million. "There has been tremendous suffering here," Sweet told Hoffenberg. "You have not accepted responsibility for these securities frauds."

Hoffenberg said he would appeal.

CHAPTER 22

Fight Like Hell in Bankruptcy Court

All Ponzi schemes eventually collapse. After a scheme has ground to its inevitable conclusion, filing for bankruptcy protection—sometimes voluntarily, but usually court-ordered—is all that's left.

In order to get anything out of the bankruptcy process, a burned Ponzi investor has to fight like hell at each of several stages. This will usually require lawyers, various kinds of professional fees and enough fellow burned investors or creditors to raise a collective voice.

Even though the effort is complex and expensive, it can be worth the effort. And you don't have to be a lawyer to make the decision whether you should fight or—within some limits—how. You only need to know a few basic points about how Ponzi schemes work their way through bankruptcy proceedings.

To start, federal appeals court judge Richard Posner has written:

> *Corporate bankruptcy proceedings are not famous for expedition.... So, the last resort for the burned Ponzi investor is to look for some restitution in bankruptcy court. The law treats Ponzi investors a little better than shareholders of a legitimate company when it comes to court-ordered liquidation...but only a little better.*

A more important distinction is the one between a Ponzi investor and a creditor of a Ponzi company. Sometimes there isn't much of one. In its 1924 decision *Cunningham v. Brown*—which involved Carlo Ponzi's original scam—the U.S. Supreme Court wrote that a "defrauded lender becomes merely a creditor to the extent of his loss and a payment to him by the bankrupt within the prescribed period...is a preference."

What's more: the Bankruptcy Code allows a court to consider *any* transaction which occurs within the last 90 days before a filing inherently preferential—simply because of the time at which it took place. This protects "those investors who transfer monies to the scheme within the ninety day pre-petition period who receive nothing in return due to the collapse of the scheme, yet whose funds are used to pay earlier investors."

Bankruptcy law discourages creditors "from racing to the courthouse to dismember the debtor during his slide into bankruptcy." Instead, it tries to set a framework within which a debtor can "work his way out of a difficult financial situation through cooperation with...creditors."

Burned investors often argue that these goals have "no rational application" in the context of a Ponzi scheme—since Congress could not have intended to protect such a debtor so as to enable it to perpetuate fraudulent activities. Courts don't always agree. As one noted:

> *[Congress's] intention to avoid a debtor's dismemberment may rationally apply even to a Ponzi scheme when one considers that creditors of such a debtor may include non-investors. For example, if a Ponzi scheme uses telephone services and its telephone company remains unpaid, preventing investor creditors from rushing to dismantle the debtor as it slides into bankruptcy would serve to protect the [telephone company's] interests....*

Avoiding preferences in a Ponzi scheme serves the primary purpose—to equalize distribution to creditors and, to a lesser extent, to discourage a race to the bankrupt company's assets. Invariably, this directs a lot of responsibility to one person.

The Trustee Determines Many Things

One of the critical aspects of a bankruptcy proceeding is the naming of a trustee[1]. This person serves as a combination of CEO and defense counsel during the liquidation. While the trustee is not directly responsible for protecting burned investors (technically, the responsibility is to the bankrupt corporate entity), he or she is instrumental in setting the tone for the proceedings.

In fact, if a trustee is found to be asserting claims belonging to creditors rather than the debtor, the court—which ultimately supervises the proceedings—can overturn any activity.

Very often, burned Ponzi investors will argue that any claims asserted in a bankruptcy case "really" belong to them. This argument usually stems from the mistaken assumption that the investors are the ones who will receive the money anyway, so they should be able to pursue the wrongdoers themselves.

That's not how bankruptcy—or a bankruptcy trustee—works. It's not a debt collection device. Indeed, the trustee's job is to investigate the debtor's financial affairs, liquidate assets, pursue the debtor's causes of action, and acquire assets through avoiding powers in order to make a distribution to creditors. Whether a trustee considers a burned investor an ally or adversary depends on the burned investor's standing in a case. And this standing isn't always clear.

There are some lessons to be learned from existing cases regarding how a trustee in bankruptcy should plead a claim against a third party participant in a Ponzi scheme. A trustee will usually be careful not to plead for a recovery based on any injury to investors or creditors, even though fraud against investors may be a part of the background allegations.

In alleging background facts, trustees often explain how investors have been defrauded. These background facts, however, should not be confused with the actual claims. A trustee will usually be careful not to plead damages as an amount equal to the funds invested in the debtor's Ponzi scheme (the investor's biggest concern); instead, the trustee will measure damages based on funds improperly paid out.

There is a difference between a creditor's interest in claims held by

1 The terms "trustee" and "receiver" are often used interchangeably. There are exceedingly slight technical differences in the terms. They mean, effectively, the same thing.

the corporation against a third party, which are enforced by the trustee, and the direct claims of the creditor against the third party. Only the creditor can enforce a direct claim; and this has to take place in civil court, not bankruptcy court.

But a receiver or trustee can protect a Ponzi company's interest, which indirectly helps burned investors get at least some of their money back. As Judge Posner has noted:

> *We cannot see any legal objection and we particularly cannot see any practical objection. The conceivable alternatives to these suits for getting the money back into the pockets of its rightful owners are a series of individual suits by the investors, which, even if successful, would multiply litigation; a class action by the investors—and class actions are clumsy devices; or, most plausibly, an adversary action, in bankruptcy, brought by the trustee in bankruptcy of the corporations if they were forced into bankruptcy.*

For a burned investor, the last of these three methods is almost always the fastest...and the most cost-effective.

The Trustee Lays Claim

If—as a burned Ponzi investor—you can convince a bankruptcy trustee to file a lawsuit (what Posner called "an adversary action") on behalf of everyone, the work has only begun.

By definition, the property of a bankrupt estate is a scarce commodity. The reason companies declare bankruptcy—voluntary or forced—is that their assets are no longer sufficient to repay creditors fully. These creditors, eager to assert their entitlement to whatever assets *do* remain, will often lay claim to the property by filing claims outside of bankruptcy court.

As the administrator of the bankrupt estate, the trustee is charged with marshalling all available assets of the estate, reducing these assets to money, and distributing this money to the estate's creditors, in a manner that ensures each similarly situated creditor of the bankrupt debtor an equitable share.

Therefore, the trustee—like the creditor—is concerned with laying claim to any property that could conceivably belong to the estate. This "any property" usually includes lawsuits against the perps who tanked the company in the first place. The trustee's concern isn't only for money, though; it's also for order. As one federal court noted, the trustee wants:

> *to avoid numerous lawsuits by individual creditors racing to the courthouse to deplete the available resources of the estate and thereby thwart the equitable goals of the bankruptcy laws.*

To accomplish these goals, the trustee is given statutory power to sue and be sued as a representative of the estate.

In practical terms, it means that money paid to Ponzi investors is the property of the scheme. The Bankruptcy Code allows "fraudulent transfers made in furtherance of a Ponzi scheme" to be reversed. Specifically, it allows the trustee to avoid a payment made within one year of filing, if the scheme "made such transfer...with the intent to defraud any entity to which the debtor was...indebted." And all Ponzi payments are made with that intent.

A Ponzi scheme is considered—by definition—to involve fraudulent intent. In the wake of a Ponzi scheme collapse, a bankruptcy court can order the reversal of any transaction that occurred within one year before the bankruptcy filing. This one-year limit is known as the "reachback period." The court can order any investor who took money out of the scheme within the reachback period to give it back.

Another Way to Overturn Ponzi Payments

The trustee can also void transfers on somewhat different grounds. If the debtor "received less than reasonably equivalent value" in exchange for a transfer of the debtor's property, the trustee may avoid the transfer if several additional elements are established.

"Value" is defined for purposes of the Code as "property, or satisfaction or securing of a present or antecedent debt of the debtor." Bankruptcy courts have concluded that a defrauded investor in a Ponzi scheme gives "value" to the debtor in the form of a dollar-for-dollar reduction in other investors' restitution claims against the scheme.

On this subject, the federal appeals court in the Ponzi scheme case *In re Independent Clearing House Co.* ruled:

> *[T]o the extent the debtors' payments to a defendant [investor] merely repaid his principal undertaking, the payments satisfied an antecedent "debt" of the debtors, and the debtors received "value" in exchange for the transfers. Moreover, to the extent a transfer merely repaid a defendant's undertaking, the debtor received not only a "reasonably equivalent value" but the exact same value—dollar for dollar. We therefore hold that such transfers are not avoidable....*

In theory, the trustee is not allowed to reverse transfers made for reasonably equivalent value because creditors are not hurt by such transfers. If the scheme no longer has the thing transferred, either it has something equivalent—which creditors take to satisfy their claims—or its liabilities have been proportionately reduced.

But a trustee has some leeway in reversing payments to Ponzi investors. If all the scheme receives in return for an investment is the use of an investor's money to continue itself, there is nothing added to the estate for creditors to share. In fact, by helping the scheme perpetuate itself, the investors exacerbate the harm to creditors by increasing the amount of claims. As one federal court observed:

> *If the use of the [investors'] money was of value to the debtors, it was only because it allowed them to defraud more people of more money. Judged from any but the subjective viewpoint of the perpetrators of the scheme, the "value" of using others' money for such a purpose is negative.*

There's an exception to this so-called "value rule": a lender who accepted scheme assets as security can still collect the money it loaned.

Ponzi investors being forced to give back distributions will often argue against the one-year limit by claiming that the United States Constitution mandates people who are similarly situated receive like treatment under the law (this argument cites the theoretically complex Fourteenth Amendment).

The theory behind this argument is that a statute may single out a class of people for distinctive treatment only if that classification bears a rational relationship to the purpose of the statute. The argument implies that all investors in a Ponzi scheme are predominantly creditors of the same class and should be treated equally.

However, this argument usually relies on non-bankruptcy cases. As one court said, succinctly, "These cases are unhelpful." The chief judge ruling in *In re Independent Clearing House Co.* offered a more specific analysis:

> *All investors in a Ponzi scheme are creditors of the same class, so in theory all should be treated equally.... The equitable solution would be either to apply the statute to all transfers to investors in a Ponzi scheme—without regard to when the transfers were made—or to apply the statute to none of the transfers. Yet this court is no more free to rewrite the statute to bring the early undertakers into its net than it is to ignore the statute to treat later undertakers equally. Courts must apply the statute as written.*

The Bankruptcy Code allows some transfers to stand because they are part of "the ordinary course of business." However, the Code insulates the transferees of an avoided fraudulent transfer who take "for value and in good faith" by providing that such a transferee has a lien, or may retain the interest transferred, to the extent the transferee gave "value to the debtor" in exchange for the transfer.

Judge James H. Williams of the U.S. Bankruptcy Court in northern Ohio wrote a number of decisions revolving around *In re Plus Gold, Inc.*—a case of a collapsed multilevel marketing Ponzi scheme. Most of Williams's decisions had to do with burned investors arguing that the court should reverse payments that earlier investors had received.

The investors' money was spent buying "spots" in the Plus Gold "matrix." A spot was the designation used for a membership or distributorship; each spot cost $265.

However, some spots on the matrix were designated as "APS" or "additional pay spot" spots. Whenever a distributor had recruited fourteen other participants, an additional pay spot would be given to the distributor for free. Periodically, the people who had these free spots would receive the same pay-outs as people who'd paid for theirs.

The trustee in the case—as well as a group of angry investors—wanted the APS people to give back the money they'd taken out. The APS people argued that they were merely being reimbursed for time and money they'd spent marketing Plus Gold's scheme.

The court ruled that, since Plus Gold had received nothing of value in return for the free spots it gave these people, the money it paid them had to come back[2].

In recognizing claims for rescission and restitution, courts usually assume that the investors had no knowledge of the fraud the debtors were perpetrating. If investments were made with culpable knowledge, all subsequent payments made to such investors within one year of the debtors' bankruptcy would be avoidable, regardless of the amount invested, because the debtors would not have exchanged a reasonably equivalent value for the payments.

Similarly, if there is a question about a recipient's innocence at the time he received a payment under a Ponzi scheme, avoidance of the transfer might be sought. This claim usually requires a court to consider the good faith of an investor who wished to retain payments, or portions of payments, received from the debtor.

Exceptions to the Code Rules

A common problem in pyramid schemes is that goods, services and cash are often shuffled among many people—including some who have little or no involvement in the underlying scheme.

The law gives innocent bystanders a break. Subsequent transferees (that is, transferees of the initial transferee), who take for value without knowledge of the original fraudulent transfer are not liable for any recovery. Nor are their subsequent good faith transferees liable.

---

[2] This ruling runs against other court decisions—particularly several mentioned in the discussion of fraudulent conveyance in Chapter 19. This conflict is an example of the court's larger conflicts over how Ponzi collapses should be handled.

The Bankruptcy Code does not define "good faith." As a result, courts applying the good faith exception have generally refused to formulate precise definitions. However, after noting that "[g]ood faith is an intangible and abstract quantity with no technical meaning," *Black's Law Dictionary* states that the term includes not only "honest belief, the absence of malice and the absence of design to defraud or to seek an unconscionable advantage" but also "freedom from knowledge of circumstances which ought to put the holder on inquiry."

The Eighth Circuit Court of Appeals has written that "a transferee does not act in good faith when he has sufficient knowledge to place him on inquiry notice of the debtor's possible insolvency."

So, a transferee who reasonably should have known of a debtor's insolvency or of the fraudulent intent underlying the transfer is not entitled to the good faith defense.

The *In re Independent Clearing House* court explained (in a mixed anatomical metaphor) the determination of good faith in a manner that emphasized objective factors: "The test is whether the transaction in question bears the earmarks of an arm's length bargain."

Bankruptcy Crimes

Often, Ponzi perps will try to hide money from a scheme in the days...or hours...before filing bankruptcy. This is certainly a major concern that burned investors have after the scheme collapses.

The Bankruptcy Code provides criminal penalties for any person who,

> *in a personal capacity or as an agent or officer of any person or corporation, in contemplation of a case under title 11 by or against the person or any other person or corporation, or with intent to defeat the provisions of title 11, knowingly and fraudulently transfers or conceals any of his property or the property of such other person or corporation.*

People charged with these crimes sometimes answer that, for an act of bankruptcy fraud to constitute a predicate act under RICO, an actual bankruptcy case must have been filed. However, the Code also allows criminal charges against a person who merely transfers or conceals assets "in contemplation of a case... or with intent to defeat the provisions of [the Code]."

All that it requires is that the defendant transfer assets with the ultimate intent to defraud a bankruptcy court, whether or not such proceedings ever actually commence.

Fraudulent Conveyance and Bankruptcy

Without any doubt, the claim most often made in Ponzi scheme bankruptcies—in fact, in all bankruptcies—is *fraudulent conveyance*. But this claim is harder to make stick that might first seem. For a bankruptcy trustee to avoid a transfer as fraudulent, four elements must be satisfied:

1) the transfer must have involved property of the bankrupt company;
2) the transfer must have been made within one year of the filing of the petition;
3) the bankrupt company must not have received reasonably equivalent value in exchange for the property transferred; and
4) the bankrupt company must have been insolvent, been made insolvent by the transaction, be operating or about to operate without property constituting reasonable sufficient capital, or be unable to pay debts as they become due.

Most people focus on the fourth of these elements. They argue some variation on the theme that: "The company was dying when it made the deal, so it can't be enforced."

But all four elements need to be satisfied before a deal—or payment—can be reversed.

On the question of fraudulent conveyance, California bankruptcy law states:

> *The trustee may avoid any transfer of an interest of the debtor in property...that was made...on or within one year before date of the filing*

of the petition, if the debtor.. received less than a reasonably equivalent value in exchange for such transfer...and was insolvent on the date that such transfer was made...or became insolvent as a result of such transfer...was engaged in business or a transaction, or was about to engage in business or a transaction, for which any property remaining with the debtor was an unreasonably small capital; or...intended to incur, or believed that the debtor would incur, debts that would be beyond the debtor's ability to pay as such debts matured.

California's fraudulent conveyance statutes are similar in form and substance to the Code's fraudulent transfer provisions. Both allow a transfer to be avoided where "the debtor did not receive a reasonably equivalent value in exchange for the transfer and [the debtor] was either insolvent at the time of the transfer or was engaged in business with unreasonably small capital."

It's likely that burned Ponzi investors will make fraudulent conveyance claims at some point in the legal wrangling that follows a scheme's collapse. However, in the *CourtTV* culture of armchair legal experts, some legal concepts get more attention than they deserve. Fraudulent conveyance claims can work for burned investors—but the claims often seem like a bigger tool than they really are.

Case Study: The Scrappy Trustee of M&L Business Machines

Beginning in the 1970s, M&L Business Machines operated as a computer sales, leasing and repair firm in the Denver area. In the early 1980s, Robert Joseph acquired approximately 50 percent of the stock in M&L. By 1986, most of Joseph's stock—and the remaining 50 percent—had been transferred to David Parrish and Daniel Hatch.

In early 1987, Joseph, Parrish and Hatch began taking in money from third parties, whom they called "private lenders" or "private investors." These investors were promised high rates of return for the use of their money to enable M&L to buy large quantities of expensive computers and office equipment.

Some investors were told that they would earn interest at 10 percent per month—120 percent per year—for M&L's use of their money.

They were told they would share in large profits upon the resale of the computers and office equipment. Some investors were actually paid the usurious interest, often in the form of post-dated checks offered as security for the loans.

However, the dividends were funded by new investor capital, loan proceeds and check kiting. By the end of 1987, M&L had become a full-fledged Ponzi scheme. The principals were able to keep the scheme running for a little more than two years—then it collapsed.

When M&L collapsed, nearly $83 million in post-dated checks remained in the hands of various private investors. In October 1990, M&L filed a Chapter 7 bankruptcy. In December 1990, Denver lawyer Christine Jobin was appointed M&L's trustee.

Unsecured claims against M&L which were related to legitimate loans from investors totaled about $21 million. In addition, the Resolution Trust Corporation (RTC) as receiver of Capital Federal Savings and Loan had an unsecured claim for about $9 million which was related to other loans to M&L. There were also some relatively insignificant unsecured claims for goods or services. On the asset side, there wasn't much. M&L had accounts receivable worth about $10,000. Most of its money was supposedly tied up in inventory.

In February 1991, Jobin removed M&L's inventory from its warehouse. Over the next several months, she opened and inspected more than 700 computer boxes. Most of them contained only bricks and dirt or hardened foam.

In September 1991, Jobin started suing people. In time, she filed over 400 adversary actions—against everyone from the Ponzi perps to investors who got money out, lawyers who gave advice and banks that made foolish loans. Rarely has there been a better example of fighting like hell in bankruptcy court.

In March 1992, a federal grand jury handed down a 41-count indictment against the M&L principals and a handful of confidantes. In announcing the indictments after a year-long investigation, law-enforcement officials credited each other for cooperation among federal, state and local agencies. In July 1993, the indicted M&L officers and employees drew federal prison terms of various lengths for what the sentencing judge called a "scam from day one."

None of this did very much for Jobin. She tried to claim all rights to sue the M&L Ponzi perps. This effort resulted in a legal tangle with some people who loaned M&L money. From its opening remarks, the court seemed soured by the tone of the proceedings:

> *Rarely does the Court have the displeasure of reviewing such antagonistic pleadings wherein at times counsel on both sides lost sight of the issues.*

In the case, some of the people who'd loaned money to M&L argued that their claims against the perps were not assets of estate and, therefore, that Jobin had no standing to absorb their claims.

Jobin argued that the Bankruptcy Code weighs in favor of allowing only a trustee to pursue these claims so that all similarly situated creditors will be treated alike. This meant that only she had the right to pursue any action against the M&L Ponzi perps. The investors countered that Jobin would only have the rights she claimed if there were voidable transfers for her to recover. Because she was not claiming that the property in the hands of the perps belonged to M&L, she had to get out of their way.

The court sided with the lenders, allowing them to proceed with their own claims against the perps. Jobin redirected her efforts.

In December 1992, she sued Gregory Lalan, an investor who'd gotten some money out of the scheme. Jobin wanted Lalan to give back money which he'd received from M&L during the year preceding its bankruptcy petition. The bankruptcy court ruled in her favor and order Lalan to return $409,476, plus costs and interest. He appealed.

Lalan had owned a dry cleaning business since 1975. He was a conservative businessman. For years, he'd had a line of credit secured by the business, but he'd never used it; he owned his home, free and clear. In the summer of 1989, a friend told Lalan about investment opportunities available with M&L. He was suspicious of the promised returns, telling the friend that "there was no way to make money that quick without a catch." But Lalan eventually visited M&L's offices and—in October 1989—invested $10,000 cash.

Lalan didn't see any of the contracts in which he was supposedly investing. He didn't ask for any detailed financial records or statements either. Whenever he invested money in M&L, he'd receive two post-dated checks—one for his principal investment, and one for his profit. This process confirmed his understanding that he faced no risk.

However, Lalan could not always cash the checks on the dates they matured. Sometimes he was told to hang on to the checks a few extra days. He became suspicious after about six months—but continued to participate because the returns were so good.

The bankruptcy court concluded:

> *[Lalan] ignored his own initial intuition and plunged headlong into the scam because of the huge profits he was promised, and which he received. Is it reasonable to expect profits of 125 percent to 512 percent? Especially when there is supposedly "no risk" for the investment? Is it reasonable to expect a legitimate business to demand cash for an investment—at a minimum of $10,000? Is it reasonable to hand over that amount of cash without at least some investigation? Is it reasonable to accept post-dated checks for large sums of money from a person, but not be able to negotiate such checks on their due dates until permission from the maker is received? The answer to all these questions is a resounding NO!*

The District Court upheld this conclusion.

For the next three years, Jobin convinced the federal bankruptcy court to void payments that M&L had made to investors. By 1996, when she finally liquidated the bankruptcy estate, she had recouped almost $10 million. So, while Jobin wasn't able to balance the accounts of the bankrupt business, she was able to mitigate the damage.

CONCLUSION

The Mother of All Ponzi Schemes

The later half of the 20th Century has seen a confusing mix of eroding public trust in certain institutions (and burgeoning trust in others), growing self-absorption among many people and an increase in material wealth that's not always evenly distributed.

The result is a favorable climate for Ponzi schemes. The uneven distribution of wealth encourages greed and fear. Self-absorption breeds secrecy and gullibility. The migration of public trust from dogged government regulators to vapid television celebrities creates a moral vertigo that makes crime all but inevitable.

With Ponzi and pyramid schemes appearing in many places, people looking to make money have to move cautiously. It's true that some of the biggest fortunes are made on the fringes of markets and industries. But these fringes can be treacherous places. "How do you know a partnership's oil properties are really there, or that they really have bank accounts?" says Bill McDonald of California's Department of Corporations. "You assume the [investment brokerage] does due diligence and that what they tell you is accurate."

If the progress of Ponzi schemes during the past hundred years has proved anything, it's that accuracy is hard to come by and trust has to be earned. This creates a conundrum: You need to be most guarded about precisely the people and situations most likely to occur. "I ask people: If it's such a good deal, why is some guy you don't know calling up to offer it to you?" says Peter Hildreth, New Hampshire's securities regulator.

To protect yourself from Ponzi schemes, remember the following, common-sense tips:

- Don't expect to get rich quickly. If an investment sounds too good to be true, it probably is.
- Most bad deals offer high yields and meaningless talk of "guarantees" to "zero risk." High returns almost always imply high levels of risk.
- Be suspicious of any investment opportunity that seems inordinately complicated. This often is intentional—it encourages consumers to make the investment on faith.
- Ask an investment advisor or accountant to review the prospectus or offer memorandum with you. Promoters who balk at this kind of review should be treated with suspicion.
- Ponzi schemes often straddle regulated and non-regulated markets—but reputations are steady things. Check out the promoters with government regulators or industry trade groups.

What's remarkable about Ponzi's legacy is that, no matter how many times investors lose money, new schemes keep coming forward. And the schemes don't recognize demographic limits. Greedy and naive people of all sorts—young and old, black and white, rich and poor—line up to throw good money after bad.

Social Security's Troubling Profile

Nobel Prize-winning economist Paul Samuelson famously wrote:

> *A growing nation is the greatest Ponzi game ever contrived—and that is a fact, not a paradox. ...the beauty about social insurance is that it is actuarially unsound.*

Pundits who want to provoke response like to call the U.S. Social Security program some variation on "the biggest Ponzi scheme in the world." And they have a point. Social Security shares many common traits with a classic Ponzi scheme. Like a Ponzi scheme, Social Security is a program that transfers wealth. It moves money from the current generation of workers to the one that came before, from people who earn a lot to those who earn a little, from single people to families and from people who die young to people who live a long time.

Like a Ponzi scheme, Social Security relies on a steady stream of new participants. As long as the number of people in the American workplace grows or the money those people are making increases, the system can continue. As soon as that stream of participants plateaus—or, worse, shrinks—the system will collapse.

Like a Ponzi scheme, Social Security's collapse can be softened and slowed by careful management and one-time infusions of cash—but it can't be prevented. The system's defenders like to point out that the federal government won't let Social Security collapse. But the Feds can't control market forces.

The growth of America's non-immigrant population slowed after 1960. About the same time, women began to have fewer children; the national average dropped from 3.5 in 1960 to 1.8 in the mid-1980s.

During the same period, older workers began to retire earlier—but live longer. When Social Security was started, the average male worker retired at 69 and then lived about eight more years. In the mid-1990s, the average male retired at 64 and then lived 19 more years.

The growth rate of the average American's wages—which exploded for a quarter-century after World War II—slowed in the 1970s and 1980s as global competition and advances in technology reduced the need for unskilled, semi-skilled and even some skilled laborers. Those left often took a larger part of their compensation in the form of fringe benefits, which are not taxed by the federal government.

Together, these factors suggest that by 2030 there will be only two active workers supporting each retiree collecting money from the Social Security system. That's a big drop from the 30 workers-per-retiree ratio which existed when the program started, 7-to-1 ratio in 1950 and 4-to-1 ratio that existed even in the late 1980s.

Still, Social Security remains a popular program. It helps millions of elderly and disabled people stay out of poverty. In the 1960s, the poverty rate among the elderly was twice as high as for all adults; by the 1990s, the rates were about equal. But this success is a double-edged sword. In 1996, 63 percent of all retirees relied on Social Security for the majority of their income. Making any reform that would reduce these benefits would be very difficult.

The Hard Numbers

Social Security participants are eligible for full benefits at age 65. They can draw reduced benefits—equal to 80 percent of the full amount—at age 62, but those benefits do not increase to the full level at age 65.

Social Security funds are invested in non-negotiable Treasury securities, which means the money is spent on current government operations. Treasury securities pay low interest—about 6 percent a year during the 1990s, as opposed to the nearly 12 percent that the Standard & Poor's 500 stock index averaged during the same period.

Social Security has already been fiddled with numerous times. To keep the program solvent, payroll taxes have been raised repeatedly. In Social Security's earliest days, the combined employee-employer rate amounted to only 2 percent on the first $3,000 of annual income. In 1996, the rate was 12.4 percent on the first $62,700.

Despite these adjustments, by the mid-1990s Social Security was already in financial trouble. According to a 1995 report published by the Social Security Administration, retirees faced a 10 percent reduction in hospitalization and retirement benefits by the year 2010, a 27 percent reduction by 2020, and a 41 percent reduction by 2040.

The primary suggestion for avoiding these cuts: More substantial increases in the payroll tax. At that point, a common suggestion was to add 2.2 percentage points to the payroll tax—raising it to 14.6 percent. The increase would buy another five years of solvency.

Structurally, this is something like the roll-over of principle or other kind of deeper investment that Ponzi perps push on their loyal investors as their schemes mature.

The First Sign of Collapse

For people who retired before the early 1990s, Social Security was a great deal. Those who began paying into the system during the Depression typically took out twice as much as they paid in. According to one study, during the 1990s an average retired two-earner couple in their early eighties would receive Social Security benefits worth a total of $208,000. That's $133,000 *more* than the value of all Social Security taxes paid by the couple and their employers, plus interest.

Many people think they are paying for their own retirement and that the money is safe because it is in the government's hands. This sounds eerily reminiscent of the complaints that burned Ponzi investors make after a scheme collapses.

In fact, the Feds use current workers' Social Security contributions to pay the benefits of current retirees. The current workers' own benefits will, in turn, be dependent on the working population in the future. This means there is no money in any account to pay any future retiree. Economists worry that, as the overall U.S. population ages, it will become impossible to come up with the money to pay promised benefits.

In June 1996, Treasury Secretary Robert Rubin announced that government projections showed Social Security would be bankrupt in 2029. The same study projected that the trust fund which pays Medicare bills for 30 million seniors will be broke in 2001. The Social Security Administration also projected that in 2013, payments of benefits to retirees would begin to outstrip payments into the system. In short, the mass retirement of baby boomers will break the system.

During 1997 and 1998, the federal government cut spending and collected enough tax to create a projected budget surplus for several years. This created much excited talk about bailing out Social Security. But even if all of the surplus is used to help the program, it won't make an unsound proposition any more sound.

Demographers and economists predict that in 2050, almost a full centruy after the peak of the baby boom, more than 15 million boomers will still be alive—and watching the mail for their Social Security checks.

The signs have already started to appear. In the 1990s, for the first time in the history of Social Security, some categories of new retirees—particularly middle- and high-income single males—could expect to get back less for their contribution to Social Security than if they had invested the same amount of money in low-risk securities.

That projection held true even if the system managed to pay beneficiaries all promised benefits into the 21st Century. Most experts considered that an unlikely proposition—unless the Feds were able to pass sizable tax increases or other adjustments to the program. So, it seemed that a growing number of retirees would likely get substantial negative returns on their contributions.

Social Security promoters insist that this doesn't mean the scheme is starting to collapse. By their reckoning, such talk is politically-motivated rhetoric. "There's been a steady campaign under way...to raise doubts about the solvency of Social Security, to lead to privatization," grumbled AARP executive director Horace Deets in 1996.

The History of the Scheme

Social Security was never intended to be an investment plan for retirement. It *was* intended to be a sort of national insurance to supplement private savings and pensions.

Franklin Delano Roosevelt and the other architects of Social Security believed that a pay-as-you-go system was needed and just, because—in the Depression Era of the 1930s—older people faced extreme poverty. But even these architects understood that the system needed limits. In 1939, Roosevelt's Social Security Advisory Council wrote that support of retirees could not come

> *at the expense of...lowering of the standard of living of the working population. No benefits should be promised or implied which cannot be safely financed not only in the early years of the program, but when workers now young will be old.*

The program's administrators didn't wait long to start ignoring that advice. And expanding the program became a routine process in Washington. One example: In the early 1970s, benefits were increased across the board by 20 percent. Another example: Almost immediately afterword, they were indexed to inflation.

Richard Nixon would later call this move one of the biggest mistakes of his presidency. Considering how his presidency played out, that's a big mistake.

When the stagflation years of the late 1970s followed, with their theoretically impossible combination of recession and inflation, the indexed Social Security benefits disconnected from workers' wages. The retirees getting government checks started catching up—and in many cases, passing—current workers in terms of disposable income and quality of life.

Eventually, Social Security benefits were adjusted again so that they were indexed against real wages. This was supposed to prevent a repeat of the stagflation decoupling. More changes came in 1983—in a series of adjustments that program administrators called the "75-year fix." This fix raised payroll taxes, taxed program benefits and phased in a higher retirement age.

But even after these changes, the system promised each successive group of retirees higher real benefits. Worse still, several generations of workers learned to expect steadily increasing Social Security benefits. Economic historians suspect that this expectation reduced savings—since people began to think that the federal government would provide for their retirement.

This trend touched yet another familiar Ponzi scheme theme. Unsophisticated investors will sometimes load their investments into one scheme that promises huge returns. That many eggs in a crooked basket are likely to be broken.

Investment banker and economist Pete Peterson dismisses Social Security as "a vast Ponzi scheme in which the first people in are big winners and the vast array of those who join late in the game lose."

Like a standard Ponzi scheme, Social Security only works if there are fresh people to bring into the system each year. Unlike a standard Ponzi scheme, the federal government *forces* people to participate.

"There is no crisis situation with Social Security," Shirley Chater, administrator of the Social Security program, told a congressional committee in 1996. She was trying to talk Congress into giving her agency more money. But her effort backfired. Like any Ponzi perp, she'd cooked the books to make a better impression. Under questioning, she confessed to having counted only workers' Social Security taxes in her analysis of the system's return on investment—not employers' matching contributions, which economists agree are paid indirectly by workers through lower wages or benefits.

One senator was so angry at the dissembling that he attacked Chater for using "Disneyland financial analysis."

Stanford economist John Shoven puts it more plainly: "The current system simply isn't financially viable. [It's] akin to an inter-generation chain letter."

Possible Solutions

"The growing disenchantment with Social Security is all but inevitable when you have a pay-as-you-go system in a low-growth world," says White House advisory council member Carolyn Weaver:

> *It's been coming for a while. [Soon] the same old, conventional fixes like raising taxes or reducing spending [on benefits] aren't going to cut it. Those tend to shift costs to the younger generation and make their rates of return worse.*

One poll, conducted by *Newsweek* magazine, found that 61 percent of adults are not confident Social Security will be solvent enough to provide benefits to them when they retire. This skepticism about Social Security, plus the fact that younger workers will not get the same favorable return rate on their investment as today's retirees, is driving people of all political persuasions to believe the system should be fundamentally restructured.

In the 1990s, Social Security's defenders have argued that the program can continue for 60 to 80 years with a few minor modifications. If retiree benefits are gradually decreased by 1 percent a year or the tax rate used to support it is increased by about 0.25 percent a year, the program could last another three generations.

The main problem with this scheme: The eventual collapse only grows bigger over time.

Raising the eligibility age would also expand the program's horizons. The move from 65 to 67 takes effect gradually, adding two months each year starting in 2003. Increasing the move from two months a year to three would mean the eligibility age would be 68 in 2012. The older starting age would lower the program's annual expenses by an additional 5 percent.

Many reform plans call for Social Security to invest its surplus funds more aggressively. In 1996, a White House advisory council on Social Security reform split on two close variations of this theme. One group supported a plan that would invest as much as 40 percent of reserves in stock-index funds, reduce average benefits by 3 percent, raise taxes on benefits, and extend coverage to excluded state and local workers.

The other group supported a plan that would replace today's system with a two-tier benefit approach. One tier would provide a flat benefit financed by almost two-thirds of the current payroll tax. A second would consist of an annuity created by mandatory personal accounts funded with the remainder of the tax. A tax increase would be needed to cover costs of a 70-year phase-in.

"We have to go to seniors, and say, Look, we can't keep this up," said Nebraska Senator Bob Kerrey. "Yes, poverty is a concern. But please don't tell me that every American over 65 is foraging in the alley for garbage or eating dog food. They're going to Vegas with their COLAS—while kids don't have computers in class."

The problem with changing from a pay-as-you-go program to a prefunded private retirement program is that one generation would have to pay twice—for the retirement of its parents and then for its own. But it's a reckoning which some generation will have to bear.

"The issue is simply that Social Security has become nothing but a giant Ponzi scheme where they're relying on new contributions to make the payment to existing retirees," says Jon Fossel, chairman of mutual fund giant Oppenheimer Funds Inc. "As with all Ponzi schemes, eventually you hit the wall when somebody wants their money back."

Allowing private investment introduces market risks into the Social Security equation, but proponents of this solution argue that a solvent system with risks is better than no system. Besides, most workers already plan to rely on other sources—separate company pensions, private 401(k) plans and IRAs—to provide the bulk of their retirement income.

In a 1996 speech, CATO Institute President Edward Crane made the philosophical case for privatization:

> *...Take Social Security. Never mind that it's the world's largest Ponzi scheme that is going to go broke in a decade if it's not privatized. Just consider what we did when we nationalized retirement income in America. ...we discouraged the personal responsibility of thrift, of saving for one's own retirement. Some people assumed the government was doing that for them through Social Security. Many more were simply unable to save because of the burdensome payroll tax which is larger than the income tax for most Americans.*

This leads to a provocative thought. Maybe Social Security *explains* the proliferation of smaller Ponzi schemes.

Be Careful, the Schemes Are Pervasive

Got a few extra dollars? Worried about the future? Thinking that the Wall Street crowd hoards all the best deals for itself? Put your money with us. We have a track record of paying out investors. And, in the remote chance anything goes wrong, we have a special mechanism for getting paid.The pitch should sound familiar by now.

It's tempting to think that the comparisons between Social Security and what law enforcement types would otherwise call a "classic Ponzi scheme" is some sort of politically-biased rhetoric. (Most of the writing that's critical of Social Security is described as politically-biased...sometimes this is true.)

But, even if the comparisons don't seem obvious at first glance, consider an interesting bit of analysis—from the SEC itself. In a prepared statement that the agency released for background on Melvin Ford's Better Life Club Ponzi scheme, the Feds are more candid than you might guess they would be:

> *Q: Why is a Ponzi scheme any different from Social Security?*
>
> *A: Social security is a compulsory savings program run by the government. If the social security trust fund runs out of money to pay back retirees, the government can raise money to make the payments through taxes. A Ponzi scheme operator...has nowhere to turn when the scheme goes bust. The last round of investors simply lose their money.*

In the 1990s, most investors realize that John Maynard Keynes died a long time ago—and the blind belief that "government" has some kind of power beyond its individual pieces died with him.

The Fed's promise that the government can enforce a *compulsory* Ponzi scheme isn't worth any more than Melvin Ford's incoherent talk about the velocity of money...or New Era's larcenous gibberish about a board or high-roller philanthropists. In the case of Social Security, taxpayers are simply the Greater Fools who are forced by law to extend the scheme.

But they can't keep the scheme going indefinitely. No foolish investor ever can. All Ponzi schemes collapse...the only question is when. Well-run schemes can last a little longer, if the perp manages the money well and takes out his or her cut slowly. But not even a savvy perp can keep prevent the final reckoning..

The questions to ask for context may be: Why are the things so pervasive? Have social welfare programs like Social Security created a lottery mentality in so much of the population that people can't resist throwing a few extra dollars of good money after bad?

Looking back over the history of Ponzi and pyramid schemes—both recent and not—the answer comes back consistently. *Yes*.

Your money is a valuable thing. As you age, more of your money will be available for investments. Don't trust it to any crook who promises big returns with little risk. Anyone making that promise—even if the *anyone* is a government agency—is lying. They're just looking for what every Ponzi perp wants...a naive person who's greedy, gullible and has some money to lose.

A Greater Fool, willing to bet heavily on a Great Idea.

Don't be that person.

INDEX

NO POSTAGE
NECESSARY
IF MAILED
IN THE
UNITED STATES

BUSINESS REPLY MAIL

FIRST-CLASS MAIL PERMIT NO. 73996 LOS ANGELES CA

POSTAGE WILL BE PAID BY ADDRESSEE

SILVER LAKE PUBLISHING
2025 HYPERION AVE
LOS ANGELES CA 90027-9849

NO POSTAGE
NECESSARY
IF MAILED
IN THE
UNITED STATES

BUSINESS REPLY MAIL

FIRST-CLASS MAIL PERMIT NO. 73996 LOS ANGELES CA

POSTAGE WILL BE PAID BY ADDRESSEE

SILVER LAKE PUBLISHING
2025 HYPERION AVE
LOS ANGELES CA 90027-9849

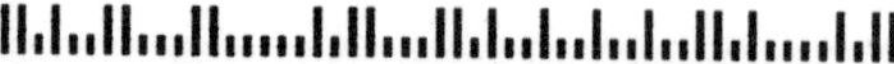